YOU ARE THE DEAD!

I, Father Jivardi Kastidine, being of the holy order of the Almin (all praise to His name) and a catalyst in the service of the *Albanara* of Sharakan, royal house of that land now lost, take up my pen with heavy heart. It is to you, the Dark Artisans, that I write. You, the Dead, to whom Life is lost and cannot be regained.

You know nothing of us—and for this reason, I write.

Our world is far removed from yours. Your world smells of metal and fire. Death cloaks you and you wear it with pride. Yet we now begin to know you. We understand your fear and your blindness, for we feared and were blind to you.

I write to bring sight to your eyes and hearing to your ears. You cannot sorrow for our destruction unless you can feel what we have lost. Only then will you know us. Only then may we speak to one another with understanding.

Thus, under the direction of His Majesty King Garald of the once beautiful Sharakan, I write to you. It is the hope of His Majesty, and the purpose of this document, to keep alive the dream and make you feel a part of it.

Bantam Spectra Books by Margaret Weis and Tracy Hickman
Ask your bookseller for the books you have missed

The Darksword Trilogy
Forging the Darksword
Doom of the Darksword
Triumph of the Darksword

Darksword Adventures

Rose of the Prophet
The Will of the Wanderer
The Paladin of the Night
The Prophet of Akhran

The Death Gate Cycle
Dragon Wing
Elven Star
Fire Sea

and from Margaret Weis
Star of the Guardians
The Lost King
King's Test
King's Sacrifice

Darksword Adventures

MARGARET WEIS
& TRACY HICKMAN

BANTAM BOOKS
NEW YORK • TORONTO • LONDON • SYDNEY • AUCKLAND

93-0401

DARKSWORD ADVENTURES
A Bantam Spectra Book / December 1988

ISBN 0-553-27600-X

Published simultaneously in the United States and Canada

PRINTED IN THE UNITED STATES OF AMERICA

OPM   12 11 10 9 8 7 6 5 4 3 2

Acknowledgments

We would like to thank Janet Pack—longtime friend, thespian, soprano, and expert on woodchuck recipes—for her work in helping us with the initial editing and refining of the text. We would also like to thank Gary Pack for having the good sense to marry Janet.

Once again, we would like to thank Steve Sullivan for his excellent mapwork, and we hope you who are enjoying traipsing about our world through his maps will pause a moment to thank him as well.

Larry Elmore's marvelous cover art has become such an integral and important part of our work that extending our thanks—once again—is like playing the refrain of a much-loved song.

Thanks to Laura Hickman who provided advice, support, and comforting smiles in times of crisis.

Finally, we would like to thank all of those who playtested our game: Peter Hildreth and Mike and Kathy Luzzi. You wonderful people worked as hard on this as we did! Thank you for all your help. It was invaluable!

Contents

Introduction

Welcome to the magical realm of Thimhallan.

We know many of you already. You are "gamers" who have visited other worlds of sword and sorcery with us before, and we're pleased that you have decided to join us again.

There are, however, many of you interested in Thimhallan who have never participated in role-playing games. Perhaps you thought they were too difficult or complicated to learn. Perhaps you were intimidated by massive, expensive volumes of rules filled with incomprehensible numbers and strange abbreviations.

We want you to join us in the fun and excitement we experience visiting Thimhallan in our imaginations. Therefore we are pleased to present a complete role-playing game and source book in an affordable, entertaining format. Everything you need to play is included in this one volume—game rules, statistics, character and monster descriptions, suggested scenarios—presented in the form of interesting and revealing reports on Thimhallan compiled by the *Duuk-*

tsarith to be given to Major James Boris. We have devised a very simple system for role-playing that you can learn easily.

There may be those of you who are not interested in role-playing but would simply like to have more information about the world and its people. You will find all that in this volume, without being distracted by a lot of rules. Included are a History of the World, a description of Thimhallan written by a young man who survived many wild adventures in the various parts of the realm, descriptions of the wondrous creatures that inhabit Thimhallan, information on the major and minor characters, and more.

Whether you journey by yourself or in the company of friends, we hope you enjoy your visit to the magical realm of Thimhallan. May your trip be an adventurous one!

Tracy Raye Hickman
Margaret Weis

Preface

I, Father Jivardi Kastidine, being of the holy order of the Almin (all praise to His name) and a catalyst in the service of the *Albanara* of Sharakan, royal house of that land now lost, take up my pen with heavy heart. It is to you, the Dark Artisans, that I write. You, the Dead, to whom Life is lost and cannot be regained.

You know nothing of us—and for this reason, I write.

Our world is far removed from yours. Your world smells of metal and fire. Death cloaks you and you wear it with pride. You called our world Kinsky-3 (itself a name reeking of technology) and marched upon it, the Dead bringing death. You slaughtered our families and sundered the beauty of our cities with your Dead devices. The terror you caused among us was not understood and not understandable.

Yet we now begin to know you. We understand your fear and your blindness, for we feared and were blind to you.

Now we are carried captive into Exile from our cherished land. You promise redress and compassion and much more: new worlds and society, a larger universe upon which we may craft our artistry as in a vast cathedral.

We care nothing for these.

I write to bring sight to your eyes and hearing to your ears. You cannot sorrow for our destruction unless you can feel what we have lost. You who have wrecked our cities must come to see their beauty and wonder. Only then will you know us. Only then may we speak to one another with understanding.

Thus, under the direction of His Majesty King Garald of the once beautiful Sharakan, I write to you. It is the hope of His Majesty, and the purpose of this document, to keep alive the dream and make you feel a part of it.

Long I have thought on how this might be accomplished— we are so very different from you and your thinking. Then, through the inspiration of the Almin, I realized why I had been chosen by King Garald to approach you.

Phantasia

The tutoring of the *Albanara* begins at a very early age. They engage in all types of activities from birth through adulthood that are designed to prepare them for their governing role. During their early years they are quickly brought to an understanding of Life and how to use the power of Life to create and shape the world about them. Especially with children this takes the form of play where games are important. As the royal child grows up, instruction becomes more formalized through their tutor.

I myself was one such tutor. An assistant to Cardinal Radisovik, I took a small part in the instruction of our Prince Garald and others of the royal household.

Early in the morning I would awake, and after performing my rites to the Almin, prepare the lessons for the day. I often prayed for some inspiration as to what I could do for the young Prince. At first nothing came to my mind except the rather disturbing picture of wringing the little heathen's neck. I ask the Almin's forgiveness, but I recall the image bringing me a great deal of pleasure at the time.

Garald was not a slow or backward child—quite the contrary. The scamp was fast and gifted. His lessons came easily to him, and the questions put to him—following the curriculum proscribed for him by Radisovik—were answered with jubilant ease. This fruit quickly soured into boredom and apathy. Things were far too easy for the boy, and his interest was difficult to keep. Radisovik ordered variety as a remedy for this affliction, but that soon got out of hand. By his fifteenth year a succession of tutors were moving in and out of the palace at an alarming rate.

So I sat. I thought. I prayed. My head wanted to sink to the desk in despair, but my elbows and arms wouldn't let it. My mind went back to the early days of our acquaintance when Garald would greet me with joy and anticipation of the games we played together.

Oh, how I love games of the mind. They can take you away from the gray drizzles of daily life to places filled with sunshine. In your imagination you can do anything.

Go anywhere . . .

Be anyone . . .

The desk tottered precariously on two legs as I leaped up from my chair. I vaguely recall hearing it clatter to the floor as I ran through the room to the great shelf of tomes in my adjoining library. I couldn't have been more excited. The Almin had answered my prayers.

My hands followed my eyes from title to title on the worn book spines. *"Warlock Conflict,"* I muttered to myself. Books fell to the stone floor as I pulled them from the shelves. Someone had not only sorted the library improperly but had placed many volumes behind other volumes. "No, no. Not in the war books. *Field Magi Economics, Tome of the Ariels* . . . no!" Dust from the cascade of books filled the room. It could not have been so thoroughly demolished had one of the *DKarn-duuk* attempted the project in earnest.

Forty minutes later I stood choking on dust, discarded books like a sea around my knees, but triumphant. The volume for which I had been searching was discovered carelessly tossed behind four outdated atlases. Next time I met Prince Garald I knew we would have our usual battle of wits, but this time I would be well armed.

Garald lay on the floating divan, one leg thrown up awkwardly over the back. The divan was as far from his work desk as it could possibly be and still be in the school-room. Absorbed in reading a book *not* on his list of recommended studies, Garald knew I had entered but chose to ignore me . . . just as he intended to ignore the lesson.

I glanced back over my shoulder. The Illusionist I had brought with me—one Frizan—stood behind me wearing a look of depression almost as deep as Garald's disinterest. Illusionists were often used by tutor catalysts to create the pictures and illustrations that were occasionally required by the lessons.

Frizan was typical of Illusionist success stories and therefore, quite miserable. Though raised in Zith-el, his talent was so obvious that his parents sacrificed much of their wealth to send him to the university in Merilon. Their investment paid off well. In the Performance Grove, Frizan's creations were often the center of attention as his shadows danced to his magic. He wrote and performed a number of intricate plays that won him critical acclaim. Frizan's bough finally bore fruit and he attained the honor of honors—House Illusionist to the King of Sharakan.

That's when his life took the typical plunge.

Being the best, he was assigned by the household to aid in the tutoring of the young *Albanara*. To have one's offspring study with a famous artist is a matter of great prestige among the royal houses of Thimhallan. Unfortunately, it is no favor to the artist. The visions he is required to create no longer come from the soul. He is now instructed to illustrate "if you put four swans with three swans, how many swans do you have?"

"Show the children a dragon," the tutor catalyst commands.

"What type of dragon? One of the southern golds or would you prefer the Outland black?" Frizan asks, warming to his art.

"Just a dragon," says the tutor.

The real problem is that the job carries with it wealth and benefits and all the Life the artist wants. He is encouraged to create things on his own time, but his art is owned and commissioned by the lord who pays him, and most rulers hate anything the least bit controversial. His family's fortunes increase as his prestige with his fellow artisans wanes. It is a job that no artist could possibly refuse . . . and one every artist hates.

Frizan whispered a sigh that came from the depths of his soul.

I walked quietly to the desk and set down the single dusty tome I had brought with me, then carefully stacked and picked up all Garald's books. The storage cabinet was close by, and as I put them away, I studied the Prince with a sidelong glance.

Still no interest, my liege?

Frizan watched me warily. The relationship between an Illusionist and a tutor is always a precarious one and in some ways not unlike a pet and his master. The tutor catalyst makes the Illusionist do the very thing the artist is loathe to do (Sit up, roll over, boy!) while at the same time it is the tutor catalyst who gives the Illusionist the Life he needs to create his art during his own time (Here's a bone, good boy!). Frizan knew something was up, and it appeared as though he couldn't decide whether to wag his tail or bite me.

I took chairs from their places near the walls and began arranging them around the table, then cleared its carefully polished wooden surface. Finally I picked up the book I had brought with me and took my place at the head of the table.

"Frizan, my old friend. Come and sit down."

The Illusionist actually jumped. Never had I, nor any of the other tutors, addressed him directly by name. He came and did as I asked, never taking his eyes off me. His robes rustled softly as he slowly sat down in his chair.

At least I had *his* attention. The Prince remained unmoved.

"Frizan, have you ever heard of the game Phantasia?"

The Illusionist stared at me warily. "Uh . . . no . . . Father."

"Oh, you'll love it." I opened the ancient text. "It's a game where you can be anything you want, do anything you wish. We're going to play it today—you and I."

My gaze was fixed on the bewildered Frizan, but my attention was on the Prince. He had looked up, but he turned back to his book the moment he caught my glancing in his direction.

"It's really quite simple. You'll help by creating the scenes for us as we play."

Frizan frowned. This sounded suspiciously like what he had been doing all along.

I began, "Once in ages now forgotten, there lived a great king. He desired the greatest of wonders, the Jewel of Merlyn, rumored to give its possessor unlimited Life. The king sent dwarves, mutated by the Life Shapers, to search under the kingdom's mountain in search of this gem. The dwarves never returned. They had roused the ire of a dragon that lived in the mountain. It rose up and began to destroy the villages of the kingdom. What do you suppose the dragon's attacks must have looked like, eh, Frizan?"

The Illusionist blinked. "Well, Father, I suppose . . ."

"Show me." I gestured toward the table.

The vague shapes of buildings began to appear.

"This is a city of great wealth and beauty, Frizan," I said.

The buildings suddenly took on beautiful shapes.

"Now, it is the middle of a very busy market day."

The streets filled with people in fine clothing, shouting their wares. Frizan added a clear, blue sky. The sounds and smells of the market came floating up off the table to surround us. It was a beautiful illusion. Frizan's mouth turned upward in a gentle smile.

I heard the Prince's book fall to the floor.

Suddenly the dragon appeared. It was beautiful and horrible. Its gleaming, scaly head thrust up through the shaped stones of the plaza. Terrified, the people ran in all directions. The beautiful buildings began to shake and collapse.

I heard footsteps behind me.

"Take us to the royal court of the king, Frizan."

The scene dissolved. There was a moment's pause, then a magnificent throne room, lushly appointed, appeared. Frizan had taken care this time. It was all there: the jeweled throne, the stately king, all the attendants at court. It was all there except—

"His daughter," I added, "the fairest woman in all the land."

Frizan pondered a moment, then there appeared, sitting

next to the king, the most exquisite girl one could imagine. Her hair fell over her shoulders in a cascade of silvery gold. Her figure was perfect. Her eyes were deep pools of green.

The Prince was standing right behind me. I glanced up. His eyes were on the Princess.

"Would my liege care to join us?"

Garald stiffened. "I think not. Is my father paying you to instruct me or tell bed-tales like House Magi?"

I shrugged. "As you wish, my lord. We are now going to become part of this illusion ourselves, just like actors in a play. Frizan, who would you like to be in this play?"

Frizan smiled genuinely. "I would like to be a catalyst, Father. I have always been interested in your profession."

"Well and done. You shall be a catalyst." I turned the book to him and showed him a page. "You will give your catalyst body and soul. These numbers tell how your catalyst relates to others in our game."

I showed him the numbers he needed, and within a moment his *dramatis personae* was complete.

"He can't be a catalyst," interrupted Garald scornfully. "One has to be born with the—"

"He can most certainly be a catalyst, my liege," I replied. "In the game of Phantasia anything is possible. I, for one, have always wanted to be a warlock—a *Duuk-tsarith*—and that is what I shall play."

Garald snorted. "You couldn't lift an apple from a bowl with the small amount of magic *you* possess!"

I turned to Frizan. "Obviously our Prince does not wish to participate in today's lesson. Would you please create a sphere to encompass us so that we may leave His Majesty to finish his book in peace?"

Frizan smiled again and created an opaque sphere that completely surrounded us. Ourselves, the court, and the Princess disappeared from Garald's view.

Frizan stood clothed in the robes of the priesthood. I appeared as one of the *Duuk-tsarith*, dressed in black robes. The court was all around us and we were listening to the king's daughter.

"My father, it is said that only woman's hand may slay this monster!"

"There are many women in this kingdom who can fight it! I'll order one of them to go—"

"Nay, Father. How would it look to our people if anyone accepts this challenge other than myself?"

I intervened in my role as warlock. "Great King, your daughter's words are wise. She will face this monster, but not alone. I offer myself to go with her. My powers are great and my Life is strong. Look, I call for fire to burn but not destroy!" I raised my hands above my head and called for flame to leap up in a column and cover the ceiling.

Frizan entered into the spirit of the game. "The Almin will walk with us!" he shouted excitedly. "I, too, will go with your daughter and this warlock."

I can only imagine what all of this must have sounded like to Garald. He experienced none of the illusion but heard all we said. Our conversations must have gotten the better of him for he appeared at my side in an instant.

"Father, you can't create fire—" Garald choked as he saw the pillar of flame rushing from my hands to the ceiling.

I clapped my hands. The flame vanished, and I turned to the Prince. "What were you saying, my liege?"

Garald scowled and did not answer.

The Princess descended from her throne and came to stand between us. "Father, I must go. The people have suffered much. Rebellion is rife among them, and unless I go forth and slay this dragon, all we have built shall be lost."

Garald turned to the Princess.

"Don't coddle the rabble," he said sternly. "Go down and rough up those rebels. That'll teach them who is in charge."

"My lord," I said quietly, "are you in this game?"

"Yes!" Garald shouted.

"What character do you wish to play in the game, my liege?"

"Make me the Captain of the Guard. I'll soon put down this rebellion. And no Princess of mine is going to endanger herself for her thankless people!"

o   o   o

By the end of the afternoon our imaginary castle was under siege, all commerce in our land had ground to a halt. The dragon was wreaking havoc in the countryside, and the Princess had been killed fighting off the invaders.

Garald, bleeding from many wounds, stood on the parapet of the castle, repelling yet another attack, when suddenly the illusion faded. We both stood in the Prince's study once more.

Frizan, exhausted and nearly bereft of Life, lay asleep on the floor.

Garald blinked, then turned to me, his face glowing. "That was a fantastic game! Much better than studying."

"Oh, but we were studying," I said. "Do you think it was right to try to crush the rebellion with armed force, my liege?"

Garald considered this long moments. "No," he answered ruefully. "I guess the Princess was right. A king should stand between danger and his people. He should protect them, not fight them."

"Does this remind you of anything?"

"Well, the Harvest Failing we read about last week. The King of Sharzad had a similar problem, didn't he? He should have worked with the Field Magi. Instead, he tried to crush them."

"Very good, my lord. Now, I want you to find me three more examples from history of this same thing. I'll see that some books are sent to your rooms. Also, I want you to report on how you *should* have handled this situation. Perhaps we will try it during the game tomorrow. We are finished for today, my Prince."

Garald nodded, then turned. As he walked from the study, I heard him muttering to himself. "Be gone from this land, foul beast, or die!" The Prince lashed out with imaginary magic at his unseen foe just as he stepped from the room.

I glanced down at Frizan. He would be asleep for some time and I doubted if I could move him. Finally I left him where he was—lying on the floor of the study. In his exhaustion he wore a vastly more peaceful look than I had ever seen upon the man. He clutched the Phantasia tome to his chest with both arms.

It took him weeks to get it copied. He refused to return it to me until he had his own.

Since that time, the game Phantasia has played an important part in the instruction of future royalty. The game itself was adapted for use at the Font in the instruction of the novitiates.

I have found it often helps one cope with his own role in life by taking on the role of others.

It was this story, then, that set me upon this course. I shall teach you the game of Phantasia as I taught it to Garald. With it, I hope I will teach you about us, of whom you know so little.

Part I

Wildreth's Wandarium

Note: Wildreth's Wandarium is an uncouth work that I would hardly have considered recommending had it not been recommended to me by the King himself.

Petar Wildreth (809–833 Y.L.) was orphaned during the early years of his life; his parents died mysteriously in a battle between Separatists and the *Duuk-tsarith*. As one of the Shadow Shapers (Illusionists), Wildreth later rose to a position of dubious respectability. He was perfecting his craft at the university in Merilon when this journey took place.

Although written in the modern style made popular in novels and travel digests, the Wandarium does have the merit of covering a considerable amount of Thimhallan's geography, politics, and social customs. The work was written in 831 Y.L., or about one year before the Turning of Joram, and is, therefore, one of the more up-to-date works, if not accurate in every detail.

Wildreth uses the measures, weights, and distances, conventions common to all on Thimhallan. For your convenience, measures of distance and size are given here, in rough equivalents to your own system:

mila = 1000 metra = just short of 1 mile
metra = 10 decimetra = just over 5 feet
decimetra = approximately 6 inches

The common year reference is Y.L. or Year of Life, which relates time to the Great Passage.

           — Father Jivardi Kastidine

Chapter One

My Travels Begin

Hail, fellow traveler in Thimhallan! Are you floating quietly in your parlor and pondering what wonders there are out in the world? Why, you have but to ask Wildreth, who, at little expense to you, will impart all of the known wonders of Thimhallan. I have walked among the giants of the Outland, have been captive of savage centaurs, have found my way into every kitchen of every palace in the known world, and I will tell you all!

Here, within these very pages, you will experience the beauty, feel the thrills, and suffer the chills of our great world. Fear not! You, lucky reader, will remain comfortably ensconced in your own home while I, on the pages before you, will take you for a walk among the greatest dangers and wonders ever to be put to pen.

Here, then, is my sad tale. Weep not! For my destiny is assured, though fate was seldom kind to me in the interim.

I was born to one of the great and noble houses of Thimhallan. My father was *Pron-alban*, a Guildmaster of some reputation. My mother was a gifted *Quin-alban* who

The Outland

The Borderland

Sharakan

Cyrsa

Valheim Mountains

Aspen Wilderness

Avidon

Vajnan Plain

Winvren

The Font
Talsin

Zith-El

Westerness Ocean

The Watchers

Merlon

Istandia

Nomish Mountains

Shgraad

The Crescent Kingdoms

also worked at home on a variety of wonderful projects. My mother's people had originally been from the City Below. Her beauty and grace had allowed her to cross that visible line between those who lived down on the earth and those who dwelt in the clouds.

Our home was in the City Above in the High Markets, just outside the Royal University on the north side. Our house was a lovely, modest dwelling done in the pre–Iron Wars architectural style. At the time these adventures begin, I was seventeen—not yet of the Age of Reliance, but within a year of that blissful date and due to begin my studies at the Royal University.

The happy memories of those days are, alas, all that I have. My dear parents were taken from me abruptly by the hand of the Almin. A group of militant Westlund Separatists were demonstrating for their cause in Mannan Park just in front of the Old Gate to the Royal Gardens. They were presenting a play designed to exhibit the poverty and oppression of their lives. *Duuk-tsarith* arrived on the scene and began to remove the rebels to the warlocks' secret places. Apparently some of the demonstrators were unwilling to leave quietly and Warrior's Magic was cast. The Separatists were powerful but unskilled. There are not many in this world who can challenge the *Duuk-tsarith* and win.

Though the battle was short, it was not without casualties. Both my parents were in the park that day and found themselves in the midst of the battle. It was reported to me that they did not suffer long before the Almin took them as His own.

Oh, the sorrow when first I learned of their fate! A *Theldara* came with the news to my home that morning, materializing in the entry garden just as I was creating a portrait of my mother out of multicolored smoke. After accepting the Druid's condolences and assuring her I had no need for her sedatives, I went inside to weep for my parents' loss and to try to make some plans, for there was much to be done.

Following the funeral I returned home, knowing that I must now continue with my own life. Fortunately my father had been a prudent man, who had laid aside money enough to support his family in case of his death. My mother had some money of her own, which I inherited as well. There was enough for me to continue my education and keep this house that they had loved so well and that had now become my only link to them. I had just vowed that I would make them proud of me when there came a thunderous beating on the door.

Thinking it was more friends of my parents, come back to offer condolences, I instructed the House Magus to let them in.

It was not my parents' friends. It was my mother's brother—Thurb Dresler.

I stared at him in amazement and disgust, for I had never liked the man. He was nothing like my mother. He was flabby in every way—both in body and mind. My mother had worked hard to obtain her position. Thurb preferred to resort to trickery and bullying. His round face glowed perpetually red from some unseen exertion (I thought it must simply have been to keep his bulk operating for I never saw him actually work). His magic appeared to be consumed in supporting his bulk and providing for his own wants.

"The funeral is over," I said coldly. "You missed it. That doesn't bother me particularly, for you were not wanted, so you have leave to go now."

He was looking about the room with an air of ownership. "Nice place. We're going to like it here."

"There is a fine inn down in City Below," I said pointedly, thinking he meant to stay for a visit.

"Good. You'll be needing a place to live." He grinned at me and, as I stood gaping, handed me a document.

"This house is mine. So's the furniture, the paintings, the china and the silverware, and, of course, your parents' fortune."

"That—that's impossible!" I cried, though I think I knew even then that somehow the unthinkable had happened.

"Take it to them legal fellows at the University," he said, shrugging his fat shoulders.

I did, and, of course, it was all legal and proper—or it seemed so at the time. According to this document, my father and mother had agreed to turn over all their property to this fiend if they died before I reached my majority.

My uncle and his family moved into my home within two weeks of my parents' death. My uncle kindly gave me a week to find a place of my own, which was going to be difficult considering I had no money. Friendless and alone, my home now filled with that detested presence, I began spending more and more time wandering the streets of the most beautiful city in Thimhallan—Merilon!

Chapter Two

The Empire of Merilon

Actually the empire has long since diminished into regional land holdings. In its time, however, Merilon was synonymous with power; its word was the Law of Life.

History: When the ancient wizard Merlyn, most powerful of the ancients and the one who made the Great Passage possible, first walked the land of Thimhallan, he came upon this grove on a plain between two ranges of mountains. So taken was he with the beauty of the land that he claimed it as the place where he would build his city and take here his final rest.

Leaving the beauty of the grove undisturbed, Merlyn—with the aid of his loyal conjurers and shapers—created a floating platform which he called the Pedestal. Made of delicately carved, gleaming, translucent marble and quartz, the Pedestal allowed sunlight to pass through it to the ground below, providing perfect weather for the health of the plant life there. It was with this Pedestal that Merlyn built his city. There the towers of his Citadel were raised, as were the first of Merilon's buildings.

Subsequently, five other floating foundations have been raised to support the rampant growth of the city. Building structures on the ground allowed even more expansion. Merilon glowed day and night as it attracted Thimhallan's best and brightest stars to its gleaming walls.

During the First Rectification the burgeoning Guilds united and began work on three additional foundations, which were called the Three Sisters. To this day the Three Sisters support the major centers of Guilds and Crafthouses in all of Thimhallan.

Toward the end of the First Rectification, the Gladewall was built. This structure served a dual purpose: it provided a defensive ground structure, and it set a definite boundary for the Grove, whose historic and legendary importance had grown in the hearts of the people of Merilon. In time the Grove became a center of culture and entertainment for the people of the city.

After the Iron War, many of Merilon's lovingly shaped buildings lay in ruins. While the Pedestal had withstood all the assaults of magic and technology, the buildings themselves were largely destroyed. Two of the Three Sisters were cracked and declared unsafe.

The renovation period of the Second Rectification restored the Three Sisters. Major improvements were made to the original designs of the city layout. Two universities were built on the Pedestal, each having its own library. The Citadel (which had been irreparably twisted by the exploding powder of the Sorcerers) was razed, and the High Garden was shaped in its place. The Crystal Palace was erected on a new, floating foundation. The Newcourt drifted cloudlike high above the city, directly over the location of the old Citadel. Its view of the High Gardens is breathtaking—a must for visitors.

With the rise of the catalysts, the Cathedral of Life was built on its own crystal floating base, its spires nearly touching the base of Newcourt. It took thirty years to shape the Cathedral, and it is considered one of the most beautiful buildings in all of Thimhallan. (Particularly wonderful are the living gargoyles. Magically constrained to perch upon the sides of the building, the gargoyles are said to be nasty in temperament and have been known to occasionally spit at church-goers.)

It was also during this renovation that an enormous, magical sphere was erected, extending from the Gladewall up and over the spires of the Crystal Place. Designed more for show than actual protection, the Stardome is primarily used for weather control.

("Everyone does something about the weather, but no one dares to talk about it" is an expression much in vogue since the weather is regulated exclusively by the royal family, who will permit absolutely no variety. It has been spring here for years, and I must say we're getting a bit sick of it.)

It was during the Second Rectification that a second sprawling city was built around the inside of the Gladewall. Common marketplaces and workshops whose goods, which were of fine quality and offered at less than half the prices charged by the Sky Guilds, gave life to the community.

Current Conditions: Merilon appears from the northern plains as a great glowing orb cradled between the mountains. The Estate Farms that surround Merilon wrap it in emerald hues, setting the city among pastoral splendor. The blue of the sky is refracted through the Stardome. It glows from crystals of the Pedestal and gleams in the crystal spires of the Palace, creating the overall effect of a gigantic, many-faceted, spherical jewel.

As impressive as the city is when seen from a distance, the jewellike effect is heightened as you enter it. The crowded streets of the City Below are utterly overwhelmed by the great, glittering Stardome.

So, at last, you reach the City of Wonder and are prepared to try your luck entering the Gates. The question remains, which one?

There were, originally, nine Gates through the Gladewall, each of them signifying one of the original Mysteries. Of these, only the Earth Gate and the Wind Gate see much usage in modern times. Since the Wind Gate is reserved for Ariels only, all others coming from and going to Merilon use the Earth Gate.

Earth Gate enters the Grove on the western side. Once you have passed the *Kan-Hanar* and their checklist

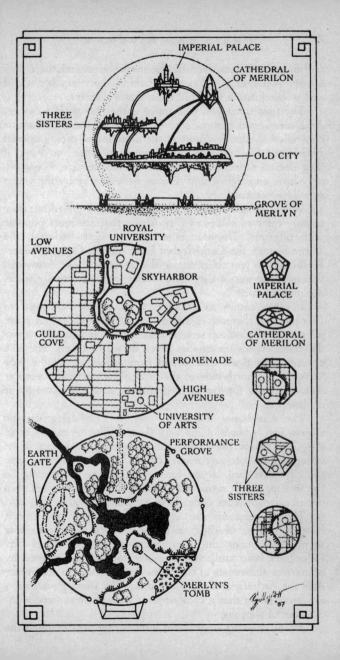

and have been approved by the invisible eyes of the *Duuk-tsarith*, you find you have left behind the everyday world and walked into a world of beauty and wonder.

The first thing you will notice is the change in weather. As I mentioned before, all weather inside the Stardome is controlled by the *Sif-Hanar* at the direction of their Imperial Majesties, the Emperor and Empress of Merilon. Even if they decide a decorative snowfall would be nice, it usually only lasts an evening and then is melted away by the warm sun. Dress accordingly.

When people talk of the wonders of Merilon, they usually refer to places in City Above that are most popular with pilgrims. These include the Old City Pedestal, the Three Sisters, the Cathedral of Life, and the Crystal Palace. So intent are you on gazing at the beauties above, however, you may not notice City Below until you are actually walking its streets.

It often comes as a shock, then, when those new to Merilon find themselves lost within the City Below. A maze of narrow, winding streets take the wanderer in every direction except the one in which he wants to go. The sole exception to this is the broad avenue leading to the Life Gate on the north side of the city. Since this gate is never opened except for heroes returning from war, the avenue is of little use.

The *Kan-Hanar* did their work well in designing the streets and byways of the City Above. The arrangement of the City Below fell more to chance and the whim of its occupants than to any master plan. One can easily navigate the city, it is said, if you can figure out the numbering on the floating street signs. All I can say is that those skilled in deciphering obscure codes have a distinct advantage!

This is most unfortunate, for these lower city streets have a charm of their own for visitors willing to lose themselves among the twisting alleys. The streets of City Below are hard and smooth, being constantly reshaped by numerous alchemists of the *Mon-alban* in order to accommodate the Airbarges of the *Kan-Hanar*. The shining walkways are grooved so that a catalyst may walk their surface without fear of slipping.

Avenues swing in graceful intersecting arcs through the

woven grass buildings on either side. The grasses of the plain form the basis for many of the structures in City Below, although an occasional building can be traced to the original rock, bush, or tree used in its construction. These crude, basic elements do not do justice to the diversity of architecture that can be found in City Below. The grasses are shaped and woven into smooth walls in which different leaves appear no more evident than the grain of wood in other structures. The ground on which these buildings stand has been reshaped into a solid base. While this means that there is a predominance of green buildings in City Below (generally this class of people does not have sufficient Life to waste changing the color of their homes to more pleasing hues), it does mean that the air in the city is constantly being refreshed by the grass homes and shops.

A wonderful variety of open-air markets exists in City Below. Here a plethora of exotic fruits from all over Thimhallan can be found. Lodging and meals can be had in City Below at surprisingly reasonable prices, although it is also true that the crime rate around the Gladewall is probably one of the highest in Thimhallan. Make certain you have cast strong protection spells over your purse!

One hostelry I can recommend is the Tarkin Inn, just three blocks from the Earth Gate entrance. Turning right just before Newmarket, you see a passage framed in brown boughs and topped by silver leaves. This leads to a gigantic brown face in the wall, flanked on either side by a pair of enormous hands clasped together. As you approach, the face identifies itself as the Tarkin Inn and inquires politely if you desire lodgings. Should you answer in the affirmative, the hands to the left of the face open to uncover an eye in the wall behind them. The hands form a bowl and the face tells you that you must deposit your payment in advance.

Once the eye has examined your money to make sure you have given sufficient for your stay, the hands clasp your coins and another pair of hands open in welcome, revealing an archway leading into the inn itself.

The common room where meals and drink are served is usually kept a bit too warm for my tastes. It is, however, a place where many pilgrims visiting Merilon can meet and discuss their various adventures. The food here is common but very wholesome, with good-size portions. The prices are most reasonable.

A pair of waterfalls—one going up and the other down—take the guests on floating platforms up through the five levels of the inn where the guest rooms are located. (Due to the normally crowded conditions of the inn, guests are not permitted to fly through the halls.) Though the platforms do move slowly, visitors may feel giddy at first and should keep a tight grip on children.

The various levels of the inn accommodate various types of rooms. The lower levels have rooms shaped primarily from stone, while the upper levels offer rooms shaped from wood. All have beds of reasonable comfort made of mushrooms grown on the premises. Bathing facilities are located at the end of every level. (You are not allowed to play in the waterfalls.)

The inn is not far from the Grove of Merlyn. A wise location, for few who visit Merilon ever wish to go farther than the Grove. A person can see more sights, hear more sounds, and experience more adventure in that Grove than in any other part of the city.

Famirash River enters the Gladewall through the Druid's Gate. Here it is split into two large streams that meander through the city. The river continues through the Grove to exit the Death Gate to the south before winding once again on its original course to the northwest.

The Famirash divides the grove into several important areas. The Earth Gate and Walk of Crafts lie on its western shores. The river splits after coming into the grove, cradling the Isle of Fihaishon on which stands the Pavilion of Healing. To the north of the island is a woodland preserve belonging to the Empress. East of where the river comes together again is the fabled Performance Grove. To the south is the Tomb of Merlyn and the Walk of Shadows.

The Walk of Crafts, just beyond the Earth Gate, is a series of paths, clearly marked in variously colored grasses, that display examples of the finest in Conjuring, Shaping, and Changing. By day visitors stroll these paths intent on viewing the finest in modern artistic achievement. In the evening, however, before the Grove is closed for the night, young people stroll these paths in search of romance.

The Pavilion of Fihaish Talisin is one of the largest houses of healing in all of Thimhallan. Surrounded by its own peaceful grounds and bordered by the river on all sides, it is an ideal place to recover from injury or illness of body or mind.

The Performance Grove is a must for all who visit the city. All of the Illusionists from the universities as well as many professionals from all over Thimhallan come to the Grove to perform. The students are always especially energetic in their displays. Their future often depends upon it (as I have good reason to know!). Patrons in the High Avenues above often watch the performances from the Promenade. If the patrons are pleased by a performance, they may offer positions of employment to the artists that will establish their careers for life.

In this area is also the famous Maze of high hedges that is changed daily to delight and confound the visitor.

Outside the Grove are many shops and cafés that have sprung up in recent times on either side of the Earth Gate. Here you will find examples of fine craftsmanship that only the wizards, magi, and alchemists of Merilon can produce. Each of the shops is shaped to best promote its own merchandise, yet all blend in harmony, one with another, in a style that is most pleasing to the eye. The fine wines of Merilon's vineyards, Sugared Ice, and the gooey treat known as Rose Willows are the most sought-after commodities.

The visions at the Gate are not limited to the wares of the city. Most of the eligible young women and young bachelors in Merilon come to the Gate to engage in their favorite pastime—flirting. Here, to the gentle whisper of the fluted wind or the ring of cymbals performed by the Music Shapers nearby, the laughing youth stroll through the shops of the gate, exchanging flowers, stealing kisses.

Lest you think it an easy thing to trifle with the affections of beautiful maidens or handsome youths, I must inform you that all marriages within the city are arranged by the parents—generally along lines of class, wealth, and social standing.

Beyond the shops you will find a stand for the rented conveyances that carry passengers up to City Above. These ships of the air are shaped with loving craft into the images of fabulous creatures. Everything from winged unicorns to fur-pelted dragons can be hired to take you to any location in the city. Often these craft are so cunningly designed that it is impossible to tell the driver from the coach, and you may find yourself talking to a giant swan who appears to carry you in the hollow of her back. Unless you want to expend your Life flying, these carriages are the only means of transportation to City Above, not counting the three Corridors near the Wind Gate that lead directly to each of the Three Sisters. These Corridors are, however, carefully watched by the *Thon-Li*, and few are authorized to use them. Visitors should note that renting a carriage is the easy part. The hard part is going anywhere in it.

While it is true that Merilon is supposedly a city for all people, it is also true that not all people can get into City Above. Only those who have a specific permit to enter City Above are allowed to travel upward to its glittering environs. Such passes include an invitation from an inhabitant of City Above, a royal pass granted by the royal family, a university pass given to students, a tradesmen's pass given to workers, or a Guild pass. Each of these must be approved and scheduled by the *Kan-Hanar* on entering the Gate. (Catalysts do not need passes, for they have leave and, indeed, are required to make their presence in Merilon known at the Cathedral.)

Unless one is a highly skilled artisan, Guild passes are difficult to obtain. Each of the Sky Guilds maintains offices in City Below for the purpose of reviewing applications for such passes. These are sometimes granted if an applicant presents a new skill or spell construction that the Sky Guilds may wish to purchase. More often these passes are issued to petitioners who desire work with one of these Guilds. The lines in these offices are always extremely long. Better pack a lunch.

University passes are issued only to the students and faculty of the two institutes of higher learning in the City Above: the Royal University and the University of Arts. There are extension offices of both schools in City Below that accept applications. The requirements for acceptance are high, and they generally take only Merilon residents. A few Outside students are accepted to add "flavor." You may obtain information and applications through your catalyst.

Royal passes are typically issued to Illusionists who wish to perform in the Grove or to pilgrims who have come simply to see the glories of Merilon. However, be forewarned that there are strict restrictions on the number of such Outsiders allowed in City Above. The demand is often so great that waiting for such a pass can try the patience of even a bishop. You should also be aware that, despite their name, these "royal" passes will not allow you to visit the Crystal Palace.

The easiest way into City Above is by invitation—either by someone you know or by someone you don't know but who is willing to take payment for such an invitation. You would be surprised at the number of acquaintances you can acquire through a little encouragement and generous amounts of money.

I have heard talk of people slipping into City Above without a pass, but I have never personally known any who succeeded. The clouds are guarded by the *Duuk-tsarith*. Need I say more?

The Old City Pedestal is home to most of the nobility and the upper middle class (the craftsmen) of the city. Its layout is that of a circle with three notches cut in it.

The western notch is called Guild Cove. Airbarges of the Kan-Hanar dock here, with their cargo from foreign lands waiting to be unloaded. On the north side, just east of the Royal University, is Sky Harbor, where the royal Airyachts are kept. To the east, the Promenade of the High Avenues carves a gentle arch into the circle. From its protected balcony the wealthy can look down into the Performance Grove and enjoy the best entertainment in Thimhallan.

Where you live on the Pedestal is as much a statement about who you are as any title you may hold. The *Albanara* dwell in the elegantly fashioned homes atop the hill east of the Old Citadel wall. These magnificent houses look down to the south on the High Avenues, where the Guildmasters and lesser *Albanara* have their homes. Mannan Park and Mannan Boulevard represent the dividing line between the High Avenues on the east and the Low Avenues on the west. The craftsmen of the Three Sisters generally live in the Low Avenues, as well as those who barely qualify to live in the City Above at all.

My home—or at that time, more properly, my "uncle's" home—was in the Low Avenues. We lived, however, in the region known as Newmarket on the north side, which is located within several blocks of the Royal University. This area, being on the approaches to both the university and the Old Citadel, was destroyed during the Iron Wars and rebuilt during the Second Rectification. Its main street runs in gentle curves, lined with quaint little shops that serve the students. The secondary streets are well kept, quiet, and tree lined.

It is along one such street that my own house is situated. It is relatively typical of most homes in Merilon, except for the truly grand dwellings of the fabulously wealthy.

With the great demand for living space within the city, there are few homes that stand alone. Eighty-five percent of City Above's buildings have at least two walls in common with another structure. There are few homes, even in the wealthy section of the High Avenues, that are completely surrounded by their own land. Nearly all of the streets that you traverse will be row after row of town houses and small shops.

The entrance to most homes is from the street, although its form may alter from time to time dependent upon the artistic whim of the Merilon Beautification Council, who takes its whims from the Empress. Sufficient Life is granted to each district, according to the station of those in residence there, to affect the changes in the house fronts. It is, of course, up to each homeowner to determine the shape and design of his or her home so long as it conforms to the current theme. The cleverness of these designs is often of considerable pride to the homeowner, and each household tries to outdo his neighbor in beauty and uniqueness.

Well I remember the time when Her Majesty wanted to have the city bathed in roses. The fronts of all homes were reshaped into many varieties of the flower. The *Sif-Hanar* caused pink petals to rain down upon the city, soon inundating all its inhabitants. The perfume was quite overpowering.

Because of the constantly changing appearances of the major landmarks, it is important to remember the location of your dwelling by using street signs and relating it to the general position of the Three Sisters, Cathedral, and the Palace. You can almost certainly count on the fact that the home in which you are staying will look nothing like it did when you first arrived.

Homeowners often like to further decorate the entrance to their home by changing its outward appearance. The doorway may be as simple as an outline etched in the wall or as intricate as an animated statue or a wall of thorny roses. This not only prevents burglary but is also something of a game played on the visitor. It is generally and rather smugly said that if you cannot figure out the door, you don't belong inside.

Once you manage to get inside, however, you can relax in a relatively stable environment. Interiors of homes follow the same general plan and are seldom changed by their owners. Homelife is considered the rock of normalcy in a sea of magical change. It is the one place where you can count on things remaining constant.

Homes in Merilon are built with their rooms surrounding a central court. Nearly all homes have two levels with an outer walkway linking the upper rooms. All these look down into the garden.

Every home in Merilon has a garden. It is the House Garden that is the glory of a home and that blesses the family. "A family's Life grows in its garden," as the saying goes. Even the meanest hovel in Merilon has at least a bed of flowers at its entry. Most houses, however, have a garden area measuring roughly three *metra* by five *metra*. Here are usually found flowers, ferns, and shrubs of all description. Guests are often entertained in the garden.

Rooms in the house include milord's bedroom, milady's bedroom, dressing rooms, the family chapel, the children's rooms, the catalyst's room for the family catalyst, guest rooms, parlor, morning room, living room, and House Magi (servants) rooms.

All homes also have a kitchen and dining room. Food is generally purchased on a weekly basis and stored in special closets where the chill of winter is maintained year round for the preservation of perishables.

Next to the kitchen is usually found the disposal room

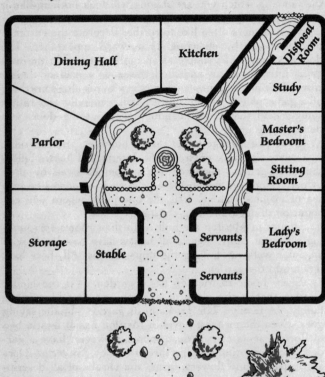

HOME OF MERILON
(first floor)

Dining Hall

Kitchen

Disposal Room

Study

Parlor

Master's Bedroom

Sitting Room

Storage

Stable

Servants

Servants

Lady's Bedroom

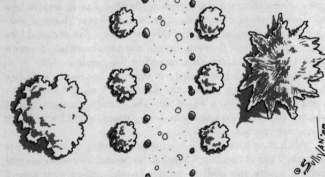

where garbage and refuse are cast. Nothing is destroyed, of course. This would be considered tantamount to murder. Through means which I do not understand, the *Kan-Hanar* have arranged that all our waste is sent far from the city. Where this location was I did not know until much later in my journeys.

The Royal University on the north side and the University of Arts on the southeast side are the pride of Merilon. From them have come some of the most renowned artists and scholars of the modern age. The universities are constructed of shaped stone and are solid, massive, dignified-looking buildings.

The Inn of the Silken Dragon is located in the Old Market's district on the High Avenue side. Its gorgeous tapestries are celebrated throughout all Thimhallan. (The prices here are extremely high! It is next to impossible to get a room—they are reserved years in advance, or so I've heard.)

The Old Citadel is where Merlyn, so legend tells us, built his residence. The original structure was destroyed during the Iron Wars. Now only the protecting wall can be seen. Inside its gates, however, is the most wonderful treasure in all of Merilon. This is the Empress's Garden. Here grows at least one of every plant that exists in Thimhallan. Huge rewards are offered for anyone bringing in a new specimen, and adventurers have been known to risk life and limb in the Outland just to bring back a hitherto unknown weed.

Once you reach City Above, if flying conveyances are not to your liking—or if you are unable to pay their price—you may travel through town by way of one of the Skybridges that extend from one Pedestal to another and to all major landmarks. The Skybridges change form almost daily. You might find yourself drifting down a waterway one day or treading on a rainbow the next.

Having described Merilon to you, I must now come to the part in my narrative where I bid my beloved homeland farewell. My uncle's tyranny was more than my free spirit could bear. The first thing he did when he moved into my parents' house was to reshape all the furniture into the ugly, modernistic style my mother had particularly loathed. Further, he made no inquiries into my parents' deaths, deaths I was beginning to find increasingly mysterious.

Slowly I became consumed with the idea of finding those responsible for that tragedy and bringing them before the justice of the Empress herself.

My first thought was to question the *Duuk-tsarith*. That is much easier said than done. While finding one of the warlocks is simple enough, there is only one place where *you* may ask questions of *them* rather than the other way round—the Font.

I was a skilled Illusionist and could perform a wide variety of musical and visual scenes. I would make my living along the way. I packed my clothing, books, six weeks' worth of food, and several pieces of essential furniture into a small knapsack and floated into the night.

How well I remember leaving my city that spring evening. Since I was an Illusionist—who are known to travel extensively—the *Kan-Hanar* let me out of the Gate with little more than a few questions and a search of my luggage to make certain I wasn't walking off with one of the Empress's prize rose bushes. I drifted over the grassy plain for some time, passing marker after marker. Near the ten *mila* mark my heart failed me and I turned around.

There shone Merilon—my world encased in glass. All that I had known and all that I had ever loved was there. Yet what I had loved was gone. Now there was nothing but heartache for me in the glorious city. Perhaps, I thought, this road will bring me to another place where I might be happy.

I turned again and floated forward once more. The stone markers placed across the Northern Plain marked the road toward the Font. Each stood within sight of the other and glowed faintly in the night. Each looked the same as I passed them, one after another. I lost track of time. When the dawn broke in the east, I fell exhausted to the ground and fell asleep against one of the road markers.

Chapter Three

The Northern Estates

*L*ight and shadow. Light and shadow. Again and again they crossed over my closed eyes. My groggy mind heard voices in the distance. My back ached as I rolled away from the stone. Light and shadow. The voices were clearer now. I stood up, but not for long.

The stone barge slammed into my back and drove me to the ground. My face was pressed through the grass into the cool, damp earth. I choked on sod, pressing close to the ground as the cold marble floated a bare inch or two above me. Should the bargemaster weaken in his Life, the stone would fall and crush me flat!

The first barge passed overhead. Cautiously I pushed myself up from the ground. White tablets were thundering down on me—

Slam! I caught hold of the next barge in the train as best I could. The muscles in my arms ached, my legs were dragged under the great stone platform as it moved over the ground. Somewhere above me I heard shouts.

The stone barge came slowly to a stop. A great rough

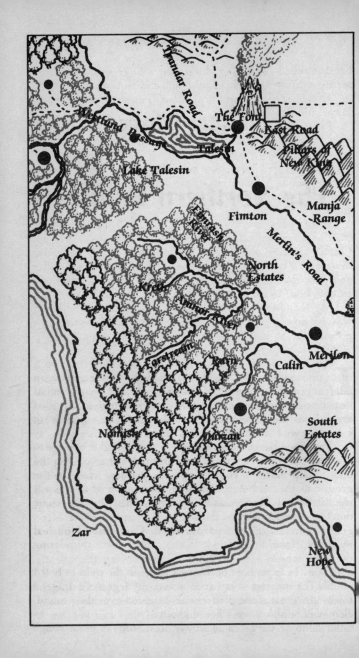

hand grabbed me by my cloak, and a huge woman hoisted me up, glaring at me in rage mingled with concern.

"Name of the Almin, boy, what possessed you to stand in the middle of the road?"

I stared with wonder into the wide face and the burning eyes. She was attractive, though minus a few teeth. (I learned later that she had lost them in a brawl and wore the gaps with pride.) Her name was Hilga Vaordigan, she was a low-ranking member of the *Kan-Hanar,* and she ran a profitable barge service between Merilon and Avidon, with stops in between.

"S-sorry, ma'am, I guess I fell asleep," I stammered.

Her voice was like gravel. "You're of Merilon, all right. Catch your kind outside the 'Bubble' and you got less sense than faeries on Moonnight." She still had hold of my collar and now she shook me slightly. "What you doin' out here, Bubble-boy? Some sort of university initiation?"

My face burned. At the time I wasn't sure whether it was because I was embarrassed at my own stupidity or proud that she had mistaken me for a college man.

"No, ma'am. I'm traveling to the Font."

She let loose of me. I had to take a couple of steps back from her just to take her all in. She was thirteen *decimetra* tall—at least two *decimetra* taller than myself—with shoulders measuring no less than five *decimetra* across. She gave the general appearance of being overweight, but from what I had just experienced, I knew that the illusion was far from the fact. She was all muscle.

"Well, Bubble-boy, the first thing you better pick up on your journey is some sense. Traffic on country roads always stays on the left of the markers. Travelers like yourself should float well clear of them, and for the Almin's peace, don't go sleeping in the middle of the road! Why are you going to such a dull place like the Font anyway? You real religious, Bubble-boy?"

"My parents were killed. I'm investigating their deaths and I've got to talk to the warlocks."

She considered that for a moment. "So, you'll ask the *Duuk-tsarith* what their black-robed ears may have heard, eh? Well, that's reasonable enough if you can get 'em to talk." She paused and looked me over.

"See here, boy. I'm flush from this last trip and the load back ain't all that heavy. I could give you a lift as far as the Font. What do ya say?"

"Well, I'd like to pay for it. I mean—I don't have a lot of money, but—well—do you like music?"

"Fine, boy, fine!" She eyed me dubiously. "You can pay your way with music. Just make sure that we don't have to pay you to make you quit."

With a lusty bellow she ordered the barge train onward. In moments the slabs were again winding their way over the grasses northward.

I hadn't had opportunity to examine the slabs before now. Each was shaped into a rectangle roughly one *metra* by two *metra* across and only one *decimetra* thick. The slabs were connected to each other by a piece of shaped marble that had been altered to allow it to bend. Floating on the left side of the slabs were several other *Kan-Hanar*. Their function was, no doubt, to aid in steering and propelling their barges. In all, there were no fewer than fifty platforms being directed in this manner.

They carried such goods as whole trees that had been removed from the ground and were being shipped north to use for housing, marble used in construction work, and a variety of other items too heavy—and, thus, too expensive—to be transported by the Ariels.

Hilga had made this trip many times before. She knew the land of the Northern Estates well and entertained me with their history as we traveled.

History: Merlyn crossed these lands many times during Thimhallan's early years. He considered them good lands and claimed them for his kingdom. Only during the Iron Wars was their ownership questioned, and then only until Merilon took them back by force within the year.

Traditionally the area was settled and farmed by Merilon *Albanara* who were granted the estates by proclamation of the Empress of Merilon. Most of these estates have remained in the hands of their original family members since the First Rectification. Large estates are cultivated and have eventually become equal to the Duchies of Avidon in their scope and power. The owners of these estates were likewise granted titles of nobility in Merilon and were considered highly influential.

The Duchies of the Northern Estates, during the time prior to the Iron Wars, often maintained armies of their own *DKarn-ðuuk*, who then served both the Duchies' own interests as well as those of Merilon.

At one point during the Iron Wars the armies of Trandar bypassed the armies of Merilon (which were defending the Font) and raced southward across this broad plain. The provisional armies of the Estates could not hope to turn aside the onslaught, and within weeks the city of Merilon itself was under siege. Relief came within the year and the city was again freed, but only after near total devastation. The Trandar armies retreated over this same land, and their rage laid to ruin much of what had been built.

Because of their continued support of Merilon in trying times, the original families of these Estates retained their lands and titles after the war by Imperial decree. Many wild, mutated creatures roamed the countryside in the chaos after the war and some of the Estates were rebuilt with a central keep and protecting castle wall. Many of these old structures remain in use today.

It is rumored that the allegiance of the Estates to Merilon is not as strong as it once was. The Dukes and Barons of these lands have recently begun to finance exploratory missions to recover ancient artifacts lost during the Iron Wars, expeditions that are frowned upon by the Church, who would just as soon these powerful relics remain forever lost.

Current Conditions: Nevertheless, the Estates today remain one of the more civilized areas outside of Merilon. Their gently rolling grounds are ideal for farming, which is carried out on a great scale by the Field Magi who serve the Barons.

As I sat on the marble slab warming myself in the spring sun, the far-off castle towers appeared serene and beautiful, their farms peaceful havens. Little was I to expect that my own experience in the days to come would prove otherwise.

The barge train took nearly a week to traverse the length of the Northern Estates. The Manja Range of mountains were our constant companion to the east as we leisurely made our way over the smooth, grassy road.

The barge people were fine companions, even if they were a bit rough in their manners and appearance. (I would see much worse before my trek was done). We broke camp around midmorning and began the process of setting the barge train in motion. This involved utilizing the magi's own Life power distributed in sparing amount evenly over the whole train. The forward, central, and back sections got particular attention as these locations carried the cargo.

We ate our lunch on the barges. Nothing stopped the progress of the train until early evening when Hilga would select the place for our night encampment. The entire train of stones was formed into a circle and we made our camp in the center.

This last custom seemed rather odd to me. Hilga explained the reason. "All this country used to be tame and peaceful. Iron Wars changed all that. Them Sorcerers let loose stuff that could kill a man before he could even figure what it was what got 'im. Then came the Night and all them creatures the Life Shapers created started to breed and grow on their own. Merilon ain't what it once was, boy. Nothin' is.

"The land's gone wild again and there's wilder things in it every day. Centaurs ain't just in books—Jeb over there lost his brother to one not four months ago. I seen it."

"Yes," I said, "but that still doesn't explain—"

"These barge is my castle, boy. My fortress. Something big, fanged, mean, and scaly comes this way, I can raise them stones up around us in a word. Messes up the load something awful when they stand up vertical like that. Still, I'd rather repack my cargo and risk a little breakage than be et for dinner."

With that she caused the fire to die out. "Night, boy."

Darkness swirled around me and I felt as if I couldn't breathe. I shivered despite my warming magic. I wished she'd raise those stones. The sounds of the night seemed far more sinister than I had remembered them before.

At last our journey came to its conclusion. Talesin, the city at the base of the Font, came into view.

I was elated, but Hilga left me with a warning that dimmed my hopes.

"This is the end of Merilon's rule, boy. Beyond the Estates, anything is possible."

Chapter Four

Talesin

I took my leave of Hilga and her caravan in Talesin and set out to discover something about that city and how I might obtain access to the Font and the *Duuk-tsarith*.

History: the oldest-known structure in all the realms of Thimhallan, the Font has undergone considerable changes during the time of its existence. Its predominance as the spiritual center of all Thimhallan has never changed, except to grow stronger.

The Font was originally a small group of buildings shaped from and delving into the mountain, most of them clustered around the Well of Life. During the First Rectification an Abbey was built on one of the summits of the Font. Here, dwelling in seclusion near the source of Life, catalysts could come from the world over to study, contemplate, and feel nearer to the Almin.

Though undoubtedly the most hotly contested prize during the Iron Wars, the Font itself was never successfully captured by any of the powers. Indeed, of all the factions which took part in that conflict, the catalysts seem to have

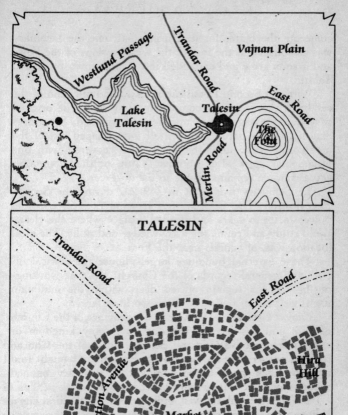

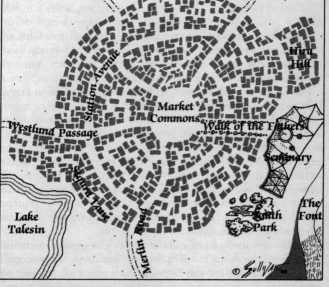

TALESIN

come out the better for it. During that time the Seminary was established at the foot of the western slope of the Font, and it soon grew and expanded into a large township called Talesin.

With the Second Rectification and the unification of the catalysts, the Font was completely renovated. The original cavernous passages were opened and widened. Structures external to the natural Font itself were shaped out of the mountain's rock, until the peaks were covered with one ornamental spire after another. Little of the mountain's actual surface remains visible to the observer.

The Seminary was built in 749 Y.L. during the Second Rectification. The Church was growing both in size and power in those years and needed a place where the clergy could study and refine their knowledge and skills. The ideal location was, of course, near the Font.

These external buildings largely house the clerical offices and general records of the Church. The true workings of the Church remain buried deep within the mountain itself, well out of the sight of the world at large.

Current Conditions: The Font is the province of the Church of Life and lies outside the domain of any kingdom or empire. The motivations and political goals of the Church itself, however, are not for me to discuss (or I might find my book taking its place among the legendary banned volumes of the Sorcerers and other heretics).

I remember Talesin well. It was, after all, the first city I visited after leaving my lifetime home.

First I noticed the smell. Never had I encountered such a mixture of spice and rot, sweat and perfume. It seemed to me that the people of Talesin were in a great hurry to experience all of life at once and to carry as much of its aroma clinging to them as possible. Vague, shifting smokes drifted from the incense shops, floating among the racks of spices from Sharzad and the fruits brought in from Avidon. All of this wonder mingled with the unmistakable odor of the open sewers that ran through the city.

After the smell, I noticed the noise. The vendors jammed the streets, and each, with his or her own unique cry, brought seething crowds around them. In time I came to recognize the vendors individually. In those first hours, walking the streets of that strange gateway to the plains, their voices tumbled about me with a roar like a waterfall.

Finally—the spectacle of it all! I found myself drifting in a river of people down narrow canyons of city streets. Around me pressed every type of humanity I had ever imagined. Dark-haired, dark-skinned people of the Vajnan Plains hawked their legendary glassware. Blond overseers from the Westlunds exhibited their crops just arrived from the fields many hundreds of *mila* distant. The colors of carefully crafted Manja cloth fluttered above the crowded street, borne on the air by golden doves. Catalysts of all descriptions were everywhere. As I was swept down the streets, I recall seeing an Illusionist creating a battle of dragons overhead for the amusement of the children gathered round about him. A battered hat stood open at his feet—the sign of an Illusionist begging for contributions. The crowd soon carried me beyond that man, yet for days his visage haunted me. I saw myself in his haggard face.

Talesin is veined by roads that radiate from its center. The path by which I entered the city was, of course, the Merlyn Road, which was originally laid out by the Old One himself. The Eastroad runs around the point of the Manja Range and across the Vajnan Plain, where it eventually splits north toward Sharakan as well as continuing through the Eastpass of Zith-el. The old Trandar Road runs northwest across the plains to eventually wind its way through the passes of the Chow-Li Peaks and beyond to Avidon. The Westlund Passage generally follows the banks of the River Fimrash to the west, although its length has never been traveled in modern times. That path of broken stones leads across unkept ground to the farms maintained by Merilon in what use to be called the Westlund. Beyond those, the Westlund Passage is said to have once gone all the way to Aronica, the traditional seaport of Merilon. Since the Iron Wars, however, the road has been overtaken by the Outland wilderness, and now only centaurs and worse walk those paths.

All of these roads pass into the city and meet in the center—known as the Market Commons. The Commons, as it is most often called, might once have been intended as a park. If such was the case, its intent was long ago overtaken by commerce. Trees continue to thrive here and flowers abound, but no one pays any attention to them. It is here that all the world's goods may be had for any price.

The Walk of the Fathers runs in a straight line from the Commons eastward to climb the hill on which sits the Seminary. The Walk of the Fathers is a broad, tree-lined avenue decorated at regular intervals with thirty-foot-tall statues commemorating the line of bishops who have shepherded the catalysts since the Great Passage.

I planned to go at once to the Font and gain an audience with one of that Dark Order, the *Duuk-tsarith*. Following inquiries in the Commons, I floated eagerly up the Walk of the Fathers and stood at last before the Seminary that lies at the base of the Font.

I presented myself at the gates of this austere cloister. Carved into the wall is a great stone sun, whose rays signify Life shining down upon all people. On a platform before this stone sun is a low altar supported by a pedestal. Written words and pictures for the illiterate instruct the supplicant in its use. Kneeling at the altar, I placed my hands under the slab and waited.

A figure in green robes trimmed in gray stepped out of the sun on the wall to the tinkle of many small glass bells. Moving gracefully, the novitiate came to the platform and reaching down, beckoned me to stand.

The hood of the robe fell back, and for the first time I saw the face that would change my life. Her eyes were large and liquid, yet there burned in them conviction and determination. Her mouth might have been pleasing had she not held it in such a tight frown of disapproval. Her lithe body would have been alluring had it not stood in such a stern pose.

Her honey gold hair was pulled back severely from her face. She had it braided into a single thick coil that fell over her left shoulder and hung down past her waist. I caught myself imagining what it would be like to see that luxuriant hair tumble freely about her shoulders.

Her name was Lilieth—Sister Lilieth—and she asked why I had come.

"T—to find the truth," I stammered.

Her head cocked to one side, a wry smile played about

her lips. "A truth seeker, eh? Which particular truth are you seeking, or do you look for them all?"

What I had in mind wasn't exactly something that could be discussed with this catalyst. Not knowing what to say, I stared into her lovely eyes.

She shook her head, the coil of hair swinging gently. "Come along, my brother. Perhaps we can find this truth you seek." She took hold of my arm and led me through the sun onto the grounds of the Seminary.

I believe that there are no uglier buildings in all of Thimhallan. The towers of the Seminary, rising from the lawns that surround them, are all made of the same uniform gray rock. Each is different in both its general architecture and design—all are overworked and overstated. As one walks through the shadows of these monoliths, the entire effect is to make you feel smaller than you were just moments before and somehow less significant.

The Seminary is the world to the catalysts who come here to study, though occasionally they may be found in the streets of Talesin, sent there on some errand. Buildings include dormitories, classrooms, laboratories, and several practice rooms for their art. There is a small library on the grounds, but the true wealth and knowledge of the catalysts is in the Font Library deep within the mountain.

We made our way past the Seminary's structures and approached a small marble structure that looked exactly like a mausoleum. I was suddenly confronted by a feeling of dread such as I had never before experienced. A pair of statues, shaped into the form of *Duuk-tsarith*, stood on either side of a shadowy archway.

"Press your hands against this granite sphere," she instructed me. I did so, and the feeling of dread left me.

I pointed at the statues and stammered, "Are—are they—"

"Alive?" Lilieth's strides were long for her short stature and I was forced to hurry to keep up. "Are they *Duuk-tsarith* who look like stone or stone that looks like the *Duuk-tsarith*? There is Life in all creations of the Almin, my brother, from the lowest stone to the highest stars. Would it make a difference either way?"

"I have come to petition the *Duuk-tsarith* to answer my question."

"They know."

"Do they know the answer?"

"That is not the issue. It is a question not of what they know but of what you know. That will determine how much they can help you." We came to a dark, cavernous room and she beckoned me to enter. "That is why they have sent me. Tell me all you know. They are listening."

In that dark, tomblike chamber I told her all my story. She listened quietly, wearing that same severe expression on her face and never once interrupting me.

I talked until I couldn't talk anymore. When at last I finished, I stared at her and waited.

She gazed at me with indifferent eyes.

"You will be notified of their decision. Thank you, brother. Go out the same way we came in." With that, she walked into the darkness.

"But how will you find me?" I cried.

She was no longer there.

The wild city of Talesin was a far cry from the beautiful, cultured environs of Merilon. To be sure there were dwellings that were as grand as though found in the City Above. These were owned by the Trade Barons, who made their homes on Hira Hill north of the Seminary.

Generally speaking, however, the Guild Houses and craft shops are clustered as close as possible around the Commons, and the tradesmen's homes are clustered as closely as possible around their businesses. The buildings in the center of town are some of the highest in Thimhallan— several over ten levels. The structures are shorter after that, standing no more than two or three levels for the most part. The buildings here also share common walls in most instances—the reason is apparently not the lack of space so much as the need to float to one's place of business as swiftly as possible. Time in Talesin is counted in coins.

The poorest section of town is the southwest area of the city known as Sigurd's Lane. During the time of the First Rectification this lane was a bustling area of trade that led from the inland port on Lake Talesin to the center of the city. In those days ships would come up the Fimrash from

Cyrsa bringing goods from distant Sharzad, Balzaab, and northern Vajnan.

However, the Iron Wars brought changes in the river's course. The lower Fimrash was wild and no longer safe to travel. Since that time, the docks of Talesin have seen little trade save a few barges sent by the farms when the overland barge trains have difficulties with centaurs or giants. Sigurd's Lane dried up, and with it the neighborhoods around it.

As one might expect, I found my own poor lodgings in this area. The Magewage Inn charges agreeable rates while remaining most disagreeable in almost all other aspects. I would have much preferred the cloud-shaped beds of the Talesin Commonview or the fine food of the House of Kazar, both located just off the Commons. Both were priced beyond my means.

I hoped it would only be a matter of days before I heard from the *Duuk-tsarith*. Days melted into weeks, however, without a word, and I soon ran out of money. Hat in hand I took to the streets to sell the only skill I possessed. There was a great deal of traffic from foreign lands, which provided an ever-changing audience. While my own Illusions were hardly on a par with those who had studied the craft for many years, I compensated for my inadequacies with my knowledge of my former homeland and drew heavily on the wonders in Merilon for my images. I returned late each night from the thronging streets, nearly devoid of Life from creating my Illusions, though a little richer for it. I would sleep in complete exhaustion until late in the morning. Only then had I rested enough to regain the Life I had spent the previous day and—once more—return to entertaining in the streets. This provided me with barely sufficient funds on which to survive.

Talesin is a city run by and for the catalysts of the Font. There is no law here except their law, which is enforced by the *Duuk-tsarith*. No other government is needed. No complaint has ever been voiced that wasn't answered—in one form or another.

I found it quite remarkable, therefore, to discover (through my life on the streets) that Talesin is the central headquarters of the Thieves Guild in Thimhallan. It seems astonishing, though somehow appropriate, that the forces of Law and the forces of Chaos should dwell within spitting distance of each other.

As one might imagine, entrance into the Thieves Guild is extremely difficult to obtain; their major fear, of course, being infiltration by the *Duuk-tsarith*. There are elaborate signs and countersigns, secret words and tests one must undergo to obtain entrance—or so I heard. The *Duuk-tsarith* play along, and about once every ten years they sweep through town and round up as many of the thieves as they can catch—mostly small fry while the big fish swim safely away. It seems to have become almost a game, providing both sides with a little light entertainment to break up the monotony of work.

Punishment for thieves is imaginative and suits their crimes. You can spot a former pickpocket by his mutated hands—now five times their normal size. A convicted robber is often festooned with heavy golden chains that he can never remove but is forced to lug about wherever he goes.

It may seem strange, my going on about thieves this way, but I began to feel like a felon myself. No matter where I went, what I did, whether it was day or night, I often felt a *presence*. That's the only way to describe it. I kept thinking someone was watching me, yet whenever I looked around, no one was there. I started at a touch on my shoulder, only to find myself alone. I would answer a voice, only to find no one had spoken.

My nerves were being drawn and stretched until I felt like a man in some ancient machine of torture.

Chapter Five

The Font

The answer came in midsummer.

I had returned to the Magewage Inn late that evening as was my custom. Standing in the entryway was a short catalyst wearing the green robes trimmed gray of the Seminary novitiate. It was apparent from his sagging shoulders and weary aspect that he had been waiting for some time.

"Master Wildreth?"

I nodded.

"Sister Lilieth bids me deliver to you a message: 'You have been granted your audience with the *Duuk-tsarith* on the morrow. Present yourself at the Seminary gates at dawn. At that time your questions and other matters concerning you will be taken under advisement.'

"May I give her your affirmation in reply, Master?"

So delighted was I at the prospect of finally redressing the wrong done to my parents that I nearly shouted for joy. My answer, I told the student, was in the affirmative and I would be at their door in the morning.

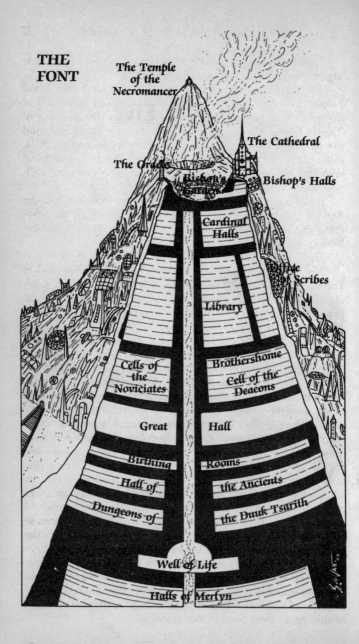

THE FONT

The Temple
of the
Necromancer

The Cathedral

The Oracle

Bishop's Garden

Bishop's Halls

Cardinal Halls

Office of Scribes

Library

Cells of
the
Noviciates

Brothershome

Cell of the
Deacons

Great   Hall

Birthing   Rooms

Hall of   the Ancients

Dungeons of   the Duuk Tsarith

Well of Life

Halls of Merlyn

I gave no thought to just what "other matters" concerning me the warlocks meant to discuss.

The next day I knelt once more on the altar that stood before the stone sun. The dawn was cool and the smell of the earth was sweet. There is a stillness in the morning of Talesin that is like no other. All of the shops are closed, and the streets, wet with morning dew, are often empty. It is, perhaps, no more quiet than in other places, but contrasted with the normal hectic pace of the city, the morning stillness there seems all the sweeter.

I was again met by Sister Lilieth, who took me into the Seminary grounds. We walked westward through the towering buildings until we came to a great stone stairway leading up into the mountain.

Here, then, was the Font.

The entire mountain is referred to as the Font and is known by no other name. Once it was the last craggy peak of the Manja Range, not greatly different from its neighbors. That, however, was many centuries ago. The Second Rectification brought power and wealth to the Church. Since that time the Font—central symbol of faith—has been reworked to such an extent that there seems no *decimetra* of its surface that has not been transformed into a spire, minaret, flying buttress, crystal wall, frieze, or sculpture. The entire surface of the mountain gives the appearance of being a vertical city.

Standing before its entrance, I stared up in wonder. High clouds streaked the blue sky with long fingers of red. They drifted quietly above the mountain, its uncounted spires silhouetted against the dawn. The Font from a distance is impressive. Standing beneath it, I felt as though its weight was crushing me into the ground. I felt as insignificant and worthless as the dust on my boots.

Lilieth gently touched my arm, bringing my attention back from the spectacle overhead. The stairs that led to the entrance and that had been carved out of the mountain itself were no less than thirty *metra* across at their base, narrowing to twenty *metra* at the entrance itself—the main doors of the Font. Twenty *metra* high, also shaped out of the side of the mountain, the doors were as wide as the top of the stairs.

In my excitement I began to float up the stairs, but Lilieth caught hold of my arm and held me back. I glanced at her questioningly. She looked away from me and, with a sigh, gathered up her robes and began walking up the steps. In my haste I had forgotten that the stairs at the Font were far from ornamentation — they were a necessity. It is the lot of those who grant the power of Life to others that they have almost no ability to use that Life themselves. Looking into Lilieth's eyes, I saw there the envy of those who have the power to use the Life that it is the catalyst's fate to give and never use.

I lowered myself to the cold granite steps and, feeling awkward, stumbled up the steps after her. I had never climbed stairs before, and I was considerably out of breath when I reached the top. Bending over, hands on my knees, I gulped down the morning air. When at last I looked up, my newly recovered breath left my body in a whoosh for there were two of the *Duuk-tsarith* looking down at me, their faces hidden in the shadows cast by the hoods of their black robes.

The warlocks spoke no word; a slight movement of a hand was a command to me to follow. Both turned at precisely the same moment and floated down the Great Hall. I started to float after them, only to receive another silent rebuke in the form of a tug on my sleeve from Sister Lilieth. Once again I sank to the cavern floor.

The Great Hall is the entrance to all the open areas of the Font. While there are several lesser-known (and many secret) entrances and exits from the Font, this is the one generally used. All those having routine business with the catalysts pass through this hall. As we moved through it, I could see shadowy entrances leading deeper into the mountain.

Never before have I seen such a profusion of staircases! Stairs spiraled upward here, downward there. With the exception of the *Duuk-tsarith* — who, unlike the rest of us, are free to use the Corridors whenever they choose — virtually everyone who comes to the Font moves from place to place on foot. The Hall was crowded with catalysts, coming and going, yet so vast was it that it seemed empty.

"Where do the stairs lead?" I whispered to Lilieth. No

one, I noticed, spoke above a hushed tone, and I was in too much awe of this place to break its holy silence.

"From this Hall you may travel to any open part of the Font," was her soft reply.

As we continued on, following the dark shadows deeper into the mountain, Lilieth took advantage of the long walk to describe the Font.

There are several distinct divisions within the Font itself. These were crafted at various times throughout the history of Thimhallan. Some of the structures were said to be shaped by the hand of Merlyn himself.

The sections that were first crafted during the Year of Dawn included the Well of Life, the Hall of the Ancients, the Great Hall, the Library, and the Temple of the Necromancer.

The Well of Life was in the center of the Hall of Life, carved deep below the surface of the ground. In the old days the Hall was called the Hall of Life and Death, but with the disgrace of the Sorcerers after the Iron Wars, the name was changed to more accurately reflect the nature of our world. The Well of Life and the Hall that surrounds it are the oldest structures in Thimhallan. Originally designed to support the Border and bring Life into the world, the Well was shaped by Merlyn with the aid of all the catalysts who survived the Great Passage.

Only catalysts and *Duuk-tsarith* are allowed to enter the Hall. I therefore pass along Lilieth's description. The Hall is shaped from the granite of the mountain's base. The domed ceiling soars nearly fifty *metra* above the Well of Life. The Hall itself is roughly circular, measuring an average of thirty *metra* in diameter. Four alcoves, large and deep, stand next to each other against one side of the Hall. A beautifully shaped throne in each of these alcoves accommodates the various Cardinals of the Realm. Opposite these is another, larger alcove, with a most magnificent throne. Here sits the Bishop of the Realm—the highest religious authority in Thimhallan. Directly between the Bishop's throne and those of the Cardinals is the Well of Life, surrounded by row after row of stone benches.

"The Hall looks as if a giant hand had reached down into rock and scooped it out in a single motion," Lilieth told me.

That perhaps accounts for the irreverent names I later heard given to the alcoves—Merlyn's Fingers—and the Bishop's Throne—Merlyn's Thumb. I leave it to your imagination what those hard, cold stone benches are called by those forced to sit upon them during long and tedious ceremonies.

The Hall of Life is accessible by stairs, but the way to it lies through the Hall of the Ancients and is no longer used. Those who enter the Hall do so by means of the Corridor.

The Hall of the Ancients refers to several levels also built far below the ground, just above the Hall of Life. These were the original dwellings used by those of the Great Passage, who sheltered beneath the mountain while the world was being restructured. Sometime during the First Rectification the Bishop ordered the entire section sealed—never to be reopened.

What was the reason? No one is certain, but it is rumored that all (or at least most) of the inherent evil in the world was captured by Merlyn and locked into rooms that supposedly exist on the same level and surround the Well of Life. Known as Merlyn's Chambers, the rooms are supposed to hold many wondrous and valuable artifacts of magic brought from the Ancient World, treasure that is now purportedly guarded by all sorts of nightdream creatures.

"House Magi tales," Lilieth scoffed, telling me this.

I might have agreed if not for the somewhat alarming story that followed. It seems that during the Second Rectification, the *Duuk-tsarith* (apparently not believing these rumors) reentered the lowest rooms of the Hall of the Ancients, intending to reclaim them for their own use. The reclamation ended abruptly. The *Duuk-tsarith* reduced their area of occupation to the top three levels of what is recorded to be no less than ten levels of living quarters, halls, Merlyn's laboratories, treasure rooms, libraries, and who knows what else.

The warlocks have never disclosed what happened to cause the end of their reclamation nor why they retreated to the areas they now occupy. Anything that could frighten them away—if that is truly what happened—must be hairraising indeed!

These three levels have come to be known as the dungeons of the *Duuk-tsarith*. This is something of a misnomer. While the warlocks do, indeed, maintain cells for imprisonment here, these levels are by no means their main dungeons.

The Library of the Font is said to be the repository of all the knowledge in Thimhallan. This is certainly *not* true. The *Duuk-tsarith*, I have learned, keep their own library. Hidden from the knowledge of ordinary men, it comes closer to fitting that description, containing — so it is whispered — records brought by those who made the Great Passage. Even so, the Library of the Font is the most extensive library among all the Mysteries. Located in the center of the mountain, halfway from its base to its crest, the Library is no less than fifteen levels in height. It is arranged in nine concentric circles that radiate from its core. The outer rings contain those books whose writings deal with routine matters — such as the uses of Life, the histories of Thimhallan, the lives of famous men and women, philosophical works, arts and crafts, cooking, and fiction. These are available to all the catalysts and students with permission to study here. The Inner Library, however, houses not only rare books, but forbidden books as well. Many of the most ancient writings of the Sorcerers of the Ninth Mystery are rumored to be housed there, although any catalyst you ask will swear that such soul-damning works of the devil were all destroyed during the Iron Wars.

During the Second Rectification when the Font underwent great changes, new sections known as the Birthing Rooms for Destitute Women, Cells of the Novitiates, Cells of the Deacons, Brotherhome, Office of Scribes, Cardinal Halls, and Bishop's Halls were crafted. As the catalysts worked to salvage what they could of the available knowledge on the now-defunct Mysteries of Spirit and Time, the Library was expanded.

The Birthing Rooms are located just above the level of the Hall of the Ancients. Despite their proximity, there are no known passages from the Birthing Rooms to the lower halls. One obtains direct access to the Birthing Rooms from the Great Hall via several downward-spiraling staircases.

The Birthing Rooms are staffed by *Theldara* and *Mannanish* of various stations. About all that can be said for these rooms, remarked Lilieth, is that they are functional. They are severe and undecorated. The appellation "for Destitute Women" is only a polite fiction. All in Thimhallan know that any woman—no matter what her class—who has an "unsanctioned" pregnancy is brought here to be delivered of her child. What happens to the babies is not known, but it is rumored that there are nurseries within these chambers that have, from time to time, been used to seclude children declared "politically ill-advised." I have heard wild stories of parents offering incredible wealth to any daring enough to break into the Font and steal back their lost children. Since these rooms are well guarded by the *Duuk-tsarith*, I put little credence in such tales.

The *Theldara* will never discuss these matters with anyone, although there have been several claims that the records of these rooms are meticulously kept and that their secrets are recorded among the pages of their tomes.

Above the Birthing Rooms is the Great Hall. This is, actually, a series of halls, some of which lead to council chambers, the Cathedral, and meditation rooms.

All of the general business of the Font is conducted on this level, as are all meetings of a secular nature. This is undoubtedly the most ornate section of the Font, although many who visit it feel uneasy in its rooms. The reason for this is undoubtedly the fact that there is little Life evident here. The catalysts are not craftsmen but must hire their shaping done for them. They dislike having their peace disturbed by workmen, and therefore what magic exists is present in the form of objects that have been donated to the Church. The total effect is one of a feeling of helplessness to those who are accustomed to using Life with such ease and abundance.

Above the Great Hall are the Cells of the Novitiates and the Cells of the Deacons. These areas provide the basic housing for those who live and work inside the Font itself. Each Novice and Deacon has a cell of his or her own measuring two *metra* on a side. In this small space is found the catalyst's cot, study table, personal books, and meager possessions. Each cell receives its light from a crystal in its ceiling, which has been connected by craft with all the other such crystals in the Font. All of these tie to several crystals on the outside of the Font that gather in the light of the sun and then distribute it throughout the structure. At a word from the person within the room, these marvelous crystals (a gift of the *Quin-alban*) channel their light back into the other crystals and thus can darken the room during daylight. The crystals radiate light slower than they absorb it, and in this way they continue to glow through the night if need be. Wind, warmed or cooled to a pleasant temperature, rushes through tunnels shaped into the rock, delivering fresh air throughout the Font. The overall effect is pleasant—the rooms are well lit, there is plenty of fresh, outside air—far from the horrors of underground life that many imagine.

All of these cells are clustered around central dining, sanitation, and transportation centers. Food is prepared by hired servants. Hot spring waterfalls provide bathing facilities. The refuse of the Font is transported to an unknown location.

Above the living quarters is located the Brotherhome. Here, the full-time Priests who serve at the Font have their dwellings. Their arrangement of cells are similar to those of the Cells of the Deacons, except that the rooms are generally more spacious and have high, vaulted ceilings. Priests' rooms generally range in size from three to four *metra* on a side.

The Office of Scribes is located above the Brotherhome and surrounds the Library. Church scribes go about the business of running the organization that reaches all civilized regions of Thimhallan. Each of these levels has access to the outer areas of the labyrinthine Library and offers research services to those in communication with the Font.

Messengers are central to the Church's survival as a political entity, the catalysts utilize the Corridors, the Ariels, the Messenger Catalysts (generally Deacons) to maintain a constant flow of information. All these keep the Bishop informed of events transpiring throughout the civilized parts of Thimhallan.

Above the Library and the clerical offices are the Cardinal Halls. Several of these luxurious apartments can be seen from outside the Font, for their exterior is shaped into large gargoyles whose bright, jeweled eyes glare down at those beneath. According to Lilieth, each of the Cardinals' apartments has a spectacular view, even those located near the heart of the mountain. The eyes of the gargoyles magically transmit what they see to false windows set inside the apartments of these select ministers.

The Font is crowned by three peaks. Nestled between the peaks is a small bowl that, ages ago, must have been the crater of the volcano. This is the Bishop's Garden. The Bishop's Halls, as his personal apartments are called, are adjacent to his garden, allowing the Bishop to take strolls among its pleasures at his leisure. Below that, on a sunny slope, is the Druid's Garden. A wide variety of herbs and plant life are grown here in part to satisfy the healing needs of the *Theldara* who work in the Font. Lilieth offered to take me to view them, following my audience with the warlocks.

All this time we had been traversing the Great Hall. Suddenly Lilieth turned and led me through an aperture that was floridly decorated with the symbols of the Nine Mysteries. We passed through this into a small hallway, whose walls were bleak and stark. Although it was dimly lit by some unseen source, it seemed dark to me after the glaring brightness of the crystal lights in the Great Hall.

Groping my way along the hall, I struggled to see. The chill in the air told me Lilieth and I had just emerged from the hallway into a vast chamber. When my eyes finally adjusted to the dimness, I saw the pit.

Gaping before Lilieth was a large hole. Looking into it by the eerie purple light glowing from an arched dome overhead, I saw that the hole was actually the top of a funnel that led down to a vertical shaft. The mouth was easily a full ten *metra* across, narrowing to the vertical shaft that I estimated was nearly three *metra* across. After staring at this in amazement for a moment, I glanced around the room. The presence of several other archways indicated to me that there were many entrances to this strange funnel-chamber. The lip of the funnel was extremely narrow, the sides looked slick in the purple light. There seemed to be no safe way around it for one who had to walk, and I was wondering why Lilieth had brought us here when, to my horror, she stepped directly out onto the downward curve of the floor.

"Lilieth! No!" I cried, floating out to grab hold of her.

The catalyst took a step toward the shaft before she turned to look sternly at me. Her body stood on the slope of the funnel at an angle of forty-five degrees, her robes falling at the same angle around her feet.

"All is well, Petar. This is the Focus of the Almin's. Blessing. Please follow me, and remember, here you must walk."

With that she turned and headed straight down the shaft in slow, measured steps. It was as if the wall of the shaft had become the floor to her. Her quiet footfalls echoed up the shaft behind her.

It took considerable courage, but I managed to take my first few steps onto that sloping floor. Soon I, too, was walking vertically, as though the wall was a floor beneath my feet.

The dimness around me was maddening. There was light enough for me to discern shapes, yet it was too dark to identify anything. I had the impression that the floor curved several times in different directions. Lilieth was like a ghost flickering before me.

At long last the round shaft—for that is what it had become in my mind—opened into a vast space of unknown dimension. The walls were illuminated with deep blue light that seemed to fade into infinity. At the very edge of my vision no fewer than a dozen black-robed warlocks stood silently, their hands folded before them.

I turned to look for Lilieth, but the catalyst had vanished from my sight.

I had reached the dungeons of the *Duuk-tsarith*.

Something in the back of my mind screamed panic. Though I knew that I was here on a mission of my own and that these people had, by allowing me to come this far, agreed to answer my questions, still I was paralyzed with fear. The sight of the *Duuk-tsarith* on a brightly lit street is sufficient to bring grown men to their knees. Here in their own street, so to speak, I thought I might well lose my senses.

In a moment, however, a voice spoke and my fears vanished.

"You, Petar Wildreth, have come to investigate the death of your parents." The voice resonated through the hall, seeming to come from no one particular form. It was the voice of a woman I think, though I really could not be certain. "Your lands and title have been usurped by your uncle—a man *you* find unfit to trod the meanest patch of ground in Thimhallan. How was it your parents were in the Mannan Park when both should have at that moment been at their offices on the Three Sisters? How were the Westlund Separatists able to penetrate City Above? Why did your uncle turn up immediately after their death?"

These last three questions startled me. I had not considered them at all.

"Yes, your—eh—your great—"

"Enforcer."

"Your great Enfor . . ."

"Just 'Enforcer.' "

"Yes, Enforcer." Being corrected by a *Duuk-tsarith* is as close to death as I care to come. "These are my questions."

"You are young, boy," the voice said coldly. "Very young and immature."

I know I felt about six at that moment.

"We could answer these questions for you, Wildreth, but we choose not to."

I cried out, but the voice continued as if it had not heard me. "You do not have wisdom enough to hear the answer. You must go into the world and learn. When you are wiser about the ways of the world and of men, then we can help you."

"But where should I go?" I asked helplessly.

"Your father has a brother in Zith-el."

"Yes, Enforcer."

"Both your parents came originally from that city."

"Yes, Enforcer."

"Perhaps you should start there."

"But wouldn't it be easier . . . if you just told . . ."

"Farewell." With that, the *Duuk-tsarith* bowed their heads. A tremendous gust of wind hit me and blew me backward into the tunnel. I slid without any grace the length of it until, at last, I ended up sprawled face down at the edge of the funnel.

Lilieth stood before me.

Beckoning, she turned away. I cast a backward glance at the funnel, thinking that I might try to make my way back and insist that the warlocks share their knowledge with me.

The funnel was gone.

There was nothing to do but follow the catalyst. As we walked, I felt Life surge around us, and suddenly a Corridor gaped open before me. Lilieth took my hand, and in an instant we both stood in the Bishop's Garden at the top of the Font.

The garden seemed to my confused sight to contain every type of healing herb and plant that could be found in the world. The flowers were even more beautiful than the Empress Garden in the City Above.

The Garden also afforded those who walked its soft paths a magnificent view of the three peaks at the top of the Font. Though startled at the sudden change, I was comforted by the peace and beauty of the place, which was, no doubt, why Lilieth brought me.

I gazed upward. Of the three peaks, the shortest has become something of a legendary monument. During the First Rectification the pinnacle was reshaped by the Diviners into a frieze that told the history of the world—both past and future—in great detail. So great was this detail, however, that those who were not Diviners could not look long at it without going mad. There are a few legendary individuals who are said to have had the nerve to climb up there and read the Oracle of the Font and receive answers to their questions about the future. I felt, however, that my answer did not lie in the ways of madness.

The second-highest peak—and the largest of the three—had become known as the Cathedral. It was shaped, during the Second Rectification, originally to provide a place of worship for the people of Thimhallan. In practice this inspiring structure has seen little use over the years. The top of the mountain has become the domain of the Bishop, and seldom does Bishop Vanya invite the ordinary people of the world into his garden.[1]

---

[1] The phrase "in your own garden" is peculiar to Merilon. It alludes to the fact that anyone who is in your garden has breached the outer wall of the home and is therefore privy to all of your secrets. It connotes an uncomfortable and/or undesirable proximity to someone you may not like or trust.

The highest of the peaks, a pinnacle of stone rising five hundred feet above the Bishop's Garden, supports the Temple of the Necromancers, where, anciently, those of that lost craft practiced their arts. It is now unused and purportedly haunted by the spirits of the dead who used to come there.

Perhaps it was the view of the crisp, clean mountain air or the fragrance of the herbs, but I suddenly felt a surge of resolution tingle in my blood. I would go forward and discover the truth! I would win back what was rightfully mine! I turned to Lilieth to tell her of my resolve. The words died on my lips.

Her expression had not changed since she had brought me through the Font. But there was something I had never before seen in her eyes—a brightness and a warmth and a hint of shyness.

"I have had the Cardinal of the Font perform the Vision[2] for the two of us. The results are pleasing and proper in the sight of the Almin. We can be married," she said.

I was astounded—pleased, but astounded.

"I—I can't m-marry you!" I stammered. "It—it's not that I'm not attracted to you. I am . . . I think. . . . It's just that—"

She stopped me. "The *Duuk-tsarith* have explained that you have yet a long road ahead of you. When you have completed your quest for your family's honor, I will be waiting here for you."

That night I packed everything I owned and set off for Zith-el.

If I had known then what lay ahead of me, I might have stayed behind to live in peace and comfort with Lilieth.

---

[2]One of the few skills of the Diviners that the catalysts were able to learn, the Vision predicts in advance of their marriage whether or not a couple will produce children and therefore their union can be sanctioned by the Church.

Chapter Six

Zith-el and the Field of Glory

The caravan of centipedes moved slowly across the broad green plain. Occasionally someone would try to strike up a conversation, but that was impossible to keep up for very long. There is simply no way you can lie on the back of the centipede in the sun and not fall asleep.

I had been traveling for twenty-three days, making my way down the Eastroad from Talesin to Zith-el.

Having made few friends in Talesin, I was traveling alone. I was on foot as well, since I did not have the price in Life to be able to afford to travel the Corridors.

My family had moved from Zith-el two years before I was born. Both my parents were from there originally, and it seemed as good a place to start as any. The road was far different from the Merlyn Road I had traveled to Talesin. This road was well traveled and its mark could be seen cutting across the gentle roll of the countryside. The monoliths that marked the road were broken and in disrepair, however. They disappeared altogether some fifty *mila* east

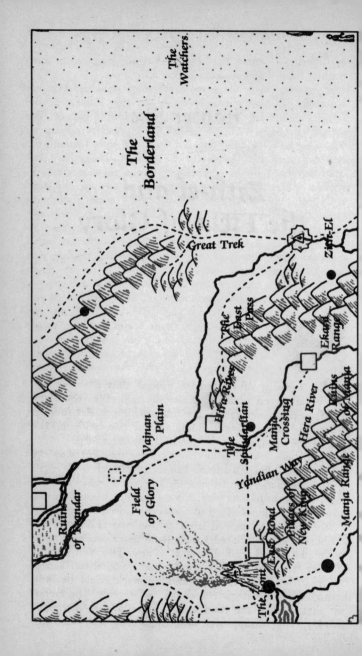

of Talesin. I hoped that I would again meet with some trading barges that would give me a lift.

I drifted above the ground eastward until the markers stopped. To the south I could see the Pillars of the Newking—all that is left of the old kingdom of Camot. The city and its keep were destroyed during the Iron Wars by tunneling demons, who dug out the earth from beneath the city and caused it to fall into the ground. The Pillars that used to stand before the Silver Gates to that city still remain, but everything else is gone. Some say the city itself still exists somewhere deep beneath the ground, its inhabitants still fighting these underworld demons. Others say that the entire city rests under a spell and will not awaken until the means to return the city to the surface of the world is found. None, however, have discovered any passage into that place, although many have searched for it, there reputedly being rich treasure lying beneath the surface.

Across those plains, beyond my sight, are the Hera and Hira rivers and the Ekard Range. To the east I saw the shifting high grasses of the Vajnan Plains and the swath that the road cut across it. Zith-el lay beyond them all.

After several days travel I was about to step once again onto that seemingly endless road when the centipede caravan, also out of Talesin, came along behind me. The specially mutated centipedes are each over ten *metra* long. Their myriad legs rumble along the ground like a hundred giant fingers drumming the edge of a table. There were no fewer than fifteen of these creatures, all heavily laden, making their way down the road. As the caravan passed me, I noticed that the masters of these animals slept soundly. I supposed that the motion of the insects lulled them into dreams.

Unseen, I jumped up onto the back of the last centipede and, in this way, joined the caravan. (I discovered later that this was an extremely dangerous thing to attempt and I would not advise it to any travelers. The masters of the caravan are able to sleep during the day because their insects are wide-awake and the bite of these giant centipedes is extremely painful! The centipede I rode must have been looking the other way for the moment.) As I lay among the trade goods strapped to the back of the bug, I reasoned that if the traders had been awake, they surely would have given me a lift. Since none of them were awake, why should I deprive them of my company due to a failing on their part? Besides, someone should look after . . . after their . . .

It was at that moment that I, too, fell asleep.

When I awoke that night, I found myself bound cocoonlike in silk from the neck down, being forced to explain to the *Kan-Hanar* in charge of the expedition why I was there at all. Since they still seemed a bit drowsy, I insisted that they had invited me to join them. They accepted my argument, and I was one of them for the journey.[1]

That was twenty-three days previous and we still had not come to the distant mountains of the Ekard Range, just visible on the horizon. How I longed to slip through the Eastpass and leave the plains behind for at last I understood why the traders slept during the day—they dared not sleep during the night.

The grasses of the Vajnan Plains are tall and soft-feeling. They wave like a sea of green during the day. Yet, as anyone who passes the plains will tell you, they are the home of terrifying things—both alive and dead! I tremble to think what might have happened to me had I not run into the caravan. No one, I discovered, travels this road alone!

History: These grasslands were once the province of the Vajnan Clans. Often warring among themselves, these dark-skinned, fair-haired people are fierce and strong and enjoy nothing better than a good fight. It was with their blessing that the Field of Glory was placed on their lands and the Rules of Warrior Conduct—also known as the Rules of War—were instituted. Much to the delight of the Vajnan people, all wars were conducted on their lands where they could watch and occasionally participate in the "sport."

Unfortunately war ceased to be "sport" during the Iron Wars. It was on the Field of Glory that the Iron Wars first escalated into unchecked destruction. Many of the War-

---

[1] More likely, they were astonished at the brazen lie and took pity on the poor fool.

changed fought and died in this land. Their spirits still haunt these plains, and their descendants still live among the high grasses.

The old national boundaries are rarely contested now, except among the small groups who live here. The Manja Kingdom, which once flourished to the south, Trandar, which once dictated its own law as far east as the Hira River, the great Vajnan clans—all are now memories.

Current Conditions: The Eastroad runs across the grasslands to Manja Crossing. Here, on the banks of the Hera River, the Eastroad intersects the ancient Yandian Way. This road, made of magically fitted stones, once ran through the very heart of the plains and was built to bring goods from Yandia to that nation's southern neighbors, the produce of the farms to the port at Yandia. Now the shining black stones of that road exist only in broken patches extending along its original route. The road that was also a great route of trade for Trandar leads only to the ruins of both those ancient nations to the north.

Indeed, the Vajnan Plain is a land of grass-hidden ruins. Here the destruction of the Iron Wars was complete. Now only the faint shadow of the wonders of ancient nations survive.

Trandar, once a capital said to rival Merilon in its wonders, was originally built upon the ruins of Yandia. Trandar styled itself as the City of Rivers. Not only was the city a port on the Mannan Sea, but its streets were crafted into navigable waterways, wide and beautiful, allowing ship captains to sail directly to the shops. Arching waterfalls and cascades graced the city, all its buildings clustered along the riverbanks. It is now said that the deadly Kij vine has taken hold of the city and locks its riches in its lethal grip. Many artistic treasures were lost with the fall of that city.

Manja was a nation located on the plains between the Manja Range and the Ekard Range. The spires of its keep swept upward to seemingly impossible heights. The last king of Manja is said to have worn a Crown of Life that had been fashioned for him by the *Quin-alban* with the aid of the catalysts. The crown is said to have given him fabulously enhanced powers of magic. It didn't help him. The king died defending his citadel against enraged griffons. They took over the land and are said to live there still. The Crown of Life lies somewhere buried in the rubble of the lost city, possibly in some griffon's bed.

Not even the brave Vajnan Clans escaped destruction. Their own Vajnan Clanhome, the Spindarlian, was conquered by savage centaurs and their darkrovers. The spirits of the murdered Vajnan are said to haunt the underground passages of their cities, guarding their treasures, always eager for a fight. It is said that any warrior valiant enough to defeat them will gain their trust and loyalty and they will make him king and grant him whatever wishes he desires.

All I know is that person *won't* be me!

Only the Field of Glory remains under any form of civilized control. This is partly due to the *Fibanish* Druids, who keep the grounds groomed, and the *Duuk-tsarith*, who keep it clear of both the dead and the living.

The Eastroad crosses the Hera River at a point where the water has been permanently frozen in order to provide passage. Winding eastward, well south of the fallen Spindarlian, the road crosses the northern tip of the Ekard Range and turns south along the Hira River. Here it eventually wanders into Zith-el.

How welcome was the vision of that city as I gazed on it from the north! The dreamlike days on the undulating backs of the centipedes and the nights of watchful terror were over. No longer would I jump in the night at every sound with visions of darkrovers leaping for my throat.

It was then that I realized how far the world had deteriorated. Once nearly all of Thimhallan was civilized, safe for travel. Now only the cities offer security from unwanted adventure. The magi have retreated behind their walls once again — as in the old days — and the world beyond those walls is wild and treacherous.

Zith-el is a compact city whose major distinction is that it is surrounded by the most wonderful Zoo in all of Thimhallan. Visitors traveling from other cities to see the Zoo's wonders provide a large portion of Zith-el's income.

History: Zith-el — a *Fibanish* druid of the Vajnan Clans — was born about 352 Y.L. He purchased a wife from a fellow clansman, who had captured the woman during a raid on

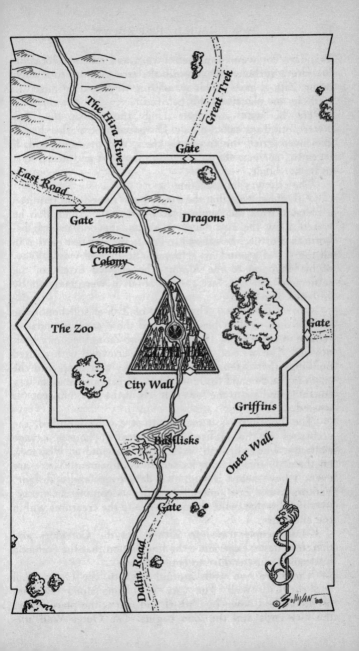

Trandar. The woman, named Tara, was a talented *Theldara*. Despite a turbulent beginning, the two grew to love each other. Zith-el gave up his wandering ways and promised to settle in one place with his beloved.

He, his wife, and their family traveled up the Hira River until Tara called a halt. Dismounting from her horse, she investigated the river, the trees, and the land, and, if legend is correct, she sat down on the spot and declared it to be her home.

The city was built around her.

Zith-el believed that the ground was sacred and required a blessing from the Almin. He vowed to the Almin that he would allow the city never to expand beyond its original borders. Further, he offered to create the greatest garden in all the world around his settlement so that all would know of his devotion to the Almin. The original extent of the settlement and the vast garden about it were laid out by Zith-el's own hand.

Current Conditions: The people of Zith-el still honor the vow of their ancient benefactor and those same boundaries remain in force today. Because of this, Zith-el is a city built upward. The area of the city itself is crowded with crafted buildings that extend high into the sky and deep into the earth in the demand for more room. Great open shafts carry sunshine and air to the lowest levels of the city. No space is wasted.

The Zoo itself is a marvel. In it can be found all the creatures of the House Magi Tales. It houses savage centaurs, whose brutish ways strike fear into all who look on them. Giants play in its secure confinement. There are even, I have heard it said, two darkrovers and a dragon. Visitors to the Zoo generally wander its confines in protective bubbles that make them invisible to the creatures within the enclosure.

Most people travel to Zith-el via the Corridors and therefore never experience the humiliation that the common tradesmen must endure to enter the city.

There are two walls around the city, the Outer Wall and the City Wall. The City Wall runs along the lines originally laid down by Zith-el and marks the place where the city ends and the Zoo begins. The Outer Wall surrounds the Zoo. Completely invisible, it allows a marvelous view of all the creatures, yet keeps them completely confined. Its nearest point to the city is some four *mila* from the city wall.

Four gates in both walls provide the only entrances and exits for overland travelers. These gates are one-way only. You step through the open portal, only to find the way back sealed shut. Gates leading into the city are located on the east and west sides of the walls, while gates leading out of the city are located on the north and south sides. It is said that all the gates through the City Wall can be deactivated by a word from the Lord of Zith-el in order to keep the city protected from attack.

The gates have a second and highly startling function. Upon entering the gate in Outer Wall, the traveler must pass through the Zoo that surrounds the city in order to enter the city itself. Since it would disturb the sensibilities of those touring the Zoo to see other humans like themselves wandering about, the gates temporarily transform the unsuspecting entrant into the illusion of some animal!

My caravan moved through one of these gates with our giant centipedes. Much to my horror, I suddenly found myself riding a black dragon, surrounded by centaurs! So complete is the illusion that not even the actual centaurs who are in the Zoo can tell the difference. I was on the verge of blind panic when I noticed that I, too, was a centaur! The centipede had become the dragon.

It takes nerves of stone to enter Zith-el in this manner.

I had never been to Zith-el and had met only a few of the family's relatives. I did not know my uncle and had no idea where he lived, so I spent several days searching the narrow streets for anyone who had any knowledge of my family. It was, quite literally, a dizzying experience. The contrasting depths and heights of the city buildings, coupled with the stuffiness of the deep airwells, brought me severe disquiet. Zith-el is not for the acrophobic.

I searched for my uncle Starg—my father's twin brother —as the *Duuk-tsarith* had recommended. I don't know what I hoped to gain from him, other than information about my father's background. Unfortunately I could find no one who knew him. I was, however, successful in tracking down my aunt on my mother's side.

I presented myself at her door, only to find that the door was loathe to let me in! After I promised that, yes, I was the person its Lady was waiting for, and no, I didn't like heights, and finally that I would shortly be making a mess of the face of the door if it didn't let me in, I gained entry.

Mother had three brothers and a younger sister, Hergris. I had never met Aunt Hergris, but I had heard something about her. She was a *Pron-alban* of only slight skill. Her in-depth knowledge of Guild politics, however, made up for her lack of talent. Her apartment was small, though well furnished, and after making her acquaintance, I told her my tale from first to last. Fortunately she had no more use for my crafty uncle Turd (as I had begun to think of him!) than I did.

She considered it all for a few moments. "You have no idea why your parents were in the park that day? Couldn't they have just gone out for a walk?"

"Father had business that day at the Guild. Besides, both of them hated the park! They said it was too quiet."

"Why do you suppose the *Duuk-tsarith* sent you here?" She flinched when she mentioned the *Duuk-tsarith*. It meant little to me at the time . . . everyone flinched at that name.

"The warlocks seemed to think that something was amiss, but they won't tell me anything except suggest that I talk to Uncle Starg."

She suddenly stood up. "We must leave at once. It's true that your uncle may be able to help you, although not in the way you might think. Your uncle was sentenced to the Turning just last month."

"The Turning! He's a Watcher on the Borderland?" I sank deep into gloom. "But that's impossible. He wasn't a catalyst. They're the only ones Turned to living stone."

"They made an exception in his case," Hergris said grimly.

"How could he possibly help me now?"

Hergris called her cloak to come to her. "It was most unusual. As he was Turned, an inscription appeared on his chest that may give you some clue. Where are your things?"

"What I wear, I own."

"Then come. Mathri, come here!" she commanded her catalyst. "Open a Corridor to the Borderlands!"

I stepped from the Corridor onto the sand. There before me stood a single row of stone figures, stretching far off into the distance. Aunt Hergris pointed to the fifth of these living statues.

"There, boy, there is your answer."

I ran quickly across the sands and stood before the statue. I couldn't bear to look up into the face of my father's twin but searched instead on the chest for the inscription.

There was none.

I turned and shouted, "Aunt Hergris, there isn't any—"

She and the Corridor were gone.

Chapter Seven

Ariels of the Borderland

All that there is—all that Lives—exists within the Border. No other place is Life possible. On the other side of the Border is Beyond—the realm of Death. To step into Beyond means to step into oblivion.

The Border appears different, yet it is the same wherever it is encountered. Some places, such as by the sea, it is a solid wall of fog that continually turns in upon itself. At the southern extremes of the Manja Range, the Border is filled with smoke, as if the forest—which suddenly ends—has caught fire. In the midst of the desert the Border turns in gentle patterns of swirling mists that seem cool and inviting. Overhead, the Border is clear and allows the sun and stars to shine upon Thimhallan.

I sat for some time at the base of that statue. The fear and panic that had at first gripped me burned away quickly in the desert sun, leaving behind numbing despair. The statue and I became friends, though he did not know it. We both stared into the mists of Beyond, not thirty *metra* to the

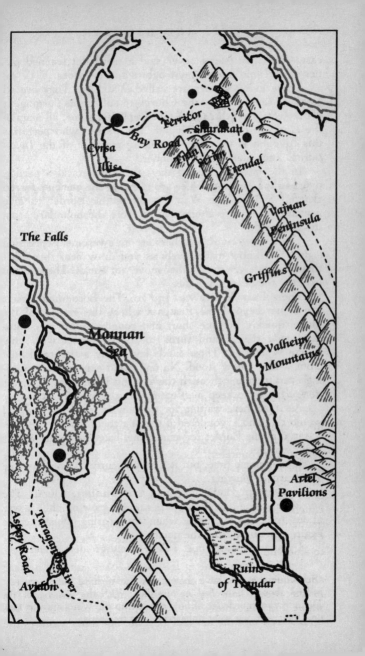

east of us. My friend never said a word but listened patiently as I told him all my troubles and my woes.

These living statues are called Watchers. They are all catalysts sentenced by the Church to suffer the Turning. It is only catalysts who are changed to living stone; all magi of the land are cast into Beyond. The person who performs this function is the highest-ranking member of the *Duuk-tsarith*, known as the Executioner.

In the most ancient of days the Diviners also participated in the Turning. Tales are told that the ancients feared Beyond and set the Watchers along the Border to give warning of anyone attempting to cross the boundary from the other side.[1]

The six-*metra*-tall Watchers are an awesome, depressing sight. You know instinctively as you draw near them that they are alive yet can neither move nor speak. They do not live, yet they can never die.

There I sat. Where was I to go? The Borderland desert starts just beyond the Eastpass where the grasses of the plains quickly become short and rough. Within two hundred *mila* the ground turns to barren desert with only sparse vegetation. Those lands lay nearly a thousand *mila* from where I now stood. No one could survive that crossing even traveling through the air, and I knew my Life was not sufficient to keep me floating for any length of time.

As I sat there waiting for the sun to set, I knew that I would die, and I wondered if the Watchers would envy me. I stared at the Border for some time, listening to the wind's shrill whistle.

It took some time, but it finally occurred to me that the wind wasn't blowing.

I stood up. Had I imagined that whistling sound? The sun was setting, the desert was rapidly growing chill. I was about to undo my pack when the soaring whistle came again—this time from the north.

I was wild with hope. I flew at my greatest speed over

---

[1] Subsequent events have shown this fear to have been very real indeed though unheeded in our day. With the passing of the Diviners the knowledge of how to listen to the Watchers was lost, and their warning went unheard during the invasion.

the Watchers, yelling for help at the top my lungs. I stopped, listened, and flew again. It occurred to me that I may be dashing directly into the gaping mouth of a Sand Dragon, but the thought didn't deter me. At least all would be over in a bite, much better than dying of thirst and starvation in the desert.

I must have flown through the air for more than four *mila* before I collapsed to the sand, nearly devoid of Life. My throat was raw and parched from shouting.

I raised up weakly on one arm, trying again to hear that sound once more. The moonlight turned the desert sands blue, making them look like a vast, dry sea.

Suddenly a great shadow rippled over the sands like a black tide. A Sand Dragon! The air was filled with a horrible fluttering sound. I rolled quickly onto my back and covered my head with my arms. A solid thud hit the ground to my right and left at the same time.

Trapped!

I kicked, rolled, and clawed at the sand in my efforts to escape.

A strong hand closed over my mouth, and I heard a voice whisper, "Do not fear, Wanderer. We mean you no harm."

Slowly I opened my eyes and looked up. Against the moonlit sky were a hundred winged men, turning from their southern route to head west into the desert. Beside me stood two of their number.

The Ariels had found me.

Griffins are the most uncomfortable beasts on which to ride. It is not that they are difficult to mount (once they agree to the idea), nor is it that they are hard to learn to ride (unless they care to make it hard). The discomfort comes in knowing that it is at least a thousand *metra* to the ground, and the griffin could care less (no matter what he says) whether you stay on his back or not.

Since the Ariels (humans mutated so they grow wings) and the griffins—two races of the Warchanged—have a mutual respect for each other, they often work together—particularly if they are after some enemy.

The Ariels are generally found working in the cities

since they are used by the *Kan-Hanar* as messengers and
carriers. Not so with the griffins. They were shaped during
the Iron Wars for sky combat, and war remains their main
interest to this day. They communicate with each other
through a mind-link inbred into the species. Griffins so
rarely communicate in spoken language that most believe
that they are incapable of actual speech.

Having determined that I was not the enemy they sought,
the Ariels called down one of the griffins. I was offered
salvation from the desert but warned that I might be involved in a battle. In my mind I pictured visiting the Field
of Glory. To watch the Ariels and griffins take on a foe on
the Field would be great sport, and I readily agreed.

Flying on the back of a griffin is also considerably
noisy. When you float through the air on the magic of Life,
you are enveloped in silence. Griffins press the wind into
their service through the strength of their wings. This ne-
cessitates that they fly fast, and such speed causes the wind
to rush deafeningly about your ears.

So I found myself on the back of a griffin flying westward across the desert sands, shouting questions into the
wind. Beside us flew an Ariel named Meteor, who, I hoped,
had more concern for my safety than the griffin. Meteor
would have been happy to talk with me. He was, after all,
used to talking while flying. Unfortunately I could rarely
understand what he said.

Much to my surprise the griffin on which I rode—one
Skirkanzhee, if I have gotten the name right—was most com-
municative for her kind. I think the heat of the upcoming
battle was running in her blood or she would not have been
so gregarious. From her halting, loud speech I was able
to learn much about the desert and the griffins who lived
there.

History: The griffins were one of the Warchanged. What
form or conglomeration of forms they were prior to being
shaped by the *Theldara* and the *Omueva* in those days is of
no consequence. They are griffins and will always be so.
They were used by all sides in the conflict, only to be
abandoned after the war ended.

During the Nightyears, griffins raided both human villages and the mountain aeries of their fellow griffin clans.

It wasn't until the very recent past (approximately 740 Y.L.) that the various clans managed to put aside their differences and band together. While there are still occasional wars between different clans of griffins, they maintain an uneasy peace.

Current Conditions: The traditional home for both the griffins and the Ariels are the Mountains of Valheim—a range that runs from the Eastpass up the length of the Vajnan peninsula. The griffins maintain their aeries in a great fortress carved from the mountain. From time to time during the Nightyears the griffins worked for humans, raiding for profit, and often trading their services for the skills of the *Pron-alban*, who shaped their fortresses.

The exact location of the aeries is a closely kept secret. Workers were flown blindfolded to and from the location so that not even the *Thon-Li* Corridor masters know where the place is.

On the details of its interior and what might be found there, the griffin remained adamantly silent. Others I have talked to since say that the plundering which the griffins engaged in during the Nightyears brought in not only food but also many of the treasures of the ancient world. Griffins will occasionally trade precious objects long thought lost to the knowledge of the world, which seems to support this story.

Do not get the idea that the griffins have become a docile group of bartering traders. Griffins still prefer to take what they want by force even though they obviously have the means of purchasing it outright. War was bred into them and time has not changed them.

Skirkanzhee interrupted her talk to shout to the Ariel: "There! Light on ground edge! Camp raider we seek."

"Are we stopping there?" I shouted over the wind.

"We stop. Take. Kill. Return . . . mate . . . Meteor!"

Certain wild images of the griffin mating with Meteor came into my mind. Fortunately I managed to make out the griffin's meaning.

"Oh! You are going to return Meteor's mate to him?"

"Raider desert take. Now we take back!" The griffin's purr rumbled beneath my legs.

"But—but the Field of Glory! What of the Rules of Warrior Conduct; the Judges; the—"

"Almin judge. Rules—Life . . . Death. *We* choose field."

With a screech that nearly split my ears, Skirkanzhee dove from the sky. I held onto her mane with all my might as we spun downward. Desert raiders are like those humans who live in the Outland. Mostly renegades, rebels, outcasts, they survive by thievery and raiding nearby settlements. Desert raiders had somehow kidnapped Meteor's mate, and both Ariels and griffins were going to get her back. This was not war as the world dictated! Someone (namely me!) might get killed!

Skirkanzhee extended her sharp-edged talons. They were a full two *decimetra* long, and the vision of their rending living flesh brought my heart to my throat. The griffin's wings pulled close to her body, she streaked down on the encampment from the sky with Meteor close behind.

Ariels and griffins flew down on the raiders from the sky. Their sentries fought back with Sorcerer's weapons (having few catalysts, they are weak in magic), but they were no match for either griffins or Ariels.

The pavilions of the desert raiders are made out of one piece of heavy canvas that magically remembers the form in which it was originally shaped and, at a word, either collapses for transport or unfolds into a dwelling. While these structures—which they call pavilions—are strong enough to keep out the elements, they cannot stop a griffin in full flight.

Skirkanzhee roared between the pavilions. Lightning flashed about us from the hands of a *DKarn-ðuuk* who had hastily awakened at the alarm. The griffin's claw tore through his robes, the beast never even slowed her pace. I looked back and caught sight of his falling amid his own flaring bolts. I also saw Meteor alight on the ground and begin battling the magi who faced him. Skirkanzhee banked again and charged the main pavilion, her wings raising clouds of sand.

More outcast *DKarn-ðuuk* came at us. Three warlocks and a renegade catalyst had barely sufficient time to concentrate their magic on the rushing Skirkanzhee. Seeing fire blaze from their hands, I tucked my head down behind the griffin's neck.

The blast stopped the griffin as though she had run into a granite cliff. I lost my grip on her and I found myself falling in a blur through the air. My voice was completely gone, as was my Life, and no scream left my lips that could be heard.

There was a tearing sound as I hit the pavilion and split it wide open. The fabric slowed my fall. I had the vague impression of a figure in black robes staring up at me in tremendous astonishment before I crashed right into him. Canvas tumbled down around me and darkness closed over my mind.

I awoke to the soft melody of the most beautiful voice I have ever heard. My hair was being stroked with smooth, gentle hands. My eyes opened to a face of surpassing radiance and beauty. The Ariels never allow their women to be seen by humans. I now know why.

She was the most incredibly beautiful being I have ever seen. White hair, the same color as her wings, framed her suntanned face. She was clad only in a short, white skirt. Her breasts were bare and of surpassing loveliness. Her wings—smaller than the male's wings—extended from her shoulders.

I lay under the Ariel's spell for too short a time, though hours may have passed in the world. Then a voice interrupted my sweet dreams.

"Willowind! Willowind!" A voice sounded outside the wrecked pavilion.

"Here, beloved!" The winged woman called, and Meteor ran into the tent.

"Are you safe, my wife?"

"Yes, Meteor! And here is the hero who delivered me!" She looked down at me. I had no idea what she meant, nor did I care. I longed to wander in her eyes forever. Later I learned that I had fallen through the pavilion wall on top of the man who had abducted her, knocking him senseless. His body broke my fall. My body broke most of his bones.

Thus I became a hero of the Ariel legion.

°   °   °

"Skirkanzhee was badly injured, but we have taken her home and she is now in the capable hands of her kin. So, friend Wildreth, where shall I take you?"

I had grown fond of Meteor. He was an Ariel of Flight rank. After their victory over the raiders and my supposedly brave and pivotal role, Meteor was empowered to give me whatever aid he could.

I told him my tale from first to last. At the mention of my uncle Starg, the Ariel stared at me intently.

"Is this uncle of yours a trader? Possibly one of the *Kan-Hanar*?"

"Yes—I believe that was his Mystery," I replied.

"I think I know him. We often have dealings with their kind, and the name is familiar to me. He was once from Zith-el, as I recall, but for the last few years he has run a ship out of Sharakan."

Could this be my uncle? The questions in my life were piling up faster than the answers. If it was, why had my aunt lied?

"I need to get to Sharakan," I said.

"It is done."

The divan was certainly a better way to travel than on a griffin. A huge dish, the divan is supported by twelve Ariels who hold fast to poles mounted on either side. A magical dome encased Meteor and me, allowing sufficient air to enter the chamber so as to sustain us, but keeping the rush of the wind outside from disturbing our conversation.

"I had no idea such wonderful things existed," I exclaimed. The mountains of the Vajnan peninsula were drifting by below us, looking like small rills in the ground. While traveling by divan is more time-consuming than taking the Corridors, it is also far more interesting from a spectator's standpoint.

"Much has been lost to human knowledge these last centuries," Meteor said sadly. "The Iron Wars were our beginning, but it was an end to much that used to be." Meteor stretched his wings as far as the limited space within the dome allowed. He was unaccustomed to being encased.

"Still, it seems to me to be far better than flashing from

one point to another without knowing the way," I said, referring to the Corridors.

"I think that you humans rely far too much on your Life to get you where you want to go. You arrive there in an instant. You conduct your business and return home in another instant. Yet you never know what has happened between the beginning and the end. Humans are too preoccupied with their destination and pay far too little attention to what happens along the way."

His words struck me. I persuaded him to tell me of his own people and their background.

History: The Ariels are, like the griffins, one of the Warchanged. Altered by the *Theldara*, they were originally used as messengers during the wars, as well as for reconnaissance. Their function quickly came to include other duties. Ariels began to be employed in flying the seriously injured people from the field of battle, removing them to areas where the *Theldara* could work their arts on them in relative safety. Ariels were also used to carry evil Sorcery devices of destruction, which they could rain down from the sky on their victims below in overwhelming numbers.

When the war ended, the Ariels were, unfortunately, remembered by many as harbingers of death rather than angels of mercy. They were hunted down and killed or captured. Consequently the Ariels—a quiet and sensitive people—withdrew into the high Mountains of Valheim. Their neighbors, the griffins, kept the rest of the world at bay while the Ariels were able to establish their own beautiful home among the craggy peaks and mountain bowls of the High Valheim.

Things changed in 724 Y.L. when Farlight, First Servant of the Ariels and the leader of all their people, took gravely ill. Her mate, Falconi, set off for the civilized lands and landed—amid great consternation—in the Druid's Garden at the Font. He begged the *Theldara* to give him aid. Farlight was saved and the grateful Ariels were again part of the greater community of Thimhallan.

Since that time, most of the major courts employ Ariels as messengers and couriers. It is said—with some truth— that they are also hired so that their rare, natural beauty will grace the courts where they work.

Current Conditions: Females of the Ariels are rarely seen outside their mountain home. Their beauty is legendary and their effect on mortal humans is hypnotic. No wonder the desert raider risked his life to steal Meteor's mate!

The home of the Ariels is in a mountain bowl deep in the heart of the Valheim Mountains. A trail leads up to it, but it is a difficult and dangerous climb, and then, near the top, one must pass a griffin stronghold. A mountain lake mirrors the marble cliffs surrounding it on three sides, and around this lake the Ariels have built their home.

Meteor described it to me, but I must confess that words fail me in explaining its beauty. He said that those humans who do find their way there decide never to return to the world of their fellow men, preferring instead to remain as servants of the Ariels. While I have heard it said that this is the Ariels' way of justifying the enslavement of those unfortunates who scale their mountain, I have only to remember the vision of his home that Meteor gave to me that day through word and song and I believe him.

Meteor claims that only the Ariels have a true perspective on the world of Thimhallan. Humanity rushes through their Corridors and they have let all the lands between their cities and their estates fall to chaos. Ruins with lost treasures abound, yet few humans remember that they exist. A world of wonder remains in Thimhallan, and people are too busy blindly passing it in the Corridors to see it.

The mountains seemed to grow as we descended. It was morning, the towering peaks cast long shadows over the plains to the west of the Valheim. Though sun would not strike its spires for another hour yet, the castle keep within the walls of Sharakan looked splendid. There is a dreamlike quality to that city. I had seen it on maps, of course, but had never visited it until now.

I remembered hearing rumors that the people of Sharakan were consorting with Sorcerers and looked about eagerly for some sign that was true.

Chapter Eight

Sharakan

The great northern kingdom of the Vajnan peninsula, Sharakan is now the rival in power and might to Merilon itself. Indeed, the ruling powers of those two houses continue to strive against each other. The matter has become an ecclesiastical one, too, for the catalysts of Sharakan, led by a renegade called Radisovik, have broken from the organized Church and are preaching such radical ideas as Free Life for all and such like.

History: The few descendants of Frea Segarson who took the Wildlands from the gore centuries earlier, were, by 482 Y.L., a large clan who had outgrown their small village. Led by Shara Phrederson, they settled permanently near the north end of the Valheim Mountains. Under Phrederson's leadership, a stout keep with a thick and formidable curtain wall was shaped from a small mountain spur near the main range. This structure, though hardly elegant by any standards, kept his clan secure from raids and other threats. A freshwater spring brought water directly into the courtyard of the citadel, and the natural caverns in the mountain were

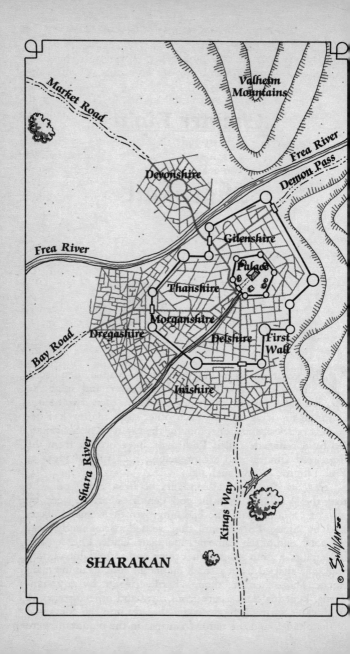

Market Road

Valheim
Mountains

Frea River

Devonshire

Demon Pass

Frea River

Gilenshire

Palace

Thanshire

Morganshire

Dregashire

Delshire

First
Wall

Bay Road

Inishire

Shara River

Kings Way

SHARAKAN

put to use storing food and other provisions. The Shara Clan, as it came to be known, was invincible within its own walls.

After the downfall of Trandar during the Nightyears, the remains of that people and many of the Vajnan Clans fled north with their families. Their fighting withdrawal into that region sapped the strength of the pursuing dragons and griffins sufficiently to halt their pursuit less than halfway up the peninsula. The beasts withdrew to lick their wounds. Finding themselves in a tenuous peace, the Vajnan army searched for a place to defend themselves should the attack renew.

Shara Clan in its mountain stronghold had also been attacked repeatedly by a number of different armies over the years of the Iron Wars. The keep had never fallen. The rumor of this might have sounded like a blessing from the Almin to the war-weary Vajnan people. They surged north toward that city and begged for protection.

The King of Shara Clan (as he had come to style himself) was no happier about a Trandar army on his doorstep than one made up of giants. Still, it occurred to him that these people might, at least, provide a buffer between his kingdom and further invasions. He did not allow them into the stronghold but gave them leave to encamp around it in various locations. Work was then commissioned to create a second curtain wall outside these camps that would make them safe as well.

Many of the *Albanara* from Trandar thought this arrangement was a little too comfortable for the King of Shara Clan. They agreed to camp outside the walls but would do so some forty *mila* from the Clan's keep. This would still give them some degree of autonomy and yet be close enough that they hoped to be able to prevail upon him to open his gates should times get rough.

As the Nightyears progressed, these various communities found themselves fighting common enemies and increasing their trade and ties. One by one the outlying communities were absorbed under the rule of the King of Shara Clan until, in 726 Y.L., Shara Clan renamed itself Sharakan (this being the way the words were spoken in the accent of the Vajnan).

Current Conditions: As the flying divan carried Meteor and myself over the sleepy city-state of Sharakan, my guide pointed out the major landmarks of the city.

The keep itself—or Palace as it is now called—stands in the middle of a large court surrounded by a thick castle wall formed of granite from the very stone of the small mountain that it once was. The structure is set up against the mountainsides of the Valheim Range and is barely discernible against the gray cliffs. The tower of the Palace looks to the southeast over the city, its walls frowning down on a rich plain that extends as far as the Mannan Sea. From our divan I thought for a moment that I could even see the waters of that great bay—a thin blue ribbon against the white cloudy froth of the horizon. The outlying communities of Tran, Terricor, Frendal, and Scrim were already awash with dawn's light, scattered like shining gems on the green of the plain.

The outer wall of the city is now called the First Wall. As in Merilon the *Kan-Hanar* are at those gates on duty with their accompanying *Duuk-tsarith* to watch those who enter the city. Meteor informed me, however, that their duties here are somewhat different than in Merilon. The *Kan-Hanar* here are required to take down the identity of those who enter and leave the city, as well as the time of their passage. They are not to prohibit entry (except in the case of known criminals or those banned by the royal family), nor may they inquire into the reason for entry into the city without cause to suspect some wrongdoing. This rather liberal attitude, I understand, is typical of the proudly independent spirit of Sharakan and her people. I simply shook my head, thinking no good would come of so liberal a policy.

Inside the First Wall, tall-shaped buildings line the major roads. The city itself is known by its sections, with these roads marking the boundaries between them. These sections are named after the encampments that originally settled there during the Iron Wars.

Delshire is the section directly south and east of the Palace. It holds most of the residential homes and is a favorite neighborhood for those of the lower stations of *Albanara* and the higher stations of the other Mysteries.

Southwest of the Palace Gates is Morganshire, a section devoted to tradesmen and their wares. Here the major *Pron-alban*, *Quin-alban*, and *Mon-alban* all maintain their Guild Houses. The business of Sharakan takes place in Morganshire.

The workers of the city live in Thanshire, west of the Palace Gate. Here respectable homes for the lower classes are maintained in a clean and orderly manner.

Northwest of the Palace is Gilenshire, where the trade barons, who keep the goods of Sharakan moving throughout the civilized world, keep their homes and what wealth they can accumulate.

Each of these shires, as they are called, is divided by major avenues with smaller streets running back from them. Kings Way runs directly south from the Palace Gates to Kings Gate and beyond, eventually following the mountains to the south and leading to Talesin. Bay Road runs from the Palace Gates to the southwest and then turns west to Bay Gate, separating Morganshire from Thanshire. Most of the major shops of the city are found along that route. Market Street runs northwest from the Palace Gates. It is lined with the trade houses and the Guilds of the *Kan-Hanar*. A spur street, Baron Street, runs northeast from Market into Gilenshire.

Outside the city walls can be found three other shires — Inishire to the south along the Kings Way; Dregashire to the south along the Bay Road; and Devonshire to the northwest beyond Market Gate. The working class of Sharakan live in Inishire or Dregashire, the two being separated by the Valvein River. Devonshire and Dregashire are separated by the River Frea, which spills out of Demon Pass north of the First Wall.

Devonshire is the newest of the shires. It is also the most feared and not without reason. The King of Sharakan determined a dark course for his nation some four years ago when he officially accepted Sorcery as a practicable and tolerated Mystery in his realm. Since that time I have heard it rumored that the people use "wheels" — whatever they may be — to run evil machines known as carts. It is even said that they found a cache of swords and armor left from the Iron Wars and are attempting to discover how they were made and learn to recreate that foul art. Tales of swords are certainly true, for I saw the Prince of Sharakan (quite a handsome young man) walking about the streets, displaying one openly. How the Church permits this evil art to flourish in this northern city is beyond my understanding.

The divan on which I had taken so interesting and entertaining a ride was gently lowered by they Ariels onto Market Street, which, at that hour of the morning, was deserted. The smoothed-stone roadway glistened with dew, and there was a slight chill in the air.

"The Windwanderers' Guild is where the *Kan-Hanar* meet. They certainly will know something about your uncle," Meteor told me.

We stepped from the divan onto the street. The Ariels who had brought us this far flew with it back into the air.

"It generally opens by midmorning, but I suggest that you will want to get some rest first. I hear that the Merryman's Inn is a good place for bed and food."

"Thank you, Meteor. I'd never have survived the Borderlands. I owe you my life." Tears welled up, unbidden, in my eyes.

He held my shoulders in his strong, slender hands. "As I also owe you. Willowind is the center of my life, and her loss would mean my death as surely as yours in the desert. We shall meet again."

He released me with a smile and, with the flutter of his great wings, vaulted into the sky.

I looked about me at the quiet street. Not even a *Duuk-tsarith* to be seen. I suddenly realized that I had entered the city without checking in with the *Kan-Hanar*! Would they let someone out whom they had never let in?

Well, I thought, cheered, surely my uncle can help me.

He did, but not quite the way I expected!

Merryman's Inn was located on Market Street, only a few hundred *metra* from the Windwanderers' Guild. Though still unsure of my own legal status in the city, I was by then too weary to fret over it—and the Inn was, indeed, a welcome sight.

The Merryman's Inn faces the street from the southwest side of Market less than two hundred *metra* from the Palace Gate and is among a variety of shops that cater to the traveler. The front of the Inn is made from the native granite of the region and is shaped into the form of two gigantic trees. The branches of the trees twine together to form a knot of incredible beauty and intricate design. A huge stone man of considerable girth stands between them. A waterfall cascades down on either side of the jovial statue, tumbling over broad steps before the water disappears altogether at the edge of the street. After a moment's observance I saw people floating through the base of the waterfall. They must get soaked, I thought, then saw other people emerging from the foot of the right-hand waterfall, perfectly dry by all appearances. For those catalysts forced to walk, the steps humbly carried them up or down from the street.

Feeling almost as weak as a catalyst myself, I stepped onto the left stairs and was carried through the waterfall (a breathtaking experience) directly into the common room of the Inn.

The interior of Merryman's Inn rivals anything in Merilon's City Below. The great central atrium is filled with all manner of plants and flowers. There are no fewer than eight levels built around this atrium. Access to these levels is via a thick vine that is constantly growing at a rapid rate. Reaching the ceiling, the vine spirals downward, sinks into the ground, then shoots up again on the other side. Those wishing to ascend (and not spend Life to do it) simply climb onto the broad, accommodating leaves and ride to the level they desire.

The common room is at the bottom of the atrium and provides weather control year-round, much after the manner of Merilon's Stardome, though of course on a much smaller scale. A staff of *Sif-Hanar* ensure that the weather in the atrium remains comfortable at all times. I have heard that the food in this common room is the finest in Sharakan, though personally I can only testify to the dawnmeal I ate that morning. The ale is renowned as far south as Talesin.

The dawnmeal was so hearty on that day that, once finished, I could hardly stay awake. I rode the vine up to my room and collapsed at once on the soft swanswing bed.

My mind wandered for a time. My uncle could, no

doubt, clear up many of the questions troubling me. It suddenly occurred to me to wonder if I hadn't been caught in the middle of some sort of family feud between the clans of my father and my mother. My parents had left Zith-el hurriedly, so I had always known, and they rarely spoke of it. But the only clues I had thus far were that my uncle had turned up most opportunely to grab my inheritance, and my aunt had lied about Uncle Starg and tried to abandon me to certain death at the mere mention of his name. I suddenly realized how very far I was from home. The dull ache in my heart to see my own room, to feel my mother's arms about me, overflowed into bitter tears that were washed away by the sweet darkness of sleep.

The afternoon sun was all the hotter for the crowds in Market Street. The Windwanderers' Guild towered over me, shaped to look like huge wings soaring into the sky. The grogginess that I experienced on waking gave way quickly to keen excitement as I came at last to the Guild's entrance.

The bright light of afternoon filtered into Mead Hall through gently hued glass windows, illuminating a large group of people, all of whom seemed to be shouting at each other at the top of their lungs. There are many offices and apartments beyond this large common room, but the true life of the Guild was here in the hall. Deals for transport were struck and sealed in this room. Tales were told, adventures exaggerated. The kitchen supplied a continuous fountain of mead to the Guildmembers. By the time I entered the Hall, the congregation was large, the air reverberating with the thunder of mirth and loud boasting. Looking into the faces of the Guildmembers, I realized that not all *Kan-Hanar* are as stern and serious as those who have the duty of guarding gates to magnificent cities. Much of the work of the *Kan-Hanar* is the transportation of goods through Thimhallan—a task that can be backbreaking and dangerous, as you have witnessed with me on my travels.

A huge man leaped suddenly on a table at the end of the hall. His voice carried easily over the entire assembly, and he got their attention—if not their silence. Most striking about his appearance were his meaty hands and his tremen-

dous red beard. The beard was obviously a point of considerable vanity with him for it was well groomed and carefully
trimmed.

"Brothers! Brothers! Great news for the Guild!"

A general roar came from the crowd.

"My good friend Sedrik Constance Percifal the Third"—a
roar of appreciation—"has come down here this day to
bring yours truly, Hravan Drew, a contract."

Another even greater shout came from the crowd. The
great, red-bearded man reached down next to him and, with
an effortless motion, hauled a thin, well-dressed, and totally
unconscious man up from the table by the back of his tunic.

"Having negotiated in good faith over numerous glasses
of mead for the last four hours, Sedrik has agreed to my
terms—am I right, friend Sedrik?"

Hravan shook the slack figure slightly. Drunken Sedrik's
head bobbed about in what the crowd thought was a
reasonable approximation of an affirmative. Cheers filled
the Hall.

Hravan released his hand and Sedrik dropped back into
his seat. Here, I thought, was a man who seemed to know
his way around. Perhaps he could direct me to my uncle. I
began pressing my way through the packed room. The
shouts and babble continued around me as I waded into
this sea of noise. The red-bearded man was still standing on
the table when I finally reached him.

". . . couldn't have been longer. So I said to him—just
before he passed out as it were—that his price was a little
steep and wouldn't he agree to a little reduction."

"Excuse me, sir," I shouted with all the conviction that
my age could muster. "I was wondering if you could—"

"Just a moment, lad—He says to me, 'Not if I have
anything to say about it.' So I tells him what I know about
his *last* shipment, that I heard it carried a few items that the
Black Robes'd be interested in obtaining. The price dropped
pre-cipitously!"

Hravan smiled as the group of men and women around
him roared with laughter. Mead sloshed from their mugs.

"Excuse me, sir." I felt a little like a child tugging on my
father's tunic. "I'm searching for someone of your Guild."

"Well, you've come to the right place, lad. Have you

business?" Hravan winked sideways at the crowd around him.

"I—well, that is—I guess I do."

"Guessin's close enough. So what can we do for you?"

"Well, sir, I'm looking for my uncle, Starg Wildreth?"

"STARG WILDRETH!"

His voice echoed. The entire Hall fell silent.

It was eerie. In a moment all the voices and motion stopped. Everywhere I looked, I saw eyes narrowed and frowning. Oh, Almin! What had I done? More to the point—what had my uncle done?

The red beard quivered. Hravan stepped down from the table, but it made little difference for he was at least two *decimetra* taller than I. His face, now nearly as red as his beard, leered down into mine.

"Starg Wildreth, ship's captain, soon to be *late* ship's captain, is not presently at home."

With each word he stepped forward. I retreated as far as I could, but the crowd blocked my movement.

"It is of considerable *doubt* if he will *ever* be *home again*!" Hravan's face shook with rage. I shrank under his baleful gaze, but he pressed his face so close that I could see nothing else. With a sneer he asked, "Well, squeak, what business is it of yours to find this (words that I refuse to repeat) uncle of yours?"

Something in me snapped.

"Look, Hravan, my parents died, my land and property were taken, I've been left to die in the desert by an aunt I hardly know, and . . . and" —I was struck with inspiration— "the *Duuk-tsarith* told me the one person who might make any sense of this is my uncle Starg—"

The crowd sucked in a collective breath. I thought Hravan paled slightly. *"Duuk-tsarith?"* he swallowed.

"Yes," I gulped.

Hravan scowled. The conversation wasn't going well. I figured that I was dead. But though he was still rough-talking, Hravan seemed to have calmed down considerably.

"So, you want to find your uncle and see if he knows what's going on. Well, kid, welcome to a large club. There's not a man in this room that didn't go in with your uncle on his last venture. Financed him goods and a ship. Never heard from him again. The pirate ran off with the loot and is, no doubt, living very well somewhere we can't find him.

"So, boy, if you ever find your uncle, tell him he owes us—big."

Hravan gripped me painfully by the arms. My fingers began to tingle. "I promise I will, sir—but how will I find him if you can't?"

He relaxed his grip and thought for a moment. "Some people can be found only when they *want* to be found. I suspect that you just might flush the bird. Jansen!"

"Sir!" A barrel-chested man roared in my ear, nearly deafening me.

"D'ya think my ship *Alacrity* could use a deckhand, Captain Jansen?"

"Aye, that she could, sir!"

Hravan shoved me toward Jansen. "Here he is. Take this boy to Avidon. Make him work his passage. I'll not have these Wildreths owing me more money than they already do."

"But, sir—" I began to protest.

Hravan glared at me.

"Sir," I continued meekly, "there's another small problem. I don't know if the *Kan-Hanar* will allow me to leave the city. I didn't come in through a gate and—"

"Ah, the Wildreths—a sneaky bunch to the last, I see. Well, son, we can help you there, can't we, mates!"

The crowd roared. Turning to the assembly, he cried, "Good friends, let's show the lad how to exit the gate!"

The bone-jarring thud shook my entire body. I tasted the dust of the street as it billowed around me outside the Market Gate. The *Kan-Hanar* jeered and laughed as I painfully rolled onto my back, only to see Jansen standing over me, both fists on his hips.

"Let's go, boy. Time's the enemy now."

We were outside the Market Gate. As I lay in the street, I was nearly run over by a most strange looking contraption of the Sorcerer's arts. It consisted of a boxlike container on both sides of which large, circular disks were attached. The disks rotated as the box was pulled along the street, and I suddenly realized that I was staring at one of the most feared symbols of Sorcery—the wheel.

I jumped to my feet. We were not far from the gate. I walked quickly to the *Kan-Hanar* watching the gate. A *Duuk-tsarith* stood behind him.

"I would like to enter, please."

Jansen shouted, "Boy, we must be off!"

"But I have to get my things!" I turned to plead with him. "I cannot practice my craft without my possessions, and I cannot leave the Inn without paying."

The captain considered for a moment, staring at the sun, calculating the time. "That much I'll do for you. We have a long road ahead of us though. Get your gear and let's be gone."

As I turned back to the *Kan-Hanar*, I noticed the *Duuk-tsarith* behind him murmur in the gatekeeper's ear. The man nodded and looked at me sympathetically. "Of course, young sir, you may enter, and may the peace of Sharakan be yours," he said with a kindly pat on the back.

I returned and settled with Merryman's Inn. By the time I was finished, there was little Life left in me, for the Inn had cost me dearly.[1] There was little food left in my pack either. I had to throw my furnishings into the bargain just to clear the bill.

And now I had to take a ship to Avidon in search of an uncle who was labeled a pirate. My heart thumping in my worn shoes, I left the Inn. Jansen was waiting for me, of course, and soon we were on our way to the distant port and the Mannan Sea.

---

[1]All trade in Thimhallan is based on the exchange of either service or Life. A person either gives service, goods, or some of his own power of Life in any transaction.

Chapter Nine

Cyrsa Seaport and Mannan Storms

The only good thing I could see about this mess was that I might, after all, be destined to find my uncle. One way or the other, the Guild would have their money. I only hoped it would come out of my uncle's hide, not my own.

Jansen was not my idea of a traveling companion. His high boots and open shirt gave him a rakish look that might have been considered handsome had not his ears been far too big for his head. They stuck out like great sails, and I caught myself wondering if this is why he had gone to sea. He told me he was a sea captain of some notable reputation, although, I began to believe—from his swaggering boasts—he was probably the only one who thought so.

The Bay Road was an ugly thing, being little more than a brown mire that cut through the grasslands of the Vajnan Plains. Twin furrows ran down its length that, for a time, puzzled me. A horrible creaking noise came our way from the west, and all too soon my questions were answered.

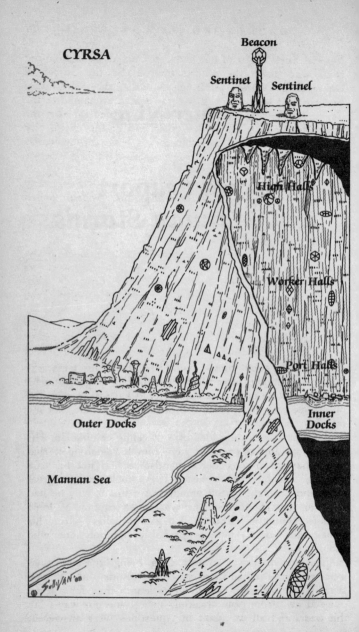

Several huge boxes of cut and constructed wood bounced their way down the road supported by the Sorcerer's contraptions—wheels. These (Jansen called them carts) were being pulled by no less than eight centaurs chained to the device by rings around their necks. Two men sat atop the assembly, holding on to the other end of the chains. By these means I understood that they guided the device by pulling the heads of the front centaurs to one side or the other.

So astounded was I by the sight that I was nearly trampled beneath the entire assembly. Jansen roughly pulled me off the road.

"What's the matter, lad? Never seen Sorcery before?" He laughed mockingly.

I turned and looked again at the horrible example of the Dark Arts that had just passed. The centaurs were, as could be seen at once, the female of their species. I wondered what terror might rain down on that caravan if the male centaurs of this region caught sight of it.

We passed several small villages with inns and taverns along the road to the sea. In general they were rather horrid places: ill kept and short on Life. Jansen and I floated along the road—me half-listening to his boasts and fretting about my own problems. Already low on Life when we left Sharakan, by the time we reached Illis, my feet were dragging through the muck of the road.

Jansen regarded me with a leering grin as we stopped before the Illis Inn. "Looks like you're done for the day, lubber. We'll rest here the night. You, lucky deck-swab, will sleep on the floor next to my bed."

"Lubber"? "Deck-swab"? I had no idea what he was talking about and was too tired to care.

I noticed, however, that he walked rather than floated into the Inn.

The Illis Inn was about as shabby as they come—a single common hall with rooms for rent shaped below the sod. No fancy entrance nor climbing vines. Just ramps and a cheerless fire.

Jansen strode into the common room. "Hail, fellows! Sit and feel no fear. None of you will come to harm this night for this Inn is under the protection of Captain Jansen the Black! Eat hearty, lads!"

No one glanced up from their suppers.

"Ah, their respect shows in their eyes. Come, boy." He motioned me into the room. "What table suits you?"

"The corner near the fire would be nice," I said, for I was chilled to the bone.

The corner table, it turned out, was occupied by a large man who was eating stew while gazing at nothing in particular. His hands were like rocks and looked to be two *decimetra* across. His arm muscles were as thick as most men's legs. "On the other hand"—I gulped—"perhaps that table over by the door might be—"

"Nonsense, boy. I am Captain Jansen the Black and I sit where I will." He swaggered over to the corner table. "Ho, varlet, take your meal to some other sty, this is my table tonight!"

The man continued to chew on his stew, staring straight ahead, though I thought I saw one eyebrow twitch.

"Captain Jansen the Black speaks to you, knave! Take your swill and be gone!"

The other eyebrow twitched.

Jansen had had enough. Disrespect he could deal with handily. Honors he soaked up like a sponge. Rage and hate he could combat. Adoration was his bread and butter.

Being ignored made him crazy.

It was over before it began. Captain Jansen the Black, scourge of the Mannan Sea, drew his sword. The iron shone in the light of the fire. The keen edge cut through the air in gliding whistles. Jansen glanced at me—making sure that I was watching.

That was his second mistake. Drawing the weapon had been the first.

"No Sorcery allowed in my Inn, Captain whoever-you-are!" announced the big man, shoving aside his bowl of stew.

Standing up, he swung his fist past the swirling blade and clobbered Captain Jansen the Black on the jaw. The sword's blade flew upward, lodging in the ceiling a full half *metra* out of reach.

The scourge of Mannan Sea hit the floor like a sack of

flour. The innkeeper hauled him to his feet, took two steps toward the door, and with both hands threw Captain Jansen the Black no less than four *metra* through the open doorway, headfirst into the mud.

I stood gaping when the innkeeper turned his glare to me. "Are you with him?"

"No, sir! J-just on my way to Cyrsa!" I stammered. "We happened to enter together, that's all."

"Hungry, boy?" He looked me over from head to toe.

"Yes," I admitted. I hadn't eaten since morning and the food smelled wonderful. "But I haven't any Life."

"How are you at washing dishes?"

I got my meal and rid myself of an unwanted companion at the same time.

Free of Jansen, I trudged my way westward again down the Bay Road. The sun was setting. I had long ago left Illis behind, and there was no other town in sight. Groves of short trees straggled across the plains. During the daylight the groves seemed pleasant and harmless enough, but I had no doubt—from the knowledge gathered along the road—that their aspect would change with the darkness.

I was just thinking that I would have to take my chances and sleep in the open when I was picked up on the road by a coach of the *Albanara*. The coach was formed of rose petals and was being pulled by an oversize cardinal. The coachman, one Halrod by name, had just delivered his Lord and Lady to Sharakan for some royal gathering there and had been sent back to Cyrsa to retrieve some of her Ladyship's things. Halrod was a pleasant fellow and had no wish, he said, to see me become a centaur's evening meal.

As the sun was setting, we came at last within sight of the Mannan Sea—colored a brilliant red from the last rays of the sun. The billowing clouds over the sea were breathtaking shades of pink and purples as night came to claim its rightful place. Where was the city? I wondered. A towering shaft of crystal glowed at the edge of the plateau, flanked by two huge stones shapings that seemed to be grotesque heads. Otherwise the plain was empty.

Halrod pulled the coach into a circle of flowers in the

grove. At his word the circle slid below the level of the ground, carrying me, Halrod, and the coach with it.

I had found the city of Cyrsa at last.

History: Cyrsa is a minor port with little known history until its expansion following the Iron Wars. With the increasing prominence of Sharakan in world affairs, the need for a seaport became more and more pressing.

Cyrsa, in an almost direct line from Sharakan to the coast of the Mannan Sea, was the perfect choice. The port was originally a small inlet at the base of a huge cliff facing the sea. Sharakan's wealth changed all of that. The natural caverns that riddled the cliff were enlarged and connected by tunnels. At the end of the Second Rectification the original inlet had become the entrance to a harbor carved into the cliff itself.

Current Conditions: The city is not visible from the plains approaching it. The land above the city is, by royal decree, a preserve where the natural flora of the area can flourish untouched. There was also some thought that this might confuse an enemy attacking Cyrsa from the land side, although the tracks the Sorcerer's carts have made certainly make this a ridiculous assumption. Circles of flowers mark the more sophisticated entry points to the upper city, while trails on the south lead down from the cliff face to the main harbor entrance below.

Here, ships sail through a large opening in the cliff to find safer harbor inside. This entrance is guarded by two large stone statues that are under the control of the *Kan-Hanar*. Vessels that attempt to enter or leave the harbor illegally (without payment) are stopped by one of these animated statues, who reaches out its stone hand and lifts the vessel out of the water. That, I heard, rarely happens.

The port of Cyrsa was occasionally the refuge of pirates and other people of questionable character, but that, I was assured, was all in the bad old days. The *Albanara* and others of privilege run the city now. Their homes are shaped out of the stalactites on the cavern roof, providing a marvelous view of the bay. Cyrsa is a wealthy city, its people profiting handsomely from the seagoing trade.

Part of the city rims the bay cavern and has its various

levels, which, in general, tend to get more and more disreputable the closer one comes to the docks.

There are a number of different inns in Cyrsa, depending upon how much Life one is willing to spend.

In the elegant part of the city the Baylord is considered the finest inn in Cyrsa. Its dancing statues are a wonder to behold, and its dreamrooms, while expensive, offer to its occupants sleep in a room that has no beds—one floats on cushions of air.

A more reasonably priced hostelry is the Waterkeep Inn, located about halfway up the north side of the cliff. The fountains there sing some of the finest melodies I have ever heard. I understand that there is also a wonderful cascade on the premises for the use of the guests who enjoy sliding down waterfalls. These falls are especially designed so that those sliding down them never have to climb back up to the top.

Sadly I had little time to take in the sights of Cyrsa. Jansen had undoubtedly headed this way, and the sooner I left this town the less likely it would be that I would run into him. Thanking the coachman for his kindness, I made my way down to the bay, passing another inn—the Sailor's Repose (a most disreputable place)—and came at last to the docks of Cyrsa Bay.

Exhausted as I was, I dared not sleep there. It was, by this time, nearly morning, so I searched for a ship. None could leave fast enough for my liking. At last I came to a particularly unsavory part of the docks and found a vessel that, though ugly and small, looked as if it would do. It was casting off just as I arrived.

"What is your destination?" I yelled through cupped hands.

A wiry man at the back of the ship looked up and called back. "We are bound for Avidon."

I threw my pack over the water to the deck and jumped. "Life for passage?"

The man glared at me as I landed hard on the deck. "Well, it certainly looks that way."

I gave him all the Life I had left within me and collapsed.

°   °   °

I was sick.

Travel by Corridor is, at first, a frightening sensation (I always feel as if I'm being squeezed to death), but you eventually become accustomed to it. Travel by air is a delightful experience that I heartily recommend.

Travel by boat is torture for both body and mind.

Ships come in a variety of shapes, primarily dependent on how they travel through the water. Some ships are shaped out of living fish. These tend to be very fast but terrible to ride, and the smell is unbelievable! Others are shaped like homing pigeons. These never get lost but are limited as to where they can go. Most ships, however, are shaped out of trees. Our ship was one of these.

The ship was manned by a crew of seven who mostly took turns at the watch. The hull was of crafted oak, the roots of the tree being stylishly knitted together to form the bow. The hollow of the trunk held trade goods and supplies, the top was shaped flat so that standing on it was not difficult for those accustomed to the sea. Aft, the trunk turned upward and swept forward, the leaves forming a sun sail.

The trunk could be turned by a word from the helmsman. The ship was steered by a branch trailing in the water. The broad, stiff silver leaves—attracted to sunlight— pulled us along with ever-increasing vigor as the day brightened. At night they curled up and so did we.

From the rakish look of her hull and the sweep of her mast, I thought at first that the ship would be one of speed, grace, and beauty. Nothing was further from the truth. The *Alacrity*, as she was misnamed (I thought that name sounded familiar, by the way, but I couldn't place it), bobbed about in the water like a piece of driftwood. Master Stamish, the man who welcomed me aboard, had his hands full just getting us out of the harbor. The ship was too short to properly cut the waves and too long to ride them out properly. She broke and crested often . . . and so did my meals.

It wasn't until a few hours out—me hugging the mast and wishing either for death or dry land, I didn't much care which—that Master Stamish came up to me.

"Captain wants a word with you, Wildreth."

I would have to move, and the prospect was not a happy thought. "I . . . I thought *you* were the cap—ulp—captain."

"Nay, I'd not be able to fill his shoes. Best get below. The captain's been recoverin' from a row he had in port. Aft cabin. Knock before ya enter."

I managed to drag myself hand over hand along the deck rail and tumbled below deck. The light shone in through windows that had once been knotholes. A desk sat at the back of the cabin where the captain rested his bandaged and poulticed head. Raising himself up on his forearms, he looked at me.

"You!" he growled.

"You!" I gagged.

Captain Jansen the Black, scourge of the Mannan Sea, leaped at me. Parchments and ink scattered as he slid across the desk and tumbled to the floor.

I told my legs to run. They responded reluctantly as I broke for the open deck. The horizon bobbed and weaved. The world and the deck couldn't seem to agree on which way they should lean. Still, my legs kept going, and I tottered down the length of the deck, glancing backward to see my approaching doom.

Jansen burst through the doorway into the blazing sunshine on the deck.

"Kill the little snipe!" he ordered. It must have cost him some pain for he looked as though someone had driven a sword through his head. Turning to Stamish, he snarled, "Toss him overboard!"

"Surely you can't be meaning that, Captain?" Stamish looked horrified, as did the rest of the crew who had gathered around. "Killing a man at sea will bring the evil curse on us for sure!"

"Damn the evil curse, you superstitious fool! I want that brat dead!"

Not a man moved. I clung to the rigging and hoped I wouldn't disgrace myself by tossing my breakfast. Jansen glared at his crew, who glowered back. Finally, seeing he was outnumbered, he was forced to give in and did so with his usual lack of grace.

"Hmm. Well spoken, Stamish! We won't kill this lubber—

who, I might add, has lied about everything he told you about me!" This brought some strange looks from everyone. I hadn't considered Jansen worthy of mention. "Still, he has cheated me, and I will not take him to his destination.

"Helmsman!" Jansen winced. "Come about to the northwest. We make for the Falls!"

The crew began to mutter among themselves. I had no idea what that might mean.

"Captain, not the Falls!" said Stamish. "He's just a little fella and there's no need to be putting the rest of the crew to danger—"

"I captain this vessel, Stamish!" Jansen's large ears flushed red. "It's the Falls for him. The brat claims to be from Merilon ... so we'll be neighborly and send him back!"

By midday the crew was getting tense. The Falls! What horror could that be? What new terror would I be forced to endure on my quest for my honor and title?

The sun was well into the afternoon sky when, checking their charts, the crew called the leaves in and waited.

They didn't wait long. Soon, to the west, a pillar of brown suddenly appeared in the sky, plunging out of nowhere into the sea and causing it to roll and foam.

Captain Jansen cried, "Thar it be, mates! Bring 'er about and make all speed. She'll be a rough one this time around for sure!"

The *Alacrity* surged ahead. The seas became more and more choppy as we neared the thundering brown of the Falls. Sea spray drenched the deck, and the crew worked in grim determination.

The column suddenly ended. Looking up, I could make out the strange vortex of a huge Corridor just opening up in the sky.

"That's one, boys! We'll go between the second and the third!"

The sea was a brown mess now. The smell around us was awful.

I suddenly knew where all the garbage of Thimhallan was sent.

"You're putting me in there?" I squeaked, looking up at the gaping Corridor that apparently stood eternally open.

Jansen smiled. "Never traveled through a sewer, eh, lubber? Don't know that anyone has, come to think of it. Can't kill you at sea—bad luck—so we're sending you home. That one leads to Merilon. Who knows, maybe one of the *Thon-Li* will come to inspect it and then you'll be found. . . . Maybe."

Corridors lead from specific places to specific places, their number almost unlimited. But there are certain things that Corridors cannot do. One of them is to transport a person to a mobile location—such as a ship. If you want to get out of a ship, you have to steer it to a location where a Corridor is located and then make use of it. There are very few Corridors at sea (for obvious reasons), but this one was here for a purpose.

A torrent of slop gushed from the sky in an ugly brown garbage-fall over six *metra* across and plunged into the sea. Refuse floated here and there before sinking below the scummy surface. The dumping occurs from time to time during the day. There are three Corridors. The first opens immediately, then the second, then the third. All remain open, after they've been emptied, and anyone who wanted to could leap inside.

"Now!" cried Jansen. "Straight for the sun and Falls!"

The broad leaves of the ship's sail spread wide. We charged across the turbulent stench of the sea directly at the third column. The torrent from the second ended as we approached. It would be the third's turn any moment now.

The leaves were pulled in by Jansen's order, and *Alacrity* wallowed in the heavy waves under the Corridor.

Jansen turned to me. I could already feel my feet lifting from the deck as his Life sent me soaring straight into the opening overhead. I had no Life left to fight him.

"I'm sure that *Thon-Li* will understand how such a stupid boy fell overboard into sea."

Stamish shouted, "Stand by to make full sail!"

The leaves spread into the shining sunlight—and failed. By the fate of the Almin a thundercloud chose that time to cross the sun. Darkened by its shadows, *Alacrity* failed to live up to her name. She drifted along slowly, lingering under the threat from above.

I stopped my upward flight and began sinking back

downward. Jansen the Black had turned his attention elsewhere. "Now, Master Stamish! Get us out of this place NOW!"

The crew ran about on the deck below me. Jansen began shouting orders: "Bring her about. Use the sunlight in the sky to the north of the storm! Master Stamish, take four men to the—"

With Jansen's concentration broken, I fell directly on top of him.

"Almin damn you, whelp!" Jansen threw me aside and leaped to his feet. "Curse or no curse, you are dead!"

His sword rang. It slashed down at me . . .

. . . just as all of Merilon's garbage plummeted down from the Corridor.

Chapter Ten

The Lost Kingdoms

When I awoke, I was staring into my father's face.

"Dad?" I cried.

"No, son." The man chuckled. "At least I don't think so. Not that I'd know for sure, if you know what I mean." He winked at me. "Girl in every port and not worrying about the catalysts. But I am glad you have come around. I don't get much company here from the world topside."

I sat up and instantly regretted it. The dull ache at the back of my head surged forward, reminding me to move more slowly. I was about to shake my head when I realized that, too, would be a bad idea. I held still while the world, or what passed for it, settled around me.

"Where am I?" My head suddenly cleared and I stood. "And who the Devon are you?"

"Starg's the name and prison's my game."

"Uncle Starg!" I cried, throwing my arms around him.

"Easy, there, boy! Don't want to get the old cloth torn now, do we?" He disentangled himself. Recognition flashed in his eyes. "Ah, you must be Dietrem's boy! My, you've

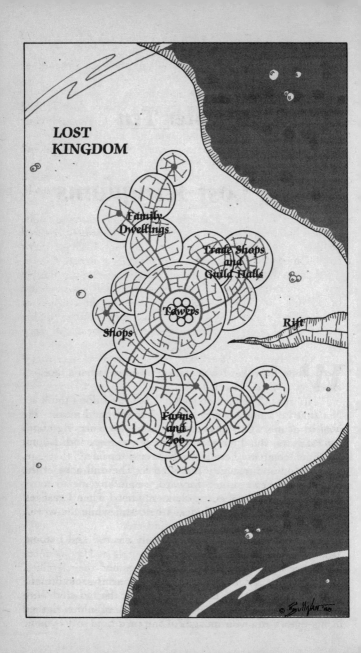

turned into a fine man, now. Tell me, how's your mother and old Trem, eh?"

"Dead, sir, these last few months."

Starg's smiling face fell at the news. "Sorry, lad. Truly I am. Trem was the best gambler I ever knew and your mother a fine, stalwart lady despite her family."

I blinked at him in confusion. Could I be mistaken? "Sir, my father was a Baron of Merilon and my mother—"

"Of course! Of course they were! Don't get so riled, son. Ah, how one's fortunes change. Look to yourself, boy. Just where do you think you are now?"

For the first time I looked out upon my surroundings. What I had supposed was a grassy hill was actually covered in fine, soft moss. Strange rock trees of brilliant color spread along the hillside. While overhead—I gaped.

A large school of fish drifted above me. A great bubble with faint rainbow hues kept our space filled with air and breathable. Beyond our bubble I could see the outlines of many more bubbles gathered around a large central bubble where stood a dark tower, silhouetted against the deep purple of the sea.

"Welcome to the Lost Kingdoms, boy. It is here that I have been held a prisoner for low these many months, and—with any luck at all—for many years yet to come."

History: Chaos ruled in the Crescent Kingdoms after the horrible Succession Wars. The *Albanara* who survived with some portion of their wealth and power intact could not hope to stand long against the roving mobs of that age. They did what they could to hold their civilization together, and when that was not enough, they fled.

Some moved to the remote southlands of the Crescent, while others crossed the sea. One group of them, however, chose another route.

Mern of Kazan led the ruling houses of Jepra, Qint, and Havlan *into* the sea rather than across it. Having spent some time in their preparations, the magi and their families, surrounded by spheres of magic that allowed them to breathe beneath the waves, walked straight into the ocean. With them they took all of their wealth, the like of which has not been seen again in all the ages of the world, or so I reckon.

What then happened, according to Uncle Starg, was the gradual changing of the Mern—as they began to call themselves—into a race of sea dwellers through magical means.

The individual kingdoms that the Mern had established along family lines were at peace with one another, largely due to the distances that separated their settlements. Jepra and Qint each established their own strongholds in the Westerness north and south of Point Aspen. Havlan took his people farthest of all, beyond the Vajnan peninsula to settle in the Frea Sea.

Mern settled in the Mannan Sea, near the center of its waters.

Looking out from their bubble-encased cities, the Mern saw the vast, unclaimed, rich lands that existed below the waves. There was Life here, unsullied by war. They loved their new homeland and wanted to leave their bubbles of air and wander it unfettered.

In those years the Mern used all of the arts of Life to reshape their race into a form more suitable to their new environment. Soon they abandoned the bubbles and built great and beautiful cities that stood far below the water, beyond the knowledge of men. There they remained until the Iron Wars.

During the Wars the seas were littered with corpses— men and women who died in disputes over the waters. It was then that the Lost Kingdoms briefly returned to the land. Enraged at the violation of their territories, they decided to stop the carnage on the surface of the oceans.

On that day the Mern came into the ports around the world and destroyed all ships they could get their hands on. Their Seadragons sundered the mightiest of the Deathships, while their sharks made short work of their crews.

When all shipping was disrupted, the Mern disappeared as quickly as they came. To this day they remain feared and respected by the men who sail the seas.

Current Conditions: The Mern remain reclusive and distrust "Lungbreathers," as they often refer to those from the world above. They no longer communicate with those above the water. Those who try to enter their realm for purposes of gain are treated without mercy.

They are not without compassion, however. Sailors who are shipwrecked, cast adrift, or fall overboard are often cared for by the Mern, who left many of their bubbles of protection intact for just such circumstances and save the drowning by this means. This was the case with my uncle, who was cast overboard by his own crew. My own salvation must surely have been through the same providence. I never found out what became of Jansen and the crew of the *Alacrity*.

The Mern's original bubble-cities, although abandoned by the general populace, are far from empty. The riches and beauty here are beyond description. Sea creatures of various kinds find their way into these cities, and many of the pets and animals that were brought here by the early inhabitants have bred, their offspring thriving in the underwater environment.

I have only seen one of the Lost Kingdom cities. Still, I would venture to say that the manner of their construction is undoubtedly similar. Uncle Starg had discovered a map carved into a prominent stone slab in one of many large parks found at most intersections of the city's roads. He had deciphered some of its symbols and could tell me much about the general layout of the city.

The entire community apparently started with the large, central bubble, onto which additional bubbles have subsequently added. The various portions of the city expanded from this central location to meet the needs of its thriving inhabitants.

The eastern bubbles of the city protect the Guild Halls and the trade shops. The abandoned halls of the *Kan-Hanar* and the *Pron-alban* can all be found here in various states of disrepair. We did not venture into those areas, however, for Starg had heard of darkrovers and other Warchanged creatures living in that area. The fact that such beings existed in this place meant that they had somehow stumbled into the Mern city from the world above. There must be ways into these cities from the world above, I reasoned. And if so, ways out. But if that were true, why was my uncle still down here?

Uncle Starg refused to take me down into the southern bubbles. These were farms and ranches originally, their food used to sustain the city's inhabitants. Now they are totally overgrown with weeds. The domestic animals have long since gone wild.

The center of the city had, of course, a mixture of all of these elements in it. Ancient stone guards kept most of the Warchanged out of the northern areas, but they ran wild in the center of the city, making the central dome a dangerous place to explore.

Looking into it, I could see the lovely coral towers that comprised the central castle of the city. Those pink and red walls no doubt contained fabulous wealth and knowledge. A moat, filled with black, brackish water, surrounded the castle. Unknown things lived in there. My uncle told me that not even the Warchanged would dare cross that swamp.

The northern branches of the city extended into family dwellings, which is where Starg had made his home. He led me back to his apartments that overlooked one of the lushest and most beautiful gardens in the northern part of the city.

It must have been the sight of the garden, for suddenly Lilieth came to my mind.

I thought back to her strong face, the lovely eyes. I imagined her long golden hair—so tightly braided—being freed by my hands. I wondered if she was as unhappy with her lot in life as I had come to be with mine. I pondered what laughter might look like in her eyes.

When I had first left the Font, I feared that I would have to return there someday and tell her that I could never be her husband.

Now, I feared that I might never walk with her again.

Though largely overgrown by vegetation from the parks, the buildings in the northern section of the underwater city remain strong and, in many instances, habitable. Those rooms that have not been vandalized by the creatures running wild through the city remain as their former inhabitants left them: orderly and undisturbed. It is a most unsettling feeling to walk the halls of those houses— abandoned hundreds of years before—and see them just as they once were long ago.

We settled down into these rooms and I recited my tale

to my uncle—beginning with the death of my parents up to my present sad condition.

Starg listened carefully.

"The *Duuk-tsarith* are right—as usual. I believe that I can help you, son. You see, your father and mother weren't exactly from the same side of the avenue. The Wildreths have always been—well—more interested in shortcuts than the long haul, if you know what I mean. Your father was good with a tarok deck—one of the best. He could turn you the Fool card four times running and you'd never suspect him of slanting the cards.

"When your father was a young man, near your age now, your mother's family moved to Zith-el. Her father was a *Quin-alban* of considerable station who had been brought in to help with some difficulty at the Zoo. He rapidly became the toast of Zith-el society, and his family was elevated in station with him."

The chair creaked as Starg leaned back, placing his hands behind his head.

"The first time he saw your mother, Trem knew he couldn't live without her. He was a *Pron-alban* by Mystery, but his station was low, despite his outward appearances (he gained his wealth through gambling, of course), and he knew that without title or lands he couldn't get near your mother. The one way he knew to win her, however, was with the cards.

"He soon found a good mark—a Baron from Merilon who didn't know when to stop playing. By the time Trem was done with him, he had the man's lands and his title of Baron."

"My father *won* his title cheating at cards?" I was aghast. "Liar! My father was a great man—a respected man—"

Starg held up his hands. "So he was, son, so he was. Now sit down, I haven't finished. The old Baron was without family—Trem chose his target well. No one contested the transfer of lands and title. Within weeks he had secured his position and began to court your mother.

"It was to her credit that she loved him not for his lands but for himself. She saw through his finery and knew him for what he was, yet she loved him with all her heart. The Church soon approved the marriage. They moved to

Merilon, living quietly with good, honest jobs. Your mother's influence for good on your father was such that he even began to plan to return his ill-gotten gains to the Baron. But fate intervened.

"Shortly after their much-publicized marriage, your mother's family in Zith-el was approached by the deposed Baron. He threatened to expose your father for the crooked gambler he was. Your mother's people had become a power in Zith-el, and such a scandal would have ruined them. They didn't like the idea of paying blackmail, and in the end, they determined to kill the Baron. The deed was done by one of your mother's two brothers."

Starg stood up and walked to the window. The park below was bathed in hues of purple and pink of the sunset far above that the Mern had caused—through their magical arts—to light the darkness of the sea. "He was caught by the *Duuk-tsarith,* of course. He disappeared, never heard from again. The full knowledge of the affair came to light, doing more damage than the Baron could ever have done on his own. Your mother's family was disgraced in Zith-el and had little choice but to move again."

Lamps in the form of large crystals in the shape of teardrops were set into the walls. Starg walked past them, lighting them in turn. The lamps lit the room in a soft white glow.

"They came to Merilon," I murmured to myself. "Of course, they had nowhere else to go." I looked up. "That's it! The Baron was dead. No one knew the truth. Father's holdings were untouched—he still held his titles and lands. Her family must have come to him, demanding that he get them reestablished in Merilon."

"Right, boy. They threatened to expose him if he didn't help them. He would have lost his job, his home, everything. There was nothing he could do but give in to them. But it didn't work." Starg sat down in the great chair opposite me. "No matter how much money your father lavished on them, the upper crust in Merilon wouldn't accept them. They remained in the City Below, their hate and envy for your father festering. They couldn't see their own faults and came more and more to blame him.

"But your father—he did well. Under the expert teaching of the Guilds in Merilon, he became one of the finest *Pron-alban* craftsmen in the city. Finally he felt secure enough in his position to stand up to his relations. Your mother backed him up. Every time he had tried to feed them, he got his hand bitten, as it were. He told them that when you came of age, they would get no more money."

Starg sat back in his chair and brooded for a while. My father had never told me this tale. Small wonder, I thought! He must have been dreadfully ashamed of it. Still, I was puzzled by something.

"Uncle—I don't see what this has to do with my parents' deaths. They were killed by Westlund Separatists in Mannan Park!"

"There's one more secret, son. As far as I know, only myself and your late father and mother knew this one."

Starg rubbed his chin and leaned his head back. He spoke quietly to the ceiling, but his words were for me.

"Your mother's people moved to Zith-el from Westlund. Your uncle—Thurb Dresler—was a Separatist."

Chapter Eleven

Avidon and Home

"**I** thought you were a prisoner here?"

We picked our way through the rubble of a tumbledown building and finally entered a partially destroyed hallway. Its darkness was lit only by the feebly glowing stone in Starg's hand.

"Well, that's mostly true, Petar. I was brought here by the Mern and they don't want me to leave. They don't like people going back to tell the world above about them. I suppose that gives me the right to be their prisoner as well as any man."

"But if you know the way out, why don't you just leave!"

Starg turned to me, his face aglow in the dim light of the crystal. "Boy, you have little idea what treasure there is in that great castle in the middle of the city! The jewels alone would set a man comfortable for several lifetimes. I've spent months trying to divine the way in and still have not yet come upon it. But I will. When I do, then I'll leave."

We turned the corner and came upon a pool. Water

poured into it from waterfalls on three sides. In its center, however, a great whirlpool spun down, leading into—an open Corridor! The swirl of the vortex was dark but unmistakable. There was a Corridor open at the bottom of the pool!

"Where does it go?" I asked in slack-jawed wonder.

"Er—well—I don't really know." Starg fidgeted a little. "But *someone* must have opened it to *somewhere*. It's the only way I know out of the city."

"But why is it still open?"

"A fine question, boy—and I'm afraid there's only one way to find out."

Jumping into an unknown Corridor is rather like leaping off a cliff in pitch darkness: you can only hope it isn't too far to the end. The prospect of doing that, accompanied by the dark, swirling water as my only companion, was a little more than I could take at the moment.

"Look—there must be another way—"

"Trust me, boy, I've tried. I've brought others here and sent them through. Not one of them returned to complain."

My face expressed my dubious opinion of that last point.

"Here," Starg said, "take this stone to the Windwanderers' Guild in Sharakan. It should more than make up for the loss of the cargo and ship."

The stone was a deep red crystal about the size of a bird's egg. But wealth was not on my mind at the time. Death was.

"You must return to Merilon, boy. Reclaim your title and your honor."

"What honor?" I asked bitterly. "Lands won in a crooked card game. Murder done to cover them up."

"Now wait a minute, son. Look over the records when you get back. I'll lay all the wealth I plan to acquire on the fact that your father stashed all that ill-gotten money away somewhere. He raised you on what he and your mother earned with the sweat of their brows. When you find it, give it to the Church, if it eases your conscience."

He paused for a moment, then wrapped his arms about me. "I see much of your father in you. I will come to you as soon as I have made my fortune. May the blessings of the Almin go with you."

With that, he spun me around and with a boot to my backside, sent me headfirst into the whirlpool.

Avidon is a city of water. Water cascades across its surfaces. Waterfalls dance to the rhythms of ice-chimed music. Pleasure boats provide the transportation throughout the city.

One of the most pleasant fountains in this city of water gushes down a myriad of levels into a vast, circular pool. It is a quiet spot set aside by the catalysts of that city for contemplation and inner searching.

It was, I presume, most startling when I bobbed up out of the center of the pool, sputtering and gasping for breath.

I coughed water for a time, lying on the edge of the pool, not having the strength to climb out. Traveling through a Corridor full of water is an experience I do not recommend.

After a time I realized that someone was standing before me on the edge of the pond. I wearily lifted my head, blinked water from my eyes, and stared into the shadow-draped face of the *Duuk-tsarith*.

Avidon is an independent city-state on the eastern boundaries of the Outland. Built on a large lake along the Taraganth River, Avidon floats peacefully on huge lilly pads. The people of Avidon boast that their city needs no moat to protect it. Detractors of Avidon say that the city *is* a moat!

Avidon can be reached by ship from the Mannan Sea by way of the wide and deep Taraganth River. A gate stands where ships enter the city from the north, guarding its waters from unwanted intrusion.

My trip through Avidon was extremely rushed. What little of the architecture I did see left me confused. All of the shaped statues—and there are more than one cares to see—are done in the modern style. The effect, I am sure, was meant to be impressive. My own impression was that the children had been given far too much modeling clay.

Still, I don't know if any other city in all of Thimhallan can boast so many waterfalls, fountains, cascades, rapids, or ponds. Many of them are quite striking. The people of

Avidon have become quite adept at exploring various shapings of water. My personal favorite was a fountain of five rings of water that floated over a pond so turbulent that its waters were capped with white. The rings themselves revolved in different directions, occasionally striking each other and causing water to explode out from them.

One might think that all this running water would make the city a noisy place, and for the newcomer that is certainly the case. However, in time the constant and unchanging noise of the waterfalls fades pleasantly into the background of one's mind.

Central to the complex of lily pads is the Uthan Palace. From within its six outer walls the Citymaster rules, advised by a Council chosen by the people of the city. The lily pad on which the Palace is built has been surrounded by a guard of mutated frogs, who prevent the uninvited from landing on the Palace grounds.

The only access to the Uthan Palace is over Starbow—a glittering span of water that connects the castle's lily pad to that of the Barter's Lane. This is the major shopping and entertainment district of the city, and it is the place with which most people will be familiar.

North of Barter's Lane is the Garden of the *Fihanish*. It is known for its works of art, fountains, and such as I have described. Indeed, it was in this section where I made my rather precipitous entry into Avidon.

The other sections of the city contain smaller markets selling quaint wares, as well as housing for the populace. Each of these is connected to the other via a series of arched water bridges, although the most popular way of getting from place to place is by boat.

The ships that I had seen in Cyrsa were great, seagoing vessels. The boats of Avidon were much smaller and more elegantly crafted. Some shaped as swans slid effortlessly through the still waters; winged horses or silver dolphins carry their patrons in swift and silent splendor.

Avidon is not without its inns and taverns. The finest of these is the Sweetwater Inn, located on Barter's Lane near Starbow. The entire structure appears to be formed from flowing water. In reality the water is shaped around clear crystals that form the building stones of the structure. The

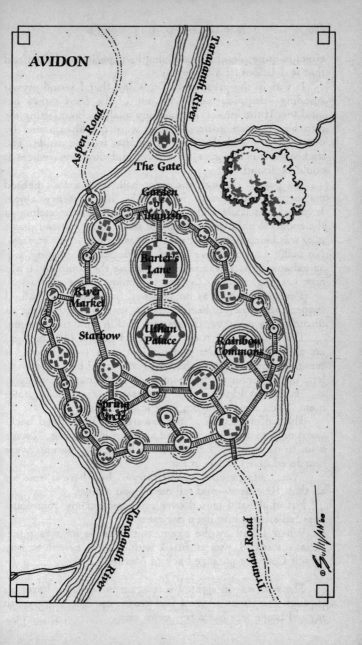

AVIDON

The Gate

Garden of Tikanish

Barter's Lane

River Market

Starbow

Ulthan Palace

Rainbow Commons

Spring Circle

Aspen Road

Taraganith River

Traranith River

Trandar Road

effect is quite pleasing. Its dining hall specializes in seafood that is delicious, if a bit pricey.

It was in the great hall of this Inn that I found myself standing—dripping wet—with one of the *Duuk-tsarith* behind me. If the innkeeeeper had any qualms about letting me into his fine establishment, they were quickly quieted by one look at the dark-robed figure that led me inside. The innkeeper quickly gave us a room and directions where it could be found.

We passed through the great hall, the warlock behind me urging me silently forward by his presence alone. Inverted waterfalls arched overhead to form the ceiling of the room. Within the contours of the water I noticed that a play was being performed with shapes formed in the streams. Normally I would have found the display fascinating, but as exhausted as I was and considering the company I was now keeping, I hadn't the heart to enjoy such a spectacle.

The room itself was far removed from the great hall—I suspect that the innkeeper didn't want his other guests disturbed by whatever the warlock had in mind to do to me.

The walls of the room shimmered gently, like the light on the surface of the water when seen from below. It reminded me strongly of the Lost Kingdoms I had so recently left. In the center of the room a soft disk floated invitingly.

"Baron Wildreth." The *Duuk-tsarith* made it a statement. "You are tired from your long journey."

The Enforcer took a step toward me. I stumbled backward only to slam into the bed and lose my footing. "I have a lot to do—please, I must return home. My parents were murdered and I can prove it—"

"Yes," whispered the *Duuk-tsarith*, "but there is time for all that. Rest now—and tell me all you know."

His chill hand closed over my eyes and my consciousness fell swiftly into deep darkness.

When I had awoke again, the *Duuk-tsarith* was gone. What's more, I was suffused with Life sufficient to buy myself Corridor passage back to Merilon!

The end was in sight. I was again in Merilon, hurrying through the street where I had grown up. The entrance to my old home was but a few *metra* away.

I knew now what I had to do. I would confront my uncle and throw him and his lot out of the house. Their greed had brought ruin to my family. Now I would bring vengeance to theirs. It might—probably would—be dangerous to encounter this man who had committed murder and who knows what other foul deeds. But I was determined to avenge my parents' deaths and carry through on what my father had tried to do in life.

I should have found it curious that the entrance to the house was unguarded and open, but I wasn't thinking clearly at the time. I ran into the entry garden, shouting out my uncle's name.

The garden was manicured and well kept. Its red and blue flowers were shaped carefully into a heart—a form that my mother had loved.

Amid the flowers stood a *Duuk-tsarith*.

We stood facing each other for a time. Then he spoke.

"Baron Wildreth, we regret our duty to inform you of a tragic loss. Your uncle, Thurb Dresler, the former master of this house, and his entire family have met with an unfortunate accident."

The Enforcer moved silently past me toward the entry. I stared him in shock.

"Am I, indeed, Baron Wildreth?"

The Enforcer stopped.

"Would you have it otherwise, Baron?"

Was there satisfaction in that cold voice? Could the *Duuk-tsarith* actually take pleasure in their work?

I shook my head, about to confess my father's crime, when the chill hand rested briefly on my shoulder. "The card game was an honest one." I heard a smile in that voice. "One of your father's few. It was the Baron who tried to cheat, then lied to cover it up."

The shadow vanished.

The *Duuk-tsarith* now had what they wanted—the explanation as to how the Separatists managed to enter Merilon. Although I would never know for certain, I guess that my uncle met them at the gate and brought them in. He must have arranged to meet my parents in the Park at the time of the demonstration, knowing full well that the *Duuk-tsarith* would arrive to break it up and that violence would be the result.

My uncle and his family were gone. Aunt Hergris disappeared, too. What the *Duuk-tsarith* did to them I neither know nor care. Their fate does not concern me.

I stood alone in the house. Everything there was just as I had remembered it. The warlocks had changed all back to its original. Yet something was missing.

Lilieth.

I pictured her working in the garden. I saw her praying in the family chapel. I saw her hair undone, her head lying on my shoulder.

As Baron, I found that I had considerable Life on account with the Church. The first of my newfound wealth, I spent on a trip through the Corridors to the Font.

Lilieth was waiting for me when I arrived.

Chapter Twelve

Other Places

As the Ariel Meteor pointed out, the people of Thimhallan are a civilization that looks at the goal and does not take the time to see what is happening all around them. Secure and safe, they hide behind their city walls. They travel from place to place through the Corridors. They have forgotten (or they do not want to remember) those lands torn asunder by the Iron Wars. From these ruins are rising new and terrible foes that, unchecked, may threaten their very existence. The land of Thimhallan was dying, even before the coming of Joram.

Baron Wildreth described some of these in his narrative, but there are many more places of romance and mystery and danger that remain to be explored.

Sharzad: The Crystal City across the Southern Sea was raised in one night by Amra and her people. No one knows if the light of her beacon still shines down on the shores of that quiet bay. All contact with the Kingdom was lost following the Iron Wars, and now fierce storms sweeping over the sea from the south keep mariners away. Prior to

SHARZAD

the Iron Wars there was considerable controversy in the *Mon-alḫan* Guild about the Alchemists in Sharzad, who were reputedly creating a receptacle that could hold the power of Life and discharge it to anyone at will. If such objects ever existed, they are now lost behind the wall of mystery that surrounds Sharzad.

Balzaab: Another scion of the Crescent Kingdoms, the city of Balzaab had isolated itself from the world since the Iron Wars. Only on rare occasions does a ship from that island nation come into one of the ports, and then only in emergencies. The sailors are tight-lipped and refuse to say anything about their homeland or conditions there.

The Wild: Beyond the cities and their estates is the Wild. Long ago there was no such place, for all lands were held by kingdoms and had names denoting law and order. Then came the Iron Wars and all the law fell before its fury.

Now law and civilization exist only in the cities and their surrounding countryside. The forests that lie outside those borders are known as the Wild.

The Vajnan Plains are part of the Wild. So, too, are the Borderlands. Those lands are but a grain of sand in the vast expanse of Thimhallan that has been left to the Wild. There is far more of the Wild than the Civilized.

In these lands the Warchanged roam free and unchecked. They answer to no law save their own. Even the griffins, intelligent as they are, are consumed by the bloodlust bred into them. Some of the Warchanged are smart, some stupid, some are brutal and savage without cause, others gentle unless roused. But in their own way, all the Warchanged are dangerous. The cities may be man's, but the Wild is the domain of the Warchanged.

Just as deadly as the Warchanged are the men and the women who have fled society for one reason or another and now make their homes in the Wild. The desert raiders of which Wildreth speaks are a nomadic band of *DKarn-ᑐuuk* who—in the absence of formal war—decided to turn their talents to accumulating wealth by any means possible. They have several renegade catalysts and may be encountered anywhere in the desert around the Border.

Within the Wild much of the wealth and knowledge of the ancient world is buried. Many of the old palaces and

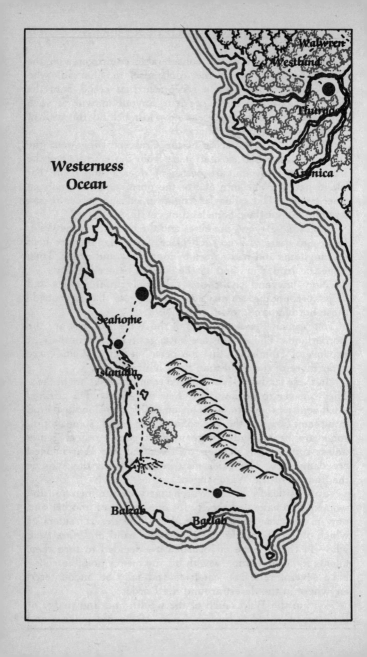

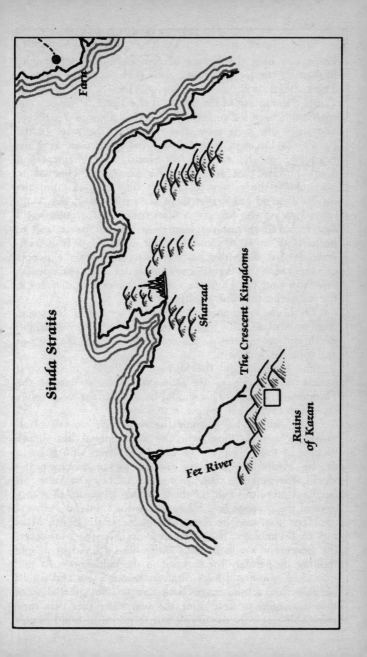

keeps are now the homes of centaurs; their streets are broken by the feet of giants; their parks are faerie glades. There exists, still, as far as anyone knows, the Spires of Truth, located far to the south in the Nomish Range. The roads that once led to the Spires were long ago destroyed, and there are none now who remember the way. In the Spires the Diviners recorded the history of man from his beginning on the ancient, lost world. The Diviners had many powers that are no longer known in Thimhallan, particularly the power to see not only the past but the future. Legend has it that there are survivors of that long-lost Mystery who foresaw a disastrous end for their world and removed themselves from it to live in peace and to prepare to meet the end in their own way. It is conceivable that they may be attempting to warn the people of Thimhallan that their doom approaches. Without a doubt, any who find the Diviners would discover the answers to the mysteries the future holds.

The Outland: Renowned the world over as a fearsome, terrifying place, this region extends from the Westlund north and west as far as the sea and is outside the laws of any king or church.

The Outland and the Sorcerer's village are described extensively in *Forging the Darksword*, volume one of the Darksword Trilogy. This should be used as the main reference in planning encounters in that area.

The Outland has become the home of criminals of all types, as well as those who are not criminal but simply victims of their society. The Dead—children who fail two of the Mysteries—are easy enough to conceal from the world at large when they are young. As they grow older, it becomes more difficult for them to hide from the all-seeing eyes of the *Duuk-tsarith*. Many flee to the Outland.

Here, too, live the Sorcerers—those of the Ninth Mystery of Technology. If encountered just after the Iron Wars, the Sorcerers would be little more than a band of people fighting desperately for survival in the wilderness. At this time they would still have catalysts among them and would be able to combine magic with any technological devices they managed to save after the war. The fact that they were able not only to survive but to go on to build homes

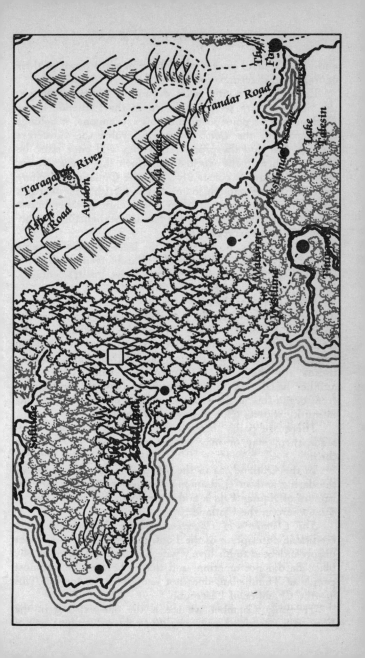

and carve a small pocket of civilization gives proof of their courage and determination and skill.

Encountered in later years, during the lifetime of Joram, the Sorcerers are well established in the Outland. If the Outland at this point in time belongs to anyone, it belongs to Blachloch, the *Duuk-tsarith* who rules the Sorcerers through fear and the promise that they will once more be able to return to the world from which they were driven. Blachloch's patrols constantly roam the Outland, searching for those daring enough to enter. The fact that the warlock loses a few men now and then to centaurs or other beasts doesn't overly concern him. He has an inexhaustible supply of villains and miscreants.

The Sorcerers, however, are the least of one's concerns while traveling the Outland. The Warchanged dwell in its glades, bogs, and woods. Dragons, ogres, giants, centaurs, faeries, griffins—all live in the Outland.

Even the plants themselves can be menacing. The shapers during the Iron Wars did not limit themselves only to the animal kingdom when they created the Warchanged. The infamous Kij vines that thrive on blood creep over the forest floor, intent on driving their lethal, blood-sucking thorns into the living flesh of man or beast. Mindfog is another hazard for the adventurer to beware. Drifting up from organisms in the swamps, it lures men to their deaths in murky waters. (See *Creatures of Thimhallan*)

There are paths through the Outland, but those who made them may or may not be glad to see you walking them.

In the Outland, as in the Wild, there are treasures for the daring and intrepid among you. Most intriguing are the rumors of Xantar Palace and Aspentown, both said to exist somewhere in the Outland.

The Chambers of Discretion: Baron Wildreth gives a creditable description of the Font, for which he is no doubt deeply indebted to his lovely wife Lilieth. But there was one place he did not mention, and that is because he, as most people of Thimhallan, does not know of its existence. This is—the Chamber of Discretion.

The only Chamber we see is the one existing in the Font. It is described in *Forging the Darksword*, volume one of the Darksword Trilogy. There are other Chambers in the world, however, though most were destroyed in the Iron Wars. Created before the Iron Wars by those of the Mysteries of Spirit and Time, the Chambers can now no longer be duplicated. Once used as a means for rulers to be able to negotiate privately among themselves, the Chambers degenerated into spy networks during the Iron Wars and are now used exclusively by the Church to keep control over the various city-states of Thimhallan.

These Chambers are strictly guarded by the *Duuk-tsarith*. Only the ruler of a kingdom would even know of its existence, and that secret is jealously kept. Each Chamber can communicate with another Chamber or with a person in the world *with whom the ruler has had previous physical contact.* The Chambers appear to have an effect on the minds of those using them, allowing them over a long period of time to perform remarkable feats of mental telepathy. It is important to note that the person in the Chamber who wishes to establish communication with someone out in the world must have met and spoken directly to that person in order to create the proper mental link.

Those speaking between Chambers may summon or call another person to the Chamber, but it is not requisite that the other Chamber reply. The ability to avoid the mental summons depends upon the strength and force of will of the person being summoned. Bishop Vanya, having used the Chamber for countless years, is extremely powerful, and ignoring a summons from him takes remarkable courage and self-discipline. Few rulers had the power to do this, one being the King of Sharakan, who—in the days just before the coming of Joram—was actually able to sever contact completely with Bishop Vanya, one reason the Bishop is so anxious to see that Kingdom driven to its knees.

The Mountain: It is never known by any other name. Located somewhere in the south, in the Nomish Range, this is the place where the *Duuk-tsarith* have their central headquarters. Here the children—both male and female—who are exceptionally powerful in the Mystery of Fire are brought for their training that begins at birth. Here they have no names, parents, or homeland. In place of identity they are

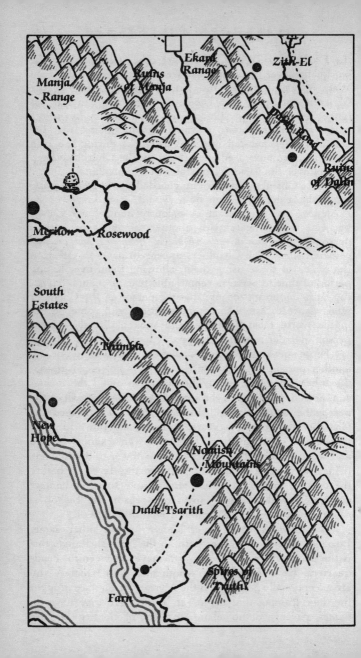

given power. Those who cannot accept the discipline are quietly removed from this world.

Criminals unfortunate enough to find themselves apprehended by the *Duuk-tsarith* may be taken to any of several locations to serve out their sentences. There is no court, no judge, no appeal.

The *Duuk-tsarith* have a central meeting hall and dungeons located beneath each city. These dungeons are generally for minor offenders—drunkards, petty thieves, pickpockets, brawlers, and so forth. The Enforcers also have extensive chambers in the Font.

The perpetrators of more serious crimes are taken to The Mountain. These include political offenders, master thieves, the Dead, and any others the *Duuk-tsarith* judge to be a menace to society at large. No one taken to this place and freed again ever has any desire to return. When asked to describe the dungeons, the most they can do is shudder and talk about the "blackness" and the "depths" and the awful impression of "vast space" that surrounds them. If pressed further, they will say that they never actually saw anything but were incarcerated in complete and total darkness. The only sounds they heard were strange and ominous ones—whispers, a muffled cry, the rustlings of rodents, the *drip-drip-drip* of falling water.

There is no escape once inside The Mountain; the only way out (if the warlocks do not set you free) is by death.

Chapter Thirteen

Creatures of Thimhallan

There are three general classifications of creatures in the world: Creatures of Life, Creatures of the Great Passage, and the Warchanged.

Creatures of Life: When Merlyn first arrived on this planet, he found a wide variety of strange and exotic plant and animal life. Many were extremely dangerous, and he knew he had to protect his people from attack. He created a small Border shield that held the worst of them at bay until the exiles could establish themselves.

After the Great Passage the Border was expanded, using the pure Life from the Well of the World. Merlyn, in unison with the Masters of Time and Spirit, enlarged the Border and sent it forth. As the Border passed over the lands that would become Thimhallan, its magic touched the plant and animal life and changed them. The result was a habitable world filled with plants and animals that appeared to have come from the Ancient World, although—as it turned out—they were not quite the same as those from Beyond. The cattle have antlers rather than horns. Tigers sprout razor-sharp spines on their back.

There were also those living upon this world who were born and bred of the magic and who were therefore not affected by the passing of the Border. The faeriefolk are among these.

Creatures of the Great Passage: When the magi came from Beyond at the time of the Great Passage, they brought with them animals from their old world. With the aid of the *Theldara* the magi were able to establish several species of Earth animals of Thimhallan. Among these were horses. The horses of Thimhallan are now believed to be extinct, all having been destroyed or mutated during the Iron Wars.

The Warchanged: These races came into being as a result of the Iron Wars. When the devices of Death rolled across the plains on their wheels, the people of Life fought back the only way they knew how—with magic. The *Theldara*, catalysts, and *Omueva* pooled their knowledge and talents to create new races of beings. These were the Warchanged: creatures with special abilities bred for war. At first the magi confined their experiments to animals, but—as the war grew more terrible—they began to mutate human beings, thinking to change them back when the war ended.

Alas, by the time the war ended, their creations had escaped their control and spread throughout the land.

The Warchanged were often shaped for specific tasks. Giants were humans enlarged in size, used to aid in sieges by breaking down city walls. The Ariels—men and women with wings—were created as messengers. Dragons rained death from the skies, while the dugruns marched with mindless precision into battle.

When the Iron Wars ended, the *DKarn-duuk* began to try to round up the Warchanged and either change them back or give them swift, merciful deaths. But it was too late. The centaurs had banded together with one dread purpose—to kill their creators. Dragons retreated to solitary caves where they are aroused only at great peril.

Presented here is an alphabetical listing of the creatures you may encounter in your exploration on Thimhallan. The list is by no means complete, and you should feel free to add to it those that you meet on your journeys.

Ariels

As the Iron Wars raged over the land, travel by the Corridors became extremely difficult and unsafe, with each kingdom exerting control of its own Corridors. Left without swift means of travel or communication, the magi created the Ariels. Formerly humans who had "volunteered" for the assignments, the Ariels were given wings so that they could act as messengers. At least that was the original intent.

Unfortunately the *DKarn-ðuuk* quickly saw their value on the battlefield. They were sent on bombing raids, dropping the exploding powder created by the Sorcerers upon unsuspecting cities and keeps. Designed to be used for peaceful purposes, the Ariels are the only race of Warchanged whose minds were left unaltered by their creators. For this reason they are the most intelligent of the Warchanged and work well with humanity.

Even though the Corridors are once again functioning, the cost in Life is high, and therefore most people prefer to use the Ariels to send messages. The Ariels are thus found in the royal courts of Thimhallan, the outlying estates, and the Church. Their duties include the confidential and swift delivery of letters, verbal messages, and transporting goods by Air. All Ariels encountered within civilized lands will be male. Female Ariels—noted for their exquisite beauty—are jealously guarded in their mountain citadel somewhere in the Valheim Mountains.

Description: Ariels are tall, slender humans with delicate features. Most male Ariels are ten to eleven *ðecimetra* tall with the females being just slightly taller. Both males and females have large, feathered wings that fold across each other at the back. Their hair tends toward white, although there have been Ariels born with shades of red or blond hair. Their eyes are large and dark, as are their skin tones. All Ariels move with a natural grace, even when walking— something they do only when forced to by circumstances.

Female Ariels are rarely seen by mortals. When encountered, they are incredibly beautiful and alluring. Human men who have seen a female Ariel have been known to choose to live among them as slaves rather than leave them.

Society: Ariel families are organized around the mother

who rears the children and sees to their instruction. Since there are few females, monogamous marriage is unknown to them. A single female Ariel may have several husbands, who are completely devoted to her and to their children.

Nearly all females of the race remain in the mountain citadels constructed for them by their mates. These females do, from time to time, however, take flight during the night to look over the greater world of Thimhallan as it sleeps.

Attributes and Abilities: Ariels can fly for hours, often days if they pace themselves carefully. They can carry into sustained flight, although for much shorter periods, an additional amount equal to their own body weight. They have keen eyesight and hearing. Their great natural attributes compensate for a lack of ability with any of the Mysteries of Life.

ARIELS
PHANTASIA STATISTICS

ATTRIBUTES

Attack	47	Defense	45	Health	45
Strength	47	Dexterity	65	Movement	5/45[1]
Intelligence	65	Intuition	45	Senses	60
Form fant/human[2]		Size	84	Resistance	34 +
Renewal	640 +	Capacity	1,460 +	Lifewell	2,400 +

ABILITIES

ABILITIES	TALENT	STATION	SCORE
Combat	5	1	6
Movement	15	5RR[3]	22 to 40
Health and Healing	4	1	5
Form and Size Altering	—	—	—
Information	2	1	3
Life Transfer	—	—	—
Tool Crafts and Skills	1	1	2
Telepathy and Empathy	—	—	—
Illusions	1	1	2

[1]Number before the slash indicates speed.

[2]Fantastic Human.

[3]This means "five plus a random number from one to ten plus another random number from one to ten." Determine two random numbers from one to ten, add them together, and then add five to that result to determine such values.

Basilisk

The legendary ability of the basilisk was brought into use for the construction and the defense of perimeters. The *Quin-alban* originally suggested that the shaping of such a creature that could, with a look, turn objects into stone would greatly reduce the demands on their Life, thus freeing them up for other duties.

The basilisk was shaped from the same large reptiles that were later formed into dragons. Unfortunately the basilisks were slow and of such limited intelligence that they could not target their gaze very well.

Caught up in the war, the lumbering basilisks often defended themselves all too well, becoming the only survivors of several seiges. When the battle passed them by, they went their own way, eventually finding more of their own kind and banding together.

Basilisks live primarily in the Outland, making their homes in swampy regions. Occasionally mated pairs may wander onto the plains in search of a suitable home in the ruins of some ancient city.

Description: Basilisks resemble large lizards with flat, bullish faces and long, flat, powerful tails. Their coloration tends toward greenish brown, making it difficult to see them in forests and grasslands. Basilisks range in size from one and a half *metra* to three *metra* in length with the vast majority two *metra* long.

Society: Basilisks mate for life in groups of four: two males and two females. Once mated, they never stray very far from one another unless separated by death. For this reason, chances are that if you encounter one basilisk, there are more somewhere very near by. Basilisks lay eggs and hatch their young.

Attributes and Abilities: The basilisk's gaze can change any solid or liquid object to stone. The creature does this by willing the Life within them to alter an object on which they are focused. This ability does not impede their normal sight, and the basilisk must consciously choose to use this magic. Because basilisks are inherently stupid, they rarely have any logic behind what they turn to stone. Two things only it will not attack: another basilisk and anything (or anyone) it thinks might be suitable for dinner. Basilisks are carnivorous. They are vicious and will attack humans on sight, first attempting to capture them to eat. Failing that or feeling threatened, they will turn them to stone.

Basilisks move very slowly on land. With their flat tails propelling them from behind, they are able to travel much more swiftly through shallow water. Basilisks cannot swim and avoid deep water at all costs. Basilisks can, however, remain underwater without having to surface for breath for several hours when they are resting.

BASILISKS
PHANTASIA STATISTICS

ATTRIBUTES

Attack	65	Defense	40	Health	80R
Strength	30	Dexterity	10	Movement	$3/5^1$
Intelligence	2	Intuition	4	Senses	10
Form	fant/lizard	Size	600	Resistance	30
Renewal	540	Capacity	1,260	Lifewell	3,200

ABILITIES	TALENT	STATION	SCORE
Combat	—	—	—
Movement	—	—	—
Health and Healing	40^2	20	60
Form and Size Altering	—	—	—
Information	—	—	—
Life Transfer	—	—	—
Tool Crafts and Skills	—	—	—
Telepathy and Empathy	—	—	—
Illusions	—	—	—

[1]The value before the slash indicates the creature's movement on land. The number after the slash indicates the creature's movement in the water or swamp.
[2]The only spell the basilisk may cast is a Living Change Flesh to Stone, which costs this creature only 1,000 points of Life to perform.

Centaurs

The most feared and terrible of the Warchanged, centaurs were humans who underwent a most fearful mutation—a cross between human and horse. Their minds were altered to turn them into merciless killers who could track and pursue an enemy with relentless skill and speed. It was assumed, of course, that after the war their Shapers would return them to human form and intelligence once more. That proved to be tragically impossible.

Left misshapen and deformed, hating their creators for what they had done to them, the centaurs survived the way that came most natural to them—by killing. Organizing into bands, they started raiding the settlements that had survived the war. For many years following the Iron Wars they roamed throughout Thimhallan, terrorizing the populace. With the return of peace to the world, the centaurs were hunted down or driven from the civilized lands into the wilderness. Now the greatest population lives in the Outland, although their kind can still be found everywhere in the Wild.

Description: Centaurs stand nearly thirteen *decimetra* tall and have a length of similar dimension. A centaur resembles a human from the waist up. His legs and body are those of the legendary horse, except that the centaur has cloven hooves. Their hair is long and lank on the head and face and sparsely covers their arms, chest, and backs. Female centaurs look exactly the same as the males except for their shriveled breasts. Their young nurse after the manner of horses. Centaur faces are human but seem to have lost all human emotions except one—hatred.

Society: Centaurs have no family unit. They roam the Wild in hunting bands, seldom staying in any one place long. Bands do, however, mark out territories for themselves and defy anyone, including their own kind, to walk their lands. These areas are distinguishable by the marks left by their hooves.

Attributes and Abilities: Centaurs have no ability in magic but do have some rudimentary skill with technology; they occasionally fashion clubs and spears for their own use or take those of their victims. Centaurs are carnivorous and hunt to provide themselves with game. Being half-human, they are fond of hunting for sport, as well, and their favorite prey is man.

Centaurs will rarely kill humans outright but will endeavor to capture and torture them first. They kill without mercy.

CENTAURS
PHANTASIA STATISTICS

ATTRIBUTES

Attack	60	Defense	40	Health	55R
Strength	65	Dexterity	35	Movement	20
Intelligence	5	Intuition	30	Senses	50
Form	fant/human	Size	256	Resistance	5+
Renewal	50	Capacity	50	Lifewell	250

ABILITIES

ABILITIES	TALENT	STATION	SCORE
Combat	–	–	–
Movement	–	–	–
Health and Healing	–	–	–
Form and Size Altering	–	–	–
Information	–	–	–
Life Transfer	–	–	–
Tool Crafts and Skills	10	5R	16 to 25
Telepathy and Empathy	–	–	–
Illusions	–	–	–

Chimera

So much manpower was being drawn off by the war that castles, keeps, and palaces could ill afford to spare men to guard treasure vaults or libraries or other places that held valued artifacts. Chimeras were created to perform this function. Though many of the ancient dwellings they once guarded have fallen into ruin and their masters are long since dead, chimeras remain loyal to their calling, still watching over the treasures of a world now gone.

Description: Chimeras have three heads: one of a goat, one of a lion, and one of a dragon. They have the body and hind legs of a lion, the forelegs of a goat, and the barbed tail of a dragon.

Society: Chimera are solitary creatures. When one is encountered, it is almost certainly alone. The species regenerates by means of larva spawned within their own corpses when they die. Of the larva spawned, only one to three will reach maturity in a process that takes a little over a year and a half. Baby chimera are easily trained, becoming excellent pets and loyal guardians. For this reason young chimera are one of the most valuable commodities in Thimhallan.

Attributes and Abilities: Chimera are loyal to those who raise them, and their owners boast that not even the *Duuk-tsarith* could guard objects of value as well as these beasts. Each of the heads has its own faculty for sight, hearing, and smell. The minds in each head can think individually, although any or all of the three heads can operate in tandem should the need arise. Since the heads look about independently, it is nearly impossible to surprise a chimera. Movement of the body—when required—is controlled by joint thinking of the three brains. Since chimera are primarily set to guard a fixed location, movement is not often necessary.

CHIMERA
PHANTASIA STATISTICS

ATTRIBUTES

Attack	72	Defense	45	Health	156R
Strength	72	Dexterity	56	Movement	20
Intelligence	62	Intuition	5	Senses	56
Form	fant/human	Size	160	Resistance	1
Renewal	100	Capacity	100	Lifewell	300

ABILITIES	TALENT	STATION	SCORE
		5–15	15–25
Combat	10	5–15	15–25
Movement	—	—	—
Health and Healing	—	—	—
Form and Size Altering	—	—	—
Information	1	1	2
Life Transfer	—	—	—
Tool Crafts and Skills	1	1	2
Telepathy and Empathy	—	—	—
Illusions	5	5	10

Darkrovers

The darkrovers are vicious two-legged dogs. Originally shaped from pet dogs of various sizes and breeds, the darkrovers became known during the Iron Wars for their relentless pursuit of their prey and unquestioned obedience to the commands issued them by their masters.

The darkrovers were one of the most economical of the Warchanged. They bred quickly on their own and grew to maturity within a few months, which was good since their high-strung temperament dictated that their lives would be short.

When the Wars ended, there were thousands of these intelligent, obedient creatures left to run loose in the wild. Many of them died, but those that did not adapted and began to thrive.

Now the various types of darkrovers can be found anywhere in the Wild and the Outland. They can be tamed if caught young, but they make extremely dangerous pets. The desert raiders use them for hunting. More often, however, they will be encountered in the wild.

Darkrovers can be categorized into the following groups:

Hunterkill

The most cunning and deadly of the darkrovers, the Hunterkill were bred as assassins. They have a tremendous talent for survival. Though their tracking abilities are not as advanced as the Squealers, their persistence is just as unyielding and their precision when attacking more exact.

Typically the Hunterkill is given the scent of the prey by its master and then released to follow its victim. Once set on its course, the Hunterkill seeks its prey relentlessly, traveling far from home if need be. The darkrover lives off the land during the course of its hunt. It travels day and night, requiring only a few hours of sleep during the hottest part of the day. Only its master can call it back by means of a talisman attached around the Hunterkill's neck.

At the end of the war many of these creatures were left searching for enemies who were already dead and buried, responding to masters who were gone as well. Without commands to return, these vicious creatures continued to roam the land, killing for food and searching for their prey.

The Hunterkill mates only with its own kind. Their racial memories give them a driving desire to search out

victims. They are quite capable of selecting a human at
random and deciding, in their confused minds, that this is
their victim and pursue that person to the death. Those
who catch them young can still train them as assassins, but
this is extremely dangerous as the Hunterkill may become
mixed up and turn around to pursue his master instead of
the target.

Description: The Hunterkill are the largest of the darkrovers. They have a long head with strong, snapping jaws and
knife-edged teeth. They have a long, prehensile tail with a
huge barb at the end, and two muscular legs and clawed feet.
Most Hunterkill measure eight *decimetra* in length, standing
nearly five *decimetra* at the shoulder. Their shining, dark
eyes are almost indistinguishable from their short, night-
black hair.

Society: Hunterkill are solitary. Once every two years they
return to the place where they were born to mate with
another of their breed. Both the male and the female then
go their separate ways.

The Hunterkill are extremely vicious. If surprised, they
will attack on sight. Fortunately, when they are encountered, they are usually encountered alone.

It is next to impossible to tell, until too late, if one has
been unfortunate enough to be chosen as this animal's target.

Attributes and Abilities: The Hunterkill moves swiftly and
in utter silence. Their black hair makes them invisible in the
darkness. Pads on their feet allow them to slip up unheard on
unsuspecting quarry. The Hunterkill attacks without warning, and either sinks its teeth into the victim's throat or
clamps its jaws around the victim's legs while using its tail to
constrict the throat. Hunterkill almost always attack by night.

DARKROVER—HUNTERKILL
PHANTASIA STATISTICS

ATTRIBUTES

Attack	75	Defense	50	Health	25R
Strength	63	Dexterity	68	Movement	25
Intelligence	1	Intuition	35	Senses	73
Form	fant/animal	Size	72	Resistance	10+
Renewal	140	Capacity	260+	Lifewell	700

ABILITIES	TALENT	STATION	SCORE
Combat	25	5–15	30–40[1]
Movement	—	—	—
Health and Healing	— —		—
Form and Size Altering	—	—	—
Information	—	—	—
Life Transfer	—	—	—
Tool Crafts and Skills	—	—	—
Telepathy and Empathy	—	—	—
Illusions	5	10	15[2]

[1]The Hunterkill may only use defensive spells, i.e., spells that create magical defense attributes. The Hunterkill does this instinctively; no other magic is possible for the creature.

[2]The only illusion spells Hunterkills can cast are those related to making their physical presence less obvious. No other spells are allowed.

Squealer

Originally these darkrovers were used to seek out the position of enemies and then give a high-pitched, squealing howl to lead pursuers to the enemy's location.

After the Iron Wars the Squealers had a difficult time surviving since they were not particularly adept fighters. They soon learned to use their tracking skills to aid them. When a Squealer finds a suitable prey, it gives its distinctive shrieking cry. Hearing the call, other creatures of the wild come quickly to kill the hapless victim. The Squealers watch and wait, taking the scraps that are left.

For this reason, those who are being tracked by a Squealer would be well advised to immediately find some way of either losing their pursuer or killing it.

Description: Squealers have rust-red pelts whose bright colors once helped their masters see them when hunting. Because of this, they are easily spotted during the day. As with all darkrovers, Squealers support their body on two powerful legs and have a long, barbed tail. Squealers usually range in length from about six to seven *decimetra*. Their jaws are small, with sharp teeth, and they have keen, black eyes.

Society: Squealers run in packs of three to ten. When

hunting, they spread themselves out at intervals occasionally approaching one to two *mila* to hunt alone. When the prey the animal has been tracking is finally killed by a centaur or some other creature, the Squealer alters its cry to call the rest of its pack together for the meal. All creatures, even the centaur, leave scraps behind for the Squealers. If Squealers do not get enough to eat, they will happily pursue their erstwhile benefactor!

Attributes and Abilities: The Squealers have similar attributes to those of the Wildrovers in terms of fighting and movement (see *Wildrovers* below), although they do not often use their speed when tracking their prey. The Squealer's scream can be heard by humans from as far as five hundred *metra* and by other darkrovers for up to three *mila*.

DARKROVER — SQUEALERS
PHANTASIA STATISTICS

ATTRIBUTES

Attack	62	Defense	43	Health	25R
Strength	39	Dexterity	68	Movement	25
Intelligence	1	Intuition	42	Senses	65
Form	fant/animal	Size	72	Resistance	5+
Renewal	50+	Capacity	50+	Lifewell	250

ABILITIES	TALENT	STATION	SCORE
Combat	—	—	—
Movement	—	—	—
Health and Healing	—	—	—
Form and Size Altering	—	—	—
Information	—	—	—
Life Transfer	—	—	—
Tool Crafts and Skills	—	—	—
Telepathy and Empathy	10	5–15	15–25[1]
Illusions	—	—	—

[1]This ability is used strictly for searching for prey.

Wildrovers

The Wildrovers were once used in all the armies of Thimhallan. They were effective attack animals for general fighting. While not as silent as the Hunterkill, they are less discriminate in their choices of target. The most common of the darkrovers, these animals can be found in packs roaming all but the most civilized locations in Thimhallan.

Description: Wildrovers are similar in stature and build to the Squealers, being only slightly larger on average by a *decimetra.* The colors of their pelts range from dark to light brown.

Society: The Wildrovers travel in packs of from five to fifty animals. They have one pack leader that is selected by deadly combat with any challengers. A den location is chosen for the pack by this leader, and the Wildrovers may live here for a period of several weeks to several years, depending upon the local hunting conditions. Ruins of ancient buildings are occasionally used as dens, as are large caves.

The Wildrovers are only occasionally found in their den. Their swift, powerful legs carry them long distances. When hunting, the Wildrovers prefer to travel individually or in small groups of three to five. They set out at various times in the day from their den in many such groups and do not return until it suits them.

If captured when they are puppies, Wildrovers can be trained as effective guard dogs, although they do not make good pets. Estate owners whose lands border the wilderness value them highly.

Attributes and Abilities: As with all darkrovers, the Wildrovers are fierce in combat and swift on foot. They can move as fast as twenty-five *milas* per hour over open ground for as long as an hour and still have strength left to bring down creatures much larger than they. Once they attack, they will not relent until they are either killed or have killed their prey. They will flee if it is to their advantage to do so but will always return to attack again. A cornered Wildrover is the most dangerous beast known in all Thimhallan.

DARKROVER—WILDROVERS
PHANTASIA STATISTICS

ATTRIBUTES

Attack	62	Defense	43	Health	25R
Strength	55	Dexterity	62	Movement	25
Intelligence	1	Intuition	32	Senses	64
Form fant/animal		Size	72	Resistance	5
Renewal	50	Capacity	50	Lifewell	250

ABILITIES	TALENT	STATION	SCORE
Combat	1	5	6
Movement	—	—	—
Health and Healing	—	—	—
Form and Size Altering	—	—	—
Information	—	—	—
Life Transfer	—	—	—
Tool Crafts and Skills	—	—	—
Telepathy and Empathy	—	—	—
Illusions	—	—	—

Dragons

Although it is not known for certain, undoubtedly the magi of the Great Passage brought with them dragons from their ancient homeland. The lives of these wondrous creatures were imperiled on Earth, and it is plausible that the magi might have attempted to save some of their kind by bringing them to a new world where they could live in peace.

As with almost all the other dreams of those ancient wizards, this one, too, was shattered by the Iron Wars.

Dragons of Gold
Description: The wise and beautiful Dragons of Gold lived in Thimhallan before the time of the Iron Wars, but whether they came originally from Earth or were in existence in the world prior to the arrival of the magi is not known.

Legend has it that when the Border had passed over the land and the magi were preparing to go forth to carve out their kingdoms, nine Dragons of Gold came and presented themselves to Merlyn, offering to be of service. Merlyn thanked them and each was given an area of Thimhallan to guard. The dragons then left, each making his or her home in the proscribed area. Although the magi living there rarely saw them, it is said that whenever they were in dire peril, they had only to call upon the Dragons of Gold to come to their aid. By what magical means this was done, no one—this day—knows. It may be that in some lost kingdom a bold adventurer might find the charm or talisman used to contact these mighty creatures.

When the time of the Iron Wars came, men called upon the Dragons of Gold and they answered. But so shocked were they by the cruelty and carnage they saw man inflicting upon his fellows that they refused to serve him anymore and retreated far back into their caves. None have been seen on Thimhallan since the Iron Wars, and it is not known if they survived or perished, as did so much else that was beautiful and good in the land.

Society: Dragons of Gold always live alone in caves beneath mountains where they can find the gold deposits off which they feed. Their life span is measured in the hundreds of years, and whether or not they produce offspring is unknown. Their caves are bright, airy, pleasant places for they have the ability to shape air shafts and skylights. The caves are often decorated with rare and lovely objects for Dragons of Gold are passionately fond of glittering, gilded, intricate things—be it jewelry, music boxes, or teapots. These were often brought to them as gifts by the grateful magi in the days before the Iron Wars, and undoubtedly many a valuable artifact could be found in their caves, to say nothing of a fortune in gold.

Attributes and Abilities: Dragons of Gold are the largest of the dragon species, measuring 40 *metra* to 50 *metra* long. They have two huge wings extending from their foreshoulders. When raised and fully extended to the sun, the wings were used to reflect the bright light into an enemy's eyes, blinding him instantly. Dragons of Gold have enchanting voices, producing songs so exquisite that even the most ferocious enemy ceases to fight and begins to weep silently, mourning the loss of his own innocence. By this and other peaceful means do the Dragons of Gold fight their enemies, for they will not kill a living being under any circumstances.

Having retreated from the world, Dragons of Gold will be loathe to return and will do so only if assured that those who find the charm and summon them are acting peacefully, in the best interests of Thimhallan. Talisman or no talisman, a Dragon of Gold always acts as he or she thinks best and is under no compunction to obey any master.

DRAGONS OF GOLD
PHANTASIA STATISTICS
ATTRIBUTES

Attack	82[1]	Defense	75	Health	106
Strength	105	Dexterity	43	Movement	4/65[2]
Intelligence	53	Intuition	47	Senses	75
Form	fant/rept.	Size	400–2,000	Resistance	65 +
Renewal	1,490	Capacity	5,260	Lifewell	3,950

[1]Dragons of Gold may attack in two ways: either for damage or directly against the spirit of the victim using its song.

Dragons who attack for damage also will blind the defender for one round on any result except a "C."

The dragon's attack with its song is conducted like a physical attack, but substitute the following TAROC results:

T =   The defender may not attack and falls to convulsive weeping for his own loss of innocence. At the defender's next opportunity to attack (either in this round or the next round) he is prohibited from doing so. The defender will also *automatically* lose the initiative for the next round.

A =   The defender is deeply moved by the song. His next attack (in either this round or the next but not in both) will suffer a −20 Force score penalty. The defender will lose the initiative in the next round.

ABILITIES	TALENT	STATION	SCORE
Combat	25	20–35	45–55
Movement	5	5–15	15
Health and Healing	15	5–15	20–30
Form and Size Altering	—	—	—
Information	10	15	25
Life Transfer	—	—	—
Tool Crafts and Skills	—	—	—
Telepathy and Empathy	—	—	—
Illusions	23	10	33

R =   The defender is moved by the song. As with result "A," except that the penalty to his next Force score will be −10.

O =   The defender is touched by the song. The next attack made by the defender in this round or the next (but not in both) will suffer a −5 penalty to the defender's Force score. Determine initiative normally.

C =   The defender is not affected by the song and may act normally.

[2]Ground/Flying movement rates.

Dragons of the Night

When the Dragons of Gold departed, refusing to participate in the Iron Wars, the magi were forced to shape their own dragons to serve them. Dragons of the Night are among the most beautiful and the most deadly of these Warchanged creatures.

After the Wars, the Dragons of the Night fled the world of light that they hated, retreating into lairs deep beneath the ground. Once the dragons have found a dwelling, they work frantically to block out any possible source of light. They come forth only on moonless nights to hunt for food. They are carnivorous but will not eat human flesh, finding it distasteful. They are particularly fond of centaur.

Description: Dragons of the Night are jet black with eyes that are the cold white of moonlight. They are 20 to 25 *metra* in length. Their wings, when unfolded, project tiny pinpoints of light that mimic stars. Thus the Dragon of the Night can blend in with the night sky when swooping down upon an enemy.

Society: Dragons of the Night are solitary creatures. They are sexless and do not breed. When those alive now die out, the species will be extinct. They do not like the company of any other living thing, including that of their own kind, and will go to great lengths to avoid it.

Attributes and Abilities: Dragons of the Night have three means of fighting. Their favorite is to cast a spell over their enemies that sends them into a deathlike sleep that only the most powerful *DKarn-duuk* can lift. When the person comes out of the sleep, he remains loyal to the magi who frees him. Thus the loyalty of entire armies was subverted by these creatures. An enemy who looks into the moonlit eyes of the dragon will immediately go insane. Finally, the small lights that flicker in their wings can be cast down upon an enemy, burning easily through flesh; less easily through stone or metal, although they may do considerable damage.

Dragons of the Night can be controlled totally by means of a charm that was placed in their foreheads. The charm can be seen only by daylight, when—because of the pain caused by the sunlight in their eyes—these dragons are comatose. Whoever lays a hand upon this charm will have the dragon's loyalty for life. Luring a Dragon of the Night from its lair and keeping it out until sunlight strikes it is a nearly impossible feat, and therefore few Dragons of the Night are seen now in this land.

DRAGONS OF THE NIGHT
PHANTASIA STATISTICS

ATTRIBUTES

Attack	75	Defense	80	Health	96R
Strength	82	Dexterity	53	Movement	4/65[1]
Intelligence	46	Intuition	43	Senses	45
Form	fant/rept.	Size	57,500	Resistance	55
Renewal	1,190	Capacity	3,260	Lifewell	3,400

ABILITIES	TALENT	STATION	SCORE
Combat	—	—	—
Movement	—	—	—
Health and Healing	—	—	—
Form and Size Altering	—	—	—
Information	—	—	—
Life Transfer	—	—	—
Tool Crafts and Skills	—	—	—
Telepathy and Empathy	25	10–20	35–45
Illusions	10	15	25

[1]Ground/Flying movement rates.

Dragons of the Sun

To counter the attacks made by the Dragons of the Night, magi shaped Dragons of the Sun. They are, in almost all respects, exact opposites of their cousins. Following the Wars, they fled to the highest active volcanoes they could find, yearning always to be near the warmth and light they crave. Whenever the sun shines, they will be out in it. By night they retreat to their lairs, where the light of molten lava dispels the darkness that they fear and detest.

Description: Dragons of the Sun are a flaming orange-red color, about 30 to 35 *metra* in length with two huge wings. They have yellow, glowing eyes. It is impossible to look at them directly without risking blindness.

Society: Dragons of the Sun enjoy company, and often several will make their homes in the same volcano. Like their cousins, they are sexless and do not breed. They are fond of humans, both for companionship and food. If not particularly hungry, they often bring their "meals" back to the lair to provide the conversation and entertainment that never fails to whet their appetites.

Attributes and Abilities: Like their cousins, Dragons of the Sun have three methods of attack. Their favorite is to cast a spell upon an enemy that creates instant insomnia. The enemy will never be able to find rest and will eventually go insane unless rescued by a powerful *DKarnduuk*. The unfortunate insomniac is henceforth doomed to be the War Master's slave. Dragons of the Sun shoot flame from their eyes that set ablaze anything it touches. When they unfold their wings, they radiate sweltering heat that will bake flesh as if it were in an oven. Over prolonged periods of time, this heat will melt stone and metal.

Dragons of the Sun are also controlled by means of a charm embedded in their foreheads. It shines only in the darkness. A Dragon of the Sun who can be caught in a completely dark environment will be paralyzed with fear. Whoever touches the charm with a hand will gain the dragon's loyalty for life.

DRAGONS OF THE SUN
PHANTASIA STATISTICS

ATTRIBUTES

Attack	72	Defense	72	Health	110R
Strength	91	Dexterity	42	Movement	4/65[1]
Intelligence	25	Intuition	62	Senses	63
Form	fant/rept.	Size	12,500	Resistance	65
Renewal	1,490	Capacity	5,260	Lifewell	3,950

ABILITIES	TALENT	STATION	SCORE
Combat	40	2	42
Movement	—	—	—
Health and Healing	—	—	—

[1]Ground/Flying movement rates.

ABILITIES	TALENT	STATION	SCORE
Form and Size Altering	—	—	—
Information	—	—	—
Life Transfer	—	—	—
Tool Crafts and Skills	—	—	—
Telepathy and Empathy	42	45	87
Illusions	10	35–45	45–55

Dragons of the Sand

With Dragons of the Night and Dragons of the Sun ruling the air, other magi decided to attack by means of burrowing under the walls and defenses of the kingdoms. For this purpose they shaped Dragons of the Sand. Although Dragons of the Sand can tunnel through any type of soil, they prefer sand, and when the Wars ended, most sought refuge in the desert.

Description: The Dragons of the Sand have the ability to take on the color and consistency of the ground. They are 10 to 15 *metra* in length. Since almost all will be found in the desert, they are sandy colored and their skin feels gritty to the touch. They have long, wormlike bodies and no wings that might impede their tunneling.

Society: Each dragon has its own territory of tunnels below ground. Extremely territorial, they will fight anyone who invades their lairs, including each other. These vicious underground battles often cause earthquakes. They are sexless and do not breed. They eat sand or soil and therefore rarely have to go above ground level.

Attributes and Abilities: A Dragon of the Sand can burrow through any type of ground with incredible speed. It leaves behind large tunnels, close to the surface, that will invariably collapse beneath the weight of an average-size human. Entire castles have been known to tumble to ruin when undermined by these dragons. Since its main preoccupation is burrowing and feeding its insatiable hunger, the Dragon of the Sand will attack only if it feels its tunnels are threatened. Its favorite method of fighting is to wrap its long body lengthwise around an enemy, endeavoring to crush the life out of him. Thus battles between Dragons of the Sand result in the two of these huge creatures twined about each other, rolling and writhing about beneath the ground.

A thick film protects their eyes from the sand; consequently they do not have good eyesight and cannot distinguish a human from another of their own kind. They are not overly intelligent and cannot be controlled by any means. They can sense the vibrations of those walking the ground above them and will, if they feel threatened, rise up out of the ground to attack, although they will immediately endeavor to drag their prey back down below into their tunnels.

DRAGONS OF THE SAND
PHANTASIA STATISTICS

ATTRIBUTES

Attack	120	Defense	47	Health	46
Strength	72	Dexterity	56	Movement	52
Intelligence	5	Intuition	15	Senses	35
Form	fant/rept.	Size	1,000–5,000	Resistance	36
Renewal	690	Capacity	1,560	Lifewell	2,500

ABILITIES	TALENT	STATION	SCORE
Combat	—	—	—
Movement	30	23	53
Health and Healing	—	—	—
Form and Size Altering	—	—	—
Information	—	—	—
Life Transfer	—	—	—
Tool Crafts and Skills	—	—	—
Telepathy and Empathy	—	—	—
Illusions	—	—	—

Dragons of the Sea

When the Mern—those magi living below the sea—were drawn into the Iron Wars, they brought with them creatures who were either shaped by them or discovered living under the ocean and subsequently tamed. These became known, therefore, as Dragons of the Sea. When the Iron Wars ended, the Mern returned to their watery depths and so did the Dragons of the Sea; both sea man and sea dragon have rarely been seen in the land since that time.

Description: Dragons of the Sea are a lovely iridescent shade of blue-green with coral-colored eyes. They are 15 to 25 *metra* in length and have graceful flippers along the sides of their sleek, scaly bodies in place of wings. They have no feet but can slide across the shore at very fast speeds, bringing with them the water of the ocean in great, destructive tidal waves. They will not venture far upon land, however, never getting out of sight of the blue water that is their home.

Society: Dragons of the Sea are either male or female. They mate (one reason that many believe they are not creations of the Warmasters) and live together for life in caves beneath the ocean. The young are born alive, very small in size, and must be carefully guarded by both parents from predators until large enough to fend for themselves. Still, the mortality rate among the young dragons is tragically high. It is said that when the Mern built their underground cities, they offered to place the baby dragons in these shelters and care for them, and it was this that won them the love and loyalty of the Dragons of the Sea. These dragons feed completely on seaweed.

Attributes and Abilities: Like the Dragons of Gold, the Dragons of the Sea will not directly kill any living thing. When they come to shore, however, they bring the waters of the ocean with them, and the resulting waves and flooding wreak havoc upon the land. They spew forth seawater from their mouths; the force of the water can knock an enemy from his feet, completely incapacitating him. Several Dragons of the Sea, working together, could wash out entire armies, lay low castles, and drown villages.

The Dragons of the Sea obey only the Mern. They are rarely seen on land, coming forth from the sea if the Mern are threatened. The Dragons are not fond of Lungbreathers but will not attack shipping, despite mariner tales to the contrary. Dragons of the Sea guard the oceans well and keep watch upon all who sail there. It is an awesome and terrifying sight to see two great coral eyes looking up at one from the depths of the ocean. If the dragon is not attacked, it will let the ship pass in peace. If assaulted, it will dive below the water with such force that the resulting whirlpool will drag ship and sailors down with it, leaving them at the mercy of the Mern.

DRAGONS OF THE SEA
PHANTASIA STATISTICS

ATTRIBUTES

Attack	94	Defense	47	Health	95R
Strength	130	Dexterity	35	Movement	15/35[1]
Intelligence	22	Intuition	47	Senses	62
Form	fant/rept.	Size	1,000–100,000	Resistance	10+
Renewal	140	Capacity	260	Lifewell	700

ABILITIES

	TALENT	STATION	SCORE
Combat	—	—	—
Movement	10	10–20	20–30
Health and Healing	—	—	—
Form and Size Altering	—	—	—
Information	—	—	—
Life Transfer	—	—	—
Tool Crafts and Skills	—	—	—
Telepathy and Empathy	—	—	—
Illusions	—	—	—

[1]Ground/Sea movement rates.

Dragons of Stone

There are now dragons in the air, dragons below ground, and dragons in the sea. Enterprising magi shaped one more—the Dragon of Stone. Made of rock with a brain to match, this dragon could move through stone as though it were butter and was used to batter down fortifications, castles, towers, keeps, and walls.

Unfortunately, these dragons were so stupid that they could retain the memory of their commands for only brief minutes. Thus the Dragons of Stone would often lumber away in the midst of a battle, forcing their magi to hurry after them and regain their attention. In time it came to be seen that creating these dragons had been a mistake, but by then so many had wandered dim-wittedly off into the wilds that it was impossible to track them down and contain them. They were able to survive due to their complete and total invulnerability. There is nothing in Thimhallan that is known to kill them, although it is generally believed

that if one were to drop a Dragon of Stone into the hottest
part of a volcano, the dragon *might* melt.

·*Description:* Dragons of Stone appear to be made of
granite and are often, in fact, mistaken for cliffs by unfortunate adventurers. They are 35 to 45 *metra* in length
and stand 10 *metra* tall. They have huge, hulking bodies,
massive heads, and thick legs. Due to their enormous size
and weight, it is difficult for them to move about, and they
do so only at very slow speeds. Once they find a location
they like (and no one has ever figured out why they prefer
one spot to another), they will sink down on top of the
farm, the castle, the city, or whatever it may be and remain
there for years on end without stirring. When disturbed by
the foot of a climber placed in the eye or someone's mistaking
it for bedrock and attempting to build a house on its back,
the dragon will get up and move, sending anyone and
anything flying. If Dragons of Stone eat at all, no one is
certain what.

Society: None. Two Dragons of Stone could rest nose-
tip to nose-tip for a century and neither would be aware
of the other's existence. They do not (thank the Almin)
breed.

Attributes and Abilities: Once it gets underway, a Dragon
of Stone can walk through a granite mountain and come
out unscathed on the other side. In so doing, it does not
displace the rock but appears to absorb it into its body,
perhaps using this as a means of sustaining life. Entire
fortifications simply melt away at its touch.

As stated, the Dragon of Stone can be controlled only
for relatively few minutes and then only at great cost in
the magi's Life. The dragon knows neither friend nor
enemy and will just as soon step on its own army as that
of anyone else's. The dragon's rocklike hide is impervious
to all types of assault. It has no means of attack other
than grinding into the ground anything that crosses its
path.

DRAGONS OF STONE
PHANTASIA STATISTICS

ATTRIBUTES

Attack	150	Defense	95	Health	480–580
Strength	175	Dexterity	17	Movement	4
Intelligence	1	Intuition	3	Senses	22
Form	fant/rept.	Size	48,000	Resistance	10
Renewal	140	Capacity	260	Lifewell	700

ABILITIES

ABILITIES	TALENT	STATION	SCORE
Combat	—	—	—
Movement	—	—	—
Health and Healing	—	—	—
Form and Size Altering	—	—	—
Information	—	—	—
Life Transfer	—	—	—
Tool Crafts and Skills	—	—	—
Telepathy and Empathy	—	—	—
Illusions	1	10–20	11–21

Dugruns

The dugruns are, without question, the vilest race to spring
from the Iron Wars.

During the closing years of that conflict, the shortage of
troops became a pressing problem for all of the kingdoms
struggling for survival. The answer was *dugruns*—meaning
"false object."

Squat savages shaped from apes, the dugruns are mindless creatures completely under the control of the only
member of their tribe that possesses any capability for
rational thought—the Dugrun Master. The *DKarn-duuk* controlled the dugruns through the Dugrun Master, knowing
that it would be obeyed blindly by its fellow tribe members.

Description: Although dugruns vary in certain respects
from tribe to tribe, they all have the same general characteristics—protruding heads, curved backs with protruding dorsal spines that force them to walk bent and stooped.
Their bodies are covered with long, matted hair. Their long
arms drag on the ground and can be used as additional feet,

which gives them the ability to run upright on two legs or travel on four if they need to increase their speed. Their brute strength is as legendary as their stupidity.

Dugrun Masters
Description: Masters are born with straight backs — a sign in that species of their genetic superiority over normal dugruns. When they mature, Masters are larger than normal dugrun by at least two *decimetra*. They alone of all dugruns are capable of human speech.

Society: The Dugrun Masters dictate the social structure of the group. This structure is generally primitive, basically dividing the tribe into those that are excellent killers and those that are simply mediocre. The Masters rule their tribes with the ruthless, merciless efficiency necessary for survival.

Dugrun Masters are cruel and hate all mankind. They will attack any human on sight.

Without the direction of the Master, the dugrun community quickly falls into chaos. Dugruns left leaderless have no direction. They occasionally go berserk when this happens, but more often they just sit down and wait for instructions that are never forthcoming. The only hope of surviving a dugrun attack is to immediately kill the Masters.

Attributes and Abilities: Masters may be either male or female. They are the only dugruns to have individual wills and thoughts. It is their orders that are carried out throughout their dugrun communities. Each Master has between twenty and thirty dugruns under his control. Tribes vary in size from fifty to one hundred, meaning that there will be at least two and possibly more Masters within a tribe.

DUGRUN MASTERS
PHANTASIA STATISTICS
ATTRIBUTES

Attack	44	Defense	35	Health	31R
Strength	57	Dexterity	73	Movement	4
Intelligence	15R	Intuition	37	Senses	68
Form	fant/human	Size	48	Resistance	10
Renewal	140	Capacity	260	Lifewell	700

ABILITIES	TALENT	STATION	SCORE
Combat	1	5	6
Movement	—	—	—
Health and Healing	2	10	12
Form and Size Altering	—	—	—
Information	—	—	—
Life Transfer	—	—	—
Tool Crafts and Skills	5	10–20	15–25
Telepathy and Empathy	—	—	—
Illusions	—	—	—

Border Dugruns

Description: Border Dugruns, or Desert Dugruns as they are occasionally called, are dark-skinned and have far less hair covering their bodies than other dugruns.

Society: During the Iron Wars, the Master Dugruns were ordered to find and destroy the Army of Timrath, believed to be hiding in the desert of the Borderlands. The Army of Timrath was already dead, but the dugruns continued to search for them and have done so ever since.

At somewhat irregular intervals the Masters of the Desert Dugruns come together to select an Overmaster from among themselves to direct all the tribes in their search for the Army of Timrath. Anyone encountered in the desert will be taken for a Timrath soldier and immediately attacked.

Attributes and Abilities: Desert Dugruns are extremely agile. They attack as an unorganized mob, fighting viciously with claw and fang, using their feet as well as their hands.

BORDER DUGRUNS
PHANTASIA STATISTICS

ATTRIBUTES

Attack	51	Defense	25	Health	31R
Strength	57	Dexterity	82	Movement	4
Intelligence	5R	Intuition	25	Senses	62
Form	fant/human	Size	48	Resistance	10
Renewal	140	Capacity	260	Lifewell	700

ABILITIES	TALENT	STATION	SCORE
Combat	1	2	3
Movement	3	7–17	10–20
Health and Healing	—	—	—
Form and Size Altering	2	6	8
Information	—	—	—
Life Transfer	—	—	—
Tool Crafts and Skills	—	—	—
Telepathy and Empathy	—	—	—
Illusions	—	—	—

Outland Dugruns

Description: The Outland Dugruns have thick hair to withstand the winters in the Outland. They wear harnesses of leather they shape from the skins of their victims. The harnesses apparently signify some sort of social standing within their tribes.

Society: Outland Dugruns are a community of females, led by from one to three male Dugrun Masters. All female Master newborns and normal male newborns are systematically put to death. Male Master newborns are also killed unless the Masters currently in charge feel the need to produce heirs.

The Outland Dugruns live in the trees, fashioning crude platforms and shelters against the winter cold. Their communities tend to be large and powerful.

Attributes and Abilities: Outland Dugruns have, from time to time, raided the villages of the Sorcerers, and thus they have acquired a knowledge of tools. In addition to attacking with hands and feet, therefore, Outland Dugruns make use of crude weapons such as sticks or rocks. Some dugruns have actually acquired spears, although they do not use them with any efficiency.

OUTLAND DUGRUNS
PHANTASIA STATISTICS
ATTRIBUTES

Attack	35	Defense	45	Health	31R
Strength	57	Dexterity	82	Movement	4
Intelligence	10R	Intuition	25	Senses	54

ATTRIBUTES

Form	fant/human	Size	48	Resistance	14
Renewal	200	Capacity	460	Lifewell	1,100

ABILITIES	TALENT	STATION	SCORE
Combat	—	—	—
Movement	—	—	—
Health and Healing	—	—	—
Form and Size Altering	—	—	—
Information	—	—	—
Life Transfer	—	—	—
Tool Crafts and Skills	2	10–20	12–22
Telepathy and Empathy	—	—	—
Illusions	—	—	—

Plains Dugruns

Description: Plains Dugruns like to wear the clothing of their human victims. Entire colonies of them can be found wearing the clothes and jewelry of those they have murdered.

Society: Plains Dugruns are not well organized and tend, therefore, to live in small groups under the control of one Master. When a Master matures, he or she invariably moves out and forms a new group far away from the old one.

Plains Dugruns are preoccupied with a desire to become human. They mimic the men and women they capture (presumably just before killing them). The concept of "trade" fascinates them. Many would-be dugrun victims claim that they have saved their lives by engaging the Master in offers to trade for whatever objects the dugrun is currently wearing. Since the dugruns have occasionally come upon ruins of ancient days, their bodies are often adorned with fortunes in jewels and other precious objects. Dugruns have no concept of value, so a trader may not only save his own life but come out rich in the bargain. Since Plains Dugrun Masters insist on selecting the items the adventurer offers in trade, this does not always work.

Attributes and Abilities: The Plains Dugruns have limited abilities in Life and can make the power of Life work for them.

PLAINS DUGRUNS
PHANTASIA STATISTICS

ATTRIBUTES

Attack	35	Defense	25	Health	31R
Strength	57	Dexterity	82	Movement	4
Intelligence	15R	Intuition	25	Senses	52
Form	fant/human	Size	48	Resistance	7+
Renewal	80+	Capacity	110+	Lifewell	400+

ABILITIES	TALENT	STATION	SCORE
Combat	2	5–15	7–17
Movement	—	—	—
Health and Healing	1	5	6
Form and Size Altering	—	—	—
Information	—	—	—
Life Transfer	—	—	—
Tool Crafts and Skills	—	—	—
Telepathy and Empathy	—	—	—
Illusions	5	1–11	6–16

Southern Dugruns

Description: These dugruns wear brown robes of rough cloth that they shape from the grasses of the foothills.

Society: Southern Dugruns organize in tribes of ten to twenty dugruns around a single Master. New Masters born into such groups eventually organize new groups of their own.

These tribes will often fight one another with their magic. This is considered great sport despite the terrible toll it exacts. In a crude mimicry of the Field of Glory, they will capture and reshape hapless animals. The sight of these deformed and tortured creatures are often the traveler's first warning the dugruns are in the area.

Attributes and Abilities: Southern Dugruns have a gift for magic. They can absorb tremendous amounts of Life and use it for their own gratification and in the destruction of others.

SOUTHERN DUGRUNS
PHANTASIA STATISTICS

ATTRIBUTES

Attack	35	Defense	25	Health	31R
Strength	57	Dexterity	82	Movement	4
Intelligence	5R	Intuition	25	Senses	62
Form	fant/human	Size	48	Resistance	50+
Renewal	1,040+	Capacity	2,260+	Lifewell	3,200

ABILITIES	TALENT	STATION	SCORE
Combat	10	20	30
Movement	—	—	—
Health and Healing	15	10	25
Form and Size Altering	10	10–20	20–30
Information	—	—	—
Life Transfer	—	—	—
Tool Crafts and Skills	—	—	—
Telepathy and Empathy	—	—	—
Illusions	5	10	15

Faeries

The faeries are the physical manifestation of magic and have—presumably—been in Thimhallan since time began. Although their colonies may be found anywhere in the world, they view themselves as one nation, united under a single Queen.

Faeries live from moment to moment, from sensation to sensation. Inherently shallow, they must gratify their lust for sights, sounds, smells, and feelings vicariously. They are particularly fascinated by humans and spy on them continually, mimicking and imitating every nuance of human life. They will often try to entrap a human and lure him into their rings of magical mushrooms that lead into their faerie mounds.

Once the human is inside their dwellings, the faeries will force him to talk about his life down to the smallest detail. They insist in hearing what you eat, how it tastes, smells, feels. They inflict pain not out of cruelty but simply to note the victim's reaction. They provide pleasurable experiences for the same reason, and a faerie captive may find himself being tortured one moment and given his heart's desire the next. Faeries have an innate curiosity about the world above that is perpetuated in the offspring of the Queen of the Faeries, who requires union with a human male to conceive her daughters.

Faerie Queen

Description: Elspeth is the Faerie Queen who rules over all the faeries in Thimhallan. Since the faeries live in separate colonies, Elspeth sends her daughters out to rule over these. The Faerie Queen and her daughters appear to human males as the most beautiful and desirable of women. They are twelve to fourteen *decimetra* in height, of slender build, with flowing hair that can be any color a man chooses.

Society: Each of the faerie daughters rules over her own colony and seldom troubles either her sisters or her mother. Faerie daughters may mate with human males for their own amusement but are not allowed to bear children. If this happens or if a daughter rebels, Elspeth moves immediately to get rid of her. This can cause Wars of the Faeries that may last for years in the underground kingdoms.

Attributes and Abilities: The Faeries are Life incarnate and their power is never more evident than in their Queen or her daughters. Since the Faeries have trouble focusing or directing their magic, there are limits to what even the Queen can do. The Faeries' greatest talents lie in the area of Illusion, and nothing seen in a faerie mound can be believed.

FAERIE QUEENS
PHANTASIA STATISTICS

ATTRIBUTES

Attack	25	Defense	61	Health	83
Strength	47	Dexterity	73	Movement	5/6/35[1]
Intelligence	72	Intuition	53	Senses	73
Form	fant/human	Size	60	Resistance	40+
Renewal	790+	Capacity	1,760+	Lifewell	2,600+

ABILITIES	TALENT	STATION	SCORE
Combat	30	20	50
Movement	35	15	45
Health and Healing	12	25–35	37–47
Form and Size Altering	17	25–35	45–52
Information	—	—	—
Life Transfer	—	—	—
Tool Crafts and Skills	—	—	—
Telepathy and Empathy	45	23	53
Illusions	56	22	78

[1]Ground/Water/Flying movement rates.

Faeries

Description: Faeries come in a variety of forms and sizes from tiny creatures that look like sparkles of light, to some that resemble butterflies with beautifully colored wings, to those that stand as tall as three *decimetra* and look like ugly imps. Since faeries are always on the search for thrills and sensations, they never stay in one place long but are continually popping in and out of existence, changing their clothes or their aspect, darting here and there. Thus it is impossible for a human to ever get a good look at any one faerie (with the exception of the Queen or a daughter).

Society: The faeries are a loose-knit, chaotic society with absolutely no structure. Although they indulge in huge orgies, the faeries never have offspring. They are bred from magic, rising from the Well of Life like bubbles in champagne. About the time the main colony gets too large, Elspeth bears another daughter. Taking the baby with them, the faeries move to another location and raise the girl until she is old enough to become their ruler. The faeries know no law except that of their Queen. They will obey her instantly, no matter what her command.

Attributes and Abilities: Faeries are masters of Illusion and can reproduce any sight, sound, smell, taste, or object that they choose. Humans very quickly lose all sense of what is real and become extremely confused and disoriented in the faerie mound. Faeries can rarely direct their own magic but act always on the whim of the moment.

Faeries never think and are therefore easy to trick. The only way to escape is by outwitting them. Fighting is useless. The faeries will think it great fun and will immediately recreate every weapon you use on them, gleefully using it on you!

FAERIES
PHANTASIA STATISTICS

ATTRIBUTES

Attack	15	Defense	43	Health	15R
Strength	8–28	Dexterity	83	Movement	5/25[1]
Intelligence	8	Intuition	35	Senses	82
Form	fant/human	Size	1–3	Resistance	1
Renewal	100	Capacity	100	Lifewell	300

ABILITIES	TALENT	STATION	SCORE
Combat	30	5	35
Movement	35	3	38
Health and Healing	27	5	32
Form and Size Altering	32	1	33
Information	—	—	—
Life Transfer	—	—	—
Tool Crafts and Skills	—	—	—
Telepathy and Empathy	45	5	50
Illusions	56	25	81

[1]Ground/Air movement rates.

Giants

Undoubtedly the most pathetic of the Warchanged, giants were created as the ultimate weapon. Under the direction of a Warmaster they could trample men underfoot, smash down walls, drop huge boulders on armies, and perform a hundred other tasks. So that they would obey commands without question, the mental capabilities of the unfortunate, enlarged humans were reduced to those of a small child. As with the others of the Warchanged, those giants were to be turned back to the normal humans they once were by the magi.

But the magi lost the ability to control their own lives in

the chaos, much less the lives of their gigantic creations. Left alone and without guidance, the giants wandered into the Wild. Their instincts led them to find food and shelter and they survive—though not in great numbers—in the Outland. They dwell in caves near a source of water.

Description: Giants range in height anywhere from 5 to 15 *metra*. They wear whatever they can for clothing, more to protect them from the elements rather than out of modesty, of which they have no conception. They are human in appearance, their faces almost invariably having the eager, curious, wistful expression of a toddler.

Society: Giants are generally solitary. If two giants happen to meet each other, they may get along fine for a while but will almost always begin to quarrel over some insignificant matter. They may lash out at each other, but this rarely results in any real harm. Both usually run off in tears, to sulk and mope until they get over their hurt feelings. They do not mate and are therefore slowly becoming extinct in the world, although their life spans appear to have increased with their size, allowing them to live hundreds of years.

Attributes and Abilities: Giants are gentle and harmless except when injured. Then they can become enraged, striking out at whatever harm them like a child throwing a tantrum. When this happens, they are truly dangerous for they do not know their own strength. Giants are fond of humans but unfortunately seem to consider them toys and will often inadvertently mangle, squash, drop, or break their "playthings."

Since giants have been hunted for sport, some can be distrustful of man, especially if they've seen one of their kind murdered. Other giants, however, may be quite trusting and come straight up to you—which means you had better be prepared to get out of their way! Treated with kindness, almost any giant will follow simple commands. They will not kill unless by accident.

GIANTS
PHANTASIA STATISTICS

ATTRIBUTES

Attack	72	Defense	47	Health	80R
Strength	82	Dexterity	37	Movement	15
Intelligence	5	Intuition	27	Senses	43
Form	fant/human	Size	1,000–7,500	Resistance	10
Renewal	140	Capacity	260	Lifewell	700

ABILITIES

	TALENT	STATION	SCORE
Combat	—	—	—
Movement	—	—	—
Health and Healing	1	10	11
Form and Size Altering	—	—	—
Information	—	—	—
Life Transfer	—	—	—
Tool Crafts and Skills	—	—	—
Telepathy and Empathy	—	—	—
Illusions	—	—	—

Gore

These creatures are not Warchanged. They are, rather, creatures of Thimhallan formed by the passage of the Border over the land in the beginning of history. When the Border was expanded, it reshaped the world's strange plants and animals into forms that would be easily recognizable by the new inhabitants. The results were, however, not always beneficial.

What fold in the Border's passage created the gore no one has ever understood. The original form of these fearsome beasts is beyond guessing. They came out of the Valheim Mountains and their numbers began to grow.

When the gore were originally encountered by the Vajnan Clans, they were called hydra or Medusae because of their many snakelike heads.

Description: The gore are about 3 *metra* in length. They have the slender body of a snake, which splits into several heads, depending on the age of the creature. Gore apparently add one head per each ten years of life. The gore are generally a lead gray in color.

Society: Gore live in family groups of varying size, all dwelling together in the tall trees of the Valheim Mountains. Each group stakes out its own hunting territory. Gore are intelligent creatures, extremely protective of their families and their territories. They have a great respect for each other, never crossing territorial lines, and disputes between gore are unknown. When humans blundered across the invisible boundaries and began attacking these fearsome-looking beasts, the rage of the gore knew no bounds. This precipitated the early battles between humans and gore.

Attributes and Abilities: When attacking, the gore rears its upper body off the ground, its heads fanning out like a cobra's hood to get a good look at its enemy. The heads strike independently of each other, however, and often seem competitive, some heads fighting others for a chance to gobble down the prize. Like a snake, the gore has four fangs—two on the upper jaw and two on the lower. The fangs sink into the victim, immobilizing him with a venom that paralyzes but does not kill—the gore preferring to eat its meal while it's still warm. Gore hate and despise man and will not only drive him from their own territories but will pursue him great distances. They eat their victims or carry them—paralyzed—back to their lairs where they store them for later snacking.

THE GORE
PHANTASIA STATISTICS

ATTRIBUTES

Attack	62	Defense	45	Health	64
Strength	45	Dexterity	45	Movement	6
Intelligence	38	Intuition	53	Senses	48
Form	fant/creat[1]	Size	180	Resistance	10
Renewal	140	Capacity	260	Lifewell	700

ABILITIES   TALENT STATION SCORE

	TALENT	STATION	SCORE
Combat	—	—	—
Movement	—	—	—
Health and Healing	—	—	—

ABILITIES	TALENT	STATION	SCORE
Form and Size Altering	1	10	11
Information	—	—	—
Life Transfer	—	—	—
Tool Crafts and Skills	—	—	—
Telepathy and Empathy	—	—	—
Illusions	—	—	—

[1]Fantastic Creature.

Griffins

Griffins were shaped during the Iron Wars for sky combat, and war remains their main interest to this day. During the Nightyears, griffins raided both human villages and the mountain aeries of their fellow griffin clans. It wasn't until the very recent past (approximately 740 Y.L.) that the various clans managed to put aside their differences and band together. While there are still occasional wars between different clans of griffins, they maintain an uneasy peace.

Description: The griffin has the head and wings of an eagle and the body and the hindquarters of a lion. They stand about 15 *decimetra* tall.

Society: The traditional home of the griffins is the Mountains of Valheim—a range that runs from the Eastpass up the length of the Vajnan peninsula. The griffins maintain their aeries in a great mountain fortress carved from the mountain. From time to time during the Nightyears the griffins worked for humans, raiding for profit, and often traded their services for the skills of the *Pron-alban,* who shape their fortresses.

The exact location of the aeries is a closely kept secret. Workers were flown blindfolded to and from the location so that not even the *Thon-Li* Corridor masters know where the place is.

In order to get humans to work for them, griffins will occasionally trade precious objects long lost to the knowledge of the world. This has led to the rumors that griffin aeries are filled with treasure. This may or may not be true.

Griffins are a close-knit society, fiercely protective of their young, each other, and their friends, the Ariels, who live near them.

Attributes and Abilities: Griffins are skilled and deadly fighters, using their ripping front talons and their sharp beaks to tear an enemy to shreds.

GRIFFINS
PHANTASIA STATISTICS

ATTRIBUTES

Attack	77	Defense	64	Health	83
Strength	72	Dexterity	47	Movement	15/37[1]
Intelligence	46	Intuition	53	Senses	72
Form	fant/animal	Size	225	Resistance	5
Renewal	50	Capacity	50	Lifewell	250

ABILITIES	TALENT	STATION	SCORE
Combat	5	5–15	10–20
Movement	—	—	—
Health and Healing	5	3–13	8–18
Form and Size Altering	—	—	—
Information	—	—	—
Life Transfer	—	—	—
Tool Crafts and Skills	—	—	—
Telepathy and Empathy	—	—	—
Illusions	—	—	—

[1]Ground/Air movement rate.

Kij Vines

So desperate were the magi near the end of the Iron Wars that they turned even the plant life on Thimhallan into a vicious predator. This was perhaps the most foolish and tragic move made in that terrible contest, for the deadly Kij vine, having no mind, could not be controlled by its creators and overgrew much of the land. From time to time teams of Druids have gone forth and fought back the weed. So far it grows prolifically only in the Outland, although it may be found anywhere in the wild, especially near the ruins of old keeps and castles.

Description: The Kij vine grows close to the ground. It

has shiny green leaves formed in the shape of a heart and what appears to be harmless-looking small thorns on its curling and twining stem. When the unsuspecting victim steps on the vine, however, the leaves clutch at him, the stem entangles him, and the thorns dig themselves into his flesh and begin to suck his blood.

The Kij vine makes travel in the Outland extremely risky since there is almost no hope for the hapless human who finds himself caught in it. All struggles to free himself will only excite the plant and drive the thorns deeper. Since the Kij vine drinks only blood, other predators—drawn by the victim's screams—wait their turn. Once its thirst is slacked, the Kij vine will disentangle itself and leave the body for others.

Society: None.

Attributes and Abilities: None.

KIJ VINES
PHANTASIA STATISTICS

ATTRIBUTES

Attack	63	Defense	62	Health	720[1]
Strength	65	Dexterity	65	Movement	1
Intelligence	1	Intuition	5	Senses	43
Form	fant/plant	Size	7,500	Resistance	5
Renewal	50	Capacity	50	Lifewell	250

ABILITIES	TALENT	STATION	SCORE
Combat	—	—	—
Movement	—	—	—
Health and Healing	—	—	—
Form and Size Altering	—	—	—
Information	1	5	6
Life Transfer	—	—	—
Tool Crafts and Skills	—	—	—
Telepathy and Empathy	—	—	—
Illusions	—	—	—

[1]This large number indicates the difficulty of killing the entire plant. The plant will release its victim if it sustains one tenth of this damage.

Mern

When the Crescent Kingdoms fell, there were certain of the *Albanara* who rescued what they could from their once-great civilization and fled to other lands.

Among these was Mern of Kazan, who forsook the world above and took his people below the surface of the sea. There they built fabulous cities under protective bubbles, their art flourished, and they lived in peace and harmony with each other.

As time went by and they grew to love their ocean home, they came to consider themselves prisoners inside their own cities and longed to freely explore the underwater realm that beckoned just beyond their domes.

So, at last the people reshaped themselves through the use of magic. They became true people of the seas and left their old, domed cities to build new ones in their newfound lands.

Though each of the races are distinctly different and have their own names, they are collectively known as the Mern.

Havlan

So enamored of the sea were the Havlan Mern that they completely denied their humanity and took fully to the water.

Description: The Havlan appear as large man-size fish covered with silvery scales. Only their human faces reveal their true ancestry.

Society: Nothing is known about their society. If the Havlan remember how to speak, they refuse to do so on those rare occasions when they've accidentally had contact with humans. Their territory appears to take up the greater part of the Frea Sea.

Attributes and Abilities: The Havlan are extremely powerful magi, making up for their lack of hands through the enhancement of their magic. A Havlan snared in a net will not only get away himself but will manage to free all fish taken with him and will warn others away from the boats.

HAVLAN MERN
PHANTASIA STATISTICS

ATTRIBUTES

Attack	53	Defense	47	Health	64
Strength	62	Dexterity	25	Movement	15[1]
Intelligence	62	Intuition	43	Senses	55
Form	fant/fish	Size	40	Resistance	40
Renewal	790	Capacity	1,760	Lifewell	2,700

ABILITIES	TALENT	STATION	SCORE
Combat	15	15	30
Movement	25	20	45
Health and Healing	15	24	39
Form and Size Altering	26	25	51
Information	—	—	—
Life Transfer	—	—	—
Tool Crafts and Skills	—	—	—
Telepathy and Empathy	—	—	—
Illusions	23	18	41

[1]Water Movement only.

Jepra

The undersea kingdoms of Jepra and Qint joined together and have since become a unified nation known as the Jepra Mern. Their kingdom extends over much of the Westerness Ocean, presumably as far west as the Border itself and north just past Point Aspen.

Description: The Jepra took the form of the classical mermen and mermaids. This gives them great mobility in the water, allows them the use of their hands, and they retain part of their human form.

Society: It is believed that the Jepra Mern are organized around strict family lines. Family units among the Jepra are reputed to be the strongest in all of Thimhallan. None have ever visited their new cities deep beneath the ocean, and nothing more is known about their life there.

Attributes and Abilities: The Jepra Mern are skilled magi, especially experienced in the Mysteries of Water and Earth.

JEPRA MERN
PHANTASIA STATISTICS

ATTRIBUTES

Attack	46	Defense	46	Health	47
Strength	42	Dexterity	68	Movement	1/17[1]
Intelligence	56	Intuition	43	Senses	63
Form	fant/human	Size	60	Resistance	55
Renewal	1,190	Capacity	3,260	Lifewell	3,450

ABILITIES	TALENT	STATION	SCORE
Combat	5	10	15
Movement	3	15	18
Health and Healing	7	35	42
Form and Size Altering	7	35	42
Information	—	—	—
Life Transfer	—	—	—
Tool Crafts and Skills	—	—	—
Telepathy and Empathy	—	—	—
Illusions	10	25	35

[1]Ground/Water movement rates.

Mern

The Mern themselves became versed in the knowledge of shape-shifting and developed the ability to change their bodies from human form to that of aquatic animals and back to humans again.

Description: In their human form, the Mern appear as blue-green humans with webbed hands and large webbed feet. They are still air breathers and are required to surface from time to time when in the open sea.

The other shapes they take vary, but their preferred aquatic form is that of blue dolphins. Often entire schools of them can be seen in the open ocean. Since the Mern are still friendly and interested in mankind, they enjoy being around ships and will often rescue shipwrecked crews.

Society: Little is known about the society of the Mern, although much can be gained through observation. They like to travel in schools and are extremely loyal to each other. They have led attacks against humans—most notably during the Iron Wars—but no such attack has been known to happen without provocation.

Attributes and Abilities: Mern are air breathers and may leave the water only for short periods of time. The Mern are able to communicate directly with humans through speech, although there is rarely occasion for this to happen. The Mern are well versed in the Mysteries of Water and, surprisingly, Fire, as well.

MERN
PHANTASIA STATISTICS

ATTRIBUTES

Attack	55	Defense	47	Health	47
Strength	42	Dexterity	69	Movement	4/15[1]
Intelligence	43	Intuition	57	Senses	62
Form	fant/human	Size	60	Resistance	50
Renewal	50	Capacity	1,040	Lifewell	3,200

ABILITIES	TALENT	STATION	SCORE
Combat	10	30	40
Movement	—	—	—
Health and Healing	20	25	45
Form and Size Altering	23	12–22	32–42
Information	—	—	—
Life Transfer	—	—	—
Tool Crafts and Skills	—	—	—
Telepathy and Empathy	—	—	—
Illusions	23	20	43

[1]Ground/Water movement rates.

Mindfog

Mindfog was the final and most diabolical crafting of the Warmasters. These magical clouds were given intelligence, Illusionary skills, and poisoning abilities, then sent to drift over enemy encampments to lure their prey to their doom. The winds of Thimhallan caught the deadly fog and scattered it over the land. Its creators had the ability to dispel the magic, but they had to find the mindfog first and then survive it!

Description: The mindfog appears at first as harmless mists drifting above the ground. When the prey steps into it, the mindfog will shift its appearance. The victim sees the person or object he values most in the world materialize in the center of the fog and will immediately be drawn toward the object.

Attributes and Abilities: The mists have limited telepathy and will call to their victim in the voice or sound of whatever may lure him deeper into the fog. The farther into the fog the victim wanders, the more and more complete the illusions become because the mindfog can more fully read the victim's mind. Unless the victim can break the spell being woven around it, he will ultimately fall down exhausted near the center of the mindfog, there to inhale the poisonous fumes and die. The mindfog feeds off the death energies released by the creature it kills.

MINDFOG
PHANTASIA STATISTICS

ATTRIBUTES

Attack	75^1	Defense	43	Health	105
Strength	—	Dexterity	—	Movement	10^2
Intelligence	10^3	Intuition	63	Senses	62
Form	fant/human	Size	10,000	Resistance	44
Renewal	890	Capacity	1,960	Lifewell	2,900

ABILITIES	TALENT	STATION	SCORE
Combat	—	—	—
Movement	—	—	—
Health and Healing	—	—	—
Form and Size Altering	—	—	—
Information	15	25	40
Life Transfer	—	—	—
Tool Crafts and Skills	—	—	—
Telepathy and Empathy	15	25	40
Illusions	10	27	37

[1] The Mindfog always attacks the Intelligence of the user, trying to persuade its victim to despair.

[2] Air movement rate.

[3] The score does not reflect its own Intelligence but rather the knowledge it has leached from its victims. Divining spells may extract this knowledge—the Mindfog itself cannot be communicated with.

Pegasus

Pegasi are one of the last vestiges of the horses that once roamed on Thimhallan. Shaped into the form of a winged horse, these small, light steeds were ridden by commanders who wanted an aerial view of the battlefield.

Nearly all of these magical steeds were killed during the Iron Wars, but legends say that some, at least, survived. The tale is told of a general from Trandar who, when he saw the armies coming to crush his nation, loosed his magnificent herd of Pegasi and commanded them to fly west to safety. There have been rumors of sightings of Pegasi in the Chow-Li Peaks.

Description: The incomparable beauty of the Pegasus in flight can only be appreciated by those who witness it. The Pegasi have white coats, although an occasional night-black stallion has been known to appear in the herd. Pegasi measure roughly fifteen *decimetra* tall and measure twenty *decimetra* long. Most have a wingspan of over four *metra*.

Society: Pegasi run—or fly—in herds. They are usually led by a stallion who seldom takes them far from their mountain meadows.

Attributes and Abilities: The winged horses' natural ability to fly and carry the weight of a heavily laden warrior is their greatest asset. They are peaceful animals unless attacked, and then they will fight fiercely, lashing out with sharp hooves.

PEGASUS
PHANTASIA STATISTICS

ATTRIBUTES

Attack	57	Defense	45	Health	75
Strength	75	Dexterity	43	Movement	18/42[1]
Intelligence	23	Intuition	62	Senses	73
Form	fant/animal	Size	1,600	Resistance	20
Renewal	290	Capacity	760	Lifewell	1,700

ABILITIES	TALENT	STATION	SCORE
Combat	—	—	—
Movement	1	15	16
Health and Healing	5	15	20

ABILITIES	TALENT	STATION	SCORE
Form and Size Altering	—	—	—
Information	—	—	—
Life Transfer	—	—	—
Tool Crafts and Skills	—	—	—
Telepathy and Empathy	—	—	—
Illusions	1	15	16

[1]Ground/Air movement rates.

Unicorns

Like the Pegasi, unicorns were shaped from horses. They were given a weapon—their horn—that could be used as a lance. They were bred to fight, and now woe betide the virgin who tries to lure a unicorn to her lap!

Unicorns are foul-tempered and vicious and will charge just about anything that moves. They proved uncontrollable as mounts, and many unicorns were loosed when their riders fell from them during the course of battle. Herds of them gathered together and found a home on the Vajnan Plains.

Description: Unicorns' coats range in color from brown to reddish brown. The hair is short, bristly. They are smaller than the legendary horse, measuring in general only about one *metra* in height and thirteen *decimetra* in length. Each animal has a horn in the middle of its forehead that measures three to four *decimetra* in length. All unicorns have blood-red eyes.

Society: Unicorns run in herds on the Vajnan Plains. Although they are herbivores, they are nevertheless dangerous to approach.

Attributes and Abilities: The horn of a unicorn allows it to cast both attack and defense magics of limited diversity but great effectiveness, in addition to using the horn itself as a weapon. The magical properties of the unicorns' horns make them highly valuable. The Church has issued bounties on unicorn horns. The price fluctuates, depending on the current Life standard. Check with your local catalysts before you go hunting.

UNICORNS
PHANTASIA STATISTICS

ATTRIBUTES

Attack	74	Defense	43	Health	62
Strength	62	Dexterity	56	Movement	18
Intelligence	5	Intuition	47	Senses	56
Form	fant/animal	Size	130	Resistance	50
Renewal	1,040	Capacity	2,260	Lifewell	3,200

ABILITIES	TALENT	STATION	SCORE
Combat	5	30[1]	35
Movement	—	—	—
Health and Healing	—	—	—
Form and Size Altering	—	—	—
Information	—	—	—
Life Transfer	—	—	—
Tool Crafts and Skills	—	—	—
Telepathy and Empathy	—	—	—
Illusions	—	—	—

[1]Possession of a unicorn horn will give the character holding it the same Combat Abilities as the unicorn. The power of Life for the spell cast with a unicorn horn, however, must come either from the horn itself (which holds the Life of the unicorn at the time of its death) or from a catalyst. To put Life back into the unicorn horn, a catalyst must be willing to act as a conduit to the horn itself. Such a conduit would be resisted by the horn with the same Magic Resistance as that of the unicorn from which it came. Such conduits are expensive.

Part II

Oracle of the Dead

The Circle of the World

The History of Thimhallan

Praeludium: At the request of Garald, King of Sharakan, with permission granted by the People of Life, we—the Duuk-tsarith—present this document to you. Though deep are the secrets, never to be revealed, that we hold in the dark places of our hearts, here we present to you, the Dead, the story of our past and the common bond between our peoples.

Think not that our loss is total nor your victory complete. We are patient. We are silent. Our time is not yet.

We watch. We wait.

Since the beginning, a sacred and secret chronicle of our years has been kept. Our recording has been faithful, despite many difficulties brought on by war and hardship.

It is to our shame that in the early and dark times of Thimhallan much of our work was lost. Originally this chronicle was kept by us under the direction of those whose Mystery was Time. The Diviners kept watch over our past and our future. But with the coming of the Iron Wars, the Diviners died out, the Mystery of Time was lost to us. The recording fell to us, and I fear we do it but imperfectly.

Caerdith Bandon wrote: "To see history is to see the road we have traveled. We cannot know where we now stand otherwise."

Walk with us this road.

Stories of the Dawn Years

-77 Y.L.[1] (aprox) *Savagery of the Mysteries:* In the time before the Great Passage, the world from which we sprang was corrupt, divided in unseen ways between the Magical and the Mundane. There were those who, from the beginning of all time, had special power—the Gift, granted them by the Almin. Their calling was as old as the world and their fates bound up in its mystery. To them, magic was Life and Life was magic. They did not know their beginning . . . but they could see clearly their end.

They saw their end in those they called the Mundane who had not been given the Gift. The Mundane's power lay in their large numbers and in their quick, technology-oriented minds. The Mundane could not understand the magic and therefore feared and were jealous of the intangible force they could neither harness nor possess.

As the world spiraled downward toward chaos and anarchy, the great knowledge of the ancients and the love of gathering such knowledge was lost in the strife. Tales from that time tell of vast libraries being burned to the ground—victims of hatred and fear and war. Battle raged over all the Earth and brought death to uncounted multitudes. Truth was no longer valued and was cast aside in favor of blind faith, misguided patriotism, and mysticism. Human thought shriveled in the winter of destruction.

In the beginning there were thirteen Mysteries of Life, not nine as we know them today. The additional four were the negative aspects of Earth, Air, Fire, and Water, known in the world as War, Pestilence, Famine, and Spirit-

---

[1]The records that count time before the Great Passage were lost with the Mystery of Time just prior to the Iron Wars. The relation of these dates to your own calendar is unknown to us. Y.L. or Year of Life was the accepted calendar until the general establishment of the Merilon Empire.

Death. The Council of Thirteen—last bastion of the ancient knowledge and keeper of the Mysteries of the People of Life—knew that their Orders and Covens were in peril. The Mundane had begun to hunt down and destroy magic in all its forms. The very existence of the Council and all knowledge of its arts was threatened.

What they did not know, at first, was that this age, called the Night of the Blind, was fueled by the four Orders within the Council known as the Dark Cults. Cult members believed that the general decay of the world was the fault of the Council for refusing to magically intervene in the history of man. Those of the Dark Cults decided that magic was the manifestation of their right to rule. Against the prohibition of the Council, the Dark Cultists began using their power to change and direct the world.

The Dark Cults had a purpose in their treachery. As the use of magic became increasingly more obvious, the Mundane grew to hate and fear those who wielded it. It was a simple matter for the Dark Cultists to direct this hatred against the Orders and the Covens of the nine Mysteries of Light. They planned to instigate conflict between the Mysteries and the greater Mundane world. Once the battle was over, the Dark Cults believed it would be a simple matter to overcome the weakened victor and establish their own rule.

At length, a famous wizard named Taliesin, after long years of dangerous and secret labor, uncovered the treachery of the Dark Cultists.

−74 Y.L. (aprox) *The Broken Council:* The Council convened. Taliesin presented the evidence against the Dark Mysteries. The powerful nine Masters of Light cast the Masters of Dark from the Council. The Council was reformed as the Council of Nine. Unfortunately the damage had been done. It was almost too late.

−73 Y.L. (aprox) *The Determination of Passage:* The Council of Nine gathered at the Foot of the World to confer over their dire plight. Merlyn, the greatest of wizards, listened to his people's desperate talk of killing and revenge and was deeply saddened. The last to speak, he rose to present his plan: that all the People of Life would one night walk among the stars to another world where they could live their lives untroubled by the Mundane. Merlyn (*DKarn-ƌuuk*), Mannanan Mac Lir (*Sif-Hanar*), Taliesin (Diviner), Circe (*Thelƌara*), Chow-Li (*Pron-alban*), Roger Bacon (Necromancer), Leonardo Da Vinci (Illusion), William Shakespeare (spirit), and Francis of Assisi (catalyst) consented to the plan.

–73 to –45 Y.L. (approx) *Search for the Way:* During this period each of the Council wandered the earth in search of the wisdom and knowledge that would open the way to new worlds. At the end of nine years they returned to the Foot of the World to pool their knowledge. Mannanan and Taliesin had between them discovered how to open magical corridors that led beyond the circles of the world. The way was far from easy. The path could be established, but its safety could not be guaranteed and the dangers facing the People when they reached their destination were unknown.

–45 Y.L. (approx) *The Ancient Leave the Circles of the World:* The Portals of Passage were established in the perpetual winter at the Foot of the World. The Masters of the Council: Taliesin, Merlyn, Chow-Li, and Mannanan, volunteered to make the dangerous journey down the magical paths that extended into the heavens in search of a new world. Each took leave of one another, departing with a catalyst and such magical protections as they guessed might be necessary to walk among the stars.

Each searched for a new world in a different way. Taliesin vowed to search out the path letting wisdom be his guide. Mannanan used knowledge as the basis for finding the world. Chow-Li determined to search guided by passion. Only Merlyn let himself be guided by Life, the Power of Magic.

Stepping between the stone columns that supported the earth, the Masters touched them, granting the columns a portion of the magis's Life, causing the stone to glow brightly, and thus the magi could find their way back.

Then each walked among the stars. Mannanan's servant, Seraphim, remained to keep watch over the portals.

A.D. −45 to −1 Y.L. *The Long Wait:* As he waited, Seraphim saw with sorrow what was taking place in the world. He chronicled his heartbreak in song. The lyrics told of the increasing ferocity of the attacks against those living by Magic. He told of the Cults losing their power over the Mundane, of witch trials and persecutions.

As Seraphim watched, the stone pillars darkened, one by one, until only Merlyn's remained alight. But as long as that pillar glowed, Seraphim knew his song was not finished.

−1 Y.L. (approx) *Merlyn Returns to Lead the Great Passage:* At last, an exhausted Merlyn stumbled through the Portal and collapsed into the arms of Seraphim. The great wizard had found a new world—he had discovered the source of Life in the universe.

Merlyn inquired after his brothers and sisters who still walked the paths. Seraphim sang for him his song. The wizard grieved over his lost comrades and mourned the lives lost to the Mundanes. He saw that this world he had discovered, though new and untamed, offered the People of Life their only hope.

It was time to leave.

1 Y.L. (approx) *Merlyn Banishes the Dark Cults:* The Dark Cultists, having lost control of the Mundanes and now finding themselves trapped, pleaded with Merlyn to grant them knowledge of the means whereby Passage to the new world could be achieved. Merlyn refused, banishing the Dark Cults from the Great Passage.

The Great Passage

1 Y.L. (approx) *The Great Passage:* One night in the early spring of that year, the People of Life who still followed the guidance of the Council of Nine received the Word and the Way. The Great Passage was opened to all magi, regardless of their location in the circle of the world. Each in his turn walked the paths away from the places they'd called home.

The world did not note the silent passing, and in a single night all the Mysteries of Light left their world to the Dark Cults and to Death.

Unfortunately, however, through torture and powerful geas spells, seven members of the Dark Cults obtained the Word and the Way and traveled the Great Passage, disguised as Brothers of Light.

The Magi arrived on the new world and found themselves standing at the base of a great mountain. Surrounded by a sphere that Merlyn set to protect them, they gave thanks to the Almin for their deliverance. Then Merlyn spoke the Last Word and the way back to Earth closed. Merlyn named the new world Thimhallan, meaning "new home."

1st Y.L. *The Well of the World Established:* The shielding dome that Merlyn had established on his first journey was not sufficient to protect the great population of magi. The world beyond the dome was a hostile place, swept hourly by terrible storms, teaming with dangerous life. Merlyn called together the catalysts and asked them to locate the source of the magic that had drawn him to this place. The catalysts told him that here within the mountain was the source of all Life.

The magi entered the mountain, the source of magic was found, the Well of the World was established. The mountain itself became known as the Font.

1 Y.L. *The Borderlands:* Using the pure magic found in the Well of the World, Merlyn spoke complex words of Life. The protective sphere he had constructed around the people changed and grew. The Masters of Time and Spirit joined him in his chant, weaving their magic into his. The other magi joined in and soon their chorus shook the very foundations of the mountain.

When at last they were done, the great sphere extended across the land. As it passed over the surface of the world, it changed all it touched. The land became as a garden bearing rich fruits. The beasts retained their aspect but were adapted to their new environs. A new continent opened up for exploration and expansion. Beyond the fruitful areas lay the old world they had found—a world of terrible storms and barren land. To keep the People of Light safe, an area was established against this world and the old world that lay somewhere behind them among the stars. This became known as the Border.

1 Y.L. *The Leavetaking:* The diverse groups who made the Great Passage brought with them their own unique cultures. Though united in their desire to establish a peaceful land of magic, they found themselves gravitating toward those of common language, customs, and experiences.

These individual groups took their leave of their fellows and went in search of places to build their own cities, to establish themselves in comfort and in peace.

So it was that the members of the various Mysteries spread across the face of the world. The land was soon populated . . . if not completely tamed.

2 Y.L. *The Year of Dawn:* During these early years the future course of Thimhallan was established. Much of what was accomplished was apocryphal rather than fact and comes to us through legend, despite the careful keeping of records prevalent at that time. This was done purposefully, for the Ancients wanted to obliterate all knowledge of the way back. The world outside the borders of Thimhallan became known simply as Beyond—a place of chaos held at bay by the Border. The events during these years (as told by legend) were the Shaping of the Almin's Throne, the establishment of Merilon (later known as Old Merilon), and the ordering of the sky.

Shaping of the Almin's Throne: The original buildings known as the Almin's Throne had their foundations near the summit of the Font. The shaping of them took ten years to accomplish. The Almin's Throne was at first a place of general worship for the people of Thimhallan but later, during the First Rectification, it became a secluded monastery.

2 Y.L. *The Council of Nine:* Under Merlyn's direction new Masters for the Nine Mysteries were chosen, reforming the Council of Nine. This was Merlyn's last act before relinquishing his position, power, and authority to the Council.

The establishing of the Border had drained his Life, and he knew it was near time for him to undertake the Final Passage.

The Council, noting the diverse needs of their people, determined only to act as mediators in magic and to become involved only in major disputes between city-states. Authority to establish their own laws was granted to local officials.

2 Y.L. *The Establishment of Merilon:* Before his death in this year Merlyn founded the Grove and shaped the Pedestals that formed the foundation of Old Merilon. The spirit of Merlyn is said never to have left Thimhallan but dwells in these crystal pedestals.

2 Y.L. *The Trial of Four:* As the various Mysteries became more organized, the presence of the disguised Dark Cultists was discovered. Three were destroyed in a terrible battle, the remaining four were captured by the *Duuk-tsarith.* The four were tried before the Council of Nine and sentenced to the Turning. Their living flesh changed to stone, they were set at the Border, serving forever as a warning to other Cultists and to sound the alarm to the Diviners should any attempt to cross the Border take place. They were the first to be so sentenced and were known as the Watchers.

3–92 Y.L. *The Ordering of the Sky:* It was during this time that the first studies were conducted by the catalysts on the positions and relationships of the stars, moons and planets in Thimhallan's sky. Astrology and astronomy both had been important factors in their magic, so it was imperative that they understand the workings of their new heaven. The very fact that all their works had to be rewritten to conform to this new sky affirmed that they had been brought to another heavenly sphere, far removed from the chaos and terror of their former existence.

22 Y.L. *Kingdom of Xantar Established:* Wan-se, one of the *Albanara,* led a group of his fellow magi north into the mountains west of the Mannan Sea. There he set up the kingdom of Xantar whose people were devoted to leading

lives of seclusion and meditation. He charged his people to record on great scrolls the knowledge of the former world for fear it might be lost. All people in his land worked at this task in addition to their other chores necessary for survival. Wan-se was no exception, and it was often told how the King of Xantar worked in the fields with his fellows, then spent laborious hours recording his memories of his former world.

25 Y.L. *Vajnan Thanedom Established:* Segar Thorveldson and his clan were the first to tame the beasts of Thimhallan and shape them to their needs. Through his magic, this *Theldara* created a herd of fleet-footed animals who carried humans on their backs and could be guided by the horns on their heads. Proclaiming himself First Thane of Vajnan (a word meaning "rolling plain" in his own dialect), Thorveldson led his people to the northeastern part of Thimhallan.

29 Y.L. *Kingdom of Yandia Established:* Yandia was an ill-fated kingdom. Onrey Durseth (also known as Onrey the First and, eventually, Onrey the *Last*) had glorious visions but little taste for the hard work that would have brought his dreams to reality.

Yandia bordered the Mannan Sea on the north and the great Vajnan River to the South. Durseth envisioned the establishment of the city as a major area of trade once there were other shipping ports along the banks of the Mannan Sea.

31 Y.L. *Loss of the Sigurd Expedition:* Sigurd was the first of the *Pron-alban* to craft seagoing vessels for the purpose of exploring the Mannan Sea and the vast western ocean of Thimhallan. His Seadragon ships set sail from Yandia with considerable celebration, being the first project by Onrey the First ever to come to fruition. Unfortunately, the ships were hastily constructed by those who did not know the craft and would not take time to learn. Their fate was never discovered.

66 Y.L. *Kingdom of Camot Established:* The Council of Nine determined that with the continuing establishment of gov-

ernments in the outlying lands, its role in governing the areas around the Font might better be handled by a King rather than the Nine.

Thus the Kingdom of Camot was established in the lands bordering Merilon to the south, Yandia to the north, and Xantar to the northwest. The River Vajnan served as the border to the east and marked the beginning of the lands of the Vajnan Thanedoms.

Lord Morthan was the First *Albanara* of Camot.

71 Y.L. *Aspentown Established:* Llewelyn ap Farestan was a *Theldara*, his wife, Krinith, was a powerful Diviner. Following his wife's visions, Llewelyn led his druidic followers out of Camot, far beyond the Kingdom of Xantar. There, in an aspen wood, Llewelyn established the village of Aspentown. All who came to Aspentown with peace in their hearts found rest among its people. Those who brought contention were never heard from again.

72 Y.L. *Nomish Country Established:* A sect of Exclusionists — a group devoted to the philosophy that teaches the total exclusion of all things nonmagical (in particular the Order of the Ninth Mystery, Technology) — departed Merilon and traveled south in search of a place to establish their kingdom.

Akthan Durzan brought them to the shores of the Southern Sea and there vowed to one day take his people across the water to a place where they could live in total seclusion. During this time they became skilled in the shaping of ships, and as their wealth grew, many became loathe to leave the land they called Nomish City and sail the seas with Durzan.

81 Y.L. *Loss of the Sinda Armada:* Sinda was a seamagus who had heard the tale of Sigurd and who claimed (despite the fact that he was not a Diviner) to have seen a vision concerning the lost ships. According to Sinda, the lost ships had actually discovered a land so fabulously rich in Life that the crew refused to return and share the knowledge with the rest of Thimhallan. Sinda spent his family's fortune to shape an armada to search for the lost ships. He, too, never returned, nor did any of his ships. This added greatly

to the legend, but it also increased the fear of the sea among the general populace.

82 Y.L. *The Spires of Truth Completed:* These twin towers were the legendary homes of the Mysteries of Time and Spirit. From them came the knowledge of the Almin that was spread throughout the land. The future was known to them, and they counseled as to the best courses to follow to ensure that it remain a peaceful and fruitful one. Here, too, the known history of the world was carefully kept. The twin towers were located "in the mountains to the south," according to the writings of Merilon's Chancellor Trestinevia, and were "crafted from the stone of the Almin."

87 Y.L. *Purist Colony Established Across the Sea:* Durzan finally persuaded a group of *Quin-alban* Purists to leave Nomish. They traveled south, making the journey inside specially conjured gigantic fish. Within three months one of these fish returned to Nomish with a messenger for the Nomish Lord. The Purists reported finding new land to the south near the Border. Their catalysts were ailing and in need of the *Theldara.* One of the healers was dispatched with the fish, which swam to the south. No further word was heard from the colony.

97 Y.L. *Yin Dynasty Established:* Yin, a *Cheuva* (enchanter), was born to a poor family in the northern reaches of Xantar. Through various magics of several followers of the Dark Cultists, who wished to take over the Xantar Kingdom, the collective fears of the people were gathered into a single personification. This became known as the Beast of the Night. The Beast killed many in the northern provinces until Yin, a peasant with great powers in his Mystery, challenged the Beast.

The Beast's whispers called forth Yin's deepest fears and threatened his life. The wise peasant used his insight and knew the Beast for what it was—his own fears turned against him. In mastering his fear, Yin defeated the Beast and saved all of Xantar.

The aging Wan-se, in gratitude to Yin for his unselfish

service, granted him the Northern Provinces. Through wisdom and courage, the peasant became a king.

152 Y.L. *Amnor Kreth's Expedition to the Purists:* Rumors and legends of Sinda's vision of a land rich in Life fired the imagination of a young man named Amnor Kreth. Supported by the King of Nomish, Kreth set sail with a great fleet of winged ships to the south. On board he carried an army led by the *DKarn-duuk* to repel any attack. Within two weeks they found the remains of the colony of Purists.

From what little Kreth could piece together, the *Theldara* arrived too late to stop the plague that ran through the ranks of the catalysts, who all soon died. The Purists had long practiced conjuring all their needs through an almost limitless supply of Life. Without catalysts, only a trickle of Life flowed into the society of the Purists. The magi lacked the Life to conjure food, maintain their shelters, or send another fish messenger to the mainland for help. They died of starvation and exposure to the elements.

Amnor had not found the colony, nor had he found the fabled land of Life for which he had hoped. What he had found, however, was a land lush with tropical growth. He returned, bringing with him a group of new colonists—this time more properly balanced in the Mysteries—to the settlement he modestly named Amnor.

172 Y.L. *Yin Joins With Xantar:* Over the years the growing prosperity of both Xantar and Yin brought increasing exchange between the two nations. It was soon apparent that their uniting into one would bring even greater prosperity.

In 172 Y.L. Emperor Yin was nearing the Final Passage. He saw that the unification of these two lands would be of benefit to both peoples. Against the advice of his *Theldara,* Yin journeyed to the Xantar Palace to give his eldest daughter in marriage to the Prince of Xantar. Yin died far from his home, but he believed he had ensured the union of the two nations and their mutual continuation despite threats of expansionism from Yandia to the south.

181–187 Y.L. *The Bluebay Plague:* A terrible sickness ending in death for more than half of those who contracted it began at Bluebay in Yandia and quickly spread to Xantar. The *Theldara* acted swiftly, calling upon the *Duuk-tsarith* to isolate the infected nations from the rest of Thimhallan.

The quarantine saved their neighboring states but proved the end of both Yandia and Xantar. Those who survived the plague had no commerce to support them. The major cities were burned in an effort to destroy any lingering traces of infection, and refugees were established in small towns in the countryside.

189 Y.L. *Aspentown Disappears:* This idyll of druidic peace disappeared mysteriously in the fall of 189 Y.L. All the paths that once led to Aspentown have vanished, and no way back to it has ever been discovered. Legends occasionally persist, even into modern times, of individuals who accidentally wander into Aspentown and never return.

191 Y.L. *The Second Passage and the Crescent Kingdoms:* The Nomish became embroiled in a dispute with the kingdom of Merilon to the north. The conjuring skills of the people in Nomish were in great demand in the northern state. The Elders of the Nomish saw many of their young people being lured away from the teachings of the *Quin-alban* to what they considered the easier and less pure ways of the *Pron-alban.*

Rather than fight their brethren to the north, the Elders gave the New Word for a Second Passage. All their nation mobilized and journeyed across the Southern Sea in a great armada of magical whales. The old Nomish kingdom was reestablished as a collection of small but unified kingdoms known as the Kingdoms of the Silver Crescent, or more commonly, the Crescent Kingdoms. Here in the lush south-lands they shaped a tropical paradise.

196 Y.L. *Kingdom of Trandar Established:* An exiled Prince of Yandia named Koranth had counseled against the Second Passage, pleading that unity of the Mysteries was necessary to the development of a thriving kingdom. He stayed in Nomish, determined to build an empire of enlightened thought on the ruins of the old. Though not taken seriously at first, Koranth succeeded in attracting many disillusioned and

idealistic magi to his new kingdom. It became the first kingdom to be established outside the direct control of the weakening Council of Nine and within twelve years was recognized as a legitimate state by every major kingdom in Thimhallan.

The First Rectification

197–382 Y.L. *The First Rectification:* This term refers to an attempt within the Order of catalysts to reshape the general political and moralistic structure of Thimhallan. The tidal politics of each of the realms was bringing about the formation of governments who were growing increasingly more independent, often defying the rulings of the Council of Nine. As the power of the Council waned, the power of the Church grew—the catalysts being the one unifying Order in the land, for the magi could not survive long without them. Divisions persisted, however, and the Church was not strong enough to halt the growing turmoil that would finally culminate in the Iron Wars.

204 Y.L. *Vajnan Crusade:* The northern peninsula of Vajnan remained largely unexplored until early in 202 Y.L. At that time residents in search of new hunting grounds came upon beasts never before seen in Thimhallan. The Vajnans called them hydra because of their multiple serpentine heads. It was discovered, however, that the creatures differed widely from the hydra of the Ancient World. They could fly, although not particularly well, and could cast magical spells (undoubtedly due to the passage of the magic border over the land centuries earlier). The creatures were renamed, called the gore.

The gore were found to be highly organized and extremely protective of their territory. When that territory was threatened by the humans, the gore retaliated.

The First Thane of Vajnan, Frea Segarson, mounted an army and rode north to do battle with the gore, leaving her younger brother in charge of the clans in her absence.

The brother, Jon Segarson, seized the opportunity to replace his sister's government with his own. Waiting until the destruction of the gore was nearly assured, he cut off support for his sister and sent his own army against her.

Frea discovered her brother's treachery as her exhausted army turned toward home. Fleeing northward with her people, she reestablished her Thanedom in the wilderness. Frea proclaimed to her clan that the northern settlement would not have a separate name from the southern, making it clear that she considered her people a nation in exile. By common usage, the northern half of the peninsula became known as the Wildlands.

208 Y.L. *The First Restoration:* (Font) The Throne of the Almin was restored to its original condition, and the Font itself was expanded and reshaped into a more ornate form similar to the cathedrals and abbeys of the Ancient World.

211 Y.L. *The Corridors Constructed:* The magical passages through time and space were created by the high craft of the Diviners and the *Aluava,* Theurgists, whose mystery was Communication.

240 Y.L. *Disappearance of Xantar Palace:* Ong-Siu, last emperor of the Xantar kingdom, watched with great sadness the slow death of his kingdom in the plague-ridden land. In despair he called his family together at the great palace library in Xantar. By his magical art, he carried his family and the palace to some unknown location. A green meadow covers the ground where the palace once stood. During succeeding years there have been many who reported seeing the palace shine again from time to time on that same spot, but none have ever found it.

242 Y.L. *The Golden Succession:* (Crescent Kingdoms) The city-state of Kazan was the wealthiest of the Crescent Kingdoms. The skills of its Houses were legendary and the light of its glory shone on all the kingdoms nearby. Unfortunately the light inspired desire among some to possess its source.

Cordist of Fez was one of those who longed to possess that light. His own kingdom was powerful but lacked the beauty and wealth of Kazan. He commanded his *Pron-alban* to shape great living statues of gold who could break down the wall about Kazan and plunder its guildhouses. This became known as the Golden Succession, so named after the golden titans created by Cordist that attacked the kingdoms of the Crescent. The unity of the kingdoms was shattered through greed and their glory dimmed by war.

248 Y.L. *Plunder of the Crescent:* (Crescent Kingdoms) The Golden Succession ended in the downfall of every kingdom of the Crescent. All that was left were the great guildhouses and several family dynasties that were able to maintain some sense of order among the chaos. Cordist began to systematically plunder all the libraries of the kingdoms, securing the books well underground.

Several of the *Albanara* of Kazan organized their own armies to protect the places of learning from the general chaos in the land. It was largely due to the intervention of these families that much of the knowledge and learning of the Crescent Kingdoms was left intact.

248 Y.L. *Lost Kingdoms:* (Crescent Kingdoms) With anarchy reigning throughout the ruins of the Crescent, many of the *Albanara* and high-ranking *Pron-alban* fled in search of a new place to establish themselves. Some went inland among the mountains to the south on the very edge of the Border. Others took to the sea.

Mern of Kazan decided upon another course. He took his people and journeyed *under* the sea rather than across it. With him went the leadership of three of the seven Crescent Kingdoms, and with them, all their knowledge. They broke off all contact with those who dwelt above and were not heard from again until the Iron Wars.

249 Y.L. *The First Estate Wars:* (Camot) The Duke of Caromway, in a dispute over weather rights, seceded from the kingdom of Camot and attempted to establish his own kingdom. Camot refused to allow him to leave, and their troops met on the field of battle. The conflict was fought using the newly accepted Rules of Warrior Conduct, marking the first time in the history of Thimhallan that combat was waged within the boundaries of rules. The Rules called

for a Field of Glory to be established on a large plain of rolling hills in the northern district of Camot. Battle was conducted by means of moving playing pieces about on a large stone board, their movements magically coordinated with real armies in the field.

The Duke of Caromway won the bloodless war with a brilliant move. He established himself and his people in the southeastern basin of Camot, calling his nation Manja after his first wife.

279 Y.L. *Trandar Absorbs Camot:* (Trandar) The kingdom of Trandar, rising from the ashes of Yandia, was celebrated all over Thimhallan for its encouragement of the arts. Because of this and its promotion of free speech and free thought, Trandar attracted many people and began to grow in wealth and power.

Camot, on the other hand, suffered greatly from internal strife and bickering. Various factions struggled against the king. No two of these factions could ever come to terms with one another long enough to overthrow their monarch, however.

The artists and philosophers of Trandar began circulating songs, poems, plays, and pieces of artwork throughout Camot. The messages inherent in all the works of art were to devote oneself to beauty and abolish strife.

In 279 Y.L. after three years of artistic propaganda, Camot's king—now turned poet—peacefully handed over the holdings of the city-state to the artist-king of Trandar.

289 Y.L. *The Division of Sisters:* (Vajnan) After the rule of Jon Segarson, tradition among southern clans passed the rulership to the firstborn son of the clan's Thane. However, in 289 Y.L., despite the herbs and potions of the clan's *Theldara*, the First Thane of Vajnan, Ekard Keilson, failed to father a son.

Born to him were twin girls—Hera and Hira Ekardson. Due to the father's disappointment in not fathering a son, no one bothered to distinguish the girls at birth. They went for days without even being named, and by that time no one remembered which had been born first. The girls were alike in temperament and ambition—when their father died, each insisted that she was firstborn and therefore the rightful ruler.

Hoping to prevent warfare, the Council of Nine intervened, offering to act as mediator. Unfortunately the Council was, by this time, weak and ineffectual. The Church, backed by the *Duuk-tsarith*, was slowly gaining control of Thimhallan.

The Council saw this and hoped that by bringing this matter to a peaceful conclusion they could show the world that they were still in command. Both sisters came before the council, each bringing testimony to support her claim to the birthright. Two *Theldara* nearly came to blows, each claiming to have been the only one present at the birth, each favoring a different sister. The Diviners—who could see into the past—either could not or would not unravel the mystery.

The Council itself was unable to come to a decision. They debated the question endlessly until open warfare broke out. This ultimately led to the sundering of the clans and the War of Sisters.

In the end Hera retained control of Vajnan while Hira claimed and held the eastern provinces from the Eastpass east of the mountains as far as the Borderlands. Hira established the Tarak Thanedom. Though she talked loudly of peace with her sister, Hira secretly plotted the overthrow of the Vajnan Thanedom.

301–343 Y.L. *The Three Sisters:* (Merilon) Situated between Nomish and the lands to the north, Merilon grew as a great trade center. After the departure of the Nomish nation across the sea, Merilon incorporated the Nomish lands and salvaged (many said "plundered") the lands of all their remaining wealth. Merilon offered homes to those Nomish who remained behind.

Merilon soon became not only a trade center but a center of Guild crafts as well. In 301 Y.L. the Guilds determined to create a monument that would symbolize their skill and provide them with much-needed security in their working environment.

For the next forty-two years, the Guilds worked to shape the Three Sisters—three floating pedestals of marble that would eventually float above the city of Old Merilon, providing a place for the Guilds to establish their halls and proceed with their work.

In 343 Y.L. the task was complete. The three pedestals were brought from the rock quarry in the hills northeast of Merilon to the city in a procession that lasted an entire month. The marble platforms were lifted into the air by the combined powers of every magi and catalyst in Merilon and hung like shining jewels above the Old City.

321–400 Y.L. *Growth of Trandar:* (Trandar) Trandar continued to expand during these years and grew ever greater in power and influence, quietly bringing the disorganized lands formerly known as Xantar and Yin under its control.

330 Y.L. *Amra's Farewell:* (Vagrad) From out of the center of the Crescent Kingdom ruins there rose in a single night a city of crystal, bright and beautiful. Amra Tariganth, a *Kan-Hanar* of the highest rank, brought her people in secret to the ruins and, through their power, caused the city to suddenly appear.

Following the plunder of the Crescent Kingdoms, nearly all society in the region reverted to primitive tribal bands filled with fear and blood lust. The scattered tribes that roamed the area saw in the city a return to the old days of oppression. A mob gathered outside the gates and threatened to demolish the beautiful city and murder all its inhabitants if Amra and her people did not turn it over to them at once.

Amra sent word to the mob: "If all your people will gather outside the city, I will open the gates and bid you farewell."

That night the city was surrounded by hundreds who had come to loot and despoil the beautiful city. Amra appeared before them, hovering over the highest spire of the city, shining in her beauty like a single bright star. Sadly Amra opened the gates and bid the mob farewell.

The plain was suddenly devoid of all that lived and moved. True to her word, Amra had opened the gates and bid them farewell. She had not said, however, who it was that would be leaving. She and her people closed the gates and lived in peace for years to come.

363 Y.L. *The Second Estate War:* (Manja) Duke Urnish of Manja had a troublesome son who was constantly looking for battle and conquest.

The Duke was old and tired but far from anxious to hand his kingdom over to his warlock son. The Duke's health was failing and he had been floating in the confines of his bed for over a year under a *Theldara*'s care. He often pleaded for some peace and quiet, but there was no muzzling the whelp. So tiresome was the lad and so insistent, that at last his father gave in.

"If you want a land of your own, then you shall have to carve it out for yourself," he said.

The son, Jendis Finth Urnish, considered his options. Trandar was growing to the north and could not be taken easily. Merilon was out of the question since to attack that prosperous trade center could lead to war against all the nations of Thimhallan. The kingdom of Tarak was weak, but Jendis would have to go through Vajnan to reach it.

Vajnan itself, on the other hand, appeared to be nothing but a loosely associated group of plainsmen who could be easily overcome in battle. Jendis took his *DKarn-duuk* and his army and stood at the border of Vajnan to make his declaration of war. The writs were sent and acknowledged according to the Rules of Warrior Conduct, and the various forces were pitted against one another on the Field of Glory.

Vajnan's ruler, Bran Hevason, was a cagey old *DKarn-duuk* who had been waging war when Jendis was cutting teeth. He lured the gullible young man into a trap, defeating him easily in one swift stroke. By the rules Hevason could claim the kingdom of Manja, and he did so. Manja suddenly came under the rulership of the Plainsmen.

364 Y.L. *Three Houses of Balzaab:* (Balzaab) Balzaab—patriarch of a large clan—was among those who fought to save the Crescent Kingdom from destruction. Even after it fell the old man clung tenaciously to his holdings until mobs eventually drove his family from their lands. Along with his sons Balzaab and Makar and his daughter, Lithinia, and

their families, the patriarch shaped a fleet of ships and sailed north. The ships landed on a previously unknown island where they were able to build new homes and kingdoms.

By 364 Y.L. these kingdoms were well enough established to be recognized by Merilon.

371 Y.L. *The Gladewall:* (Merilon) With the growth of Merilon as an empire, so, too, came the growth of Merilon the City. Old Merilon, standing on its famous pedestal, became over-crowded and almost unlivable.

In 371 a solution was devised—the Gladewall. Ostensibly designed for defense, it established a visible boundary between the privileged and the working classes. The *Albanara* further gave permission for housing for the workers to be constructed on the ground below the pedestal, as long as the dwellings were kept outside the sacred grove of Merlyn.

The wall was completed in that same year, and Merilon was divided along class lines into City Above and City Below.

391–587 Y.L. *The Night of Nine:* This refers to the period of about two hundred years at the end of the First Rectification. During this time sorcery, brought about in concert with the other Mysteries, gained great prominence. Technological advances in all the fields outstripped the wisdom of man to utilize them. Most frightening was the invention of an exploding powder that could level city walls and topple the strongest fortress. The Council of Nine could not agree on an effective method of controlling or using technology. The magi all over Thimhallan became bitterly divided over the issue, some advocating technology, others insisting that it be banished from the world. This culminated in the Iron Wars and the ultimate destruction of technology as an acceptable Mystery.

404 Y.L. *The Newking War:* (Camot) Certain descendants of the king of Camot claimed that the Trandar lords were siphoning off the wealth of Camot for their own personal gain. This small group, led by one calling himself Ardith Newking, began to wage guerrilla warfare in the state of

Trandar. Ardith demanded a separate state of his own, to be built around the base of the Font.

Though sick of fighting the guerrilla war that was draining its resources, Trandar dared not set a devastating precedent by giving in to Newking's demands. Trandar invited the guerrillas to do battle on the Field of Glory. Though outnumbered, Ardith accepted in the hope that there would be many in Thimhallan who would champion his cause.

That hope proved unfounded. The Newking forces of Camot were on the verge of defeat when Marshal Withrin Zen of Trandar suddenly surrendered to the astonished Ardith. The Rules of Warrior Conduct assessed the position of all forces on the field at the time of surrender and granted to the Newking a comparable area—of ten square *mila* around the Font.

Thus did Trandar rid itself of a malcontent without losing anything more than its dignity.

409 Y.L. *The Third Estate War:* (Vajnan) The cultures of the plainsmen and the city dwellers of the Manja region were not compatible, and this eventually led to open revolt in the combined kingdom of Vajnan. The Rules of Warrior Conduct were never designed to accommodate such insurrection, and hasty revisions had to be made so that the revolt could be played out in the relative safety of the Field of Glory. The battle ended with the once-united kingdom of Vajnan split into several uneasily allied factions.

420–450 Y.L. *The War of Spheres:* (Merilon) The Merilon Empire by this time occupied most of the southwest territories of Thimhallan. The rapid growth of Merilon ultimately resulted in friction between the agricultural regions, the highly technological estates, and the magnificent city of Merilon that they supported.

Despite the rhetoric of Chancellor and Historian Trestinevia III, who proclaimed these differences to be "natural perspectives from Spheres of Influence," a revolutionary war was demanded on the Field of Glory. Due to apathy on the part of the Merilon civilian population, the war was only moderately contested, and the western territories were granted their own representation in the Merilon Council. Ultimately this resulted in the establishment of Norlund, and later Newlund, as independent western territories.

430–500 Y.L. *Decline of the Diviners:* (Spires of Truth) With a high confidence in their own abilities and the upsurge in hedonism and self-gratification (particularly in Merilon), the people of Thimhallan had no desire to remember their own dark past, let alone contemplate what the Diviners and the Necromancers were increasingly warning would be a dark future.

The Church had long been displeased at the power of these two groups, and the catalysts did what they could to encourage the people to cease to follow them. Pilgrimages to the Spires of Truth and the Temple of the Necromancer became less and less frequent, and both fell into disrepair. The old members of both Orders began to die off. Children born to the Mystery of Time and Shadow were encouraged to develop other talents, or if they stubbornly insisted on pursuing their art, they conveniently disappeared.

452 Y.L. *Gathering of Nine:* (Norlund) The Sorcerers of the Ninth Mystery—Technology—had long worked for many different nations and rulers. At the beginning of this century, however, they began gathering in the western territories of the Merilon Empire to fully develop their craft. The land there was rich in timber and mineral ore. There were rivers that could be used for transportation and harnessed for power.

By 452 Y.L. the northwest territories of Thimhallan held the greatest concentration of Sorcery ever known in the history of the magi. There, the craft advanced with an accelerated pace, causing no small amount of alarm to neighboring states and, in particular, the city of Merilon.

501 Y.L. *Consolidation of Westlund:* (Norlund & Newlund) Merilon began making secret alliances with Vajnan and Trandàr to bring either Norlund or Newlund back under its control and thus divide the growing power of the territories. Word of this was brought to the knowledge of the Sorcerers who ruled in Norlund. Before Merilon could

complete its plan, Norlund and Newlund joined together under a single flag and became the unified nation of Westlund.

556 Y.L. *The Birth of Aris Devon:* Greatest of the Ancient Technologists and the last Master of the Ninth Mystery. Prior to the Iron Wars, Aris led the last great advances during these years that came to be called the Night of Nine, including the invention of exploding powder.

Following the Iron Wars he was captured and brought to trial. Accused of crimes against humanity by the Church, he was cast into Beyond. Mention of his name alone is considered a traitorous offense in all the lands of Thimhallan.

The Iron Wars

589–643 Y.L. *The Iron Wars:* The rise of powerful armies in many realms, combined with the alarming growth of the power of Sorcery, created an increasingly unstable political climate. The warlike posturings of Merilon and Trandar added fuel to an already volatile situation. Both nations had grown wealthy and powerful and were locked into a constant struggle for supremacy. To this end they invested in engines of destruction made by the Sorcerers, paying for them with the granting of large amounts of Life. The great influx of Life among the Sorcerers, in turn, allowed them to make greater and more terrible creations.

The two nations were unable and unwilling to resolve their political differences. They called for support from their allies, and one kingdom after another fell into the maelstrom of the Iron Wars.

At first, the warring nations met on the Field of Glory. Here they unleashed the first of their powerful weapons of Sorcery. As greater weapons of technology came into play, the Council of Nine was forced to revise the Rules of Warrior Conduct. The revisions of the Council were quickly outstripped by the events on the Field of Glory—which required, of course, further revisions. The war soon got out of hand and boiled over from the Field of Glory into actual and destructive warfare between the nations involved.

As all the Mysteries were brought to bear in the struggle, it was determined by the *DKarn-duuk* that the best way to counter the Dead creations of the Sorcerers was with living creations of their own. The most powerful of the *Theldara* were matched with powerful catalysts and Omueva. First in Merilon, then in Trandar, the *Theldara* began to reshape many of the creatures of Thimhallan into new and terrible forms for the purpose of warfare. These came to be known as the Warchanged. Not all of these reshapings worked out as had been predicted. They did, however, add a new and terrible dimension to the war.

The few remaining Theurgists came forth, uttering dire prophecies. It was their hope that knowledge of the dark future that their people were bringing on themselves would result in an early end to the war. Their words were unwelcome, however, to those who longed for victory and conquest. The Diviners and Necromancers were ridiculed, imprisoned, and ultimately put to death. By the end of the war, the Mysteries of Time and Spirit had all but vanished from the face of the world.

When the Iron Wars dragged to its conclusion five decades later, nearly one fifth of the population of Thimhallan was either dead or destitute. The magically altered creatures who had been summoned into existence had grown too powerful for their weakened makers to control and were roaming the land. Much of the glory of Merilon had been destroyed during the sieges, but the Pedestal of the Old City remained unaffected. The Font, though the object of repeated campaigns, remained safe through the loyalty of the *Duuk-tsarith*. Anarchy ruled Thimhallan and brought about the Nightyears.

643–720 Y.L. *The Nightyears:* A period of chaos reigned after the battles of the Iron Wars. Merilon continued under its original rulership, although much of the city lay in ruins and had to be abandoned. Trandar disappeared. No vestige of its original leadership remained; its buildings had been destroyed by the exploding powder of the Sorcerers. Desperate bands of survivors lived by raiding the countryside, occasionally laying siege to an isolated stronghold of some *Albanara*.

666 Y.L. *The Prophecy:* In an effort to calm the chaos and give the people hope for the future, Bishop Philinous III, with the aid of the last of the Theurgists, undertook a prophecy. After a year of preparation he knelt before the Well of the World and called upon the Almin to grant his prayer.

He was successful beyond his expectations. He failed beyond his nightmares.

Those present claimed that the Almin appeared and spoke to the Bishop these words that he repeated as he heard them:

"There will be born to the Royal House one who is dead yet will live, who will die again and live again. And when he returns, he will hold in his hand the destruction of the world—"

At this point the Bishop—horrified perhaps by what he saw—pressed his hand over his heart and fell dead. The Prophecy's dark images were kept secret from the war-ravaged populace and, in time, became the joint province of the *Duuk-tsarith* and the Church to protect against its fulfillment.

720–810 Y.L. *The Second Rectification:* It was left to the Church to bring about the salvation of their people. The catalysts began by unifying the Church under one central authority operating out of the Font.

At this time was forged the alliance between the catalysts and the *Duuk-tsarith*. The warlocks had the power to keep in line those who were tempted to rebel against the authority of the Church. The catalysts held the source of Life power that the warlocks needed. Though neither side ever came to fully trust the other and both maintained their separate autonomies, they found it to their mutual benefit to support one another.

723–782 Y.L. *Blame of the Dead:* Central to the restructuring of the civilization of Thimhallan was the focusing of the hatred that ran wild across the land. By providing a common enemy, the *Duuk-tsarith* and the Church could more easily unite the diverse factions. The Sorcerers were the perfect choice.

The Church soon began preaching the purity of Life.

The cause of the Iron Wars, they claimed, was the perversion of Life by the Sorcerers who gave Life to that which was Dead. To a fearful and war-ravaged populace, the Sorcerers were soon viewed as the cause of all their strife and pain.

The Ninth Mystery was abolished by the Church. The Sorcerers were declared outlaws, their records and creations were confiscated and purportedly destroyed (in reality, much was retained in secret by the *Duuk-tsarith*). The Sorcerers—men, women, and children—were cast into Beyond or, if captured by mobs, met horrible deaths.

For fifty-nine years the persecution of Sorcerers continued. Numerous small crusades were launched to hunt down those who had fled into the countryside. The Sorcerers who fought back with their technology simply fanned the flames of hatred against their kind. In the end, all Sorcery was driven from Thimhallan, except for a few pockets where the remaining survivors fled.

726 Y.L. *Sharakan Established in Vajnan:* (Sharakan) Nobles from various houses who fled north during the last days of the Iron Wars were at last able to establish kingdoms in the northern reaches of what was once Vajnan. By 726 all of these smaller dominions were, by one means or another, brought under the banner of Sharakan and its ruling house. Though not apparent at the time, the Church and the *Duuk-tsarith* had done much to bring this about.

The rulership of Merilon had remained largely intact, and the Church feared that this nation would soon rise up to dominate the world without any opposition. In Sharakan the Church foresaw a force that would maintain the balance of power in Thimhallan.

747–800 Y.L. *Expansion of the Font:* (Font) As the catalysts unified themselves, the Font—their power base—was greatly expanded, including a seminary for the training of their Order.

650–751 Y.L. *Renovation of Merilon:* (Merilon) At the end of the Iron Wars, Merilon was left severely damaged. Cracks in two of the Three Sisters made them uninhabitable. The buildings on the Old City Pedestal were laid to waste. As Merilon grew, the city was rebuilt to the order of Empress Halnava into a more glorious form. Two new pedestals, smaller than the original Sisters, were shaped. On one was built a cathedral for the catalysts. Floating in the air above the city was a grand new Crystal Palace for the Emperor and Empress.

The gardens of Merilon were restored as was the Tomb of Merlyn. The Three Sisters were repaired, and most wondrous of all, the Gladewall was not only restored, but a dome of magic known as the Stardome rose from its upper spires to encompass all of the city.

So beautiful did Merilon become that the artists of the world naturally gravitated to its gates. Two universities were founded within the city, and Merilon once again became the hub of civilization.

810 Y.L. *Birth of the Dead:* Following the Second Rectification, all legitimate births were sanctioned and carried out in their conception by the Church with the aid of the *Theldara*. The population of Thimhallan had been dangerously depleted as a result of the Iron Wars. Through what few remaining Diviner spells the catalysts knew, they could predict whether or not a union would provide issue and sanctioned only those that did. Since children were in such demand, the ceremonial test given each infant to determine if the child had Life became largely a matter of custom and tradition.

Around the year 810 Y.L. there were several incidents of children being born who failed two of the three tests and were declared Dead. These incidents increased in frequency up until the fulfillment of the Prophecy.

815 Y.L. *Birth of Joram:* Empress Evenue of Merilon gave birth to a male child. The child, named Gamaliel (God's reward), failed not one or two but all three tests of magic at the ritual following his birth. The child was declared Dead and taken to the Font by Bishop Vanya to await its Final Passage to the next world.

The Bishop, being one of those entrusted with the knowledge of the Prophecy, knew full well the terrible import of the child's coming. He determined to hide the child and keep the baby alive, since to let it die would fulfill the beginning of the Prophecy.

A woman of high birth in Merilon happened to be at the Font at this same time. Her name was Anja, only daughter of Baron Fitzgerald. Anja and the family's House Catalyst fell in love with each other. The Vision was undertaken. Anciently, the Vision could tell much about the future issue of any couple but since the loss of Diviners, only a shadow of its former power remained. As a preliminary to any proposed union in Thimhallan, the Vision can tell only whether there will be any living children of a marriage, though nothing of the Mystery or Power of Life in the child. In the case of Anja and her love, the Vision failed utterly. Since no living issue was seen, their marriage was disallowed. In an effort to prove the Vision wrong, the two mated after the manner of heathens and beasts. They were discovered in the act. The catalyst was sentenced to the Turning. Anja was taken to the Font to await the birth of her child. When the child was born dead, as the Vision had foreseen, the woman went mad.

The *Duuk-tsarith* took her child away for burial and left Anja supposedly sedated in her room. She escaped however, and roamed the Font until she came upon the Dead child of the Empress, who was still crying frantically for love and nourishment. Snatching up the baby, Anja fled into the countryside.

Bishop Vanya, returning to take the child into captivity, was horrified to find the boy had disappeared.

832 Y.L. *Turning of Joram:* Anja's child, whom she named Joram, grew to young adulthood in the farm holdings of Merilon near the Outland. When the overseer discovered that Joram was Dead and threatened to reveal this to the *Duuk-tsarith*, Anja attacked the man, who accidentally killed her.

Furious, Joram killed the overseer and was then forced to flee for his life into the Outland. He was saved from centaurs by the Sorcerers and joined their secret coven hidden in the woods.

Here it was that Joram discovered darkstone and with

the help of Saryon, a catalyst, forged the Darksword that absorbed the magic of the world.

Along with Saryon and several companions, Joram returned to Merilon to seek his inheritance, still believing that Anja's family fortune was his for the claiming. By means of Saryon's betrayal, with the aid of a mysterious prankster known as Simkin, the *Duuk-tsarith* apprehended Joram.

He was brought to secret trial before Bishop Vanya, who planned to get rid of him before his true identity was known. Joram was sentenced to the Turning, but owing largely to the abilities of his own Darksword and the sacrifice of Saryon, Joram chose to step across the Border and into the Beyond rather than live longer in a world he felt had betrayed him. A young woman he had met in Merilon — Gwendolyn of the House of Samuels — followed him into the void of her own volition. As none had ever returned from the Beyond, this was generally considered the end of the matter. Those familiar with the Prophecy, however, were of a different opinion.

833 Y.L. *Return of Joram:* Joram returned to Thimhallan with Gwendolyn — now his wife. He opened the Border. The forces of the world Beyond came after him, which history is better left to others to tell.

Part III

The Mystican

Chapter One

Life Is Magic, Magic Is Life

Magic is the substance and essence of Life—that is the philosophy of this land and all who dwell here. Life and magic are one and the same. They are inseparable and indistinguishable.

All things have Life within them. Rain makes the crops grow because the rain itself has Life and gives that power of Life to the crops. The crops nourish the people because it transfers that Life force from them to the people.

Life granted by nature to the living beings of Thimhallan is called Inherent Life. People have an inherent ability to walk, to breathe, to pick up an object with the hand. These actions do not require any further expenditure of Life than that which comes from the foods they eat and the general health of the body. All save the most unfortunate have Inherent Life, granted them freely by the Almin.

The other type of Life is generally called the Life of Almin. For our lessons, however, it will be known by its formal term—Acquired Life. Acquired Life is slowly absorbed by all who live in Thimhallan. The amount absorbed is dependent upon a great many factors: class, station, wealth, Mystery.

It is through this Acquired Life that all magic functions. All Acquired Life in Thimhallan springs from the Well of Life centered at the Font.

People in Thimhallan utilize Life in varying ways, depending largely on the Mystery to which they are born. There are Nine Mysteries of Life: Earth, Water, Air, Fire, Time, Spirit, Shadow, Life, and Technology. While a person has some degree of skill in all the Mysteries currently in use in Thimhallan today, a person is born with specialized skill in one of the Nine.[1] All magic, no matter which Mystery governs it, follows the same general form in its execution.

The first aspect is that of *Mystery*, defining which of the talents is being called upon. *Form* is the second aspect and determines the general direction or function of the spell. A single spell may have many Forms in its construction, but such talent is possible only among the gifted and the powerful. Third is *Class*, which determines the complexity, power, and precision of the spell being cast. Several Classes under the various Forms are possible in a single spell, but, here again, this compounds its complexity.

The people of our world are gifted with the Mysteries by the Almin. It is the Almin alone who determines the extent and direction of this gift. Yet it is important to remember that a gift in one area does not mean a lack in others. All those who enjoy Life in our world share in some part of all the Mysteries. The *Duuk-tsarith* can move silently—a manifestation of the Mystery of Air. The *Albanara* can shape a chair for himself (Mystery of Earth) or strike down enemies (Mystery of Fire). The chair he shapes is probably not the piece of craftsmanship that the *Pron-alban* would have produced, but he can sit upon it. The *Duuk-tsarith* would have dealt with his enemies with greater speed and accuracy, but the *Albanara* managed to save his own life. It is important to remember that the Mystery and

---

[1] Only six Mysteries are currently in use in Thimhallan today. Two Mysteries, those of Time and Spirit, have disappeared. The Ninth Mystery of Technology has been banned.

Station to which the Almin has called each person in Life manifests their best destiny through their gift of one of the Mysteries. It does not prevent them from calling upon their innate skills in any of the others.[2]

---

[2]The exception is the Mystery of Life, which is the function of the catalyst alone.

Chapter Two

The Economics
of Life

The economy of Thimhallan is based on the exchange of Life—either in the direct form of giving the power one possesses within himself to another, giving something crafted by Life or with equivalent value, or giving the coinage of the Church, which is backed by the value of the Life.

The giving of Life for services is the sole province of the Church. Only the catalysts can create the Conduits through which the power of magic is transmitted. When the Church is asked to give Life in exchange for services, a medium for the exchange has to be set up. The best way to illustrate this is through an example.

Baron Wildreth wants to stay the night in an inn. At the door he is required to give a part of his Life in payment for his room. The Life flows into the inn itself but does not become part of the woodwork. By a means that the Church keeps a carefully guarded secret (lest counterfeiters spring up), the catalysts measure the amount of Life the Baron gives and keep it on account. Some of that Life is absorbed by the Church, the remainder is returned to the inn for use in maintenance, upkeep, and so forth.

A catalyst himself may grant a service in exchange for Life, which he returns to the world (if he is in the wilderness) or to the Church (if he is in a city). The most common example of this is the opening of a Corridor by a catalyst. This service requires the giving of Life to the Catalyst who then discharges the Life back into the world at large.

The most common form of exchange in the Wild as well as in the Estates surrounding the major kingdoms is that of traded goods. In this, people may exchange goods, services, or both for Life. The only standard for such exchanges is the adeptness of the bargainer and the shrewdness of the trader.

The most common form of exchange in the cities and kingdoms of Thimhallan is the *Glindar,* a system of coinage minted by the Church of Life and used almost universally for exchange. The Glindar is minted in a variety of denominations:

100 Glindar	= 1 Pria (P.)
10 Glindar	= 1 Decinar (Dc.)
10 Krol (Kr.)	= 1 Glindar (Gl.)
100 Dekrol (DK.)	= 1 Glindar

The Glindar is the common point of exchange for Life. Calculations for the amount of Life a catalyst grants for any given spell construction are all based around the Glindar or a percentage of it. The money in circulation, then, is a physical representation of the amount of Life due to the bearer of the coin.[1] Coins may be redeemed on a one for one basis (usually) for Life from a catalyst. Some catalysts may charge a profit over the actual rate of exchange, but the Church frowns on such practices.

Following is a partial list of the most common exchanges and their value in Glindar:

[1]This is one reason the Church felt threatened by the revolt in Sharakan. With catalysts going about giving away free Life, the eventual collapse of the world monetary system was inevitable.

Food

(Poor) Meal	5 DK.
(Good) Meal	1 Gl. (100 DK.)
Feast	17 Gl.(170 Kr.)
Banquet	27 Gl.

Drinks

Ale	5 DK.
Mead	25 DK.
Wine (Good)	50 DK.
Wine (Poor)	25 DK.

Traveling Food

1 Week	5 Gl.
3 Days	3 Gl.

Transportation (Contracted)

Corridor	2 Dc. per *Mila*

Carriage

In town	1 Kr. per *Metra*
Between cities	3 Dc. per *Mila*
Ariels	5 Dc. per *Mila*

Lodging

Substandard Inns	5-12 DK. per night
Moderate Inns	2-3 Dc. per night
Excellent Inns	8 Dc. per night
Albanara Suites	2-5 P. per night

Goods

Clothes

Simple Tunic	3 Kr.(30 DK.)
Belt	15 DK.
Soft Boots	1 Gl.
Hard Boots	2 Gl.
Leggings	2 Kr.
Soft Cap	5-10 DK.
Field Worker	5 Gl.
City Trademan	2 Dc.
City Guildmember	3-5 Dc.
Albanara	1-3 P.

Sundry Items

Illumination Stone	5 DK.
Lifelantern	12 Gl.

Amulets

Protection	1-20 Gl.
Warning	1-3 Dc.

Rings

Lightning	4-14 Dc.
Warning	1-3 Dc.
Invisibility	1-3 P.

Wands

Command	7-17 Dc.
Becalm	15-35 Gl.
Paralysis	3-13 Dc.
Icemirrors	5 Gl.

Chapter Three

Acquisition of Life

*L*ife is acquired through one of two ways: either through the natural acquisition of Life by an individual during the course of the day or by being granted Life by the catalysts through a Conduit.

Life is acquired naturally while a person rests each night. The Life that is in all things in the world is absorbed into the body of the Living and suffuses them with its force.

How much Life an individual can absorb depends upon his station. The higher the station that each individual attains through the practice of his art, the greater the amount of Life his body can hold at any given time. Those of higher station may also discharge more Life into a given task with much lower risk and higher accuracy than the lower stations. *Albanara,* for example, can absorb more Life at a faster rate than Field Magi. It further holds that an Emperor can absorb more Life than a Duke, while an overseer can absorb more Life than a Field Magus.

The second way Life may be obtained is through the catalysts. Born to the Mystery of Life, a catalyst's gift is to give Life in abundance to those who are in need of it. Catalysts take Life directly from other objects and transfer it to another through a process called the Conduit.

Catalysts rarely open a Conduit, however, without charging a price. It is the strict rule of the Church that balance must be maintained in all things.

Part IV

The Chronocon

PREFACE: Life, or magic as you call it, is the center of our existence. No understanding of us is possible without a comprehension of how Life functions.

The following is translated from a Merilonian text for the older children of the Albanara. *Entitled* The Chronocon, *it deals specifically with aspects of social class and distinctions in magical ability. It does not deal with history except in terms of its relationship to the social classes.*

I have also inserted in the text, rules and equations needed for the game of Phantasia, which — according to King Garald — you think many of your people would like to play. It is my prayer to the Almin that the combination of these rules and text may go far toward our mutual understanding.

Praeludium

"Tell me, Old One, of the Orders of the World."

Lord Mannara[1] knelt low at the feet of the Servant of All Mortals. Even Mannara—a great and proud king—could not help but feel humble before this Master of the Mysteries. He wondered vaguely if this effect was enhanced by Merlyn's magic.

Ancient hands touched him. Lifting his head, Mannara looked into the face of the Old One, as he was called. Great was Merlyn's magic and far his sight. Mannara felt as though he were standing next to a precipice of unseen depth.

"What is it you truly seek, Mannara?" Merlyn sounded amused. "You know of the Nine Mysteries. You recited them in your classes to your instructors—not, as I recall,

[1] Lord Mannara is a fictional character used in this work to represent the reader. The text is written in the form of "Magic Fiction" so as to be more appealing. Merlyn certainly no longer walked among men at the time when the Three Sisters of Merilon were built. Such allowances in "Magic Fiction" are common. The essential message of the text, however, is accurate.

without some difficulty. Even now I see them burning in your mind."

Mannara smiled inwardly. No shadow in any man's soul is hidden from those eyes. I am twenty years old, a king in my land, yet to him I am a child again at the feet of my teacher.

"What is it you truly seek?" Merlyn asked again.

"I seek an understanding of what I already know, Old One. I can tell you well each Station of each Mystery and what their crafts accomplish in our world. I seek to comprehend their essence and their relationship with one another."

Merlyn nodded, seemingly pleased.

"We stand, Lord Mannara, in the midst of a great Circle of Magic."

"I do not understand. Where is this Circle?"

"Look about you and tell me what you see."

"I see the mountains of my home. I see the lands of my people stretching from east to west between the mountains' cradling arms. Is this Circle to be found among my lands?"

Merlyn did not answer. "What else?" he persisted.

"I see the sun overhead. Is this your Circle?"

"What else?"

"The ground—its grasses and flowers. Perhaps their eternal cycle of life, death, and rebirth is your Circle."

"Below the ground, above the sun, beyond the shores of the world—there it is that the Circle is completed. There is where our journey to understanding will take us. The path to knowledge is not without its rocks and pitfalls. Will you chance it?"

Mannara's eyes flashed with excitement. "I will!"

Nodding, a glint of fire in his eye, Merlyn lifted his staff, and the world began to spin in the sight of Mannara.

Cantus I

Mystery of Fire

The artisans of Witchcraft are the Fire Shapers. They are known as warlocks and witches and they are the Guardians of the World. They have the power to call up terrible and destructive forces. They also have the power to protect the innocent against these forces.

The Mystery of Fire is divided into two separate disciplines:

DKarn-ðuuk: (Warlock; Warrior Class)
Duuk-tsarith: (Enforcer; Guardian Class)

The *DKarn-ðuuk* (D'karn-dook) are the Guardians of the State. They are generals, War Masters. Each kingdom, empire, or state within Thimhallan has its own organized army led by *DKarn-ðuuk.*

The *Duuk-tsarith* (Dook-sa-rith) are the Guardians of the People. Known as the Enforcers, they ensure the general stability of the realms and the productive peace of Thimhallan. When a threat to the order of the world is suspected, they act swiftly and efficiently to end the threat.

When a child is born to the Mystery of Fire, the catalysts notify the *Duuk-tsarith*, who arrive within hours. The warlocks give the child further tests to determine if he or she is qualified to become a member of their Order. If the child passes these rigorous, secret tests, the warlocks take the baby directly to The Mountain, their labyrinthine headquarters.

Although all know The Mountain is somewhere in the Nomish Range, its exact location remains a mystery to all except the *Duuk-tsarith* themselves. Here the training of the Enforcers and the War Masters is undertaken in complete secrecy. The only thing generally known about the training is that less than ten percent of those who begin the training survive it.

The *Duuk-tsarith* reenter the world at the age of eighteen. No matter which realm they serve, warlocks and witches wear black (black representing disciplined thought), floor-length robes with wrist-length sleeves and deep hoods that leave their faces in shadow. The only part of their bodies visible are their hands. The similarity in dress the world over serves as a reminder to all who see them that their allegiance is first and foremost to their Order. Their second allegiance is to the Dream of Merlyn—a harmonious and unified world. Their third allegiance is to the lord they serve.

Thus the primary duty of the *Duuk-tsarith* is the enforcement of order in the world. The Enforcers consider overall harmony and order more important than justice. The transient rights of one are nothing, in their minds, compared to the good of the many. To this end the *Duuk-tsarith* carry out their orders in a cold and ruthless fashion, with the end justifying any means.

Training of the *DKarn-ðuuk*, the warriors, is both different and similar. The War Masters are those members of the *Duuk-tsarith* whose talents indicate that they would be suitable for further study in the art of war. Instead of going out into the world at the age of eighteen, they remain in The Mountain for another two years, studying strategy, weapons of war, history of warfare, and practicing those skills needed to fight upon the Field of Glory or wherever they may be called. They are then assigned by the Conclave (the ruling body of the Mystery of Fire) to serve either a realm or the Church. The DKarn-duuk are known by their red robes.

History

Before the magi left their ancient world to begin the Great Passage, they packed what they considered essential to making their lives in a new world. Much of what they brought were physical objects: spellbooks, scrolls, flasks, beakers, clothes, furniture.

All of these things were mortal, of course, and with time crumbled into their baser dust and elements. Scrolls were copied and knowledge was passed on. New chairs were built to replace the old. Soon the trappings of their former world were but a memory to them.

They brought, in addition, something from their old world that might have been left behind—their differences. Merlyn's dream of creating a unified kingdom of magic was soon sundered as the various diverse peoples of Thimhallan banded together along the same racial or social lines that had divided them on their original faraway planet.

So it was that Thimhallan quickly polarized into various states and kingdoms, each realm having its own set of customs. Had it stopped there, the realms might have dwelt in peace. But it didn't. Each realm decided that its way was The Way and that all other ways were wrong and false. The realms began arguing among themselves, each trying to impose Their Way on the others.

During this time, several warlocks and witches particularly gifted in their Mystery came together in secret council called the Conclave. It was in this meeting that they determined their allegiances: to the Order, the Dream of Merlyn, and, finally, their individual Lords. They took upon themselves a mission to restore and try to maintain order and balance. Calling themselves *Duuk-tsarith*—meaning "Fire Enforcers"—they went forth into the world, always knowing that they could come together at any time should such be required.

During the first century, the *Duuk-tsarith* operated as a powerful branch of the Council of Nine, enforcing their decrees and keeping peace between nations. As time went on, however, the Council became a diminishing force in world affairs and began turning over more and more of its actual power to the *Duuk-tsarith*. Ultimately the Council of Nine disbanded, and only the *Duuk-tsarith* were left to carry on the dream.

Since that time there have been *Duuk-tsarith* and *DKarn-duuk* at the side of every ruler, there have been *Duuk-tsarith* walking all the streets in all lands, there have been *Duuk-tsarith* keeping watch within the Church.

Lives of Fire

Life of the Duuk-tsarith: Not a single fold of his black robes shifted as he stood in the Conclave, silently waiting. This was his place. As far back as he could remember, this is where he wanted to stand.

He did not know his beginning, just as he did not know the name his mother had given him, or the country in which he'd been born. It was in the Records of the Order—had he cared to look it up—as all is in the Records.

His father was a warlock serving the courts in Zith-el. Marriages among the *Duuk-tsarith* are not handled the same way as other marriages in the land. For one thing, it is a marriage in name only. The husband or wife of a warlock never sees or knows his partner. They are brought together for one purpose only—to perpetuate the Mystery of Fire. The Church chooses a partner they deem suitable for the warlock or witch. The Vision is performed and if issue is foreseen the two "marry."

The female is impregnated with the seed of her husband. The child is taken away at birth. In the case of this particular warlock, his mother's family objected but were summarily notified that the marriage was in the interests of the state. The marriage and ultimately the birth of the child went according to plan. The child was born and passed all tests. Within hours of the birth and the testing, the *Duuk-tsarith* took the child to The Mountain. The father never saw his son. The son knows neither father nor mother.

There followed the Years of Shadow as they are known. During this time the boy moved from one Illusionary situation to another, learning to hone his combat crafts and other skills.

They were long years. Many of his friends had gone insane or simply disappeared there in The Mountain. But when the years were done, he was as dark as the mountain depths, as cold as the snow on its peak, as hard as its granite.

He would give his life for the Order, The Dream of Merlyn, and his Lord.

DKARN—DUUK (WARLOCK & WITCHES)
PHANTASIA STATISTICS

ATTRIBUTES

Attack	50R	Defense	47R	Health	50R
Strength	53R	Dexterity	54R	Movement	5
Intelligence	60R	Intuition	60R	Senses	47R
Form fant/human		Size	55R	Resistance	10
Renewal	100	Capacity	100	Lifewell	300

ABILITIES

	TALENT	STATION	SCORE
Combat	15R	1	17+
Movement	5R	1	7+
Health and Healing	2	1	3
Form and Size Altering	2	1	3
Information	—	—	—
Life Transfer	—	—	—
Tool Crafts and Skills	—	—	—
Telepathy and Empathy	—	—	—
Illusions	5	1	6

DUUK-TSARITH (ENFORCER)
PHANTASIA STATISTICS

ATTRIBUTES

Attack	50R	Defense	47R	Health	50R
Strength	53R	Dexterity	54R	Movement	5
Intelligence	60R	Intuition	60R	Senses	47R
Form fant/human		Size	55R	Resistance	1
Renewal	100	Capacity	100	Lifewell	300

ABILITIES	TALENT	STATION	SCORE
Combat	15R	1	17+
Movement	10R	1	12+
Health and Healing	—	—	—
Form and Size Altering	10R	1	12+
Information	—	—	—
Life Transfer	—	—	—
Tool Crafts and Skills	—	—	—
Telepathy and Empathy	20R	1	22+
Illusions	10R	1	12+

Cantus II

Mystery of Earth

Generally divided into two separate classes, the Earth Shapers are the workers of the world. The Mystery of Earth is divided into three stations—Magic, Alchemy, and Wizardry.

Quin-alban: (Conjurers; Bringing into existence)
Pron-alban: (Magicians; Craftsmen of Thimhallan)
Mon-alban: (Alchemists; Base changers of craft)
Albanara: (Wizards; Ruling-caste Shapers)

History

Prior to the Great Passage, Conjurers, Magicians, and Alchemists were held in little respect by those of the other Mysteries. There skills, after all, were widespread among the rest of the Living; their special talents were seldom needed.

The Great Passage changed that.

Suddenly there was an entire world to be shaped. The

Sorcerers of Technology and the Shapers of Magic were in great demand, building castles and keeps, cities and houses, furniture and toys. The highest of the rank, the *Albanara*, brought their talents to creating governments.

As time passed, Shapers began to specialize in one particular aspect of their craft. They became Stone Shapers and Wood Shapers and Gem Shapers. In order to maintain standards in their workmanship, ensure fair wages, and establish apprenticeship programs in their crafts, the various groups banded together to form Guilds.

The Guilds grew in power, either absorbing or forcing out the independent concerns, until they controlled all crafting of material goods in Thimhallan. This might have resulted in the Guilds demanding exorbitant fees for their labors had not the Church stepped in and controlled pricing. What it did result in, however, was the unfortunate severing of ties between the Shapers and those of the Ninth Mystery—Technology.

As the Sorcerers became more and more advanced in the art, the Guilds began to fear that their services would no longer be needed. It takes Life and several days to lovingly shape a chair from a tree. With their tools the Sorcerers could put a chair together in a matter of hours. Because they expended hardly any Life in so doing, they were able to charge less for the article.

The Exclusionists were spreading the idea that Magic was good and Technology evil. The Guilds quickly began promoting this view. Angry, the Sorcerers withdrew from the Guilds and formed their own close-knit group, determined to prove their worth to the world.

This was one of the factors leading inevitably to the Iron Wars.

Lives of Shapers

Life of the Quin-alban: Thar Solverdon collapsed into his chair in his study with a suddenness that made even its finely crafted structure creak. Never had there been such a day!

Thar had been a Conjurer all his life, but there were times—oh, yes, there were times—when he seriously thought about packing it all in and retiring to the country! Bad enough that he had to put up with that meddlesome whelp from down in Barging. There hadn't been a day go by when that little snip of an overseer hadn't come to him with complaints about slow production and shortages. The young upstart was obviously bucking for some type of station elevation—probably Thar's own Masters Station.

No, a Conjurer's life is far from an easy one.

Thar leaned back on his creaking chair (he'd have to get it reshaped, he noted irritably) and looked out on his House Garden. There was a sweet summer breeze—ordained by the Empress—and the stars were out. Unfortunately he didn't have the proper tranquillity of mind needed to enjoy either.

Of all the crafts in the Mystery of Earth, Conjuring was by far and away the most difficult to master. That was Thar's opinion, at least. And it was—he was certain—the least appreciated. The *Pron-alban* and even the *Mon-alban* started with *something* when they set out to create. The *Quin-alban*, on the other hand, must produce an object using the power of Life alone.

This was a most expensive proposition. One did not just "create" without a high cost in Life. The work was draining and exhausting for both shapers and their catalysts. No catalyst ever worked for the *Quin-alban* Guild House for very long. It seemed that just when Thar got one trained, the catalyst would be called back to the Font for reassignment and another sent in his place.

Thar supposed, grudgingly, that at least the life of a *Quin-alban* was more interesting than the life of a *Pron-alban*. At least he wasn't shaping fainting couches day in and day out. Orders coming into the *Quin-alban* were often for specialized items that couldn't be formed out of material existing in nature. But as such, the *Quin-alban* were often subject to the whims of the public. Thar recalled—with a shudder—two months ago when the rage in Merilon had been for black lilies. No one wanted to wait for the Druids to grow them; they wanted black lilies and they wanted them now!

The *Quin-alban* conjured black lilies by the hundreds, and soon every home in Merilon had vases of black lilies sitting on the dining table or were wearing them in hats and lapels. Of course the Guild had been able to charge a hefty amount of Life for their services, but now that the fad was over, Thar was stuck with a warehouse full of black lilies. It would cost additional Life to get rid of the things, cutting down considerably on the Guild's profits.

Thar thought with regret back to his days in the military. Although he'd griped and complained about it at the time, he missed the excitement and adventure. The *DKarn-∂uuk* invariably take several *Quin-alban* along if they are, say, going out to defend an Estate being attacked by dugruns. In an emergency situation such as this, what the *DKarn-∂uuk* need, they need now! They don't have time to wait for a Shaper to shape it. Because of this, most young *Quin-alban* see service with the military. Not a bad idea, Thar thought. It gives the youngsters practice at their art and provides gainful employment at the outset of their careers.

Thar grinned as he recalled one particularly hair-raising incident. He and a small patrol were on what was supposed to be a routine scouting mission when they came upon an entire tribe of dugruns. Outnumbered, they could do nothing but fly for their lives. When their Life gave out, they were forced to run on foot. The dugruns were closing in on the patrol when they came to a large, deep stream with no way across!

To this day Thar did not remember conjuring up the huge log that led them to safety. It was truly said that the *Quin-alban*'s life in the army was one of long boredom punctuated by brief moments of terror-filled responsibility.

Remembering that log, Thar closed his eyes and smiled. He'd done it, he'd saved the patrol. He'd been a hero. That loudmouthed overseer wasn't going to be such a problem after all.

If he doesn't shut up, thought Thar sleepily, I'll create another log—right through his mouth!

Life of the Low-Caste Pron-alban: Cyrus Gran's Gem Shaper's shop was a small one located not far from the keep of the Duke of Blandis. Although Gran's shop was small and the Duke's Estate was out of the way of most travelers, Gran was gaining a growing reputation for the fine quality of his work.

This reputation led to the momentous event that was happening to Cyrus Gran today. It was a proud and terrifying moment, exhibiting his lovingly shaped rubies and sapphires and diamonds to the Guild representatives of Merilon. If his work was fine enough, the Gem Shapers Guild would move him and his family—at Guild expense—to the wondrous city of Merilon. He, Cyrus Gran, would at last fulfill his lifelong dream—working in the halls of the Three Sisters.

The Guild representatives took their time, minutely examining each jewel, searching for the slightest flaw. When they left without a word either of praise or blame, Gran knew it was all over and his heart sank.

But then the Duke himself walked into Gran's shop.

"Well, old friend, it appears you will be leaving this out-of-the-way place for Merilon. My congratulations!"

Tears streamed down Gran's cheeks. Thanks be to the Almin! he wept. Thanks be!

QUIN-ALBAN (CONJURERS) PHANTASIA STATISTICS

ATTRIBUTES

Attack	42R	Defense	42R	Health	43R
Strength	43R	Dexterity	52R	Movement	5
Intelligence	45R	Intuition	42R	Senses	47R
Form	fant/human	Size	55R	Resistance	10
Renewal	100	Capacity	100	Lifewell	300

ABILITIES	TALENT	STATION	SCORE
Combat	5	1	6
Movement	5R	1	7+
Health and Healing	2	1	3
Form and Size Altering	20R/10[1]	1	22+/11
Information	—	—	—
Life Transfer	—	—	—
Tool Crafts and Skills	1	1	1
Telepathy and Empathy	—	—	—
Illusions	7	1	8

[1]The score before the slash indicates the character's score whenever casting a conjuration spell in this mystery. The score after the slash deals with all other types of spells of the mystery.

PRON-ALBAN (MAGICIANS)
PHANTASIA STATISTICS

ATTRIBUTES

Attack	43R	Defense	43R	Health	43R
Strength	43R	Dexterity	50R	Movement	5
Intelligence	45R	Intuition	42R	Senses	47R
Form	fant/human	Size	55R	Resistance	10
Renewal	100	Capacity	100	Lifewell	300

ABILITIES	TALENT	STATION	SCORE
Combat	5	1	6
Movement	5	1	6
Health and Healing	2	1	3
Form and Size Altering	25R[1]/10	1	27 + /11
Information	—	—	—
Life Transfer	—	—	—
Tool Crafts and Skills	2	1	3
Telepathy and Empathy	—	—	—
Illusions	7	1	8

[1]The talent before the slash indicates the character's talent whenever casting spells dealing with *permanent* conjuration in this mystery. The score after the slash indicates the character's talent whenever dealing with any other type of spell structure in this mystery.

MNON-ALBAN (ALCHEMISTS)
PHANTASIA STATISTICS

ATTRIBUTES

Attack	43R	Defense	42R	Health	43R
Strength	43R	Dexterity	52R	Movement	5
Intelligence	45R	Intuition	42R	Senses	47R
Form	fant/human	Size	55R	Resistance	10
Renewal	100	Capacity	100	Lifewell	300

ABILITIES	TALENT	STATION	SCORE
Combat	5	1	6
Movement	2	1	3
Health and Healing	5	1	6
Form and Size Altering	20R[1]/7	1	23 + /8
Information	—	—	—

ABILITIES	TALENT	STATION	SCORE
Life Transfer	—	—	—
Tool Crafts and Skills	1	1	2
Telepathy and Empathy	—	—	—
Illusions	7	1	8

[1]The talent before the slash indicates the character's talent whenever casting spells dealing with alteration of an already existing object. The score after the slash indicates the character's talent whenever dealing with any other type of Wizardry.

ALBANARA (WIZARDS)
PHANTASIA STATISTICS

ATTRIBUTES

Attack	41R	Defense	41R	Health	47R
Strength	46R	Dexterity	42R	Movement	4
Intelligence	47R	Intuition	47R	Senses	52R
Form	fant/human	Size	55R	Resistance	10
Renewal	100	Capacity	100	Lifewell	300

ABILITIES	TALENT	STATION	SCORE
Combat	5R	1	2
Movement	5R	1	7+
Health and Healing	5	1	12+
Form and Size Altering	5	1	6
Information	1	1	3
Life Transfer	—	—	—
Tool Crafts and Skills	1	1	2
Telepathy and Empathy	1	1	1
Illusions	5	1	6

Cantus III

Mystery of Water

The Mystery of Water is divided into two classes—Druids and Shamans. The Druids hold the life of plants in their care and are experts not only in agricultural matters but in the natural healing properties of all creatures. Shamans, on the other hand, are primarily concerned with humans and the more advanced healing arts.

> *Fihanish:* (Druids of the Fields)
> *Mannanish:* (Druids of Healing; minor health)
> *Theldara:* (Shamans of Healing; major health)

The *Fihanish* are the lowest station of the Druids, often found working on the Estates and farms that supply the cities with their food. They assist in the ordering of the fields and see to the health of the crops. They are also responsible for organizing plant life to come to the defense of a settlement.

The *Mannanish* are the Druids of Minor Healing. They use the herbs of the field as well as Life in practicing their mending of the sick or afflicted. The *Mannanish* are, however, limited to accelerating the natural defenses of the body. They have little effect on more serious maladies or injuries. They are responsible, too, for caring for the body when its spirit has departed. The *Mannanish* take charge of funerals and are the overseers of all burial sites in Thimhallan.

The *Theldara* are able to use the direct application of Life in the healing of the sick. Their knowledge of the human body is most extensive. All serious problems in physical health are treated by the *Theldara*. Their healing arts are, however, expensive in Life and occasionally time consuming.

History

Those of the Mystery of Water weave their way intimately through the history of Thimhallan. They traditionally take no sides during a war, no matter what their allegiance, but are bound to treat the dying and bury the dead of all involved. Their most desperate hours came during the Iron Wars, when there were not enough people of this Mystery to treat the seriously wounded and dying, and they despaired that the world itself was coming to an end. Yet out of this terrible time came some good, for the Healers learned a vast amount that would later enable them to save more lives.

Lives of Water

Fibanish (Druids of the Fields): Lying on his bed, Caern Ulnith tried to get the rest he so desperately needed. Yet, in his excitement, sleep would not come.

He had succeeded where they had been sure he would fail. He had brought forth fruit from what had been a wild, untamed wilderness. Yet even he'd had doubts.

When land for a new farm is to be cleared, the Druid in charge calls for the attention of all the trees and shrubs and commands them to pick up their roots and find new homes. He must deal with saplings who want to run wild. He must argue with stubborn old oaks who have been in one spot for a century and refuse to budge. He must remove the dead wood and see to it that it is taken to where it can be put to further use.

It was an exciting time, and Caern set about the task with relish, driving both himself and the catalyst assigned to him to the point of exhaustion every day. As the pines skulked away into the brush and the oak trees finally gave way to his persuasions, Caern felt his pride and satisfaction in his work increase.

After the ground had arranged itself into furrows, the Field Magi came into the field and planted. Caern watched them impatiently, anxious for the seeds to begin to sprout.

Then he had walked the fields under his care, listening to the plants, talking to them, finding out what they needed. Was the soil too acid, too wet, too dry? He had listened and reassured them, then used his own judgment. You couldn't always rely on what plants said. They tended to complain a lot during the early growing season.

In the early summer, the time for battle came—weeds began to encroach upon the fields, stealing the nutrients from the crops, attempting to take over the rich ground. Usually the Field Magi can deal efficiently with weeds, but now and then a particularly vicious enemy will attempt to take control of an entire field at once. When this happens, it is war, and the *Fihanish* march to battle with formidable weapons.

On this occasion Caern had been forced to inflict a blight on the weeds, and even then it had seemed—for a few nerve-shattering days—that the weeds might win out in the end.

At last they'd given up and retreated. Harvest came, and Caern watched with pride the stores of crops being gathered in.

He had all winter now to sleep and dream of spring.

FIHANISH (FIELD DRUIDS) PHANTASIA STATISTICS

ATTRIBUTES

Attack	41R	Defense	41R	Health	47R
Strength	46R	Dexterity	42R	Movement	5
Intelligence	41R	Intuition	46R	Senses	45R
Form	fant/human	Size	55R	Resistance	10
Renewal	100	Capacity	100	Lifewell	300

ABILITIES	TALENT	STATION	SCORE
Combat	2	1	3
Movement	5R	1	7 +
Health and Healing	10R	1	12 +
Form and Size Altering	5	1	7 +
Information	2	1	3
Life Transfer	—	—	—
Tool Crafts and Skills	1	1	2
Telepathy and Empathy	—	—	—
Illusions	5	1	6

MANNANISH (DRUIDS OF MINOR HEALING)
PHANTASIA STATISTICS

ATTRIBUTES

Attack	41R	Defense	41R	Health	47R
Strength	43R	Dexterity	45R	Movement	5
Intelligence	45R	Intuition	46R	Senses	45R
Form fant/human		Size	55R	Resistance	10
Renewal	100	Capacity	100	Lifewell	300

ABILITIES	TALENT	STATION	SCORE
Combat	2	1	3
Movement	5	1	6
Health and Healing	15R	1	17 +
Form and Size Altering	1	1	2
Information	1	1	2
Life Transfer	—	—	—
Tool Crafts and Skills	1	1	2
Telepathy and Empathy	—	—	—
Illusions	5	1	6

THELDARA (SHAMANS OF MAJOR HEALING)
PHANTASIA STATISTICS

ATTRIBUTES

Attack	41R	Defense	41R	Health	47R
Strength	41R	Dexterity	46R	Movement	5
Intelligence	47R	Intuition	45R	Senses	45R
Form fant/human		Size	55R	Resistance	10
Renewal	100	Capacity	100	Lifewell	300

ABILITIES	TALENT	STATION	SCORE
Combat	—	—	—
Movement	2	1	3
Health and Healing	25R	1	27+
Form and Size Altering	—	—	—
Information	1	1	2
Life Transfer	—	—	—
Tool Crafts and Skills	1	1	2
Telepathy and Empathy	—	—	—
Illusions	2	1	3

Cantus IV

Mystery of Air

The Shapers of the realm of Air are always thought of as practitioners of Magic. Those among their ranks are referred to as magi and archmagi.

Magi oversee the shaping of air, weather, and transportation from place to place. They are in charge of commerce in Thimhallan.

Kan-Hanar: (Air Motion/Transportation)
Sif-Hanar: (Weather Direction)

Being able to demonstrate abilities in the Mystery of Air at birth is not sufficient to enter this Mystery. Both the *Sif-Hanar* and *Kan-Hanar* require all who want to join their ranks to prove their abilities before being accepted into the Guilds. Since all legal shipments of goods in Thimhallan are arranged through the *Kan-Hanar,* being an accepted member of the Guild represents the difference between a comfortable life as a legitimate trader or the chancy life of a smuggler.

The *Kan-Hanar* maintain Guild Houses in all the cities of

Thimhallan. Here anyone of their Mystery is welcome to free food and a free place to sleep. The houses are maintained by the dues that each member must pay, amounting to five percent of any transaction. Guests of a Guildmember may also stay at the houses, provided they pay an amount equal to half the amount they would pay at the nearest hostelry.

The *Kan-Hanar* direct all shipments by air (through their associations with the Ariel), land, and sea. The only aspect of transport not directed by the *Kan-Hanar* are the Corridors. Those are controlled and maintained by the *Thon-li,* much to the regret of the Air Shapers.

High-ranking members of the *Kan-Hanar* are responsible for guarding the gates into and out of every major city in the world of Thimhallan.

The *Sif-Hanar,* those magi responsible for weather control, are a reclusive and elitist group, prone to wearing robes that flow in the gentle breezes they craft for themselves. They are also noted for their short tempers, probably because they are the one Mystery that seems to be under unceasing attack from the public. No matter what the weather is, someone is certain to complain about it. If it rains, the city dwellers complain that their holidays are ruined. If the sun shines, the farmers complain that they don't have enough rain. The *Sif-Hanar* can strike like lightning — literally — and storm on their detractors unceasingly.

The major concentration of high-ranking *Sif-Hanar* is in Merilon since the demand for their services in the great Stardome is almost continuous. *Sif-Hanar* of lower station are relegated to assisting with the raising of crops out in the field and reclaiming the Wild.

History

The knowledge and the skills of the *Sif-Hanar* were particularly useful in the new world following the Great Passage. They controlled as best they could the violent storms that swept the land and made it possible for that original small group of exiles to survive long enough to establish the Border.

During the Iron Wars the *Sif-Hanar* of the various

realms began conducting private battles among themselves, refusing to cooperate with their own military in their desire to wreak havoc upon the foe. Violent storms swept the land—cyclones, hail, lightning—all did as much or more damage than invading armies.

The *Kan-Hanar* saw their business of commerce fall apart completely during the Iron Wars. At first the magi despaired, but they soon discovered that they had skills much in demand. Since they were one of the few groups of magi to travel throughout Thimhallan, they were familiar with almost all cities and villages, and were welcome almost everywhere. The *Kan-Hanar* became invaluable as spies.

Lives of Air

Kan-Hanar (Air Motion/Transportation): Breck nervously awaited his turn to enter the gate of Sharakan. It wasn't that he particularly worried about his pass. It looked in every respect like one of the official Guild passes. Chang-ye did good work, though one paid well for it. No, it wasn't the pass. It was the waiting. Breck detested waiting for anything, and he had to remind himself—as he did every time he stood in line—of his father's teaching: the best time to enter the city is when there is a long line. The Gatekeepers will not look at you as carefully as they might otherwise.

Breck had deliberately chosen this time to enter Sharakan—in the late evening when travelers hurried to get inside the safety of city walls before nightfall. All the same, it was time wasted, standing here in line. Breck had a brief, fleeting dream of being a legitimate member of the Guild and walking into this city anytime he chose. He saw himself strolling freely into the Guild Hall. He saw himself handing over his five percent . . .

That ended the dream. He wasn't going to share his profit with anybody!

Breck moved several steps closer, pulling his floating handcart behind him. Like his parents before him, he was what is politely known as an "independent" *Kan-Hanar*. The official term was "smuggler," but Breck considered that insulting. If he chose to make his way in this world without benefit of the Guild—and without handing over five percent of his earnings—then why shouldn't he?

"State your name," said the Gatekeeper, speaking so rapidly that the words blurred together.

"Breck Drevin Sprengler," said the young man. Hat in his hand, he stood humbly before the archmagus.

"Business?"

"I am a street peddler come to show my wares in the market tomorrow."

"Pass?"

Breck handed over the forged pass—a small, round, white stone, completely smooth, with no writing on it. When the archmagus at the Gate took it in his hand, however, it began to glow a bright orange. Satisfied, he handed it back to Breck.

"What do you sell?"

Breck flushed. "Lady's undergarments," he mumbled.

"Speak up! What?" the archmagus barked.

"Lady's undergarments!" Breck shouted.

A fellow standing behind him laughed jeeringly.

"Would you like to inspect the cart?" Breck offered, casting a swift glance at the silent, black-robed *Duuk-tsarith* standing in a shadowy corner. It was impossible to see the warlock's eyes in the shadows, but the hood was facing in the direction of the man standing behind Breck—a man wearing a wooden wheel on a leather thong around his neck.

"No, that won't be necessary," growled the archmagus. "Move along."

Breck started forward, pulling the cart behind, when a "yip-yip-yip" sounded from inside the cart. The fingers of the *Duuk-tsarith* twitched. The archmagus rounded on Breck swiftly.

"Since when do lady's undergarments bark?" the Gatekeeper demanded sternly.

Cowering before the archmagus in apparent fear, Breck reluctantly pulled aside the tarp that covered his cart. Amid piles of lacy, beribboned finery, a bright-plummaged parrot skittered back and forth on a perch. "Yip-yip-yip!" cawed the bird rakishly, and made a snap at the hand of the archmagus.

"He's company for me," said Breck apologetically.

"Get a move on!" shouted the Sorcerer standing behind Breck. "It's almost nightfall!"

People standing behind him took up the grumbling chorus.

"Oh, go along!" said the archmagus irritably. "I'll be watching for you to leave, though, and you better have that bird with you. Trading in exotic animals is illegal in Sharakan."

"Oh, I wouldn't sell him!" Breck said earnestly. "He's far too valuable."

"A parrot that barks like a dog!" The archmagus sneered, and waved the young man through the gate.

Tugging the cart behind him, Breck entered the city, moving neither too fast nor too slow—just as his father had taught him. He sneaked a peek at the Black Robe, but the *Duuk-tsarith*'s attention was completely focused on the Sorcerer trying to enter behind Breck.

The Gatekeeper refused him admittance. The Sorcerer began to argue vehemently. Grinning, Breck disappeared into the crowd, pulling his cart behind. He and his partner— the Sorcerer—would meet later to split the money.

Ducking into an alleyway, Breck brought his cart to a stop and lifted the tarp. The illusion of dainty clothing vanished. Curled up on a pile of rags, three Hunterkill puppies blinked in the sudden light and begin yipping frantically—a sound that caused the parrot on the perch to join in.

Scratching the puppies on their ugly heads, keeping his fingers carefully away from the slashing teeth, Breck lifted the parrot to his shoulder, drew the tarp over the cart, and set off for the Thieves Guild to make his sale of the illegal assassin-dogs.

Sif-Hanar (Weather Direction): The Duke of Millan greeted his two visitors in the morning room of his Estate. A mild man who had inherited this property from his father and been told to do something with it by his King, the Duke would have much preferred a quieter life—something in the Shaper line perhaps. But he had been born *Albanara*. Today he confronted two *Sif-Hanar*, who were making it clear that they considered this all far beneath them.

"Yes, my lord, if we could just get on with this," said one *Sif-Hanar* briskly, cutting the Duke off in his long-winded apology. "What seems to be the problem?"

"It's the rain," said the Duke.

"Too much," pronounced the *Sif-Hanar*.

"Er . . . no . . . not enough." The Duke seemed highly embarrassed at contradicting his important visitor.

"Are you certain?" The *Sif-Hanar* frowned; his partner shook her head.

"Yes," the Duke said, flushing. "I'm sorry, but the crops . . . er . . . they're turning brown and—"

"What type of rain did you have in mind?"

"Just . . . rain," said the Duke helplessly.

The *Sif-Hanar* and his partner exchanged long-suffering glances. "Gentle rain, moderate rain, driving rain, rain mixed with snow, sleet and rain, thunderstorms . . ."

"I-I don't know," stammered the Duke.

"How about a sample?" said the second *Sif-Hanar*. At her gesture, gentle of drops began falling on the Duke's bald head.

"That's . . . that's fine!" said the Duke.

"Now then, how long? Day and a night? One week? Can't be over the weekend," said the first *Sif-Hanar*, consulting a small book. "Your neighbor's daughter's getting married. They've asked for a sunny day in the 70s, with a mild south wind and picturesque puffy clouds."

"A week, I suppose, said the Duke, wiping his face with a handkerchief.

The *Sif-Hanar* gravely recorded it. "It will start in exactly one hour, so close you windows. We'll be by each morning to collect the amount of Life you owe." He raised a warning finger. "No Life, no rain. Farewell, my Lord."

"Good day," said the Duke politely.

The *Sif-Hanar* raised an eyebrow. "That depends entirely on *us* now, doesn't it, my Lord?"

KAN-HANAR (MAGIC)
PHANTASIA STATISTICS

ATTRIBUTES

Attack	42R	Defense	52R	Health	42R
Strength	47R	Dexterity	49R	Movement	5

Intelligence	48R	Intuition	42R	Senses	45R
Form	fant/human	Size	55R	Resistance	10
Renewal	100	Capacity	100	Lifewell	300

ABILITIES	TALENT	STATION	SCORE
Combat	5	1	6
Movement	15R	1	17+
Health and Healing	2	1	3
Form and Size Altering	1	1	2
Information	—	—	—
Life Transfer	—	—	—
Tool Crafts and Skills	3	1	4
Telepathy and Empathy	—	—	—
Illusions	5	1	6

SIF-HANAR (WEATHER MASTERS)
PHANTASIA STATISTICS

ATTRIBUTES

Attack	42R	Defense	52R	Health	42R
Strength	47R	Dexterity	49R	Movement	5
Intelligence	48R	Intuition	42R	Senses	45R
Form	fant/human	Size	55R	Resistance	10
Renewal	100	Capacity	100	Lifewell	300

ABILITIES	TALENT	STATION	SCORE
Combat	2	1	3
Movement	5R	1	7+
Health and Healing	1	1	2
Form and Size Altering	25/10[1]	1	27+/11
Information	3	1	4
Life Transfer	—	—	—
Tool Crafts and Skills	1	1	2
Telepathy and Empathy	—	—	—
Illusions	5	1	6

[1]The number before the slash indicates the character's talent concerning any Wizardry related to weather or atmospheric conditions. Any other wizardry uses the number after the slash.

Cantus V

Mystery of Life

The magi have always used catalysts—those people born to the Mystery of Life. Although not able to use much magic themselves, catalysts possess the ability to draw magic from the world around them, focus it within themselves, then extend that magic to their wizards. In ancient times, before the Great Passage, many catalysts were known as Familiars. In that dangerous world, where magi were often persecuted, the powerful wizards disguised the weaker catalysts as animals. Thus the catalysts could be protected from harm, and the magi could more easily carry their catalysts with them.

After the Great Passage such measures were no longer needed and the practice was discontinued.

The Divisions of Catalysts: Following the Second Rectification, the last two orders were united.

Thon-li: (Conduit Masters; the Gifters)
Daran-li: (Enlighteners; Enhancer)
Sharak-li: (Directors; Knowledge of Life use)

History

Before the Great Passage catalysts possessed little power and wielded little control over Life. Unorganized and weak in magic, they worked generally on a one-on-one basis with their individual magi.

The arrival in Thimhallan changed that, however. Immediately on entering the new world, they felt themselves suffused with Life. Led by one of the greatest of their Order, a Bishop Carli, the catalysts realized that here was their chance at last to acquire ascendancy over the people and, hopefully, guide them toward a better life.

It was Carli who discovered that—while the magi could absorb some Life from the world—the catalysts now had the ability to greatly enhance the magi's natural Life through means of the Conduit. Carli convinced the Council of Nine that it was in the best interests of the world for the catalysts to guard the Well of Life. The Church's power began from that time and has grown steadily since.

Part of the reason for this growth is that the catalysts—much like the *Duuk-tsarith*—owe their allegiance first (ostensibly) to the Almin and second to those who might claim their allegiance. When the various races and factions of magi split up and went their separate ways, the catalysts who went with them remained—more or less—a unified force. All catalysts, no matter where they were born, were required to spend years in study at the Font. Here they dedicate their lives to the Almin, not to man.

Had the catalysts been stronger at the time, the Iron Wars might have been prevented. Unfortunately a series of Bishops whose minds were more on heaven than the world below ruled the Church just prior to and during the Iron Wars. Instead of forcing the warring rulers to come to peaceful terms by such means as excommunication (shutting off their source of Life), Bishop Philinous III wrung his hands and prayed to the Almin to stop the war. Catalysts who looked to the Church to unite them found no one home and so were drawn into the Iron Wars in desperate efforts to save themselves and their people.

It was Philinous III who undertook to see into the future, giving out the Prophecy just before he died.

Succeeding him was a strong-minded man known as John of Avidon. As a Cardinal, John had seen clearly the weakness of the Church and how detrimental that weakness was to the world. He took firm control, and it was under his leadership that the Second Rectification began.

John of Avidon immediately abolished two of the three Orders, unifying the Church. He ordered the catalysts to salvage what they could of the now extinct Mysteries of Time and Spirit. Bishop John was also responsible for the banishment of the Ninth Mystery. By laying the blame for the war on the Sorcerers, John was able to wipe out any lingering vestiges of hostility between realms. "You were all duped by the Sorcerers," he told the people. "You have no quarrels with each other anymore. Your only quarrel is with them—the evil Technologists who brought us to ruin."

In this, John gained the help and support of the *Duuk-tsarith*, who saw that by making the Church the power in the land and using their own might to back it, they could come close to fulfilling Merlyn's Dream.

Bishop John introduced the monetary standard to Thimhallan, thereby putting the Church in control of the economics of the land.

Finally, by Bishop John's direction, the Font was enlarged and made to symbolize the new power in the land. Catalysts were strengthened in their allegiance to the Almin—or rather to the Church. Their power and might have grown down to the present time.

The revolt of catalysts in Sharakan came as a bitter blow to the Church. Led by a wise, intelligent, and benevolent man named Radisovik, the catalysts in Sharakan renounced the Church's involvement in politics. They advocated, among other things, the free dispensing of Life to anyone who asked for it and the need to bring Technology back into the world.

THON-LI (CONDUIT MASTERS)
PHANTASIA STATISTICS

ATTRIBUTES[1]

Attack	41R	Defense	41R	Health	47R
Strength	45R	Dexterity	46R	Movement	5
Intelligence	52R	Intuition	45R	Senses	46R
Form	human	Size	55R	Resistance	10
Renewal	100	Capacity	100	Lifewell	300

ABILITIES	TALENT	STATION	SCORE
Combat	—	—	—
Movement	—	—	—
Health and Healing	—	—	—
Form and Size Altering	—	—	—
Information	—	—	—
Life Transfer	$25/10^2$	1	$27 + /11$
Tool Crafts and Skills	1	1	2
Telepathy and Empathy	—	—	—
Illusions	5	1	6

[1]Unlike other character classes, a catalyst's Renewal, Capacity and Lifewell do not change as the character gains stations but, rather, remain the same as listed. Only the catalyst's Resistance score increases with station.

[2]The score before the slash indicates the character's talent when opening corridors. The score after the slash indicates the character's talent for other aspects of the catalyst mystery.

DARAN-LI (ENLIGHTENERS)
PHANTASIA STATISTICS

ATTRIBUTES

Attack	41R	Defense	41R	Health	42R
Strength	43R	Dexterity	46R	Movement	5
Intelligence	54R	Intuition	55R	Senses	42R
Form	human	Size	55R	Resistance	10
Renewal	100	Capacity	100	Lifewell	300

ABILITIES	TALENT	STATION	SCORE
Combat	—	—	—
Movement	—	—	—
Health and Healing	—	—	—

ABILITIES	TALENT	STATION	SCORE
Form and Size Altering	—	—	—
Information	10R	1	12 +
Life Transfer	10R	1	12 +
Tool Crafts and Skills	—	—	—
Telepathy and Empathy	10R	1	12 +
Illusions	10R	1	12 +

SHARAK-LI (DIRECTORS)
PHANTASIA STATISTICS

ATTRIBUTES

Attack	41R	Defense	41R	Health	47R
Strength	45R	Dexterity	46R	Movement	5
Intelligence	52R	Intuition	45R	Senses	46R
Form	human	Size	55R	Resistance	10
Renewal	100	Capacity	100	Lifewell	300

ABILITIES	TALENT	STATION	SCORE
Combat	—	—	—
Movement	—	—	—
Health and Healing	—	—	—
Form and Size Altering	—	—	—
Information	—	—	—
Life Transfer	30R	1	32 +
Tool Crafts and Skills	—	—	—
Telepathy and Empathy	—	—	—
Illusions	—	—	—

Lives of Life

The Life of Catalysts: The training of catalysts begins in their youth. Like those of the Order of *Duuk-tsarith,* a catalyst pledges his or her life to the Church. Unlike the *Duuk-tsarith,* this is seen as a great blessing to any family fortunate enough to have a child blessed with the Mystery of Life. The catalyst is not only raised and educated at the expense of the Church but is almost always (unless he falls out of favor) guaranteed to be able to support not only himself but his family.

The sign of a catalyst is the shoe. Since all magi on Thimhallan have the ability to travel the winds through the power of Life, they rarely walk on the ground and therefore have no need to protect their feet from anything other than cold.

The catalyst, however, has little Life of his own. His function and natural ability is to grant Life to others. Traditionally he has been portrayed as a selfless individual, sacrificing his own needs to the needs of the people. "The catalyst walks humbly on the ground that others may fly" is a homily taught to children. Catalysts do have the ability to open and walk the Corridors that are now maintained by those of their Order, but otherwise, when a catalyst wants to get somewhere, he walks it on his own two feet.

A catalyst's position within the Order is known by the color of his or her robes.

Color of Robes

Trim Color	Green	Red	White
None	Field (Deacon)	House (Father)	Font (Seminarian)
Grey	Font (Novitiate)	Font (Deacon)	Font (Deacon)
White	Font (Deacon)	Font (Undermaster)	— —
Silver	City (Priest)	House (Lord Father)	Realm (Cardinal)
Gold & Silver	Region (Bishop)	Realm (Bishop)	Master (Lord Bishop)

At age six a catalyst is assigned to a local catalyst for training. Most are taken to schools established within the realms for this purpose. Here the young catalysts live apart from their families, learning early on to dedicate their lives to the Church. During these years the basics of mathematics are taught to the child in the form of games and puzzles. By the time the children reach the age of fifteen, they begin their more advanced training and testing, which may include work at the universities or the Guilds, depending upon their specialties. At the age of twenty-one all catalysts travel to the Font for three more years of training before their assignment into the world. They enter as a Novitiate, attaining the station of Acolyte with the successful conclusion of three years of study. At this time they are either sent out into the world or are invited to stay in the Font for additional study.[1]

Assignments for catalysts vary. Those who show exceptional abilities are retained at the Font as instructors or to study advanced mathematics and other areas designed to enhance the general understanding of the catalyst's art. These fortunate ones are those most likely to be promoted to higher offices within the Church.

The unfortunate catalysts are those sent out to work as Field Catalysts. This particular duty generally means the catalyst has committed some minor infraction, although there *are* catalysts who enjoy life outdoors and occasionally request this assignment.

Catalysts may be taken into the homes of the wealthy nobles and the upper-middle classes. Here they devote themselves to serving the family, granting Life, conducting religious services, and assisting in the education of the children. Catalysts are also assigned to work with the Guilds and universities, or they may be sent to the abbeys and cathedrals located throughout the realm to conduct the Church's business on a local basis.

Catalysts joining the Order of Thon-li are sent to work within the Corridors.

Life of a Font Seminary Catalyst: The Deacon rises in the early hours of the morning. After gathering with his brethren for the Ritual of Dawn, he hurries off to his first class of the day—the Theorum.

Taught in the seminary of Talesin, the Theorum provides the Deacon with the theory and abstracts of the catalyst trade. He learns ancient and living languages, classical formulati, history, astrology, social sciences, and advanced mathematics. The basis of his life, this class lasts until the Highhours.

At the beginning of the Highhours the Spiritum begins. The Deacon enjoys this as a break from the studies of the

[1]There are those catalysts who, at this stage, disappear. No one knows what happens to them, but it is presumed that they are taken to The Mountain where they work with the *Duuk-tsarith*.

morning. During the Spiritum the students explore Life as it relates to all the Mysteries (with the exception of those lost or banned). Sports are also encouraged during this time as a necessary element in maintaining the body as well as the soul.

Following this is a free time during which the catalyst is encouraged to meditate and reflect. Bells call him to chapel, where he is taught the doctrines of the Almin.

The Highhours conclude and the Falling Hours begin.

This begins the Practicum. The Deacon hastens through the Font, arriving at last at the entrance to the Labyrinth. Here, in these tunnels, a maze of Illusionary sequences provide the catalyst with practical problems that apply to the theories learned during the Theorum portion of the day.

CATALYSTS
PHANTASIA STATISTICS

ATTRIBUTES

Attack	41R	Defense	41R	Health	47R
Strength	42R	Dexterity	51R	Movement	5
Intelligence	51R	Intuition	48R	Senses	45R
Form	human	Size	55R	Resistance	10
Renewal	100	Capacity	100	Lifewell	300

ABILITIES	TALENT	STATION	SCORE
Combat	—	—	—
Movement	—	—	—
Health and Healing	—	—	—
Form and Size Altering	—	—	—
Information	5R	1	7+
Life Transfer	10R	1	12+
Tool Crafts and Skills	1	1	2
Telepathy and Empathy	5R	1	7+
Illusions	5	1	6

Cantus VI

Mystery of Shadow

The Illusionists of this world are of the Mystery of Shadow. Everything that exists in Thimhallan and a thousand things that do not may be reproduced or created by Illusion. There are no subclasses in this Mystery, since Illusionists find their talent within themselves. Artists and musicians are almost universally of this class. Illusionists are also used as instructors for children and to aid in the training of catalysts and warlocks.

History

Since their art is transitory and fleeting in nature, Illusionist contributions to history tend to be those of an impractical nature designed to benefit the soul more than the body. After the Great Passage, Illusionists went off with their separate races and factions during the early years of Thimhallan. Since Illusionists were always in search of new and different ways of expressing their art, however, they did not isolate themselves away from the rest of the world, but wandered it freely. Their allegiance is and has always been to Art.

During the Iron Wars, Illusionists and their skills were in great demand by the *DKarn-đuuk*, who used them to confuse and frighten the enemy. Many of the Illusionists were opposed to the Wars, however, and refused outright to fight. They were ridiculed, imprisoned, and in some cases tortured for holding to their pacifist beliefs.

Lives of Shadow

For further information on the lifestyles of Illusionists, we recommend the Merilon section of *Doom of the Darksword*, volume two of the Darksword Trilogy, and the opening preface to this book.

ILLUSIONISTS (SHADOW SHAPERS)
PHANTASIA STATISTICS

ATTRIBUTES

Attack	43R	Defense	48R	Health	42R
Strength	44R	Dexterity	53R	Movement	5
Intelligence	52R	Intuition	48R	Senses	55R
Form	human	Size	55R	Resistance	10
Renewal	100	Capacity	100	Lifewell	300

ABILITIES	TALENT	STATION	SCORE
Combat	—	—	—
Movement	5	1	6
Health and Healing	—	—	—
Form and Size Altering	1R	1	3 +
Information	1	1	2
Life Transfer	—	—	—
Tool Crafts and Skills	2	1	3
Telepathy and Empathy	5R	1	7 +
Illusions	20R	1	22 +

Cantus VII

Mystery of Time

Those who practiced this Mystery were called Diviners and they were the rarest of all the magi, there being only a few born each year in the entire population with this gift. While some of their knowledge survives with the catalysts—in particular the ability to foresee whether or not the union of two people will be fruitful—the majority of the Diviners' powers perished with their passing during the Iron Wars. Today, if there are any on Thimhallan who can foretell the future or look back into the past, they hide themselves well.

History

Despite being few in number, the Diviners were powerful in the forging of the new world. This, perhaps, is what led to their downfall.

Possessing the ability to see forward in time as well as backward, the Diviners were said to be closest to seeing the Mind of the Almin. They did not see the future as one long path stretching out before mankind, but as a series of paths. Using their knowledge of the paths, they were able to recommend the correct path for man to walk. Whether man chose to walk it was up to him.

The Diviners warned against the separation of the factions that they saw must lead, eventually, to the Iron Wars. Few paid heed to their words, or, if they did, they maintained that they alone knew the right way to save the world.

Since the Diviners were so few in number, it is not surprising that their Mystery was completely wiped out during the wars. A child of that Mystery must have a Diviner for a parent, and so it is generally believed that no children with this talent have been born since.

DIVINERS
PHANTASIA STATISTICS

ATTRIBUTES

Attack	41R	Defense	39R	Health	38R
Strength	42R	Dexterity	42R	Movement	5
Intelligence	55R	Intuition	58R	Senses	55R
Form	human	Size	55R	Resistance	10
Renewal	100	Capacity	100	Lifewell	300

ABILITIES	TALENT	STATION	SCORE
Combat	—	—	—
Movement	—	—	—
Health and Healing	—	—	—
Form and Size Altering	—	—	—
Information	25R	1	27+
Life Transfer	—	—	—
Tool Crafts and Skills	—	—	—
Telepathy and Empathy	5R	1	7+
Illusions	10R	1	12+

Cantus VIII

Mystery of Spirit

This Mystery, too, perished during the Iron Wars, although under much more sinister circumstances than that of the Diviners. Those of the Mystery of Spirit were responsible for communication with the realms beyond the mortal boundary. They were divided into three classes:

Aluava: (Necromancers) These dealt with communicating directly with those who had passed before.

Cheuava: (Enchanters) Those responsible for the spiritual health and well-being of the dead as it affected the living.

Omueva: (Theurgists) Direct intervention with the Almin was the province of the Theurgists.

History

Living on two planes at the same time, the Necromancers (as they were generally known) were able to bring the living and the dead into close touch. They could ease troubled spirits, help assuage the grief of the living by maintaining contact with those who died, and help the dead keep in touch with their survivors. Through the Necromancer, mankind could easily come to terms with his own mortality.

The Necromancers were also able to provide glimpses into the future of individuals as it came to be known by their ancestors, who would then communicate this through the Necromancers. Although not as accurate a vision of the future as that obtained by the Diviners, this tended to be much more personal in nature and so was very popular.

Because of this popularity, the Necromancers began to wield great power over not only the general populace but over their rulers as well. No one viewed this with less liking than the Church, who saw its own influence beginning to wane in consequence.

Whether the Church, with the *Duuk-tsarith* as their instrument, had a hand in removing the Necromancers from the world is not known. Certainly it was greatly to the Church's benefit that the Spirit Shapers disappeared.

ALUAVA (NECROMANCERS)
PHANTASIA STATISTICS

ATTRIBUTES

Attack	43R	Defense	42R	Health	46R
Strength	42R	Dexterity	47R	Movement	5
Intelligence	45R	Intuition	52R	Senses	43R
Form	human	Size	55R	Resistance	10
Renewal	100	Capacity	100	Lifewell	300

ABILITIES	TALENT	STATION	SCORE
Combat	—	—	—
Movement	5	1	6
Health and Healing	—	—	—
Form and Size Altering	—	—	—
Information	5R	1	7+
Life Transfer	—	—	—
Tool Crafts and Skills	—	—	—
Telepathy and Empathy	25R/10[1]	1	27+/11
Illusions	5R	1	7+

[1]The number before the slash indicates the talent of the character when attempting telepathy or empathy with the dead. The number after the slash indicates the talent for all other types of Telepathy & Empathy.

CHEUAVA (ENCHANTERS)
PHANTASIA STATISTICS

ATTRIBUTES

Attack	43R	Defense	42R	Health	46R
Strength	42R	Dexterity	47R	Movement	5
Intelligence	45R	Intuition	52R	Senses	43R
Form	human	Size	55R	Resistance	10
Renewal	100	Capacity	100	Lifewell	300

ABILITIES	TALENT	STATION	SCORE
Combat	—	—	—
Movement	11	1	12
Health and Healing	—	—	—
Form and Size Altering	—	—	—
Information	—	—	—
Life Transfer	—	—	—
Tool Crafts and Skills	—	—	—
Telepathy and Empathy	20R/10[1]	1	27+/11
Illusions	5R	1	7+

[1]The number before the slash indicates the talent of the character when attempting to create a magical ability to alter the thoughts and desires of another creature. The number after the slash is used in connection with all other spells of this mystery.

OMUEVA (THEURGISTS)
PHANTASIA STATISTICS

ATTRIBUTES

Attack	42R	Defense	41R	Health	48R
Strength	43R	Dexterity	45R	Movement	5
Intelligence	45R	Intuition	52R	Senses	48R
Form	human	Size	55R	Resistance	10
Renewal	100	Capacity	100	Lifewell	300

ABILITIES	TALENT	STATION	SCORE
Combat	—	—	—
Movement	11	1	12
Health and Healing	—	—	—
Form and Size Altering	—	—	—
Information	15R	1	17+

ABILITIES	TALENT	STATION	SCORE
Life Transfer	—	—	—
Tool Crafts and Skills	—	—	—
Telepathy and Empathy	15R	1	17+
Illusions	5R	1	7+

Cantus IX

Mystery of Death

Those of the Ninth Mystery, the Forbidden Mystery, are called Sorcerers and Technologists. Each of these terms is thought of as being synonymous and interchangeable; both are now considered degrading.

The major divisions of the Death Shapers are as follows:

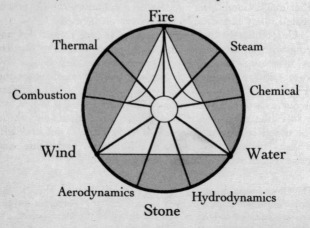

These classifications are used as general reference points for various individual studies. Note that missing from these divisions are medical sciences. This is primarily due to the fact that Life Shaping was traditionally and adequately handled by the Druids, thus technology missed its application to this field altogether. Following the Iron Wars, however, the Sorcerers were forced to develop skills in medicine in order to survive. Advances in this area were classified as a subcategory of Fire and Water.

History

The Shapers of Death or Technology came to this world with the other magi in the Great Passage. According to what the Church would have you believe, this class of magic has always belonged exclusively to the provinces of evil. However, that was not always so. In the old world, those of the Ninth Mystery were the scientists and tinkerers of their trade. It was they who fashioned the magical devices such as wands, golems, and swords.

Legend holds that the Border surrounding and protecting Thimhallan was fashioned by the Sorcerers of that time, although Church text tries strenuously to discount what they term a myth. After the First Rectification the power of the Technologist branches grew far beyond the powers of the other magi. Combining magic with mechanics, the Sorcerers created many remarkable and powerful devices.

Unfortunately the wisdom to utilize this power did not grow with equal speed. During the Iron Wars the Sorcerers' inventions took the form of engines of destruction. By Wars' end the people—refusing to blame themselves for the terrible destruction—blamed the Sorcerers. The catalysts encouraged this belief and used it to help unite a world left in shambles. The Ninth Mystery was banished, and those who practiced it were persecuted, hunted down, put to death, or sent Beyond. Everything the Sorcerers had made was destroyed, as were all their writings and books.[1]

---

[1]The Church first made copies of these texts, keeping them in the Font. Additional copies as well as many of the Sorcerers' inventions are believed hidden in The Mountain of the *Duuk-tsarith*.

Lives of Death

For a complete description of life in a Sorcerer's village, please refer to *Forging the Darksword*, volume one in the Darksword Trilogy.

All the homes in a Sorcerer's village are arranged according to the divisions of the Wheel. In the center—at the Wheel's hub—is a central plaza. Here stands an arch made of black stone. Hanging from the arch is a huge gong.

Radiating out from the central plaza are three paved roads that lead directly to the Temples of Wind, Water, and Fire. Along these roads may be found windmills, waterwheels, reservoirs and aqueducts, and, most prominent, the forge.

The rest of the community is arranged around the hub in concentric circles. First are found the various shops of the community, each according to its place in the Wheel. Beyond these are warehouses, and then, lastly, the living quarters. On the outside circle of the community is a defensive perimeter where a variety of mechanical traps and other mechanisms secure the village from unwanted intrusion.

The Scianc: This is the weekly ritual of dance and song (pronounced alternatively SEE-ans or SEE-ank) that recites the learning and sciences of the Coven of the Wheel. The Scianc came about when the Sorcerers, forced into hiding in the Outland, realized that they needed some way to hand down what they had learned to future generations. They had books, but because of their struggles just to survive, they were unable to take the time to teach their children how to read and understand them. They put what they knew into song, therefore, and chanted it each evening so that their children would learn it and remember. The children learned the song but unfortunately lost the key to its translation.

The entire coven gathers together at the hub of the community where the roads of Fire, Air, and Water converge. The dance begins in a slow chant and then builds to the accompaniment of drums and various other crafted instruments into a wild, chaotic litany of knowledge. By the culmination of the chorus, the song reaches an almost hysterical frenzy. To a catalyst or any other magi this song would seem to come from the depths of Hell.

SORCERERS (TECHNOLOGISTS)
PHANTASIA STATISTICS

ATTRIBUTES

Attack	49R	Defense	49R	Health	52R
Strength	53R	Dexterity	49R	Movement	5
Intelligence	42R	Intuition	47R	Senses	45R
Form	human	Size	55R	Resistance	10
Renewal	100	Capacity	100	Lifewell	300

ABILITIES	TALENT	STATION	SCORE
Combat	3	1	4
Movement	2	1	3
Health and Healing	1	1	2
Form and Size Altering	5R	1	7+
Information	—	—	—
Life Transfer	—	—	—
Tool Crafts and Skills	15R	1	17+
Telepathy and Empathy	—	—	—
Illusions	5	1	6

[1]These abilities are for typical Sorcerers who may not be Dead to the ways of magic. There arose in the final days of Thimhallan those who were truly Dead. For characters of this type, list zeros for Renewal, Capacity and Lifewell and figure the Resistance Attribute as "20R". Such characters will not have any of the listed abilities except for Tool Crafts & Skills as listed. Dead characters *never* increase their Life Attributes as a result of character advancement. As a Bishop in the Church of Life, I strongly urge you not to trifle with characters that are devoid of all magic.

Postludium

Mannara blinked and opened his eyes. The motion of
the world had ceased. Once more he stood upon the
hill from where he and Merlyn had started their journey.

"King and Ruler of Many, did you find understanding
in what you have seen this day?"

"Yes, Master, I see that all are indeed part of a great
circle. But alas, I see that the circle has been broken, much
to our detriment. Will the circle ever again be one?"

"That, my son, could be answered only by a Diviner."

The Nine Mysteries

> EARTH: (The Foundation; Craftsmen)
> AIR: (The Transporters and Weather Crafters)
> WATER: (Plant and Animal Life; Healers)
> FIRE: (Warriors; Enforcers)
> SPIRIT: (Spiritual Life)
> TIME: (History and Prophecy)
> SHADOW: (Illusion)
> LIFE: (Catalysts)
> DEATH: (Technology)

Part V

Phantasia

What Is Phantasia?

Phantasia is a game that allows you and your friends to experience the world of Thimhallan.

We have all played "Dugruns and *DKarn-ðuuk*" as children. Choosing up sides, we'd skulk about the House Gardens casting imaginary Fireblossoms (if we were pretending to be the Warriors) or wielding imaginary clubs (if we were pretending to be the dugruns). We chose a section of garden and defended it mightily until the House Catalyst came out to drag us back inside to study.

No one ever really won or lost the game. The purpose was just to have fun, and when we were finally able to escape those long, boring sessions on the theory of Life, we were out into the garden again, hiding behind plants that in our own minds had magically become the dark forests of the Outland.

That we can still remember those times so clearly tells us how important they were to us—and perhaps, how much we learned from them. We didn't know it at the time, but we were learning how to interact with each other in our "make-believe" world.

Eventually we grew up and began watching other people do our pretending for us. The artists in Merilon's Performance Grove can be seen each night giving their interpretation of the latest play. We enjoy them and wistfully long to be up there again pretending—just for a little while—that we are a princess, an emperor, or one of the powerful *Duuk-tsarith*.

Phantasia is a lot like playing "Dugruns and *DKarn-duuk*" because you get to pretend that you are someone else. This time, though, there won't be any arguments about "my spell worked and yours didn't" because the rules of Phantasia solve that for you impartially.

Phantasia is also very similar to being in a play, but with an important difference—it is a play whose plot you create with your own actions. One person—the Gamejudge—will provide the sets, the extras, and other necessities, but it will be the players themselves who will determine the outcome.

Phantasia is important in another sense: the Adventure takes place in your mind. You can battle centaurs without ever leaving your chair. You can cast the powerful spells of the *Duuk-tsarith* without ever using one drop of Life. You can learn from your experiences—suffer the consequences of your own poor choices or thrill to your triumphs—without risking your life.

And most important still—you get to share these experiences with friends.

How the Game Is Played

To play Phantasia you need a group of people comfortably seated, pencils and paper, and this book. One person in the group is designated the *Gamejudge*. This person prepares the Adventure and referees the game. All other participants become *Player Characters* (PCs), taking the role of make-believe individuals in the game.

The following is a summary of game play.

1. Preparation for Play

The Gamejudge prepares the *Adventure*.

An *Adventure* is the skeleton "plot"—a set of guidelines outlining various aspects of the story in which the players of the game will participate. The Adventure includes such things as maps of the various areas the players will explore, descriptions of what the players might feel, smell, touch, hear, or see, as well as Phantasia ratings for the player's various attributes and abilities. *Extras*—called *Nonplayer Characters* (NPCs)—are characters who are controlled by the Gamejudge. Determining which NPCs the players will encounter is part of designing the Adventure. Goals and objectives of the Adventure—if any—are also included at this stage of development.

The Adventure is written and designed by the Gamejudge. This can be a simple task or an involved process depending upon how detailed and interesting an Adventure the Gamejudge has in mind.

2. The Play of the Game

It is here that the Player Character and the Gamejudge come together to create the course of the tale.

The words of the Gamejudge create—in the PC's imagination—the sets, costumes, props, and supporting cast of the play. He also provides the basic plot of the tale by describing the setting in the beginning. Although the Gamejudge may have some idea of the direction he or she wants the plot to take, the Gamejudge should try to allow the PCs as much freedom as possible in determining the outcome of the Adventure.

When the Adventure begins, the PC takes on the role of his character, speaking his words and describing his actions. Through his actions the PC travels the make-believe world of the Adventure in an effort to reach—when present—the goal of the game. Occasionally just the experience of the play is enjoyable, and thus goals are not always necessary.

3. Conclusion of the Game

The end of the game comes when the goal of the Adventure has been reached or—in the instance of a complex Adventure—whenever everyone feels that it is time to quit for the day. The game may always be continued in subsequent sessions. If there is no conclusion or goal stated in the game, then play may continue on indefinitely as the players find other realms to explore.

At the Conclusion the Gamejudge gives *Experience Awards* to each PC (if these awards have not been given during the course of the game).

Each of these three parts of the game are now explored in greater detail.

Preparation for Play

Gamejudge Preparation

Phantasia is an easy game to teach to others because it does not require that the Players have any knowledge of the rules in order to have their PCs participate in the game. It does require, however, that the Gamejudge be knowledgeable regarding the rules and fully prepared with an Adventure. For this reason the Gamejudge preparation for a game is extremely important.

Knowledge of the Rules

Players may direct their characters through an entire game of Phantasia without ever really understanding how the rules work or how the results are determined except in general terms.

This requires, therefore, that the Gamejudge be familiar enough with the rules to be able to handle all the requirements of the game. This is the province of the Gamejudge, who will be the final arbiter in everything that takes place in the course of the game. A Gamejudge who knows the rules of Phantasia is essential in providing an enjoyable game.

1. It is less important to KNOW the rule than it is to know WHERE the rule is located in the book.

2. Knowing WHERE the rule is in the book is less important than making sure the game is being enjoyed by the Players! If you find yourself spending too much time looking for a rule while your Players are sitting around yawning, you should use your general knowledge of the rules, give it your best shot, and let the game continue.

Designing the Adventure

Where do ideas for Adventures come from? They come from your own dreams and hopes, fears and nightmares.

They come from within you. They come from outside you. They are all around you!

Before the Players assemble for the game, it is the Gamejudge's responsibility to create the Adventure to be played. The Adventure is the key to an exciting game—the better prepared an Adventure, the more enjoyable it will be for your Players. You cannot be *too* prepared!

But where do you start? Often it's difficult just to sit down and think up a wonderful story filled with villains and monsters to challenge your heroes and heroines. How do you make up a setting for the Players to act in?

The following ideas are by no means the only way to go about creating an Adventure, but they should give you a start.

1. The Story
All good Adventures begin with a story. The story can be as simple as the finding of a lost golden ring to as vast as all the history of Thimhallan.

The story for an Adventure does not dictate to the Players what is going to happen to them. Instead it indicates (1) what has gone on before they arrived, and (2) what is going on *around* them currently. The story should then pose a problem that the character can try to solve. The story may indicate possible solutions to the problem, but a good Gamejudge will use the story as a guideline for what *may* happen in his Adventure without restricting the Players' freedom to choose their own course of action.

Where do you get ideas for a story? Our own history of Thimhallan provides you with many hints that might fire your imagination. What lurks in the sealed-off areas of the Font? What wonders might be found in the ruins of Trandar? What mysteries await PCs in the dark Towers of the Lost Kingdoms? Is there a band of adventurers hardy enough to go into the Outland in search of a weed for which the Empress of Merilon is offering 600,000 Glindars? Any of these might prove a good basis for a tale.

2. The Setting
Once you have in mind the general story you wish to tell, it is time to set the stage.

Maps are an excellent place to start working out your design. Maps take the abstract visions of your mind and make them more concrete. Map out the areas where you think that the Players may go during their Adventure. This may be one map of a room in a castle, the castle itself, or a series of maps of the castle and the countryside around it done in various scales. You may use the maps we have included in this book or design your own or a combination of both.

Map out the entire complex where the Players will adventure and label the individual areas, just as we have done with the maps in this book.

3. Filling the Adventure

Note on a separate piece of paper all of the different labels of areas you have put on the map. It is time to start filling the Adventure with challenges and rewards for your Players.

The easiest place to start is with the Treasures. These can be anything that the Players will find during the Adventure. If a Treasure is the objective of the game, then place it now in the section you consider to be the heart of the game. Make certain it is well-guarded and not too easy to reach. After you have placed all the treasures, note down on your paper their locations, their value, and any other information.

Traps come next. Doors that bite, illusionary floors, fireballs crisscrossing a hallway—all of these are traps. Generally your traps should be designed with some sort of logic behind them, and there should always be some way of disarming a trap. Traps should allow thinking Players to use their minds in overcoming the obstacle. Note the location of the trap and any descriptive information on the paper.

Monster NPCs follow. You will need to take care to populate the Adventure with NPC monsters that are of roughly equal or somewhat weaker nature than the PCs who will be adventuring there. Note on the parchment any statistics for these monsters as well as any special habits or other considerations that will have a bearing on how the monster behaves and attacks.

Finally, you should place any special NPCs who have specific information about the Adventure as well as any clues that might be discovered upon the way. These should help advance the basic story line.

4. Polishing the Game

Finally, you need to polish what you have designed. This may come in the form of creating set pieces for the game (generally miniature in size) that can be used for special scenes in the game.

Actual props can often liven up the game and be important clue pieces as well. For example, make up a scroll with a crudely scrawled map on it, and rather than describe the map in the game, allow one of the PCs to "find" it.

Starting the Game

Starting a game can be as simple as beginning a story.

"Once there was a queen in the city of Trandar during the terrible time of the Iron Wars. Her name was Amy the Stouthearted, and she was known far and wide for her courage. Often she walked the battlements, bolstering the morale of her troops. Then one day she received a scroll. Upon reading its words, she fled into the highest tower in the castle of Trandar. Shutting the door, she bolted it behind her. She spoke to no one after that, and in time her generals were defeated and the country brought to ruin. There are those who say that she remains in that tower today. You stand on the outskirts of that fabled ruin—"

If you have Players who have not participated in the game before, a good way to get them instantly participating is with combat.

"You stand on the edge of the ruins of Trandar. In the distance you see the great tower rising up from the ground that appears to be covered with the deadly Kij vines. Suddenly ten dugruns leap from the brush—"

Starting a new game with combat will help your Players work together from the outset as they band together to defeat the menace.

Settings for Play

Phantasia is a game that can be played without any other materials than those in this book and the imagination to make them come to life in your mind. You can, however, do a great deal toward helping your Players visualize the Adventure.

Keep your props hidden until the dramatic moment.

You want your PCs to explore your underground citadel.
Let them anticipate what is around the corner. Don't reveal
the layout of the castle to them. Describe it as their characters would see it—room by room, passage by passage. It is
a good idea to provide your Players with paper and pencils
so that they can draw their own maps as they go along.

Dice are helpful if you have them, although this game
offers its own system of hand signs to simulate dice. If you
would like, you may use ten-sided dice. If you cannot find
ten-sided dice, then use the hand signs shown in this book.

Finally, a display—like a small stage with the sets in
place—can also be helpful. This usually takes the form of a
large piece of paper covered with one-inch-wide squares.
By placing small figures (miniatures) on this display, you
can easily see the distance relationships between the PCs
and any NPCs they might encounter. The movement rates
for PCs and NPCs can be easier to translate, PCs know who
is front of them and behind them, and combat is thus made
much simpler. The display can also be used to help your
Players understand the distance to objects, walls, and doors.

Player Preparation

Prior to the start of the game Players must select a Character whom they want to portray. In the Character section of
this book we offer descriptions of Characters that Players
might choose to become. Players may decide (and should
be encouraged) to think up their own personae instead.
Character Sheets are provided to help Players create their
Characters and to remember the Character's abilities and
attributes during the play of the game.

In order to make it easier for the Gamejudge to determine what a PC can do in the game in relation to other PCs
and to NPCs, a Player's attributes and abilities are reduced
to a series of numbers called stats. Sometimes these stats
have been predetermined. A *Duuk-tsarith* and a catalyst will
obviously have different stats in regard to how each is able
to use magic. On other occasions, however, the stats will
reflect the individual PC's attributes and abilities. A high-
ranking member of the *Duuk-tsarith* will, because of her
experience, skill level, and other factors, have different stats

than a low-ranking member of the same Order. These stats are easy and generally fun for the Players to figure out, so allow plenty of time at the beginning of the game to develop each Character fully.

Mystery

A Player should first decide upon the *Mystery* of the Character who will represent them in the game. A Player may choose from among the Mysteries of modern Thimhallan (catalysts, warlocks, Druids) or may choose from the mythical mysteries (Necromancers, Seers). If the setting and the Gamejudge allow it, Players may choose from the Creatures (giants, centaurs, faeries). The choice of Mystery will determine the relative strength of the PC's beginning attributes and abilities.

You might want to begin by briefly describing each of the Mysteries from the Chronocon. The Players should then select the Mystery that they would like to play. You will note in the book that each Mystery has its own preassigned stats. Have each Player copy down the stats that represent his particular Mystery on a separate sheet of paper. Allow the Players freedom in making their selection. However, if everyone wants to be a warlock, you might point out the advisability of having a catalyst along or mention that a Sorcerer might be useful.

Example

Michael has always been fascinated by the mysterious *Duuktsarith*. Kathri, on the other hand, has always wondered what it would be like to be a catalyst. Each of them creates a copy of a blank Character Sheet found on page 429 and prepares to fill them out. Michael turns to the section in the *Chronocon* that describes and gives the statistics of the *Duuktsarith* while Kathri turns to look at the section providing statistics and descriptions of the catalysts.

Attributes

After choosing the Mystery, Players must generate the *Attributes* for their characters. Attributes represent natural aptitudes that your PC possesses. Attributes, unlike Abilities, are not learned. Generally, they represent what a Character can do *without* using the power of Life (walking, runing, fighting with fists, etc.). To generate Attributes, go through each of the Attributes listed on the Character Sheet. Players will see either a number listed for the Attribute or else a formula for determining the number. Those that have only a number in the space should be left as they are — that number is the Attribute.

Attributes with formulas are determined randomly. The "R" in a formula represents a random number between one and ten. For example: A Fire Attack attribute might be listed on the Character Sheet as "40 + R." The formula is asking for the result of forty plus a random number from one to ten.

The random number may be determined by rolling a ten-sided die, or by using the hand signal system described on page 305–307. Find the difference between the signaled numbers and consult this chart to determine the random number from one to ten.

HAND SIGNAL DIFFERENCES FOR RANDOM ONE TO TEN RESULTS

Differences	0	1	2	3	4	5	6	7	8	9	10	11	12	13	14	15	16	17	18	19
R-Number	10	1	2	3	4	5	6	7	8	9	9	8	7	6	5	4	3	2	1	10

The Attributes for characters in *Phantasia* are described in more detail under the Rules of *Phantasia*. The following brief description, however, will aid players in developing their PCs:

FIGHTING:

Attack: Used to determine how effectively a PC can physically assault or otherwise overcome an opponent during the game. Represents everything from a slap in the face to a roundhouse punch.

Defense: Used to determine how effectively a PC counters attacks made by Monsters, NPCs, or other PCs.

Health: Measures the physical well-being of the PC. This number changes often during the course of the game as successful attacks against the PC reduce it. If this number reaches zero, then the PC has "died" and is removed from play.

PROWESS:

Strength: This score determines whether the PC can lift a boulder or break down a door or needs help picking a flower.

Dexterity: When the PC swings over a chasm on a slippery vine, this Attribute is used to determine if the PC reaches the other side or falls into the gorge.

Movement: This score tells the maximum number of *metra* the PC can move in a single round.

INFORMATION:

Intelligence: This Attribute Score measures what the PC knows or what the PC can work out intellectually. Can the PC read the ancient writing on the wall? Can the PC recall the old legend told about the castle?

Intuition: Sometimes a hunch is more important than a sure thing. Does the PC have a "bad feeling" about walking into that dark cave? Does the PC have a "hunch" that the old man in the corner of the inn may know where the treasure is buried? A good Intuition Attribute will help the PC determine such things.

Senses: How well the PC sees, hears, smells, tastes, or feels by touch are all determined by his Senses Score. Can the PC see the griffins approach? Can she over-hear the whispered conversation at the next table?

SHAPE:

Form: The general shape and category of the PC is described here. Most will be human — at least at the beginning of the game! This score acts as a guideline for use in possible magical transformations described under Abilities later, such as the PC turning herself into a were-tiger, for example.

Size: This number represents the PC's two largest mea-surements in square *decimetra*. A human, for exam-ple, may be 12 *decimetra* in height, 5 *decimetra* in width, and 2 *decimetra* in depth. The two largest measures would be his height and his width. There-fore, his size would be described as sixty (12 × 5 = 60). This number is used in determining combat results between opponents of different sizes and as an aspect of certain magical constructions.

Resistance: This is the PC's Resistance to unwanted magic. The PC may *willingly* reduce this resistance to zero if the spell being cast on the PC is desired by him: a warrior requesting that a *DKarn-ðuuk* turn him into a were-wolf. If the PC is resisting the effect, this Ability may prevent the unwanted change: a *Duuk-tsarith* attempting to turn the PC into custard.

LIFE:

Renewal: How much Life the PC can acquire naturally after a good night's sleep.

Capacity: How much Life the PC can use in casting a spell at any one given time.

Lifewell: The maximum amount of Life the PC can carry at any time. Any additional Life acquired by the PC is discharged at once back into the world and cannot be used.

Example:

Kathri finds the entry for catalysts in the *Chronocon* and sees the following stats for attributes:

CATALYSTS
PHANTASIA STATISTICS

ATTRIBUTES

Attack	41R	Defense	41R	Health	47R
Strength	42R	Dexterity	51R	Movement	5
Intelligence	51R	Intuition	48R	Senses	45R
Form	human	Size	55R	Resistance	1
Renewal	1	Capacity	100	Lifewell	300

Kathri fills out her blank Character Sheet, starting with the Attack Attribute and working her way down to Lifewell. The Attack Attribute is listed as being "41R." ("R" = a random number from one to ten.) This means that catalysts have an Attack Attribute of forty-one plus a random number from one to ten or, in other words, a range of scores from forty-two to fifty-one. (41 + 1 = 42, 41 + 10 = 51)

To determine the Attack Attribute for her own PC, Kathri

finds a random number between one and ten either by rolling a ten-sided die or by using the hand-signals. When Kathri rolls the die, the result is a seven. Kathri's PC has an Attack Attribute of forty-eight (41 + 7 = 48). (The seven was a lucky roll: the higher the number, the better the PC will be at performing that particular Attribute during the game.)

Kathri moves on to the second Attribute on her form: the Defense Attribute. This, too, is listed as "41R." Kathri rolls the die again and the result this time is three. Kathri's character will have a Defense Attribute of forty-four (41 + 3 = 44). Even though all catalysts on the average have about the same Attack and Defense Attributes, Kathri's particular catalyst is slightly better at finding the weaknesses in other's defenses than in providing for her own defense. This would make her an excellent choice to assist a *DKarnduuk* or *Duuk-tsarith* in battle.

The catalyst's health is listed as "47R." Kathri rolls a ten and her catalyst has a Health Attribute of fifty-seven.

Kathri continues filling out her form, adding a random number whenever an "R" follows the number. In some places, where the number alone appears, she simply writes down the number that is listed. Catalysts have a Movement Attribute of "5." This means that they can, on the average, move five *metra* per round. Kathri writes the number "5" in the box for Movement Attribute.

Abilities

There are three types of Ability scores—Talent, Station, and the Ability Score. The Talent for each Ability is determined when the PC is created. The Station for each Ability represents additional levels of expertise that the PC will acquire during the course of the game. The Ability Score is a combination of the PC's Talent and Station scores and determines how successful the PC will be when using that Ability.

Talents are found in the same way as Attributes: using either the number or formula listed.

Michael has filled out the Attributes section of his PC form and is now ready to proceed with the Abilities. He thinks, "This should really be fun. *Duuk-tsarith* have good statistics for Attributes, but this is where I acquire the real power—Magic!" Michael looks at the *Phantasia* statistics listed in the *Chronocon* and finds the following:

DUUK-TSARITH
PHANTASIA STATISTICS

ATTRIBUTES

Attack	50R	Defense	47R	Health	50R
Strength	53R	Dexterity	54R	Movement	5
Intelligence	60R	Intuition	60R	Senses	47R
Form	human	Size	55R	Resistance	1
Renewal	1	Capacity	100	Lifewell	300

ABILITIES	TALENT	STATION	SCORE
Combat	15R	1	16+
Movement	10R	1	11+
Health and Healing	—	—	—
Form and Size Altering	10R	1	11+
Information	—	—	—
Life Transfer	—	—	—
Tool Crafts and Skills	—	—	—
Telepathy and Empathy	20R	1	21+
Illusions	10R	1	11+

All of the Abilities, with the exception of Tool Crafts & Skills (the Lifeless craft of the Dead Sorcerers) deal with the power of Life and its channeling into Magic. Having already determined the stats for his PC's Attributes, Michael is now ready to determine his stats for Abilities.

Talents represent the PC's natural aptitude for the Abilities. Talents never change during the game once Michael determines their value.

Michael fills out his PC's Abilities on his form, beginning with Combat. The *Duuk-tsarith* have a Combat Talent listed as "15R." The Combat Talent for Michael's PC is determined in the same way as his PC's Attributes. A random value from one to ten is found and added to the number before the "R" to determine the PC's Combat Talent. Michael rolls a five with one of the ten-sided dice and

thus determines his PC's Combat Talent to be fifteen
(10 + 5 = 15)

· Michael completes his Character Sheet by adding his
PC's listed Station to each of his Abilities to determine
an Ability Score. It is the PC's Ability Score that will
determine how successfully he performs magic. Michael's
PC has a Combat Talent of fifteen with a Combat Station
of one. This means his PC has a Combat Ability Score of
sixteen (15 + 1 = 16). Michael continues down the list of
Abilities, determining the Ability Score for each, based on
the Talents he has determined and the Stations listed.

Making Characters Come to Life

Stats represent the skeleton of the character, giving shape
and consistency to the Character in play. Now it is up to
the Player to flesh out this skeleton. The Player may now
take some time to give personality to his Character. What
does the Character look like? Where is she from? What is
the age? What does he wear? What are her likes and
dislikes? These are the kinds of questions a Player may
want to answer for himself about his Character before play
begins.

The Gamejudge should have each Player tell the others
something about himself or herself at this point, with the
Players taking the role of their Characters. Please note that
there are some things Players may wish to keep secret
about their Characters. For example, if the Player's Character happens to be a rogue *Kan-Hanar* smuggler who finds
himself in league with a high-born *Albanara*, it might be in
his better interests to keep his past a secret from such
royalty. Of course, players are free to tell anyone anything
they like about their Character—regardless of whether it is
true or not.

The Course of Play

Once the Characters are generated and introduced, the
game is ready to begin. The Gamejudge describes the starting point of his Adventure and tells where each of the PCs
are in relation to it. Then he asks the Players how their PCs

are reacting to that description. Since it is traditional for the Players to take on the roles of their Characters in the game as though they were acting in a play, the Gamejudge would ask of a Player "What are you going to do?" rather than "What is your Character going to do?" Each Player in turn designates what his Character is going to do or say. The Gamejudge must then evaluate the consequences of the Character's actions. Helping him in this judgment are the Rules of Phantasia and its Comparative Probability Standard (CPS). These rules determine the probable outcome of physical, magical, and, occasionally, social conflicts in the game and thus help determine the consequences of the actions described by the Players. The Gamejudge then tells the Players what has happened, what changes may or may not have affected their Characters, any new information or descriptions that their actions have generated, and then asks for further action descriptions on the part of the Players.

This quickly takes on the form of mutual storytelling held within reasonable bounds by the restrictions of the game itself. Back and forth these descriptions and actions go until either the Adventure is conquered, the Characters playing in the game are all vanquished, or all participants defer the conclusion to another night.

A sample might go something like this:

Gamejudge: "You come to a closed door. What do you want to do?"

PC: "I put my ear to the door and listen. Do I hear anything?"

Gamejudge: "You hear growling and sounds like claws scraping across stone. What do you do?"

PC: "I try to open the door."

Gamejudge: "You try, but the door won't budge. Something heavy is leaning against it. You now hear screams coming from the other side of the door. The growling sound is getting louder."

PC: "I hurl a ball of fire at the door."

At this point the Gamejudge will determine, using the CPS, whether the PC successfully burns down the door or sets his robes on fire.

Using the Comparative Probability Standard (CPS)

The heart of the game Phantasia is the Comparative Probability Standard—CPS. This mathematical probability system compares the various elements in any situation and determines the probable outcome. It is used to simulate magic, to fight without doing real damage, to travel without ever leaving your chair.

There are two things to keep in mind when using the CPS. First, the system does not perfectly simulate individual aspects of Thimhallan. Veteran gamers will be familiar with games that can tell you that the crossbow bolt the PC fired at the castle gate struck the third plank from the left side two *decimetra* lower than the casing and penetrated the wood to a depth of four *decimetra*. Such accuracy in detail involves complex calculations and is obtained at the cost of fast-moving play. CPS is designed to do all things with general accuracy rather than individual things in detail.

In addition, individual results from the CPS reflect a range of PROBABLE outcomes. You won't get a feeling for the world of Thimhallan just on the basis of one or two numerical comparisons. A true understanding of life on that world can be achieved only through a series of general simulations and role plays. This will give you a much better statistical feeling for the results.

Force and Resistance

With this in mind, the CPS is referred to whenever Force meets Resistance in the simulation. "Force" can be defined as "anything attempting to change the state of its environment." Strength may represent force to move a rock. Dexterity may represent the force a juggler needs to keep four globes in the air at the same time. Attack represents the force used to overpower an enemy. A PC's sense of sight may represent force to see something far away. The PC's intelligence may represent force needed to read an ancient language or understand the function of a technological device.

To counter the Force, Resistance also takes many forms. Defense, of course, represents resistance to attacking force.

Strength may represent resistance to another PC's strength in a wrestling match. The stranger's intuition may resist the PC's intelligence. The Gamejudge may also determine more abstract Resistance Scores. The weight of a boulder is represented by a High Resistance Score against the PC's strength force trying to move it. The complexity of a technological device has a high Resistance Score to the PC's intelligence force in trying to understand how it works.

The Result of any comparison of Force vs. Resistance is, effectively, the degree of change that the Force exacts upon the Resistance. In order to determine the result for any such required comparison, follow these steps:

Step 1—Compare Force/Resistance Abilities
CPS Refer to chart on page 309.
Find the Force and the Resistance statistics that apply to the situation in question. If the PC attempts to move a rock under which the treasure is buried, the Force is the PC's physical strength. The rock's weight is the Resistance. RESISTANCE IS ALWAYS SUBTRACTED FROM FORCE. This results in the Differential (DIF). The DIF determines the row of the CPS where the result will be found.

Kathri's catalyst wants to move a rock under which, she believes, is buried a book that contains ancient Diviner spells. Consulting her chart, she sees that her Strength is forty-five (42 + her die roll of three). The rock weighs forty-six pounds. The Gamejudge subtracts forty-six (Resistance) from forty-five (Force applied to move the rock). The result on the DIF row (reading down) is –1.

Step 2—Generate Force/Resistance Random Factor
Having determined the DIF row that is to be used, the column for the result is discovered randomly. (This represents the random events that occur naturally to help or inhibit a PC's actions.) There are two methods for generating random numbers, both of which give identical results. The first method is to use ten-sided dice. The second is to use differential hand signals.

Using Dice: Ten-sided dice can be obtained at most hobby

stores. To determine the column for the result using dice, simply roll a single ten-sided die and match the resulting number to the column on the CPS Table. Only one person rolls this die, normally, the PC exerting the Force. However, occasionally the Gamejudge will roll the die if for some reason he or she wants to keep the result of the actions secret. An example of this would be the use of Intelligence or Intuition and is explained in the Abilities section.

Using Hand Signals: A system of hand signals can also be used to determine randomly the column to use.

Results from one to ten are indicated with right hand signals as shown on the next page. By using the left hand as either open (signaling no change) or closed (signifying to add ten to the number of the other hand), a number from one to twenty is thereby shown.

For example: if your friend were to show you the number ten in this system, he would close his right hand in a fist and open his left hand, as shown below.

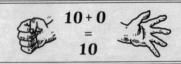

$$10 + 0 = 10$$

The left hand can only have a value of either zero or ten. The open hand means to add zero. Therefore, ten (the right hand) plus zero (the left hand) makes ten.

If, on the other hand, your friend clenches his left hand, then its value becomes ten. Ten (the right hand) plus ten (the left hand) equals twenty—as shown below.

$$10 + 10 = 20$$

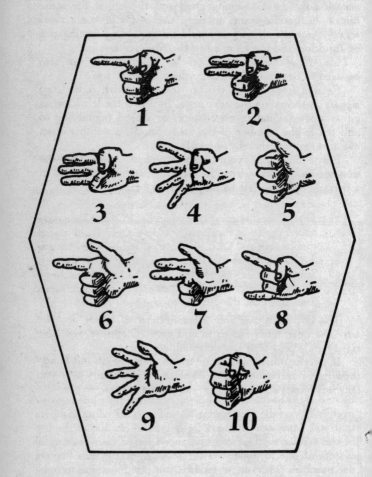

This same addition works for all other numbers between one and twenty.

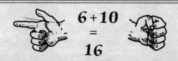

$$6 + 0 = 6$$

$$6 + 10 = 16$$

Once everyone understands these signals, the column can be determined by using these quick steps:

1. The PC who is using Force and the PC (or Gamejudge) applying Resistance both display their hand signals simultaneously. Each displays a number. For example, the PC signals ten and the Gamejudge signals thirteen.
2. Subtract the lower number from the higher number to obtain the difference. In the example, ten is subtracted from thirteen, the difference is three $(13 - 10 = 3)$.
3. Find this difference along the top of the CPS Table to determine the column to use. For the example, the column labeled "3" is used.

NOTE ON THE HAND-SIGNAL SYSTEM: One might think that a system where two participants consciously determine a number would be biased and easily manipulated by one of the parties. If PCs begin choosing the same number over and over, the Gamejudge should start signaling numbers that will work against the PC. The numbers across the top of the CPS are statistically balanced based on a numerical system of one to twenty. Thus it is important that Players use numbers from one to twenty, not just from one to ten.

In our example, Kathri's randomly picked number is three. The Gamejudge finds the DIF number (–1) and follows it across to the Random Differential number (3). This is an

"R." The Gamejudge the consults the Probable Result Chart in Step 3, looking for the "R" result.

Step 3—Determine Probable Result
Cross reference the row (determined in Step 1 above) with the column (determined in Step 2 above). This will yield a letter result. In general they have the following application:

Once again, our PC is attempting to move a rock to find the treasure buried beneath.

$T = Total:$ This is the most successful result of Force over Resistance. This usually reflects 100% success. The PC moved the rock into the next county.

$A = Almost:$ While not as successful as Total, this result usually reflects a satisfactory result inside projected tolerances. Normally this result refers to a 75% success level. The PC moves the rock off the treasure.

$R = Reasonable:$ The application of force was partially successful. This result generally means approximately 50% success level. The PC moves the rock halfway.

$O = Off:$ Only partial success is indicated. Generally this reflects a 25% success level. The PC manages to wiggle the rock.

$C = Canceled:$ Resistance overcame the Force in total. The effect of the force was lost. The PC couldn't even make the rock budge. To refer to our example a final time, Kathri's Probable Result was "R." Consulting the Chart, the Gamejudge sees that "R" stands for Reasonable. He announces that Kathri has managed to move the rock half-way off the book. The next round, she may try to move the rock again.

The exact interpretation of the TAROC result is dependent, of course, on the Force and Resistance to which it is referring. Part of this document's purpose is to aid you in determining the results from such Force/Resistance comparisons. The Attributes and Abilities sections that follow will give you specific examples of how these are used as Force and/or Resistance scores and the types of TAROC interpretations that result.

COMPARATIVE PROBABILITY STANDARD DIFFERENTIAL (DIF)

Random Differential

DIF	0 / 10	1 / 19	2 / 18	3 / 17	4 / 16	5 / 15	6 / 14	7 / 13	8 / 12	9 / 11
-50	R	O	O	C	C	C	C	C	C	C
-40	R	O	O	O	C	C	C	C	C	C
-30	R	R	O	O	C	C	C	C	C	C
-25	A	R	O	O	O	C	C	C	C	C
-20	A	R	R	O	O	O	C	C	C	C
-16	A	A	R	O	O	O	C	C	C	C
-12	A	A	R	R	O	O	O	O	C	C
-8	T	A	R	R	R	O	O	O	C	C
-5	T	A	A	R	R	O	O	O	C	C
-3	T	A	A	R	R	O	O	O	C	C
-1	T	A	A	R	R	R	O	O	O	C
0 EVEN	T	A	A	R	R	R	R	O	O	C
2	T	A	A	A	R	R	R	O	O	C
4	T	T	A	A	A	R	R	O	O	C
6	T	T	A	A	A	R	R	R	O	C
10	T	T	T	A	A	A	R	R	O	O
14	T	T	T	A	A	A	R	R	R	O
18	T	T	T	T	A	A	A	R	R	O
22	T	T	T	T	A	A	A	R	R	O
27	T	T	T	T	T	T	A	A	R	R
35	T	T	T	T	T	T	A	A	A	R
45	T	T	T	T	T	T	T	A	A	R
50	T	T	T	T	T	T	T	A	A	R

Scale—Time Weights, Distances, and Measures

All distances and ranges in the game are stated in *metra*—roughly equal to one and a half meters or five feet. *Mila* refers to "a thousand *metra*" and is roughly equivalent to a mile. All rates are stated in *mila* per hour.

A round begins when the PCs state what they intend to do and is concluded when all PCs have performed their stated actions.

There are several different units of time used in the game.

1 round = 7.2 seconds
1 turn = 5 rounds or 36 seconds
1 sequence = 10 turns or 6 minutes
1 hour = 10 segments

A Movement Attribute of 1 *mila*/hour translates into a movement of 2 *metra* per round. A person moving at a speed of 5 *mila*/hour would cross 10 *metra*/round.

Adjusting Scales

If you are using grid paper as the "game board," the markers that show the relative locations of all the game elements are usually placed on a grid of lines one inch apart. This works fine for people moving at rates of 10 *mila*/hour (10 inches on the board), but there are few areas large enough to properly show rates of 5,000 *mila*/hour (or 5,000 inches).

Equally important is the task of figuring times for rates of travel and actual distances between empires and kingdoms in Thimhallan. Trying to show on a table the distances between Merilon and the Outland (some 2,000 *mila*) would require more table space than the Field of Glory.

Fortunately both of these problems can be solved by adjusting the scale of the playing surface and time.

Adjusting Distance Scales

When distances are being played out simultaneously between one group that is moving very fast (requiring a large scale of 1 square = 10 *mila*) and a second group moving normally (requiring a normal scale of 1 square = 1 *metra*) the Gamejudge may wish to divide the play surface into two separate sections using two separate scales.

This technique can prove most successful in many situations. Two groups of PCs are standing several *metra* away from their winged carriages. Group A suddenly leaps into their carriage and flies west at top speed. Group B takes time to gather their belongings before walking to their carriage, and then they fly west at top speed. The proper distances between the carriages can always be maintained. The faster movement of Group A is tracked on a scale of 1 square = 10 *metra*. The slower movement of Group B is tracked separately at a scale of 1 square = 1 *metra*.

It is important, however, that the time scales of all parties involved remain the same.

Adjusting Time Scales

It is not required nor is it advisable that the Gamejudge always use the time scale of 1 round for everything that happens. When traveling safe roads without any difficulty, it is not required that the Gamejudge describe every *metra* of the way. Often it is as effective to simply tell the PCs: "You travel for several days without incident before coming to the outskirts of Merilon."

The important thing to remember is that *when interesting things happen, time slows down,* and *when boring things happen, time speeds up.*

Rules of Phantasia

Attributes, Inherent Life

Everyone in our world, even those who are Dead to the ways of Life, have Inherent Life. They have what might be termed physical or natural characteristics. Everything found within creation has Inherent Life and has what we will call *Attributes*.

All things within Phantasia have this Inherent Life. These Attributes, defined by a set of numbers for purposes of play, are:

> *Combat: Attack, Defense, and Health*
> *Prowess: Strength, Dexterity, and Movement*
> *Information: Intelligence, Intuition, and Senses*
> *Shape: Form, Size, and Resistance*
> *Life: Renewal, Capacity, and Lifewell*

Everyone or everything encountered in Thimhallan can be defined by these Attributes.

In some instances an Attribute will be zero. AN AT-TRIBUTE THAT IS NOT LISTED HAS A VALUE OF ZERO. A rock, for example, will have Attributes for Defense (how much movement it can resist), Health (how much damage it can take before crumbling), Size, Form, and Lifewell. Since the rock has no intelligence, this factor is not listed and therefore is counted as zero.

Each of these Attributes has a score by which it can be compared relative to the same Attribute in other people or objects. In general, normal humans are found to have a score of 50 for each of these Attributes. Remember that it is the *differences* between these Attributes that count, not the actual stats on their own.

Don't worry if you're feeling confused. Keep going. Each of the Mysteries and their attendant Attributes are discussed at length in following sections. How each affects play in the course of the game is also explained in detail.

Attribute Checks

Walking down the street is something that everyone can do practically without thinking about it. Opening a door or reading a road sign probably doesn't require much thought or effort on your part. Such events are ordinary actions and PCs in the game may perform them and many others without having to resort to the CPS Charts or Attributes for their resolution. If a PC says he is reading a road sign, tell him what it says and leave game rolls out of it.

However, whenever the PCs attempt to do something extraordinary, they may be required to resolve the action with an "Attribute Check."

Attribute Checks are a check against the specific attribute that is being used. A PC who wants to climb a sheer wall must make a "Dexterity Check." A PC who wants to read an ancient scroll must make an "Intelligence Check."

Whenever an Attribute is listed with the word "Check," for example, "Movement Check" or "Senses Check," the Gamejudge should compare the Force of the Attribute listed against any Resistance to that Attribute and determine a TAROC result from the CPS Table.

Fighting: Attack, Defense and Health

Whenever a creature or object attacks another creature or object, the conflict is defined in terms of Attack (Force) and Defense (Resistance). Each object in the game that has the capability of combat is given a value for these two basic combat forms.

When attempting to ascertain the effects of any such confrontation, the Defense number of the person/thing being attacked (Resistance) is subtracted from the Attack number of the person/thing (Force) attacking them. These numbers translate directly to the CPS system rows to determine the outcome.

It is the relative scores of the combatants that determine if and how well any attack worked. How much damage is done, however, depends upon the actual type of attack that was made.

How to Attack and Defend

Whenever any type of attack is made, you should follow this procedure to determine its outcome and effect.

1. Declare Attack

Any PCs who are going to perform an action in the current round should declare what their actions are at this time. Those who are going to attack others must declare who they are attacking and how they are attacking them. The declaration and description of their intended attacks will be important in determining the result at the end of the round. Different types of attacks are listed under "Attack Forms," below.

2. Determine Initiative

The person who has initiative is considered to move first during the current period of combat. To determine initiative, the participants in the combat choose up sides in the conflict. The Gamejudge uses the CPS chart to determine who has initiative using the even row. Situations may arise that will require the Gamejudge to alter the row of the initiative up or down. If one group is surprised by the other group, obviously the surprised group has a much lower chance of gaining initiative than the group that did the surprising. Any result of T or A means the person on the Gamejudge's right will be the first to act, a result of O or C means that the person on the Gamejudge's left will be the first to act, while a result of R means that both sides act simultaneously.

If the action is between PCs and NPCs, a result of T or A means the PCs have the initiative. O or C gives the initiative to the NPCs. An R result is the same as above.

The PCs who have the initiative may then choose to attack as their action, or they may attempt to flee, talk—whatever they can accomplish in the space of three seconds. If there is simultaneous combat, any damage done in combat and its effects are taken *after* all blows are struck by both sides.

If combat is avoided, then the game resumes. If combat takes place, however, then continue with the following steps.

3. Subtract Defender Attribute From Attacker's Attribute

If the Attack is being made using the Fire Attribute (i.e., is a physical attack), then the defender's Defense Attribute for Fire (i.e., their physical defense attribute) would be subtracted in order to determine the row on the CPS chart.

4. Add or Subtract Any Situational Modifiers

There are many situational modifiers that apply during combat. These could include distance to the target, relative size of the target, and intervening objects. How to determine these modifiers will be explained later. Apply these to the difference found in step 1 above in order to determine the final row on the CPS.

5. Determine the CPS Result

Randomly determine (by the method previously explained) the column on which the result will be found. Cross-reference this with the row previously determined to find a letter result: T, A, R, O, or C.

6. Apply Any Indicated Effects

The results of this are generally interpreted in terms of damage done. All damage is expressed in terms of Full, ½, ¼, and ⅒ the amount of damage the attacker is capable of doing. How much damage the attacker will do is determined by the Attack Score on the Damage by Score chart.

For example: an attacker with an Attack Attribute of fifty (50) will do 10 points of damage at Full Damage, 5 points of damage at ½, 2 points of damage at ¼, and 1 point of damage at ¹⁄₁₀. Subtract the amount of damage shown from the Health Attribute of the PC who suffered the attack.

Find the result on the CPS scale.

T = *Total:* The Defender takes full damage.
A = *Almost:* The Defender takes ½ damage.
R = *Reasonable:* The Defender takes ¼ damage.
O = *Off:* The Defender takes ¹⁄₁₀ damage—a flesh wound. The PC probably just hurt it enough to make it really mad.
C = *Canceled:* The Defender takes no damage.

7. Determine Results

If the defender's Health Attribute drops to zero or below, then the defending character will be incapacitated. See the section on Health to determine the consequences of Health reductions.

ATTACK FORMS

Melee Combat

Any combat that takes place within physical reach of a PC is known as Melee Combat. Normally this means that the Attacker and Defender are located in squares that are adjacent to each other on the *metra* scale. Hand-to-hand combat or spells that are transmitted through touch use Melee Combat to determine their effects.

Melee combat is usually the easiest to resolve, since there are few modifiers that apply. Simply compare the Attack and Defense Attributes of the involved PCs and determine the result.

Example:

Kathri has named her PC Lindar. Lindar is walking down a path in the Outlands when she is suddenly accosted by a wounded Centaur. Since both Kathri's PC and the Centaur are adjacent, the Combat will be Melee Combat.

Kathri realizes that flight is useless and announces that Lindar will attack. The Gamejudge announces that the Centaur will also attack. Both parties have declared their actions for the round.

DAMAGE BY SCORE

ATT	1/10	1/4	1/2	FULL	ATT	1/10	1/4	1/2	FULL
10	1	1	1	2	110	40	100	200	400
20	1	1	2	4	120	60	150	300	600
30	1	2	3	6	130	100	250	500	1k
40	1	2	4	8	140	200	500	1k	2k
50	1	3	5	10	150	400	1k	2k	4k
60	2	4	8	16	160	600	1500	3k	6k
70	5	10	20	40	170	1000	2500	5k	10k
80	10	20	40	80	180	1500	3750	7500	15k
90	15	30	60	120	190	2000	5k	10k	20k
100	25	50	100	200	200	3000	7500	15k	30k

k = multiples of 1,000
ATT = Attribute

Initiative for the round is then determined. The Gamejudge rules that although Lindar was keeping close watch while walking down the path, she was nevertheless surprised by the Centaur, who had been concealed behind some bushes. The DIF will, therefore, be "6" on the CPS, with the "T" and "A" results favoring the Centaur. Kathri and the Gamejudge are using hand signals to make their random determinations. Both display their numbers for initiative at the same time. The Gamejudge displays a seven while Kathri shows a fifteen. Subtracting the lower number from the higher gives a difference of eight. Checking the column on the CPS under "8" against the row "6" gives a result of "0." Initiative is given to Lindar! (Lindar heard the rustling of the bushes as the Centaur leaped out and so was able to prepare for the attack.) Lindar, therefore, may perform her action—that is, attack—before the Centaur can attack her.

Lindar's Attack Attribute is forty-eight. The Gamejudge notes that the Centaur's Defense Attribute is forty. The Centaur's Resistance (Defense) is subtracted from Lindar's Force (Attack), resulting in a DIF of eight (48 − 8 = 8). Since "8" lies between "6" and "10" on the CPS, the DIF row that will be used is "6." Again, the Gamejudge and Kathri display hand signals, giving them a Random column result of "10." The DIF row of "6" cross-referenced with the column "10" gives a CPS result of "T."

Looking at the Damage by Score Table, the "T" or Full result does eight points of damage to the Centaur. Eight is subtracted from the Health Attribute of the Centaur. The Gamejudge notes that the already wounded Centaur only had five points of health remaining. The Centaur's health drops below zero and the Centaur dies at once.

Lindar is grateful, for if the Centaur had been in full health, it would have survived Lindar's blow and been able to complete its own attack on Lindar—probably doing great damage.

Ranged Combat

Any time damage is inflicted from a distance, it is called Ranged Combat. Stones thrown from the walls of a castle at

Range/Attribute Chart

ATT	Short	Medium	Long	EXT.
10	1m	1m	1m	2m
20	1m	1m	2m	4m
30	1m	2m	3m	6m
40	1m	2m	4m	8m
50	1m	3m	5m	10m
60	2m	4m	8m	16m
70	5m	10m	20m	40m
80	10m	20m	40m	80m
90	15m	30m	60m	120m
100	25m	50m	100m	200m
110	38m	75m	150m	300
120	63m	125m	250	500
130	125m	250m	500m	1M
140	675m	1250m	2500m	5M
150	1250m	2500m	5M	10M
160	2500m	5M	10M	20M
170	12,500m	25M	50M	100M
180	125M	250M	500M	1KM
190	625M	1250M	2500M	5KM
200	1250M	2500M	5KM	10KM

m = *Metra* / M = *Mila* / KM = *Kilomila* or 1,000 *Mila*

the troops of the enemy below are an example of Ranged Combat.

In Ranged Combat the accuracy of the thrown object must also be considered. The longer the distance, the more resistance to accuracy is encountered.

There are four divisions of Ranged Combat: short, medium, long, and extreme. Each of these carry a modifier that increases the difficulty of hitting the target.

General Combat Modifiers

Distance to Target	
Short	None
Medium	−10
Long	−25
Extreme	−50
Relative Size of Target[1]	
For each 10 larger/smaller up to 100	+1/−1
For each 100 larger/smaller up to 1000	+2/−4
For each 1,000 larger/smaller up to 10,000	+3/−6
Attacker's Movement	
Standing still or lying prone	None
Walking	−5
Running	−15
Avoiding while moving (dodging)	−30
Defender's Movement	
Standing still	+5
Walking	None
Running	−7
Avoiding while moving (dodging)	−15
Intervening Cover (objects blocking the attack)	
Rubble	−5
Soft cover (overturned wood tables, wooden door)	−15
Hard cover (stone wall)	−30

[1]Determine the difference between the smaller and the larger and then apply the modifiers listed. Positive modifiers will apply for the smaller creature attacks while the negative modifier will apply to the larger creature attacking the smaller. These results are cumulative. Therefore, a faerie (size 3) attacking a griffin (size 225) would have an attack modifier of +14 (+1 × 10 for each 10 increments plus +2 × 2 for each 100 increments). The griffin would attack the faerie at a −18 (−1 × 10 for each 10 increments plus −4 × 2 for each 100 increments).

Michael's *Duuk-tsarith* finds himself in trouble. He is being stalked by a Hunterkill, his magic is depleted, and all he has left to defend himself is a Technologist's spear. Michael decides to throw the spear at the Hunterkill. Since this attack will mean attempting to do damage to a Hunterkill that is several *metra* away, the attack is considered Ranged Combat.

The *Duuk-tsarith* has an Attack Score of fifty-four while the Hunterkill has a Defense Score of fifty. Normally, this would result in a DIF of four. However, the General Combat Modifiers may change that. The target will be at medium range (3 *metra*), which means a −10 modifier to the DIF. Though the Attacker—the *Duuk-tsarith*—is stationary (no modifier), the Hunterkill is running at full speed (−7 modifier). All the modifiers together work out to a −17 (−7 + 10 = −17). The DIF of 4 is altered to a −13 by the modifiers (4 − 17 = −13). Since −13 falls between −12 and −16, the DIF row used will be "−16."

Possessional Combat

This type of combat takes place when two or more PCs or a PC and an NPC are struggling to determine which of them is in possession of an object. Two PCs with their hands gripping a single spell book would involve Possessional Combat.

The Defender is considered the PC who last had possession of the object. In this instance, the Gamejudge may use the strength and/or dexterity Attributes of those fighting for the object. The difference in the PCs' Attributes is then determined and the result read on the CPS. They are interpreted as follows:

T = *Total:* Attacker takes possession of the object and may use it during the next round of action.

A = *Almost:* Attacker may add 5 to his next attempt.

R = *Reasonable:* Both PCs are locked in the struggle without outcome.

O = *Off:* The Defender may add 5 to his next attempt.

C = *Canceled:* The Defender maintains possession and may use the object during the next round.

A thief grabs Lindar's prayer book and runs away with it. Lindar pursues and catches him. She grabs the book. The thief hangs onto it. The two begin to struggle.

Lindar's Strength is forty-six; the thief has a Strength of thirty-eight. Since the thief last had possession of the book, he is considered the defender in the struggle.

After comparing both characters' Strength statistics and determining the CPS result of "A," the Gamejudge rules that Lindar regains possession of her book and will be able to add 5 to any struggles with the thief for the book in the next round.

Nonlethal Combat

Occasionally a PC may announce that he wants to overpower an opponent, not kill him. This is considered Nonlethal Combat.

Run the combat as usual, but keep track of the damage done separately as Subduing Damage. Each round, subtract half of the damage done in that round from the Defender's Health Attribute while accumulating, on a separate piece of paper, the full amount of Subduing Damage. Whenever such damage is done, find the difference between the Defender's remaining Health Attribute (Resistance) and the accumulated amount of Subduing Damage (Force) that has been done to determine a TAROC result on the CPS. Determine the results as follows:

T = *Total:* The Defender falls unconscious and cannot be revived for another 3R + 10 minutes.

A = *Almost:* The Defender lapses into a daze. He is still able to communicate but will not be able to fight the Attacker.

R = *Reasonable:* The Defender is weakening. The next attempt at subduing will be at +5 on the Attacker's score.

O = *Off:* The Defender remains in control of himself. The next attempt at subduing the Defender will be at –5 to the Attacker's roll.

C = *Canceled:* The Defender remains in control of himself and will not submit to the force of the Attacker. No modifiers to the next roll.

Michael's *Duuk-tsarith* intends to try to knock out a smuggler and take him to the dungeons for questioning. The warlock announces that he plans to attack using Non-lethal Combat.

The Combat is run normally, resulting in damage to the smuggler of eight points. The smuggler has a health of thirty-two points. Half of the eight points of damage is done as actual damage so that four points are subtracted from the smuggler's Health Attribute. The full eight points of damage is written down by the Gamejudge on a separate piece of paper, however.

The smuggler's health is now twenty-eight points (32 − 4 = 28). This health is subtracted from the total damage already done (eight points as written separately), resulting in −20 (8 − 28 = −20). The TAROC result on the " − 20" row is found to be "C." The smuggler is still conscious, although his return attack this round comes to no result.

The next round, the *Duuk-tsarith* again attacks with Nonlethal Combat, this time doing ten points of damage. Half of this is actual damage of five points, which is subtracted from the smuggler's health making it now twenty-three points (28 − 5 = 23). The ten points of damage is added to the eight points already noted on the separate paper, bringing the total to eighteen. Again, the comparison is made of total Subduing Damage (force of eighteen) to current Health (Resistance of twenty-three) to determine a CPS row of –5 (18 − 23 = –5) The TAROC result is then found to be an "A." The smuggler is dazed and the *Duuk-tsarith* is able to apprehend him easily.

Other Types of Combat
How does Combat handle the PC who wants to temporarily blind an opponent? What about the PC who wants to break an opponent's weapon instead of his opponent's head?

Any type of combat will work with the CPS system; it is simply a matter of determining which Force and Resistance scores apply, as well as what modifiers should be enforced for difficulty.

In all cases the Gamejudge is the final arbiter of which Attributes or Abilities apply in Combat to Force and Resistance and of the value of any modifiers. A Gamejudge should be fair and impartial in his application of modifiers and in judging the various merits of Force vs. Resistance.

If the PC can describe the specific type of attack he wants to perform, the Gamejudge has the responsibility of determining the parameters for resolving it based on Force, Resistance, and Situational Modifiers.

Health

PCs with Health are alive. PCs without health are considered "dead": i.e., no longer part of the game.

Whenever damage is done, either through combat or calamity, add it to any previous damage done and write the resulting number next to the PC's Health Attribute. When the damage done to the PC either equals or exceeds the Health Attribute, the PC has died from wounds and is removed from play permanently.

The body has a natural ability to heal up to one point of damage per each day of bed rest. The body cannot naturally heal damage that has dropped to within three points of the Health Attribute score. Such healing is the province of the *Theldara*.

Through the magic of Life, *Theldara* can cause miraculous healing far beyond the natural ability of the body to heal itself. Such healing is discussed under Abilities later.

Regardless of how the healing takes place, subtract any healed points from the total of damage that the PC has taken.

Prowess: Strength, Dexterity, Movement

Strength

The power of muscle is the PC's strength. Use this Attribute to determine how well the application of physical force works.

Strength Resistance Examples
Lifting Objects

Small stone	size ×2
Large stone	size ×2
Boulder	size ×2
People	size of the person

Forcing Open

Locked wooden door	65
Locked stone door	85
Locked metal door	120

Pushing Objects

Boulder	size of boulder
Table	35
People	½ size of person

There are many more objects and situations that will resist a PC's physical strength. It is the province of the Gamejudge to create these resistance factors as situations arise.

Check the Strength Force against the Resistance of the Object then compare the TAROC result against the following chart:

T = *Total:* The object is lifted or moved easily. Forced doors are opened and serviceable.

A = *Almost:* The object being lifted can be held for only three rounds. Forced doors open but are broken and cannot be used again.

R = *Reasonable:* The object is moved only one fourth of the intended way. Lifted objects can be held for that round only.

O = *Off:* The object moves slightly but then rebounds on the Player attempting to move it. The boulder rolls back over the PC's foot; the PC trying to force a door bruises his shoulder (both doing some minor damage).

C = *Canceled:* The object is not affected at all.

Dexterity

How nimbly the PC moves or how well he manipulates objects is a function of the PC's dexterity. Resistance to dexterity is anything that increases the amount of dexterity needed to perform the action. This may include tossing an object through a small hole, walking a thin line, leaping over a table.

The Resistance Score for any Dexterity Check is determined by the Gamejudge based on the circumstances. Use the following for a guideline.

Dexterity Resistance Examples
Moving
Resistance Factors for Radical Movement
Types of Movement (Force Modifiers)

Walking (carefully: 1 *metra* per round)	+ 15
Walking (casually)	None
Running	–10
Dodging	–10
Changing direction gradually	+5
Changing direction immediately	–10

Terrain
  Terrain Types (Resistance Scores)°
    Earth (across ground)

Flat	5
Gravel	15
Broken: Large rocks & occasional boulders	25
Gentle slope (climbing speed at ½; descent speed at 1½)	20
Steep slope (climbing speed at ¼; descent speed at ×2)	40

    Water

Calm	5
Gentle waves	7
Choppy (speed ¾)	15
Whitecaps (speed ¾)	25
Deep swells (speed ½)	35
Stormy (speed ¼)	50

    Air

Calm	10
Breeze	20
Stiff wind	35
Gale	55
Turbulent	65
Rainstorm	55
Thunderstorm	75

  Terrain Conditions (Resistance Modifiers)
  (Applies both to movement & footing for a jump)

Stable and unmoving (floor, wall, etc.)	– 15
Unstable and movable (chair, table, etc.)	+5
Smooth and dry	– 10
Slippery/icy	+ 15
Sandy (speed at ¾)	Normal
Running through a crowd	40
Jumping over tables	50

°These scores are cumulative: i.e., a broken, steep slope would
have a resistance score of 65 (40 + 25).

Swinging from rope to rope	68
Climbing	
Sheer cliff	80
Tree	30
Dodging boulders	75
Standing upright	
On a flat, stable surface	None
On a ball	65
On a pitching deck in high seas	70
Manipulation	
Catching an egg without breaking it	
From 10 feet	50
From 20 feet	85
Balancing a book on the head	40

Compare the Force of the PC's Dexterity Score against the stated Resistance and check the TAROC result against the following chart:

T = *Total:* The feat is performed perfectly. Allow the PC another action during the same round due to her deftness. The Warrior leaped over the table with such skill that she can cast a magic spell during the same round.

A = *Almost:* The feat is completed satisfactorily. The Warrior leaped over the table and landed on her feet, but she will need time to recover from the jarring. She may cast the magic spell during the next round.

R = *Reasonable:* The feat is completed but without all the desired results. Impose a small penalty on the following round of action. The Warrior falls over the table but regains her feet. She can cast a magic spell next round but will be penalized.

O = *Off:* The feat has not only failed but failed in a most spectacular fashion. The Warrior falls over the table and tumbles headfirst into a barrel of ale. Impose a more severe penalty next round for the spell-casting attempt.

C = *Canceled:* The feat has failed. The Warrior fails to leap over the table and falls flat on her face. She will be able to move the next round, but she cannot cast a spell.

Movement

The Movement Attribute indicates in *mila*/hour how fast a PC can move. Five times this number is the number of squares maximum the PC can move in a single round. Note that such movement would require a human PC to be running as fast as he could without taking any other actions. Normal movement, in which a PC could perform other actions, would be moving the number of squares indicated by his Movement Attribute in a single round.

Example:
Kathri's PC has a Movement Attribute of five. She can run as fast as twenty-five (5 × 5) squares in a turn. Kathri knows that doing so might be hazardous, for PCs who run that fast over any but ideal terrain are assured of having to make a Dexterity Check. If they fail, they will probably fall down and take subsequent damage. Kathri's PC limits her movement to five squares per round, so that she can perform attack, defense, and other actions without penalty.

Most questions of how well a PC moves are determined by Dexterity Checks. A Movement Check is only made when a Dexterity Check has failed while the PC is moving.

A PC involved in a collision must immediately make a Movement Check using his movement in one *metra* squares per round as the Force Score and the Resistance Score of the Terrain he hits with the following results:

T = *Total:* Full damage
A = *Almost:* ½ of the full damage
R = *Reasonable:* ¼ of the full damage
O = *Off:* ¹⁄₁₀ of the full damage
C = *Canceled:* Damage avoided altogether

Full damage is calculated as equal to the PC's speed — in 1 *metra* squares per round — at the time when he failed his movement. This damage may be modified by other circumstances as dictated by the Gamejudge.

The size score generally reflects the size of the object in square *decimetra* measured over its two largest proportions. To determine size, picture the object or creature as a flat portrait showing its largest measurements. Men, for example, would be measured by their height and their width although some very fat men might be measured by their height and their depth. A Pegasus would be so pictured as from above with its wings extended. Count the number of square *decimetra*[2] which it would take to cover the object or animal. The number of squares equals the size of the creature. Humans have a size of about fifty (50) square *decimetra*.

Information: Intelligence, Intuition, and Senses

Intelligence
Intelligence is an indicator of what the PC knows about the world in general, culture, history, and the arts. Intelligence is used in the game to help determine what the PC could reasonably be expected to know.

Although the PC is the one who "has" the information, it is the Gamejudge who will generally supply that information for the PC. The PC is not required to make it up on the spot! It is by this means that the Gamejudge is able to control the amount of information given about an object. The Gamejudge will usually impart such information to the PC in a note. The PC may or may not choose to share such information with the other PCs.

The actual knowledge the character has will vary among the different Mysteries. For example, a group of PCs arrive at a ruined temple atop a mountain. A catalyst would recognize this as the Temple of the Necromancers. She will have some knowledge of it, mostly what she has gained through rumor or her own research. A *Duuk-tsarith* may have the same information, plus additional, secret knowledge concerning the fate of the Necromancers that is known only to those of his Order.

Information Resistance Examples

History	Before Iron Wars	After Iron Wars
General Facts	60	40
Names and Places	70	50
Specific Events	75	68
Obscure Details	80	70
Individual Objects	95	75

[2]In your terms, squares that measure six inches on each side.

Customs		
General Facts	70	60
Warchanged Creatures	n/a	85
Other Kingdoms	85	70

Whenever the Gamejudge needs to determine the extent or accuracy of PC's knowledge on a subject, he compares the PC's Intelligence Force against the Information Resistance number set by the Gamejudge. The PC and the Gamejudge then determine the random number for the TAROC result on the CPS. The Gamejudge then uses the following guidelines in determining what the PC may know about a subject:

T = *Total:* The PC has a complete knowledge of the subject or object in question. He is able to identify most of its properties and relate its history.
A = *Almost:* The PC has a general knowledge of the subject or object in question. He can identify only one or two of its properties and has only a general knowledge of its history.
R = *Reasonable:* The PC has only a small amount of knowledge of the subject or object. He cannot identify any of its properties but does have some idea of its history.
O = *Off:* The PC has a mistaken idea about the subject or object. He will misidentify it and will give completely inaccurate information regarding both its history and its properties.
C = *Canceled:* The PC cannot identify the object and has no knowledge of either its properties or its history.

In this instance it is important that the Gamejudge keep the actual result of the TAROC secret from the Players. Since the result is occasionally a mistaken belief, the Gamejudge should limit his response to giving the information without any comment as to its veracity.

For example, a player asks the Gamejudge what her Character knows about the Temple of the Necromancers. The Gamejudge asks for her Intelligence attribute score. He then applies any modifiers (as explained above) and determines the row for the CPS system. He does *not* tell the player which row has been determined as that might clue the player into what chance her character has of knowing about the Temple. The Gamejudge and the player then compare random numbers and come up with a difference. The result, in this case, is "O"—an "Off" result.

The Gamejudge does *not* tell the player that her information is "Off." Instead, the Gamejudge gives her false information. He might tell her that the halls of the Temple are haunted by the restless dead spirits of ancient worshipers when—in fact—no such thing exists. He might tell her that the Temple is a place of peace and security though the truth is that deadly traps abound.

PCs are allowed only THREE such attempts on any one object or subject.

Intuition

Occasionally a PC may wish to search his intuition for guidance. In these cases the Intuition Force is applied against a Resistance Factor imposed by the Gamejudge.

For example, the PC steps into a dark and gloomy wood and asks the Gamejudge, "Do I have any feelings about this place?" Or a PC encounters an extraordinarily beautiful woman wearing nothing but vines and flowers and asks the Gamejudge, "When I see her, what am I feeling now?"

According to the numbers generated, the Gamejudge may say, "You have the feeling that this wood is an extremely dangerous place" or "You know only that you are looking at the woman of your dreams."

INTUITION RESISTANCE FACTORS

All modifiers are for the Resistance Score

Situation

Peaceful surroundings without danger	10
Threatening surroundings	None
An encounter with an NPC imminent	
Friendly to Player Characters	−10
Uncaring toward Player Characters	None
Dangerous to Player Characters	+ 10
Catastrophic event about to take place	+ 10

Encounter

Emotional state of the encountered NPC

Calm	−10
Friendly	−5
Excited	none
Enraged	+ 10

Compare the force of the PC's intuition to the resistance of the situation to obtain a TAROC result, then consult the following chart:

T = *Total:* The PC has a clear, vivid feeling about the subject or object. If danger is imminent, she will have an overwhelming sense of foreboding. If encountering an NPC, the PC will be able to divine the NPC's intentions toward her.

A = *Almost:* The PC has some feelings about the subject or object. If danger is imminent, she will feel uneasy. If encountering an NPC, the PC will have an impression about the NPC's intentions toward her.

R = *Reasonable:* The PC has only vague impressions about the subject or object, which arise more from what is obvious than from what she senses. If encountering an NPC, she will judge it by outward appearance more than any inner feelings.

O = *Off:* The signals get crossed. PCs will have dark forebodings in the middle of entirely peaceful surroundings or will feel truly at ease just before plunging into terrible danger. If encountering an NPC, the PC will have completely wrong ideas about the NPC's intentions.

C = *Canceled:* The PC senses nothing about the subject or object. She has no sense of foreboding if danger is imminent. She will feel nothing about any NPC encountered.

As with Knowledge, the Gamejudge should keep the actual result of the CPS determination secret since the result will occasionally ask the Gamejudge to provide the PC with misinformation.

Example:
Michael's *Duuk-tsarith* is exploring the rooms known as Merlyn's Chambers in the Font. Entering a dark room, he discovers that no light of any kind will illuminate it. The *Duuk-tsarith* decides to use his Intuition Ability to see if he can discover if there are monsters waiting to attack him.

Even though Michael's PC is the one exerting the Force (Intuition), the Gamejudge rolls the die behind a screen so that the result cannot be seen by Michael. The result is an "O," an Off result, which requires the Gamejudge to impart false information to the *Duuk-tsarith*.

The Gamejudge tells Michael, "You feel perfectly safe and, in fact, you get the distinct impression that a fabulous treasure is just waiting for you to discover it." Pleased with his own intuitive sense, the *Duuk-tsarith* steps boldly into the dark room and immediately feels unseen hands grab him around the ankles and start pulling him to a pit!

Senses

How well the PC sees, how much the PC can hear, how well the PC identifies objects by taste or smell or touch are all related to the Senses Attribute. The Senses Attribute covers all five senses with one score. Whenever the PC has a chance of seeing something that normally would not catch his eye, a Senses Check is used. Whenever there is a chance that a faint crackle of leaves will give away an enemy's position to a well-tuned ear, the Senses Check is used.

The following lists several examples of Sense Resistance Factors and possible modifiers. The numbers alone represent Resistance Scores; numbers with plus or minus signs represent Modifiers.

SENSE RESISTANCE FACTORS

Sight
Size of the target[1]
Size difference 0–40	50/50
Size 41–60	40/55
Size 61–100	30/60
Size 101–1,000	10/80
Size 1,000–10,000	5/100

Lighting (Resistance Modifiers)
Bright Day	− 10
Hazy Day	− 5
Cloudy Day	None
Stormy	+ 5 to + 15
Twilight	+ 15
Moon-light night	+ 10
Star-filled night	+ 20
Cloudy night	+ 50

Light Room	None
Dim Room (Torchlight)	+15
Dark room (slivers of light from door cracks)	+50
Unlit Cavern	+100

Sound

Small tinkle of glass touched together	71
Gravel underfoot	52
Dry Leaves Underfoot	43
Whisper	65
Muttering	55
Normal Voices	50
Loud Voices (shouting)	35
Small Battle	20
Large Battle	10

Smell and Taste

Faint Odor/Taste (single rose/faintly tainted water)	53
Strong Odor/Taste (many roses/bitter drink)	45
Stench/Rotting	10

Touch

Gentle Breeze	45
Slight shift in the still air	65
Subtle change in temperature (1–3 degrees)	45
Sudden change in temperature (4–10 degrees)	10

Distance to Target (Modifiers for Sight, Sound and Smell)

1 *metra*	None
2–3 *metra*	+5
4–5 *metra*	+10
6–10 *metra*	+15
11–30 *metra*	+20
31–50 *metra*	+25
51–100 *metra*	+35
100–500 *metra*	+50
501–1,000 *metra* (one *mila*)	+75

[1]Use the number before the slash if the target is larger than the character doing the Sense Check. Use the number after the slash if the target is smaller than the character doing the Sense Check.

Whenever a Senses Check is called for, subtract the appropriate Resistance score with Modifiers from the PC's Sense (Force) to determine the DIF row for the result on the CPS Table. Use this to figure the TAROC result and then apply the result using the following guidelines.

T = *Total:* The PC sees, hears, smells, tastes, or feels whatever is the target of the Senses Check and, if it is known to him, can identify it in general terms. The direction or distance (not both) can also be determined in a general way.
A = *Almost:* The PC can see, hear, etc. the target of the Senses Check. The PC can identify the smell in a general way. Direction and distance are not determined.
R = *Reasonable:* The PC notices *something* but cannot determine what it is. There will be a +2 to the PC's subsequent attempt at this same Senses Check.
O = *Off:* The PC fails to see, hear, etc. entirely and MAY MAKE NO FURTHER ATTEMPTS at this Senses Check.
C = *Cancel:* The PC senses nothing.

PCs may make only THREE attempts at any one Senses Check. If they fail to notice the sight, sound, etc. in three tries, further attempts will be of no use.

Variable Senses: There are blind people who have exceptional hearing. Some people have highly developed senses of smell. In other words, not all people have equal abilities in their senses. The Senses Attribute works, as all things in Phantasia, in a general way.

If, however, you would like your PC to have more detail in this area, you may use modifiers to give variety to the different types of senses you use. You might have a +5 modifier for your sight, for example, which would increase your effective Senses Attribute by five whenever you were looking for something. If you do this, however, it is MANDATORY that you also have a negative modifier of the same value for some other sense.

Shape: Form and Size

Form
Form gives a general idea of the appearance and ancestry of creatures in the game. This not only gives some guidance as to the appearance of the creature, but is also used to determine the effects of magical transformation of the creature encountered.

Everything in the game is classified by five levels of form: Attributes, Sex, Species, Genus, and Kingdom. However, in most instances, these levels are not all written on the PC sheet. "Human," for example, doesn't refer to the sex or specific attributes of a PC, nor does it give the full Kingdom/Genus/Species structure of its grouping. Still, when you see "Human" in the Form slot of the PC, you have a pretty good idea what all these others are.

Each of the five levels of form is described in detail in the Abilities section. Form has little effect on Attributes other than as an aid in describing the PC. Its more important effect is its stabilizing influence on Transformation Magic, which is dealt with in the Abilities section.

Life (Lifewell, Renewal, Capacity & Resistance)
The Attributes of Life define the holding places and capacities for the magic that a character takes with him or can safely use. These scores regulate the Abilities—excluding Technologic Sorcery—by showing the limits of general Life and its passage in the individual users.

All of the Life Attributes will increase with the rise of the character's station. New and young characters of low station will have to make do with what they have until they earn sufficient experience to increase their station.

The Lifewell attribute has four scores. These are *Renewal, Capacity, Lifewell,* and *Resistance.*

All creatures of magic have a natural ability to renew their own Life over a period of time. The Renewal score indicates how many points of Life may be added to the character's Lifewell after one night's rest. Points renewed over and above the character's Lifewell maximum are lost—a character can only hold as much as his Lifewell maximum.

Capacity reflects the maximum amount of Life which

the character can use at any one time without being dammaged by its use. This may limit the amount of Life the character may use from his own Lifewell as well as from other sources such as catalysts.

The Lifewell score shows the current amount of Life which the character can hold. The score is in two parts. The score before the slash represents the amount of Life the character currently is holding while the score after the slash indicates the maximum amount of Life the character can hold at any one time. This limits the amount of Life available to the character unless he uses a catalyst.

Finally, all Living creatures in Thimhallan not only use magic, but have learned how to resist its use upon them as well. In this way, unwanted drainings by rogue catalysts and some types of magical attacks can be avoided. Whenever the Power of Life is used *directly* against a character, this score provides a base Resistance Score for the attempt. The character who is having the magic cast upon him may choose, however, not to resist the magic—in such cases, the Resistance Score is considered to be zero.

Acquired Life (Abilities)

The PC is considered to be born with certain Attributes. Abilities, to a large extent, are learned. While you are born with Talents in certain Mysteries, they are improved in your life through your Abilities.

There are two types of Abilities: Magical and Technological. Magical Abilities use the power of Life to create new scores that temporarily—sometimes permanently—replace or alter your Attributes. The Technological Ability—the dark arts of Sorcery—can also create new scores to replace or alter your Attributes. Technological Ability does so without the power of Life, however.

Example:
Michael's *Duuk-tsarith* has an Attack Attribute of fifty-four. He is about to be confronted by a Dragon of Night, which has a Defensive Attribute of eighty. Michael's score of fifty-four will not give him very good odds against the Dragon's defense of eighty, so the warlock decides to create

a Combat Magic Spell that will effectively alter his Attribute to a far higher number. Suffused with Life, the *Duuk-tsarith* prepares to do battle with the Dragon. He creates a Fireblossom spell that has an Attack Attribute of eighty-five and does a damage maximum of 120. The warlock had better hit the first time, because such a powerful spell will cost him dearly in Life!

Magical Abilities in Phantasia

Magical Abilities are used to create spells. These spells, in turn, generate Magical Attributes that replace the PC's original Attribute in the game for as long as the spell lasts. When the PC casts a Combat Spell, the magic in the spell creates Magical Attributes for Attack or Defense. When the PC casts a knowledge spell, the magic in the spell creates a Magical Attribute for Intelligence, Intuition, or Senses. These Magical Abilities work *exactly* the same way as their natural counterparts; the only difference is that Attributes may be created without any cost of Life points to the PC, whereas using Magical Abilities requires the draining of the PC's Life Points.

All Magic works the same way, but it has different effects, depending upon the Magical Attributes created.

Unless he is one of the Dead, the PC will be able to cast magic spells from any of the Mysteries, but only with various degrees of success. A *Duuk-tsarith* will not be particularly adept at commanding trees to move. A Druid will have difficulty casting Fireblossom explosions. Similarly, a Druid of high station in his Order will be able to command giant oaks to pull up roots and move on, while a Druid low in his Order may have to work very hard in order to persuade a weed to get out of his tomato patch.

Your Talent plus your Station determines your Ability in any Mystery. If your Talent is relatively low, you will have only moderate success even with the more basic and simple spells of the Mystery. If your Talent is high, then your success will be much greater.

There are eight different types of Magical Abilities: Fire, Water, Air, Earth, Life, Spirit, Time, and Shadow. Each type of magic has a different effect in the game, but all work in the same way.

There are three different types of spells:

(1) *Conjuration* — the use of magical force to temporarily affect an object; (2) *Alteration* — the permanent changing of an object through the power of magic; and (3) *Illusion* — appearance without substance.

Conjuration magic uses the power of Life directly. Examples of this are Lifeshields which create magical Defense Attributes, and Fireblossoms, which create magical Attack Attributes. These spells last only as long as the PC wants them to last (or has the Life Points to maintain).

Alteration magic deals with modifying or reshaping an object. This is either very easy or very difficult, depending upon how radically the PC wants to change the object. Changing a grape to a raisin is relatively easy. Changing a man to an Ariel is not.

Illusion is the Mystery of Shadow. Through Illusion the PC can *appear* to Conjure or Alter an object at a fraction of the Lifecost required for real Conjuration or Alteration. All Lifecost multipliers — except for duration — are ignored when crafting an Illusion. Illusions may occasionally confuse or frighten, but they do not change the actual Attributes of a person or have any permanent damaging effects.

All spells are constructed using the same process. The steps by which a spell is created are:

1. Determine the Attributes of the spell you are casting.
2. Calculate the spell's Force and Lifecost.
3. Expend Life for the spell.
4. Determine whether or not spell was successful.
5. Determine the result of the spell.

Each of these steps is explained in greater detail below.

1. Determine the Attributes of the spell you are casting

The spell you are going to construct is defined by the Magical Attribute it creates. A spell that causes damage to your enemy creates a magical Attack Attribute. A spell to divine the history of an object does so by creating a magical Intelligence Attribute.

PCs in Thimhallan are all of certain Mysteries. These

Mysteries are actually labels of titles that reflect the PCs' Talents in the various kinds of magic. Warlocks are especially gifted when it comes to combat spells. *Theldara* are especially gifted in magical healing. The fact that the various Mysteries cast different spells with different levels of success is reflected in the Ability Scores for each of the Mysteries.

PCs may attempt to create spells in any Mystery in which they have at least one point of Ability. How well those spells will work is determined by their Ability score in that Mystery.

Each Mystery that deals with Life is listed below. The type or types of spells that are permitted to that Mystery are shown in parenthesis after the name. For example, the FIRE: ATTACK & DEFENSE Mystery lists Conjuration as the only type of spell that may be constructed using that Mystery. How each of these spells is constructed is given, along with examples of each type.

FIRE: ATTACK & DEFENSE (Conjuration)

Fire conjurations are among the simplest spells to perform. Determine the value of the Magical Attack Attribute the PC wants to create with the magic. This number will also be the value used later in determining spell costs. If the spell is successfully cast, simply use this Magical Attack Attribute number in place of the PC's normal Attack Attribute to determine the effect of the spell.

Example:
ATTACK: Michael determines to cast a Fireblossom spell in order to stop the Desert Raider who is fleeing from him. He arbitrarily decides that sixty points should be enough to stop the Raider. Sixty will be the value used later to determine the Lifecost of the spell. Sixty will also be the Magical Attack Attribute if the spell is cast successfully.

DEFENSE: The Desert Raider sees the *Duuk-tsarith* closing in on her. The Raider decides to cast a Lifeshield defensive spell. She hurriedly calculates that she will need at least a Defensive score of seventy to counter whatever the *Duuk-tsarith* has in mind. Seventy will be the value used later to determine the Lifecost of the spell. It will also

be the Magical Defense Attribute if the spell is cast successfully.

Basic Fire spells are conjurations; they last only so long
as the power of the spell holds out. To be made permanent
Fire Spells must be combined with other Mysteries. See
"Combined Spells," below.

MAGICAL ATTRIBUTES USING FORCE AND RESISTANCE

All following spells are cast using either Force or
Resistance to modify the spell's effects. For example, a PC
casting a Dexterity spell on a rope can declare Force,
which will make the rope easier to climb (putting knots
on it), or Resistance, which will make the rope extremely
slippery. A PC casting an Intelligence spell on an unread-
able scroll may use Force, in which case the scroll will
become understandable, or he may use Resistance, in which
case the scroll will be completely indecipherable.

The PC must declare which — Force or Resistance — he is
using when casting the spell.

AIR: MOVEMENT (Conjuration)

Air spells may be cast either by the PC on other objects
or by the PC on himself. An Air Mystery spell can be cast
on a teapot (to make it float), or another person (to help
him float over a wall), or on the PC himself (to allow him
to float over a wall).

There are three types of Air Mystery spells: *Strength*,
Dexterity, and *Movement*.

Strength spells create a magical Strength Attribute. These
are useful in moving heavy objects or forcing open doors.
By creating a strength spell on herself, the PC may be able
to break down doors. By casting a strength spell on the
door, the PC may be able to reinforce it against others
who are trying to break it in!

STRENGTH: Carey runs a PC *Kan-Hanar* named Klint.
Klint is faced with a large boulder blocking the road. His
caravan of one hundred floating platforms could be lifted
over the boulder but at an enormous Life cost. Better just
to move the rock.

Klint summons up a Strength Force spell. He guesses

the boulder's weight to be about sixty and decides that a Strength of eighty should be able to move it. Eighty becomes the value of the magical Strength Attribute and will also be used to determine the Lifecost of the spell. The spell is successful and the result is that Klint is able to lift the huge boulder and move it to one side of the road.

Dexterity may be enhanced with a spell of this type. This is useful when trying to throw a rock through a particularly small hole in a wall. It is an *essential* part of any Movement spell. Dexterity cast on the PC makes climbing walls much easier. Dexterity Force cast on the wall will fill it with hand and footholds if the spell is successful. Dexterity Resistance will cover the wall with oil and make it difficult for enemies to follow up after you. Dexterity cast on an object in conjunction with Movement (Combined spell) may make the rope move to avoid being climbed in the first place.

Example:
DEXTERITY: Klint has successfully moved the boulder; now he finds his caravan facing a difficult and winding path up a mountain. His caravan platforms are large and they must move very slowly or continually run up against the rocks. Since their cargo is needed desperately in Avidon, Klint cannot afford the time to move the caravan slowly. He calls together his companions and each of them casts a Dexterity Force spell on the platforms to imbue them with a Dexterity of sixty for three hours. They now move over the rocky terrain with the grace of mountain goats.

Movement spells provide the capability of either velocity or stopping. They do not add Dexterity, which often comes into play when moving. Casting a Movement spell on an object that does not have its own Dexterity is like putting a rocket engine on a wheeled vehicle and neglecting to add a steering mechanism. When combined with Dexterity, however, Movement spells allow an inanimate object to move at the magus's will. A Movement Resistance spell will keep the object immobile.

Living creatures who have their own Dexterity Attribute may use their own Dexterity for purposes of movement — if the caster of the spell wills it. This means that a flying Movement spell cast on another person will give her the ability to fly with a Dexterity the same as her Dexterity Attribute. However, if the caster of the spell declares the movement to be under his own control, then a person with a Movement spell cast on her will float about at the will of the spellcaster, unless she can resist the magic. If no such declaration is made, however, the Movement remains under the control of the person or creature on whom the spell is cast.

There are three kinds of Movement in Phantasia: Surface, Flight, and Water. Surface refers to travel across the ground, Flight to movement through the air, and Water to any movement through the water. When casting a Movement spell, you will need to state the kind of Movement the spell will create.

Example:
MOVEMENT: Klint needs real speed to get these platforms over the mountains before the Dexterity spell he has cast wears off. He again brings together his companions and they cast another spell on the platform—this time, a Movement Force spell. The platforms are given a Movement of twenty-five. Klint and his companions leap on top of the platform, where they cast the magic and begin guiding the platforms quickly and with great dexterity over the rocky terrain.

WATER: HEALING AND LIVING CHANGE *(Conjuration and Alteration)*

The Mystery of Water and its spells are the only ones that affect existing Attributes either temporarily or permanently in living creatures. The affecting of Attributes in inanimate objects is the province of the Mystery of Earth (see below).

There are two types of water spells: *Healing* and *Living Change.*

Healing: The Water Mystery is used most often for healing PCs who have been damaged in combat. This is the simplest type of water magic. The Resistance to healing is equal to the amount of damage the PC has taken. PCs who are dead can *not* be healed.

As with other spells, Healing uses either Force or Resistance, and the spellcaster should declare which is being used when casting the spell. Healing Force will heal a person injured in combat. Healing Resistance has the opposite effect and could be used by Druids to wilt weeds in a berry patch or to inflict a disease upon their enemies.

Example:

HEALING: Lutz is playing a *Theldara* named Crandel. Michael's *Duuk-tsarith* has nearly died in combat with a gore and another attack is likely any moment. Crandel casts a spell with thirty Magical Attribute points. In healing, this will erase thirty points of damage from the *Duuk-tsarith*'s Character Sheet. If the spell is successful, the Enforcer should be up and around in time for the next battle.

Living Change: Any natural Attribute can be changed either temporarily or permanently through the use of these spells. A PC may change a comrade or himself into a dragon for a short time—or permanently if he has the Life to do so.

Living Change only affects certain Attributes. The Shape Attributes (Form and Size) will be automatically altered by the spell to coincide with the effective change. Living Change will *not* affect any of the Life Attributes (Renewal, Capacity, Lifewell, or Resistance). The Gamejudge will decide exactly what form and size the receiver of such a spell will take, based on the success and result of the spell as determined by the CPS Chart.

(Since Living Change changes Attributes, it does not use either Force or Resistance and these do not need to be declared when casting this spell.)

Follow these steps to determine the values for a Living Change spell:

A. Determine specific Attributes that the PC wants changed

Because Living Change spells alter the object into another form, they modify the object's previous stats. For example, a human with a Physical Attack score of forty could be magically altered into a were-tiger with an attack score of sixty-five. To do this, the human's Attack Attribute must be altered fifteen points.

The number of different Attributes and the number of points the PC may change are limited by the type of Alteration. Use the following Forms and Attributes table to determine these limits.

Forms and Attributes Table

Level	Name	Max Number Attributes Changed	Max Number Change in Score	Lifecost Modifiers
1	Lycanthropy	3	20	None
2	Sex	4	10	×2
3	Species	4	30	×10
4	Genus	6	50	×100
5	Kingdom	All	Unlimited	×1000

Examples:
  Lycanthropy: man to were-beast.
  Sex: male to female or vice versa
  Species: lizard to dragon
  Genus: pig to dragon
  Kingdom: man to stone

Maximum number of Attributes changed: This represents how many different types of Attributes may be changed by the spell. A Lycanthropy spell may only change three Attributes. For example, the change may affect the Attributes of Strength, Attack, and Dexterity if the PC casting the spell chooses those three. A Genus spell, however, allows for the altering of up to six separate Attributes.

Example:
Michael's *Duuk-tsarith* decides to enhance his own Attributes magically. A pack of dugruns is attacking him. In order to defend himself, he decides to become a dragon. A Genus change allows him to select up to six different Attributes to change. He chooses Attack, Defense, Health, Strength, Dexterity, and Movement. All his other attributes will remain

the same except for his Form and Size, which the Game-judge will decide upon, based upon the success and result of his spell as determined by the CPS Chart.

B. Determine the number of Positive and Negative numbers of changes to make

Maximum Number Change in Score: This is the maximum number of change that can be made in any one Attribute. (Refer to Forms and Attributes Table.) A PC with an Attack Attribute of forty who is doing a Lycanthropy change can raise that Attribute to as high as sixty (40 + 20 = 60) but cannot raise it any higher. PCs doing a Genus change would be limited to fifty. Kingdom changes are unlimited number.

These changes can be either up (raises Attribute scores) or down (lowers Attribute scores). Write down which Attributes will change and by how many points.

Example:

In order to become a dragon, Michael's *Duuk-tsarith* now has to determine the changes he wants to make in his Attribute scores. He decides to raise his Attack by twenty-five, raise his Defense by twenty, increase his Health by thirty, pump up his Strength by ten, lower his Dexterity by thirty, and increase his Movement fifteen.

C. Determine the spell's total value

Separately total all the positive numbers (those that increase the receiver's Attributes) and all the negative numbers (those that decrease the receiver's Attribute scores). If the lower number is *more* than half the larger number, the value of the spell is one-half the larger number. If the lower number is *less* than half the larger number, then the value for the spell is the larger number minus the lower number.

Example:

Michael's *Duuk-tsarith* is ready to change from man to dragon. His positive changes are taken from his increases in Attack, Defense, Health, Strength, and Movement Attributes. These total exactly one hundred (25 + 20 + 30 + 10 + 15 = 100). His negative changes were limited to the decrease in his Dexterity by thirty, so his total negative change is thirty. One hundred is the larger number and thirty is the lower number. Since the lower number is less than half the larger number, Michael subtracts it from the larger number and gets the result of seventy (100 − 30 = 70). Therefore, the value for Michael's Alteration Spell is seventy.

The Life Change spell, unlike other spells, does not create a Magical Attribute of its own. Instead, it enhances the Attributes the PC already has either for the duration of the spell (Conjured Living Change) or permanently (Alteration Life Change).

EARTH: STANDARD CHANGE (Alteration)

This Mystery, which deals with changing the Attributes in inanimate objects, is called *Standard Change*. It is conducted in precisely the same way as Living Change but may be performed on inanimate objects only.

Example:

STANDARD CHANGE: Michael has two other PCs he occasionally plays named Tucker and Twine. The PCs are twins. Tucker is a *Theldara* (a healer) and Twine is a *Quinalban* (a conjurer of inanimate objects). Tucker can perform Living Changes but not Standard Changes. Twine can perform Standard Changes but not Living Changes. This means that Tucker can change dogs into cats or people into lizards. Twine can change dead trees into homes, rocks into furniture, twist marble into fantastic shapes, and when duty calls, he can change the stone walls of an enemy fortress into ice so that by morning they will melt.

To accomplish the latter, Twine would have to change the Defense Attribute of the wall to zero. The description of what that means is up to the Gamejudge, although changing stone to ice is as good a description as any. See "What does the spell look like?" on page 366.

TIME: INTELLIGENCE & FARSIGHT (Conjuration)

The Mystery of Time was, anciently, the province of the Diviners, who were powerful in the art of seeing and understanding both the past and the future through their magic.

Today, their Mystery is lost, although there are some who still have Talent in this Ability. There are two types of Time spells: *Standard Intelligence* and *Senses*.

Standard Intelligence spells generate a value that both replaces the PC's natural Attributes and is used for the value of the spell to determine its success. Standard Intelligence spells may be cast concerning knowledge of the past (smaller modifiers) or the future (large modifiers). Standard Intelligence deals with information about the object. It differs from Telepathic Intelligence, which deals in knowledge and motivations taken directly from the mind and spirit.

Example:

STANDARD INTELLIGENCE: Michael's *Duuk-tsarith* wants to know the history of a crown he has found in the vaults of the Font. He casts an Intelligence spell of eighty points, which will be both the magical Intelligence Attribute and the value for the spell. The modifiers for this spell will be small since he is trying to learn the past history of the object. If he were trying to learn the future history (fate) of the object, the modifiers will be much higher and it would be far more costly in terms of Life!

Casting for knowledge of the future is always a tricky proposition at best. When a Gamejudge is required to give knowledge of the future, it simply means that he must tell the PC something that *may* happen—not necessarily something that is guaranteed to happen. This means that the Gamejudge, knowing the trouble the PC faces, will give the PC a warning about a certain situation, but nothing more conclusive.

For example, the Gamejudge knows that if the PC enters a certain cave, he will face a Night Dragon. There is the possibility, though, that the PC will bypass the cave completely. If he enters, he may fight the dragon and win.

Therefore, the Gamejudge will warn the PC that he *may* be killed by a Night Dragon. The Gamejudge will not say specifically that the PC *will* be killed in a fight with a Night Dragon.

Senses spells also generate a value used for both a score to replace the PC's natural Attribute and to determine its success and costs. In casting the spell, regardless of whom the spell is cast upon, the caster of the spell must say which sense (hearing, sight, taste, touch, or smell) is being affected.

Example:
SENSES: Michael's *Duuk-tsarith* wants Klint to see a battle taking place clear across the valley. The Enforcer casts a Senses spell, telling the Gamejudge that the spell is for seeing. The spell will have a value of 120, which will also be the Magical Attribute of the spell if it is successful. The Gamejudge rules that if the spell is successful, Klint's eyes will see as if through a magical window that magnifies objects miles away.

SPIRIT: TELEPATHY & EMPATHY (Conjuration)

Though nearly a lost art in modern time, the Mystery of Spirit was once a powerful force in Thimhallan. With it the dead could be contacted and people's true inner thoughts and feelings known. In more modern times, those of this Mystery have disappeared from the world and its secrets have gone with them. Only a small Talent for that Mystery remains to be found among the Living today.

There are three kinds of Spirit Magic: *Telepathic Intelligence*, which deals specifically with gaining information directly from the mind of a living creature, *Intuition*, which has like effect to the Intuition Attribute of the PC, and *Persuasion*, which acts as a special new Attribute.

Telepathic Intelligence is like Standard Intelligence, listed above, except that it deals with information that can be gained from the mind of the living—or occasionally the dead. A Telepathic Intelligence spell, also called a telepathy spell, creates a Magical Intelligence Attribute that may receive information from the mind of another. The value of the spell acts as the score of the Magical Attribute and helps one determine its success and costs.

If the spell is successful, the Force of the Magical Intelligence Attribute will be resisted by the Intelligence of the target. The target cannot lessen the Resistance through his or her own will. The results of the spell are similar to those for the natural Intelligence Attribute Checks.

Example:
TELEPATHIC INTELLIGENCE: Kathri runs a PC named Nardia who is a Necromancer from ancient days. Nardia is confronted in a dark street by a rather shabby-looking old man in rags. The Necromancer is supposed to meet a stranger here with information about her past. Could this be the man? Nardia decides to use a Telepathic Intelligence spell on the stranger to read his thoughts. She determines the value of the spell to be seventy-five. She hopes the intelligence of the man is not too high for her spell to be successful, for the man's intelligence will fight her telepathic attempt to invade his mind.

Intuition Spells act to create magical Intuition Attributes. The results are read as in using the Intuition Attribute. How the results appear may be determined by the Gamejudge or the PC. See "What Will the Spell Look Like?" on p. 366.

INTUITION:

Persuasion Spells actually create a temporary new Attribute called Persuasion. This Attribute is used to persuade another creature to follow you and obey any instructions you give him. The value of the spell becomes the Force in the attempt. This is resisted by the Intelligence of the victim or target of the spell—assuming the spell works in the first place.

If the spell is successful, subtract the victim's Intelligence Attribute from the force of the Persuasion spell (the Force being the same as the value determined by the spell's success) and determine a TAROC result from the CPS. Read with the results as follows:

T = *Total:* The victim of the spell falls completely and totally under the sway of the spellcaster. The victim will do anything that the magus requires of him for the duration of the spell.

A = *Almost:* The victim of the spell will do anything requested of him until he sees that his life is being placed in jeopardy or until he takes damage, at which point the spell will be broken. The spell will last only so long as the duration of the spell in any event.

R = *Reasonable:* The victim can see the logic in the PC's actions and will act for the PC during the next course of events. Thereafter, the victim will be free to act on his own.

O = *Off:* The victim knows what that the spellcaster is trying to charm him and becomes enraged. The victim may take what action it deems necessary to avoid having the spell cast on him—either fleeing or attacking.

C = *Cancelled:* The spell has no effect.

Example:
PERSUASION: Kathri's Necromancer Nardia has been captured by a party of dugruns. She is now being held in a cavern guarded by one of the vile creatures. Nardia decides to cast a Persuasion spell to convince the dugrun that she is his friend. Kathri decides that fifty points will be sufficient, since the dugruns are notoriously low in intelligence. When she is successful, she persuades the dugrun to help her escape.

SHADOW: ILLUSION (Conjuration and Alteration)

Things that appear to the senses as something other than what they truly are are Illusions.

The Force of the Illusion is the Shadow Ability Score of the PC casting the spell. The Resistance is the Intelligence *or* Intuition Attribute of the PC or NPC viewing the Illusion. Subtract the Resistance from the Force to determine the CPS row. Use the TAROC result as follows:

Declared Action: The PC creates the Illusion of an attacking dragon in order to frighten away a centaur.

T = *Total:* The Character viewing the Illusion believes it and will act accordingly. No further checks against this Illusion will be necessary until it ends.

The PC creates the Illusion of an attacking dragon and the centaur flees in terror.

A = *Almost:* The Character viewing the Illusion hesitates to believe it. The PC may attempt to cast the Illusion again next round with a –2 penalty to the Force Score. This penalty is cumulative until the Character either believes the Illusion or disbelieves it. For example, if the Force Score on the first round was 50 and the Character viewing the Illusion scores an A on the CPS table, that Character will believe the Illusion for one round. On the following round the Force Score is checked again—this time with a score of 48 (50-2). The next round after that, the score is 46.

The PC casts an Illusion of an attacking dragon. The centaur halts in his own attack on the PC and stares at the dragon uncertainly. The PC must successfully cast the Illusion next round or the centaur will realize it has been tricked.

R = *Reasonable:* The Character viewing the Illusion is unsure about its authenticity. Attempt this again next round with a –5 penalty to the Force Score. This is a cumulative penalty to any other penalties already accrued.

The centaur's attack is halted by the Illusion of the dragon, but the centaur seems very skeptical and continues to look menacingly at the PC. The PC better hit this Illusion next round or be prepared to do battle.

O = *Off:* The PC creates an Illusion but not the one he intended. He may try for the Illusion he wants again next round with a –10 cumulative penalty subtracted from the Force Score.

The PC wanting to create the Illusion of an attacking dragon creates the Illusion of an attacking bunny rabbit. The centaur—after a fit of laughter—attacks the PC.

C = *Canceled:* The Illusion is not believed in the slightest. No further checks against this Illusion will be necessary for as long as it remains operating.

The PC creates the Illusion of an attacking dragon, but the centaur knows that there are no dragons living within a hundred miles of this place and so doesn't believe it for an instant. The centaur attacks the PC.

The Five Levels of Shape
There are five levels of shape that define each person, animal, or object.

1. Attributes and Lycanthropy: The first level of shape deals with the specific Attributes of the PC—those listed on the Character Sheet.

Lycanthropy (defined here as a human changing to any sort of an animal) deals with the magical alteration of an Attribute's maximum values. Growing fangs (i.e., increasing physical attack score) or a thick coat of fur (i.e., increasing physical defensive score) would be a level-one shape change, or, in other words, a lycanthropic change.

2. Sex: This refers to the male or female sex of the PC or object in question.

In terms of magical alteration from one sex to another, the process takes place throughout the entire body (as opposed to the teeth's growing larger) and is, therefore, more expensive in terms of Lifecost.

3. Species: The classic test for whether creatures are of the same species is whether, if they were mated, there would be any offspring. Humans and Ariels would be considered in the same species. Centaurs and humans would not. Changing within a species—turning a human into an Ariel —requires more Life than changing a male human into a werewolf (lycanthropic), but it costs less Life than changing a human into a centaur.

4. Genus: Groups of species form a genus. All reptiles would be a genus, which would include the species for crocodiles and alligators as well as a separate species for dragons and basilisks. Centaurs would be found in the genus of War-changed Radicals rather than in either the genus for horses or humans. Changing a lizard into a dragon costs less Life than changing a pig into a dragon because lizards and dragons are both reptiles.

5. Kingdom: This refers to the broadest category. The Kingdoms of Thimhallan include Animal, Vegetable, Mineral, and Ethereal. Changing a human to stone (the Turning) costs an incredible amount of Life.

LIFE: LIFE TRANSFER

The Mystery that deals with the transfer or the gifting of the power of Magic is known as Life. All the magic of Thimhallan is powered by the essence of Life.

Catalysts are the fountains of Magic in the world. The catalyst's function in society is to dispense Life. In a sense, a catalyst, through the Conduit, alters the Lifewell Attribute of the PC by refilling it when it is depleted.

Catalysts have two actions they can perform: (1) the opening of Corridors for quick passage throughout Thimhallan and (2) the forming of *Conduit* which channels the power of Life directly into another person for use.

CORRIDORS

Corridors go nearly everywhere in Thimhallan. The art of creating them was long ago lost but they still remain in use today.

The amount of Life required to open a corridor and the success of its opening depends upon several factors including distance from the present location, whether the target location is currently inhabited and how secure the location is supposed to be.

Determine a TAROC result on the CPS using the amount of Life spent by the person asking the corridor to be opened as the Force. Use the following table to determine the resistance to the opening of the corridor.

Corridor Resistance Scores and Modifiers

Distance to target location
    1 to 100 *metra* . . . . .2 per 10 *metras*
    101 *metras* to 1 *mila* . . . . 20 + 2 per 100 *metras*
    More than 1 *mila* . . . . 40 + 1 per *milas*
Obscurity of Location
    Civilization
        Private Residence . . . . ×10
        Important or Wealthy person's residence . . . . . . ×100

Royal Residence .... × 1,000
Wilderness
   Ruins .... × 500
   Secret Location .... Gamejudge Determines
Description of target location
   Destination in same structure/building .... None
   Destination in same city/town .... × 2
   Raw Wilderness .... × 100

Once you have determined the force and the resistance for the Corridor opening, find the TAROC result on the CPS and use the following to judge the effects:

T = *Total:* The corridor is opened. Characters may pass. The corridor may remain open for a number of turns equal to the force of the opening.

A = *Almost:* The corridor is opened. Charactes may pass. The corridor may remain open for a number of rounds equal to the force of the opening.

R = *Reasonable:* The corridor is opened. It will close immediately after the characters have passed through it to their target destination.

O = *Off:* The corridor is opened to an alternate and unplanned location. It will remain open for R-3 rounds. (A random number from one to ten minus three rounds. Any result of less than zero is considered zero. Zero means that the corridor will close immediately after the characters pass through it.) The Gamejudge determines just what that location is.

C = *Cancelled:* The corridor does not open. The life is expended anyway.

CONDUITS

Catalysts have very small lifewells of their own, their duty being not to take but to give. Catalyst grant Life through the *Conduit*, which allows the catalyst to draw Life directly from one source and transfer it to another.

To utilize this ability the catalyst follows these steps:

1. Open the Source Conduit

Check the Conduit Resistance Chart to determine the Source Resistance to the Conduit. The source of the Life may be anything from rocks beneath the catalyst's feet to an enemy warlock with his own catalyst.

Conduit Resistance Chart

Description	Resistance	Life Available
Source	+1 per *mila*	
The Font	from Font	Unlimited
Living Woods	60	5000
Water	70	6000
Earth/Stone	40	4000
Willing Donor	None	Lifewell of Donor
Unwilling Donor	Life Resistance	Special[1]
Catalyst's Strength		
½ normal	−10	Unlimited
¼ normal	−30	Unlimited
¹⁄₁₀ normal	−70	Unlimited
Distance to Receiver	+5 per *metra*	Unlimited

[1]The Life available from an unwilling donor is limited to either the targets' own Lifewell or any Conduits that he has available to him.

Subtract the Resistance from the catalyst's Life Ability Score to determine the row on the CPS. The TAROC results will be as follows:

T = *Total:* The magic flows freely. All the points available in the area can be accessed by the catalyst.
A = *Almost:* The magic flows well. Half of the points available in the area can be accessed by the catalyst.
R = *Reasonable:* The magic is inhibited. A fourth of the points available in the area can be accessed by the catalyst.
O = *Off:* The connection is difficult. One tenth of the points available in the area can be accessed by the catalyst.
C = *Canceled:* The blockage is total and no connection is made. There are no points available to the catalyst.

If faced with the possibility of combat, it might be wise for a catalyst to draw Life prior to rather than during a battle since this action counts as one round. The catalyst cannot perform any other action this round. (The catalyst cannot transfer Life to anyone until the next round.)

2. Open the Output Conduit

The PC or NPC who is to accept the magic from the Conduit is called the Receiver. Make a TAROC check using the catalyst's Life Ability as a Force Score minus any distance-from-the-catalyst Resistance modifiers.

Declared action: The catalyst wants to transfer magic from the world around him to a *Duuk-tsarith* who is fighting a Hunterkill.

T = *Total:* The magic flows freely. All the points available from the catalyst can be accessed by the Receiving Character. The catalyst is able to give all magic intended to the *Duuk-tsarith*, who uses it to cast a spell that defeats the Hunterkill.

A = *Almost:* The magic flows well. Half of the point available from the catalyst can be accessed by the Receiver. The catalyst is able to give only part of the magic required to the *Duuk-tsarith*, who must therefore modify the spell she intended to cast at the Hunterkill for one that requires less Life.

R = *Reasonable:* The magic is inhibited somewhat. A fourth of the points available from the catalyst can be accessed by the Receiver. The *Duuk-tsarith* looks for an even lower Lifecost spell.

O = *Off:* The connection is difficult. One tenth of the points available from the catalyst can be accessed by the Receiver. The *Duuk-tsarith* looks for another catalyst.

C = *Canceled:* The blockage is total and no connection is made. There are no points available from the catalyst. The *Duuk-tsarith* looks for a Corridor!

Remember that this effect is cumulative. For example: A catalyst opens an Input Conduit to a source hoping to draw 1,000 points from it for his warlock. He gets an Off result and can only draw 100 points. Next round he opens the Output Conduit to his warlock. The bumbling catalyst then gets a second Off result when opening the Output Conduit and can only give one tenth of what he is receiving — i.e., 10 points. This catalyst is going to have a lot of explaining to do!

Once opened, the Conduit and its flow of energy will remain constant for that round so long as the Conduit is kept open.

3. Adjust Catalyst's Strength

Keeping the Conduit active is a difficult and exhausting prospect. For every round the Conduit remains open after the first round, the catalyst must determine another TAROC result. Use the catalyst's current modified strength as the Force Score. The Resistance will be a cumulative stat of ten per round that the Conduit remains open. The results of this will be the *temporary* draining of the catalyst's strength Attribute. Keep track of this drain separately from the Attribute itself as you will need to be able to compare the two scores for future Conduit Resistance modifiers.

T = *Total:* The magic is flowing well. No changes in the catalyst's strength at this time.
A = *Almost:* The catalyst can feel the effects of the magic he is giving. Subtract five from the catalyst's strength. The Conduit remains open if desired.
R = *Reasonable:* The effects of the magic's running through the catalyst is beginning to take its toll. Subtract ten from the catalyst's strength. The Conduit remains open if desired.
O = *Off:* The catalyst is weary. Subtract twenty from the catalyst's strength. The Conduit remains open if desired.
C = *Canceled:* The catalyst collapses. The catalyst's strength falls to zero and the Conduit is forced shut.

Catalysts can regain their strength from the Conduit's effects at a rate of one point per hour of rest.

4. Close All Conduits

Conduits will remain open until either (1) the catalyst or the Receiver decides to close them or (2) the catalyst's strength fails.

Too Much Power: Receivers take 1R points of Physical Damage whenever they receive by Conduit more Life than their Station will allow.

The relationship between a catalyst and his magus is one of the most interesting and important aspects of this game. In most role-playing games, whenever the group faces danger, it is usually every man for himself. In this game a magus must act to defend not only himself but the weaker catalyst or risk losing his source of Life.

Catalysts and their magi should refer to Prince Garald's Teachings on the Art of Warfare in *Triumph of the Darksword*, volume three in the Darksword Trilogy, for tips on how the two can work together successfully to defeat an enemy. Gamejudges should also encourage PCs to work out their own systems.

Gamejudges are encouraged to add a realistic aspect to the role-playing. If the catalyst is transferring Life to his magus through touch, for example, then the Gamejudge should insist that the two actually clasp hands or the catalyst should put his hand on the magus's arm.

The Gamejudge should make certain that at least one person in the group is a catalyst. Don't allow the group to insist that the Gamejudge run the group's catalyst as an NPC. This might be all right in an emergency (the group's catalyst is studying for a final exam), but remember that this game is about relationships between the PCs as much as it is about fighting centaurs.

2. Calculate the spell's Force and Lifecost

Some spells have specific values and specific Force stats that will not vary. Other spells have variable values for variable effects. There are also modifiers attendant upon some spells.

Multiply the value of the spell by any type modifiers to determine the Lifecost of the spell. Note the Lifecost and the Force score.

Magic Modifiers

Variable	Lifecost Modifier	Force Modifier
Conjuration Duration		
1 round	None	None
Successive rounds < 10	×2 per round	−5
Successive turns < 10	×5 per turn	−10
Successive sequences <10	×8 per sequence	−15
Successive hours	×10 per hour	−25

(chart continued on page 364)

Spell Summary Table

Block & Elements	Force	Lifecost
Fire Conjuration		
ATTACK	V	2 per point
DEFENSE	V	2 per point
Air Conjuration (Strength, Dexterity, and Movement)		
STRENGTH	V	1 per point
DEXTERITY	V	2 per point
MOVEMENT		
Across the ground	V	1 per point
Through the water	V	2 per point
Through the air	V	1 per point
Water Conjuration (Healing and Living Change)		
HEALING	V	2 per point
LIVING CHANGE		
Lycanthropic	V	2 per point
Sex	V	10 per point
Species	V	50 per point
Genus	V	100 per point
Kingdom	V	1000 per point

Earth Conjuration (STANDARD CHANGE)
Shape Only .... V ... 2 per point
Shape and Size .... V ... 10 per point
State of being (solid, liquid, gaseous) ... V ... 50 per point
Attributes .... V ... 100 per point
Kingdom (Metallic, Lithic, Organic) .... V ... 1000 per point
Time Conjuration (Intelligence and Farsight)

STANDARD INTELLIGENCE
Past Knowledge (Divining from no intelligence source)
Of specific object present .... V ... 6 per point
Of person present .... V ... 4 per point
Of object not present .... V ... 8 per point
Of person not present .... V ... 6 per point
Present Knowledge
Of specific object present .... V ... 4 per point
Of person present .... V ... 2 per point
Of object not present .... V ... 6 per point
Of person not present .... V ... 4 per point
Future Knowledge
Of specific object present .... V ... 10 per point
Of person present .... V ... 10 per point
Of object not present .... V ... 12 per point
Of person not present .... V ... 12 per point

SENSES

Spirit: (Telepathy, Intuition, and Persuasion)

TELEPATHIC INTELLIGENCE (Knowledge about subjects from Intelligence source)		
Surface Emotions	Equal Victims Intelligence + V	2/point
Inner Emotions	Equal Victims Intelligence + V	5/point
Surface Thoughts	Equal Victims Intelligence + V	10/point
Inner Thoughts	Equal Victims Intelligence + V	20/point
Subconscious/Inner Motives	Equal Victims Intelligence + V	100/point
Memories	Equal Victims Intelligence + V	20/point
INTUITION		
Current Events		
Of specific object present	V	2 per point
Of person present	V	1 per point
Of object not present	V	3 per point
Of person not present	V	2 per point
Future Events		
Of specific object present	V	5 per point
Of person present	V	5 per point
Of object not present	V	6 per point
Of person not present	V	3 per point

PERSUASION

	V	
Agreement	Equal to Victim Intelligence	3 per point
Quest (must fulfill before free)	Equal to Victim Intelligence	10/point
Change Allegiance	Equal to Victim Intelligence	50/point
Emotion Alteration		200/point
Becalm	Equal to Victim Intuition	5/point
Enrage	Equal to Victim Intuition	1/point
Paralyze	Equal to Victim Intuition	50/point
Instill fear	Equal to Victim Intuition	20/point
Forget/amnesia	Equal to Victim Intuition	150/point

Death Conjurations (Persuasion and Enhancing Technology)[1]
Enhancements of technological devices through Conjuration are at the same costs listed above in each block. Treat the device as though it were a Living creature for purposes of this game.

[1] Acts such as these are crimes against the state and the church. While they are included here for purposes of the game, we feel bound to remind you that using magic with technology is an evil practice punishable by the Turning.

Variable	Lifecost Modifier	Force Modifier
Alteration	× 00	None
Lycanthropic	None	None
Sex	× 2	− 10
Species	× 10	− 20
Genus	× 100	− 40
Kingdom	× 1000	− 80
Shadow	× ¹⁄₁₀ & Special[2]	+ 10

[2]*ALL* other Lifecost modifiers with the exception of duration are ignored.

3. Expend Magic for the spell

Spells receive their energy from Life. Subtract the Lifecost of the spell from either (1) the Lifewell of the PC casting the spell, (2) from the Life being granted the PC by a catalyst, or (3) a combination of the two. Life, once spent, can be regained only through time or the aid of a catalyst.

4. Determine the success of the spell

Take the Ability score of the Mystery of the spell being cast (Force) and subtract the Resistance (if any) of the object, animal, or person that the PC is casting the spell on. This gives the DIF for the CPS Chart. Determine randomly the column number and find a TAROC result as follows:

T = *Total:* The spell is completely successful. All Force points are applied to Result of spell (Step #5).
A = *Almost:* The spell is partially successful. Only three quarters of the Force points are applied to Result of Spell.
R = *Reasonable:* The spell is only halfway successful. Only half the Force points are applied to Result of Spell.
O = *Off:* The spell is one-fourth successful. Only a quarter of the Force points are applied to Result of Spell.
C = *Fails:* The spell fails completely. No Force points can be applied to Result of Spell.

Once success of the spell has been determined, carry the points earns to Step #5.

5. Determine the result of the spell

The results of the spell are figured differently depending upon whether the spell was one of Conjuration, Alteration, or Shadow.

Conjuration Spells: These create Magical Attributes which replace the character's attributes for as long as the magic lasts. For example, a spell of the Mystery of Fire (Combat) that creates a Magical Attack Attribute of ten will cause the same damage to the target as the PC with an Attack Attribute of ten. This is true with all other Mysteries as well. A PC trying to divine the history of an object casts a spell of the Divining Mystery. The Magical Intelligence Attribute created by that spell will be the same to the PCs using an Intelligence Attribute.

Therefore, the Gamejudge should use the results tables from the various Attributes to determine the results of a Conjuration spell. For example, use the TAROC results from the Intuition Attribute section to determine any Intuition spell results. All modifiers still apply.

Alteration Spells: The Force Score is compared to the Resistance Score of the Target to determine the row on the CPS to be used. Determine the TAROC results as follows:

Declared action: The PC wants to change himself into a werewolf.

T = *Total:* The change is effected as desired. All the points that have been listed as being changed are altered. The PC becomes a werewolf and will attack with increased power.

A = *Almost:* The change retains all the power of the alteration but misses a few Attributes, resulting in a slight unbalancing of the object. If only one Attribute is being changed, then treat this result as a "T" result above. If more than one Attribute is slated to be changed, the Gamejudge randomly determines one out of every five Attributes being changed that will remain unaffected by the spell. *A minimum of one Attribute must remain unaffected.* The points that would have gone to those unaffected Attributes MUST be reassigned to the other Attributes that were affected. They may not be assigned to Attributes that were not going to be changed by the spell in the first place.

The PC's Attack Attribute is reduced. The PC changes

into a werewolf with the exception that he retains human-type teeth. (Therefore his attack will do less damage.)

R = *Reasonable:* Reduce the points that are to be added to or subtracted from each Attribute by half and then assign them normally. The PC looks to be about halfway between wolf and man. He may have nice silky fur, a long tail, wolf ears, and incredibly sharp claws on his hands but be human in all other respects.

O = *Off:* Reduce the points that are to be added to or subtracted from each Attribute by half, then randomly assign those values to the various Attributes of the PC *regardless of whether the Attributes were slated for change or not.* The Gamejudge is encouraged to have fun with this result. He may add all the points to the PC's Attack score for example. The PC, wanting to become a werewolf and requesting fangs, may grow huge, elephantine tusks that weigh more than he does. He may remain human but suddenly find that he has a row of sharp spines protruding from his back.

C = *Canceled:* The change does not take place at all.

It is important to note that *any* successful Alteration will result in some sort of appearance change—the more powerful the spell, the greater the change.

Gamejudges are encouraged to use their imaginations and provide vivid descriptions. Simply announcing that the spell has failed is boring. It is much more exciting and fun for the players if the Gamejudge describes the action thus:

"Mosiah casts his spell turning himself into a werewolf and leaps at the *Duuk-tsarith.* Unfortunately the spell fails, and the witch is now lying on the ground with Mosiah on top of her, nibbling at her neck."

What Will the Spell Look Like?

The answer is—whatever the PC or the Gamejudge wants it to look like!

A difference that *makes* no difference *is* no difference. This is the guiding rule when dealing with any Conjuration, Alteration, or other magic. Whenever a spell is cast, the Gamejudge and Players should feel free to be imaginative describing what the spell looks like, sounds like, or feels like.

A dugrun and a snake both have a Physical Attack

Score of 42. Their appearance—one being apelike and the other reptilian—makes no difference to the score of 42. Both have the same probability of hitting their opponent and doing the same amount of damage. The Gamejudge could say that the PCs are being attacked by a monster with a Physical Attack Score of 42. Yawn. It is much more exciting if the Gamejudge tells the PCs they see a giant snake slithering toward them across the sand, its forked tongue flicking in and out between its poisonous fangs.

Likewise, if the PC magically increases his Character's Physical Attack Attribute from 56 to 72, it makes little difference whether he does so by growing fangs or claws—the probability of the result will remain the same. The Gamejudge should encourage the PC to describe exactly what he does change to increase his attack score and should relate the results of the attack in similar exciting detail.

Death (Technology)

In the darkest reaches of our land there are covens of Technologists or Sorcerers. Anciently they were highly regarded and possessed great power. In these times, however, Technology has been exposed as a vile tool of the Dead.

The game of Phantasia simulates the effects of Technology without having to dabble in that terrible and evil art. The fact that Technology is included in this game should not be construed as condoning actual acts of Technology. This is a game of make-believe. Imagination is a healthy activity for both young and old, but even such exercise should never persuade the young and impressionable to enter into its Dark Arts.

Normally I would have been tempted to leave this part of the game completely out of this book. However, given the recent history of our lost home, it is impossible to comprehend us without its dark effects.

—Father Jivardi Kastidine

Those of the Ninth Mystery are called Sorcerers or Technologists. They practice the dark and secret craft of Technology. Using objects of Death called Tools, a Technologist of sufficient arcane learning can perform feats of wonder that rival the greatest power of magi. The Death

Mystery requires no Life, for all that it shapes and uses is Dead. Wood hewn from a once-living tree must be dead before it can be of use to a Technologist. The rock of theground is melted in their furnaces, draining it of all Life before it is then given a most horrible life of its own through its user.

Use of Technology

Technological devices either (1) increase a PC's Attributes (acting as a modifier to one's current Attributes) or (2) replace a PC's Attributes.

For example: A sword *increases* a PC's attack Attributes, a lever or pulley *increases* a PC's Strength Attribute. A gun *replaces* a PC's attack Attributes, a cart on wheels *replaces* a PC's ground Movement Attribute.

The following table lists common Technological items and their respective Attributes and Force Scores and Modifiers. Numbers that have a plus or minus sign before them are modifiers of the PC's existing Attribute. All other numbers replace the Attribute listed.

AUTHOR'S NOTE: I have taken the liberty of adding some of your own devices and giving equivalent scores here. Hopefully this will help you better understand our relative powers in the world.
                                                —*Father Jivardi Kastidine*

Select Technological Items Table

Description of Item	Attribute	Score of Modifier
Weapons (Technological Attacks)		
Personal Weapons		
Axe	Attack	+25
Bow & Arrow	Ranged Attack	+30
Gun		
Grenade Launcher	Ranged Attack	120
Handgun	Ranged Attack	70
Laser Pistol	Ranged Attack	75
Laser Rifle	Ranged Attack	95
Long Gun (Rifle)	Ranged Attack	80
Machine Gun	Ranged Attack	45[1]
Hammer		
Normal	Attack	+10

Description of Item	Attribute	Score of Modifier
Warhammer	Melee Attack	+25
Knife	Attack	+10
Spear	Attack	+30
Stone		
Boulder	Melee Attack	+30
Hand held	Ranged Attack	+15
Small	Ranged Attack	+5
Sword		
Broad sword	Melee Attack	+25
Long sword	Melee Attack	+22
Rapier	Melee Attack	+20
Heavy Weapons		
Cannon	Ranged Attack	120
Catapult	Ranged Attack	130
High-Energy		
Cannon	Ranged Attack	160
Laser Cannon	Ranged Attack	150

[1]May be used three times each round.

Armor (Technological Protection)
  Personal Armor

Chain-Mail Armor	Defense	+8
Helmet	Defense	+2
Plate-Mail Armor	Defense	+15
Reflective Armor	Defense	+2
Shield		
Large, Metal	Defense	+8
Large, Wooden	Defense	+6
Small, Metal	Defense	+5
Small, Wooden	Defense	+3
Heavy Armor		
Heavy Metal	Defense	120
Light Metal	Defense	80
Wagon, Wooden	Defense	60

Vehicles (Technological Movement)
  Ground Vehicles
    Small Vehicles

Chariots	Movement/Dexterity	15/20
Wagons	Movement/Dexterity	8/8
Carts	Movement/Dexterity	10/10
Wheelbarrows	Movement/Dexterity	5/25

Description of Item	Attribute	Score of Modifier
Scout cars	Movement/Dexterity	70/10
Large Vehicles		
Wagons	Movement/Dexterity	8/8
Freight Wagons	Movement/Dexterity	5/6
Armored Carriers	Movement/Dexterity	50/7
Gravitic Laser Tanks	Movement/Dexterity	50/6
Tread Laser Tanks	Movement/Dexterity	40/5
Water Vehicles		
Surface		
Pleasure Boats	Movement/Dexterity	15/10
Shore Assault Craft	Movement/Dexterity	25/20
Gunboats	Movement/Dexterity	50/6
Subsurface/submarine	Movement/Dexterity	40/5
Air Vehicles		
Aeroplanes	Movement/Dexterity	120/8
Assault Landers	Movement/Dexterity	230/6
Gliders	Movement/Dexterity	55/9
Jumpjets	Movement/Dexterity	450/7
Fire Vehicles (Jumpships)	Movement/Dexterity	100/2[2]

[2] The movement score is the speed through the ether. This is deceptive, for distances between locations are shorter through the ether than in the physical realms, and therefore much more distance can be covered in a much smaller space of time.

Medicine (Technological Healing)
Minor Healing

Bandage	Healing	+5
Medkit	Healing	+30
Splint	Healing	+7
Stitching	Healing	+6

Major Healing

Plasmatank	Healing	83
Plaster cast	Healing	+20

Crafting (Technological Shaping)
Strength Aids

Hydraulic Lift	Strength	60
Lever	Strength	+10

Description of Item	Attribute	Score of Modifier
Pulley	Strength	+12
Winch	Strength	+20
Dexterity Aids (Tools)	Dexterity	+2 to +18

Calculator (Technological Knowledge)

Abacus	Intelligence	+5
Books	Intelligence	+1 to +20
Computer	Intelligence	+1 to +100

Construction of Technological Items

From time to time a PC may desire to construct a Technological device. This is much the same as crafting a spell, except that no Life is involved in the process.

To craft a Technological device, follow these steps:

1. Select the type of device to construct

Use the Select Technological Items Table as a guide for determining the type of device you wish to construct. Determine the points for the device's Attributes just as you would for spells.

2. Determine the availability of materials

The Gamejudge should determine if the required materials are available for the construction of the device. If not, then the PC may be required to find these materials. NOTE: the availability of materials will decrease as the complexity level of the device increases. A PC wanting to make a simple set of bow and arrows with his own hands will be fairly well assured of finding the material he needs in order to produce his weapon. A PC wanting to manufacture a sword will have a more difficult time finding iron, a forge, and a blacksmith, while a PC wanting to construct a nuclear bomb will undoubtedly have to spend years simply searching for the plutonium!

Use the following guidelines to determine the availability of the materials. Total all of the attribute points for the device and compare that total to the following Table.

Total	Number of Rare Parts	Quest Required?	Cost in Life	Distance to travel	Area of Quest
1–10	1	No	R × 1	1 *mila*	Any
11–15	1	No	R × 20	10 *mila*	Wilderness
16–50	2	Yes	R × 100	50 *mila*	Town
51–100	3	Yes	R × 1,000	100 *mila*	City
101–150	4	Yes	R × 1,500	200 *mila*	Ruin
151–200	5	Yes	R × 2,000	500 *mila*	Lost Ruin

200 +   May only be made by combining different devices.

Number of Rare Parts: This is the number of different rare parts which the device requires and which cannot be manufactured by the characters. Each of these must be obtained separately and, most likely, at vastly separated distances.

Quest Required: If yes, then the character must, for each required part, participate in a separate adventure whose ultimate goal is the obtaining of the required part(s).

Cost in Life: This is the value of the part being looked for. This gives the Gamejudge a guideline as to how important this part will be to the NPC's and monsters who may be encountered on the quest.

Distance to Travel: Again, this is a guideline as to how far a quest regarding the part should take the character looking for it.

Area of the Quest: This guideline gives the probable setting for such a quest.

ONLY after the character has participated in all these adventures and quests in search of the required items should final construction of the device be attempted.

3. Find the TAROC result

Use the PC's Craft Score for the Force, the total of all points of the device's Attributes as the Resistance. Find the TAROC result and apply it as follows:

T = *Total:* Device is constructed as designed.

A = *Almost:* Device is constructed but with half of the points originally assigned to it. The PC who constructed the device may reassign the points in any way he chooses so long as (1) the points are only assigned to those Attributes for the device that were originally in the design, and (2) no single Attribute for the device is given more points than were originally assigned to it.

R = *Reasonable:* As with result "A" above except the total number of points is one fourth of the original numbers assigned to it.

O = *Off:* As with result "A" above except the total number of points is one tenth of those originally assigned to it.

C = *Canceled:* The device does not work at all. Start again from the beginning.

Repair or Understanding of Technological Items

As in the case of the Executioner's learning to use a gun in *Triumph of the Darksword*, volume three of the Darksword Trilogy, occasionally PCs may come across Technological items that they have never before encountered and will want to experiment with their use.

Anytime a PC wants to understand or repair a Technological device, use the PC's Crafting Ability Score as the Force score, and the normal modifier or Ability score of the device as the Resistance score. Find the TAROC results as follows:

T = *Total:* The device is understood and/or fully repaired. The PC may use the device normally. If the device was damaged, the Gamejudge may restore the device's points to their original scores.

A = *Almost:* The device is partially understood and/or partially repaired. The device can be operated at a penalty of –5. If the device was damaged, determine the difference between the original points and the current damage points. Restore half of the difference.

R = *Reasonable:* The device is partially understood and/or partially repaired. Use as result "A" above except the use penalty is − 10 and the restored damaged points are one fourth.

O = *Off:* As "A" above except the use penalty is –20 and the restored damaged points are one tenth.

C = *Canceled:* Use of the device is not understood nor is it repaired. .

Conclusion of the Game .

Experience Awards

When the session of gaming is completed, either by adjournment or the conclusion of the Adventure, the Gamejudge will give PCs an Experience Award. This is important because each player's character will gain power and heightened abilities through these awards. Experience Awards reflect the growth of the character in the game setting.

Following are guidelines to help the Gamejudge make this award.

Gamejudges should award points for the following actions:

HEROIC DEEDS
COMPASSIONATE ACTS
USE OF A PC'S ABILITIES
CREATIVE USE OF LIFE
ACHIEVING ADVENTURE GOALS (SMALL
    AND LARGE)
INVENTIVENESS
ACCURATE AND CREATIVE PORTRAYAL OF
    CHARACTER

Points may be awarded individually or to the group at large. The Druid who turns aside from the quest to come to the aid of a sick child may receive 15 points for a Compassionate Act. The group that achieves the Adventure Goal — rescuing the King and finding the Long-Lost Scroll of Divining — will receive a total of 30 points to be divided evenly among group members. The group that only partially achieves the Adventure Goal — saved the King but lost the Scroll — may receive 15 points. The person who failed at every task but who kept the group enthralled by her accurate portrayal of a witch may be awarded 10 points for her acting abilities alone. The group who failed in achieving any Adventure Goals but still did some good in the world may be awarded points.

The amount of the Experience Award is entirely up to the Gamejudge. An arbitrary limit of 5 points per act and a maximum gain of 50 points per night's adventuring is fairly standard.

Character Advancement

Whenever strange PCs meet in Thimhallan, the correct way to introduce themselves is by giving their names, their Mystery, and their Station level in that Mystery.

"I am Jana, Fourteenth Station *Sif-Hanar.*"

Two *Duuk-tsarith* meeting for the first time would say simply "I am Twelfth Station" or "I am Ninth Station." (This would instantly determine for them who is the leader in a particular situation; the warlock of the higher station would assume command. Two of equal station would go by age, the elder assuming command.)

Experience Award points, therefore, are extremely important in advancing the PC in his or her station. The PC should keep a running total of these Experience Award points on his Character Sheet. These points can be thought of in terms of coinage needed to "buy" another Station level.

A character may purchase stations in any Mystery in which he already has a station of at least one. (If the character does not have a station of at least one then no stations may be purchased for that Mystery.)

Note that a single character will, therefore, have various stations in the various mysteries. A *Duuk-tsarith* for example, may have a station of nine in witchcraft, seven in magic, and three in Illusion. In terms of describing such a character, the *character's station* is the largest of the station numbers. In this case, the character's station is ninth station. This is important in determining the Life Attributes of the character.

Whenever a PC has sufficient Experience Award points, he may purchase from the Gamejudge additional Stations in the various Abilities of the Player's Character. Follow these steps:

1. Find Award Cost on Station Advancement Cost Table

Each Station has an increased cost. The PC's first Station, for example, will cost him only 10 from his Experience Award. Station 5 will cost him 120 points (if he is in Station 4).

If the PC is advancing more than one station at a time, he MUST PAY THE COST OF EACH INCREASE. For example, if the PC has a warlock Station of 2 and he wishes to raise it to 5, he will have to pay the costs for Station 3, Station 4, and Station 5. This is equivalent to $60 + 80 + 120 = 260$ points.

2. Adjust the Revised Scores for Each Mystery

The PC writes the new Station number in place of the previous one on his Character Sheet. Add the PC's Talent in that Mystery to the new Station to determine a revised Ability Score for that Mystery.

3. Adjust the Character's Attributes:

Whenever a Character increases his or her station, the player may also increase certain of the character's Attributes. This reflects the character's physical learning and growth as he or she reacts to the environment.

For each Station the character increases, the player may add one point to one of the following attributes: Attack, Defense, Health, Strength, Dexterity, Intelligence, Intuition or Senses.

Attribute Station Increase Chart
Combat

Increase Any Attack Attribute Score	1 point
Increase Any Defense Attribute Score	1 point
Movement: Increase existing Attribute Score (NOT speed)	1 point
Health: Increase existing Attribute Score Maximum (NOT actual points remaining)	5 points

Form

Increase Existing Dexterity Score	1 point
Increase Existing Strength Score	1 point

Knowledge

Increase Existing Intelligence Score	3 points
Increase Existing Intuition Score	3 points

4. Adjust the Character's Life Attributes:

Whenever a character increases his character station, the Life Attributes change as well. The more powerful a wizard becomes, the more power he may wield.

If the *character's station* — in other words, his highest station in any Mystery — increases over his previous station, then not only does the Station and Score increase for that Mystery but his Life Attributes increase as well.

The Life Attributes by Station Table below shows the effects of these changes as the character station increases. All numbers are given as modifiers to the character's previous number. Note that these effects are cumulative. For example: if a character's station should change from three to six, that character's Resistance would increase by three (+1 for station four, +1 for station five, and +1 for station 6) and his Renewal would increase by four (+1 for station four, +1 for station five, and +2 for station six). His capacity would be increased by forty (+10, +10, +20) and his Lifewell maximum would increase by eight hundred (+200, +200, +400).

LIFEWELL ATTRIBUTES BY STATION TABLE

STATION	RESIST-ANCE	RENEWAL	CAPACITY	LIFEWELL MAXIMUMS
1-5	+1	+10	+10	+50
6-10	+1	+20	+50	+100
11-15	+2	+30	+100	+200
16-30	+2	+50	+100	+100
31-50	+1	+30	+200	+50
51+	+1/4	+20	+100	+20

Deduction of Points

Under rare conditions a Gamejudge may elect to deduct points from a PC or the group of PCs. This should be done only in the most dire circumstances. A group should not, for example, have points deducted if they fail to achieve Adventure Goals provided they gave the attainment of these goals their best efforts. A group that elects to go on an Adventure to save the King and search for the Scroll of Divining, then completely abandons the Goal to go hunting giants, might have points deducted.

A PC who acts in a manner completely out of character (a Druid setting fire to a forest, a catalyst committing an unwarranted, brutal murder) may have points deducted.

In all cases the penalty is determined by the Gamejudge.

Station Advancement Cost Table

Station Score		Station Score		Station Score		Station Score	
1	10	27	2,100	53	7,560	79	16,400
2	30	28	2,240	54	7,830	80	16,800
3	60	29	2,400	55	8,120	81	17,220
4	80	30	2,550	56	8,400	82	17,630
5	120	31	2,720	57	8,700	83	18,060
6	150	32	2,880	58	8,990	84	18,480
7	200	33	3,060	59	9,300	85	18,920
8	240	34	3,230	60	9,600	86	19,350
9	300	35	3,420	61	9,920	87	19,800
10	350	36	3,600	62	10,230	88	20,240
11	420	37	3,800	63	10,560	89	20,700
12	480	38	3,900	64	10,880	90	21,150
13	560	39	4,200	65	11,220	91	21,620
14	630	40	4,400	66	11,550	92	22,080
15	720	41	4,620	67	11,900	93	22,560
16	800	42	4,830	68	12,240	94	23,030
17	900	43	5,060	69	12,600	95	23,520
18	990	44	5,280	70	12,950	96	24,000
19	1,100	45	5,520	71	13,320	97	24,500
20	1,200	46	5,750	72	13,680	98	24,990
21	1,320	47	6,000	73	14,060	99	25,500
22	1,430	48	6,240	74	14,430	100	26,000
23	1,560	49	6,500	75	14,820		
24	1,680	50	6,750	76	15,200		
25	1,820	51	7,020	77	15,600		
26	1,950	52	7,280	78	15,990		

Appendix I

Major and Minor Characters

This section is designed primarily to be used by the Gamejudge for portraying Nonplayer Characters whom the Players might encounter during the course of an Adventure. However, the section can also be used by Players in search of a Character. In this case they may choose only those designated as Player Characters. The reasons for this are that certain characters are so powerful that they would upset the balance of the game. In all cases, those listed as Player Characters may also be run as Nonplayer Characters.

If, as Gamejudge, you choose to "play the novels"—that is, to use the plot of the novels as the basis for your game—it is important to remember to let the PCs have freedom of choice even if that freedom seems to be taking the plot in an entirely different direction from the plot in the books. You and your friends will often discover many new aspects of the characters of Thimhallan if you do this.

Joram (Nonplayer Character)

Early Childhood: Anyone meeting Joram at this time will be struck instantly by the child's remarkable beauty. The boy's face is framed by a mass of black, curly hair that is shiny and well cared for. The hair is long, for his mother refuses to allow it to be cut. The boy's eyes are a deep brown and very large, shadowed by long, black lashes. The child's eyebrows are dark and thick, giving the boy a solemn air that is accentuated by the piercing, intelligent gaze of the eyes. Up until the age of nine, Joram's skin is white and he has the fragile, sickly look about him of one who is kept sealed inside a dwelling and rarely allowed out into fresh air. After the age of nine, when Joram is working in the fields, his skin color changes to deep tan and he is stronger and healthier in appearance.

There is little likelihood any player would have a chance to talk to Joram, beyond more than a few words. Anja guards the boy jealously and will permit no one to get near him.

Joram begins his training in sleight of hand at this early age and becomes quite proficient in it, having little else to occupy his time. This and reading the books Anja finds for him are his only outlets. Anyone seeing Joram working with other children in the fields would not notice a difference in the magic skills of the Dead boy and his Living companions.

He is dressed like the other children, in peasant clothes. His might be more tattered or less clean than others.

JORAM (AS A CHILD)
PHANTASIA STATISTICS

ATTRIBUTES

Attack	35	Defense	32	Health	26
Strength	33	Dexterity	59	Movement	5
Intelligence	25	Intuition	55	Senses	49
Form	human	Size	60	Resistance	25
Renewal	0	Capacity	0	Lifewell	0

ABILITIES	TALENT	STATION	SCORE
Combat	—	—	—
Movement	—	—	—
Health and Healing	—	—	—
Form and Size Altering	—	—	—
Information	—	—	—
Life Transfer	—	—	—
Tool Crafts and Skills	22	1	23
Telepathy and Empathy	—	—	—
Illusions	—	—	—

Early Teens to the Forging of the Darksword: At the age of
twelve Joram begins to experience periods of depression.
Deep inside, he knows he will never acquire the magic
he longs to possess. He has to face the fact that his mother
is completely insane. He also realizes that he is different
from others in this world and that he will always be alone.

At this age Anja no longer has to keep Joram apart
from others; Joram is only too happy to isolate himself.

PCs meeting Joram anywhere between the ages of twelve
and sixteen in the village of Walren and during his years
spent in the Sorcerers' town will find him to be a sullen,
angry, and rebellious youth. He is physically attractive,
with a strong, muscular body that comes from hard labor.
His hair is thick and black and tangled, for he cannot be
bothered to care for it. His face is handsome, although the
smoldering anger seen burning in the eyes and in the perpetually frowning thick, black brows mars its beauty.

Joram is well educated and can be well spoken when he
chooses. He has an air of superiority that comes from deep
within. Despite the fact that he is Dead, he is *Albanara* —
born to rule. He is a natural leader but seldom chooses to
do so.

When the fits of melancholia come on him, he lies upon
his bed, staring at the ceiling, for as long as a day. During
this time he refuses all contact with anyone. When he
comes out of these fits, he appears more talkative than
usual, but otherwise there is no noticeable change in him.

Joram has few friends, and those that he does have he
does not treat particularly well. He is never cruel or hurt-

ful, he merely gives the strong impression that he would prefer to be left alone. On rare occasions, however, he will open up to a close friend. Joram dislikes and distrusts all strangers, he hates catalysts and will manifest this hatred openly. He despises all those in authority, with the exception of Andon, leader of the Sorcerers.

In the Sorcerers' village Joram works in the forge from dawn to dusk. What leisure time he has he spends reading the hidden texts pertaining to Technology or playing tarok. Consumed by his lust for power and his ambition to return to Merilon, Joram has little interest in anything else. Though many young women in the Sorcerers' village sigh with admiration when he walks by, there are none who manage to catch his attention.

Joram's skill at sleight of hand is good enough that even his best friend, Mosiah, does not know Joram is Dead. Joram knows the limits of his skills and will not attempt to do something that might expose his lack of magic—such as fly. His lack of Life will not be readily apparent in the Sorcerers' village, since without catalysts these people utilize only a small portion of their Life.

Because he is *Albanara,* Joram has a deep, inborn need to champion people weaker than himself. Blachloch's raid on the village disturbs him (although he claims it does not). His feeling that he should protect Andon and the other Sorcerers from the warlock is a motivating factor in his forging the Darksword. But there should be no doubt that Joram's primary reason for creating the Darksword is his desire for power and his need to compensate for his lack of magic.

JORAM (EARLY TEENS TO FORGING OF DARKSWORD)
PHANTASIA STATISTICS

ATTRIBUTES

Attack	56	Defense	53	Health	62
Strength	53	Dexterity	62	Movement	5
Intelligence	52	Intuition	55	Senses	51
Form	human	Size	60	Resistance	25
Renewal	0	Capacity	0	Lifewell	0

ABILITIES	TALENT	STATION	SCORE
Combat	—	—	—
Movement	—	—	—
Health and Healing	—	—	—
Form and Size Altering	—	—	—
Information	—	—	—
Life Transfer	—	—	—
Tool Crafts and Skills	22	5	27
Telepathy and Empathy	—	—	—
Illusions	—	—	—

Joram in Merilon: Following his meeting with Prince Garald, Joram undergoes a personality change. In the Prince, Joram sees suddenly the man he would like to be—noble, respected, admired. At first he is jealous and detests Garald for having these qualities. Beneath all the anger and inner turmoil Joram is basically a rational person, however, and he soon sees that he can learn valuable lessons from Garald.

It is important to note that Joram at this point in his life is very "I-centered." He views everything in relationship to himself and what effect it will have on him. He rarely thinks of others or is sensitive to their feelings. Although he fondly imagines it to be otherwise, even his love for Gwendolyn is a selfish love—taking everything from her and giving little in return. Thus Joram sees that it is to his benefit to change his personality, to become less abrasive, to hide his anger and rebellious nature beneath a veneer of charm. Just as he tricks people with his magic, so he now learns that he can trick them with his charm. He uses and manipulates people, often without even knowing it.

It takes a series of shocks—believing himself nameless and abandoned, then knowing himself to be the son of the Emperor and Empress, then the bitter realization that his true father will once again sacrifice him—to force Joram to start looking both inward and outward. The sacrifice of Saryon and the knowledge of the great love the catalyst bears him finally leads Joram's soul out of darkness into light.

PCs meeting Joram in Merilon will find him charming, but they will receive the impression that he is constantly watching them with a wary, suspicious eye. On the surface he is agreeable and polite. Cross him, and his anger is quick to flare. Only Saryon has the ability to calm him. Joram's adolescent infatuation for Gwendolyn is combined with his sexual desires and is therefore completely irrational and totally obsessive.

JORAM (IN MERILON)
PHANTASIA STATISTICS

ATTRIBUTES

Attack	56	Defense	58	Health	62
Strength	53	Dexterity	62	Movement	5
Intelligence	52	Intuition	60	Senses	51
Form	human	Size	60	Resistance	25
Renewal	0	Capacity	0	Lifewell	0

ABILITIES	TALENT	STATION	SCORE
Combat	—	—	—
Movement	—	—	—
Health and Healing	—	—	—
Form and Size Altering	—	—	—
Information	—	—	—
Life Transfer	—	—	—
Tool Crafts and Skills	22	15	37
Telepathy and Empathy	—	—	—
Illusions	—	—	—

Joram: The Return: Joram ages ten years in the time he spends in Beyond. During this time he comes to manhood. He grows and matures. His life in Beyond has not been an easy one, although it is unlikely that he will ever reveal any specific details about it. Knowing that few on Thimhallan could even begin to imagine what life in Beyond is like, Joram will only discuss portions of it with his most trusted friends, and these would be portions that would relate directly to the war in Thimhallan—such as his relationship with Menju the Sorcerer.

During the ten years that Joram lived in Beyond, he never forgot Thimhallan. As time went by, he forgot the ugliness in the world, however, and remembered only its beauty. He hopes that he can bring about a merger of the two worlds—Technology and Magic—and this is his reason for returning to Thimhallan.

On his arrival, however, his old anger is kindled by his discovery that Saryon has been tortured in attempts to wrest the Darksword from him. Joram travels through the world, finding more evidence of corruption and disease brought on by the suffocating lives of the magi. He is ready to leave Thimhallan and return to the world Beyond when he discovers that it, too, has betrayed him.

He plans to let both worlds go their own separate ways. At the end, however, Joram comes to understand that if allowed to do so, both worlds will die. One world is suffocating for lack of the magic. The other world is suffocating from a surfeit of magic. Joram must free the magic, send it back into the universe for life to continue to flourish.

He does so, but the cost to him is enormous. He must forsake both worlds, not out of anger, but out of love.

PCs meeting Joram during this time will find him brusque and businesslike. He will never volunteer information about himself and will most likely refuse to answer all questions about the world Beyond except those that bear strict relevance to the current threat faced by Thimhallan. He is very gentle with and protective of Gwendolyn. For him there is and can be no other woman in his life.

JORAM (THE RETURN)
PHANTASIA STATISTICS

ATTRIBUTES

Attack	56	Defense	58	Health	72
Strength	53	Dexterity	62	Movement	5
Intelligence	62	Intuition	65	Senses	51
Form	human	Size	60	Resistance	25
Renewal	0	Capacity	0	Lifewell	0

ABILITIES	TALENT	STATION	SCORE
Combat	—	—	—
Movement	—	—	—
Health and Healing	—	—	—
Form and Size Altering	—	—	—

ABILITIES	TALENT	STATION	SCORE
Information	—	—	—
Life Transfer	—	—	—
Tool Crafts and Skills	22	40	67
Telepathy and Empathy	—	—	—
Illusions	—	—	—

Saryon (Player Character)

Saryon is tall and thin, slightly stoop-shouldered, even in his youth, as though he wished to be able hunch down and hide himself in the crowd. His robes are too short and show his bony ankles. His tonsured hair is sparse and of a nondescript color, turning gray early in his life. He is a mild spoken, gentle man—the kind children and animals approach without fear. The only time his face ever becomes animated or his talk ever grows excited is when he is discussing some new mathematical theory. He will go on happily about this for hours, never noticing that he is boring his audience to the point that most will quite literally disappear.

The color of the catalyst's robes will vary depending on when and where the players meet him and under what circumstances. (See *Catalysts*, page 269, for details on the catalysts' dress.)

Although Saryon appears to be a very open, guileless, and honest man, he is, in reality, a man with many secrets—most of them dark and terrible (or so he believes). Raised by a strict and deeply religious mother, Saryon was taught to keep all emotions hidden and suppressed. He magnifies his faults and because of his studious, retiring nature, he has few friends. He takes refuge in his studies, finding happiness only in his books, and it is this that leads him down the forbidden path to the study of the Dark Arts of Technology.

Saryon's life, until he meets Joram, is empty and sterile. The only person he has ever loved was that small baby—the Emperor's Dead son. The love for the child and trauma of the child's "death" mark Saryon deeply, leading to the unconscious bond that develops later between the catalyst and Joram.

PCs meeting Saryon prior to his journey in the Outland will find that the Priest is a crashing bore. He will talk about mathematics and that is all. Although he has been to court, he knows nothing about the people of Merilon and beyond the Emperor and the Empress, could probably not name more than half a dozen of the nobility. Gossip goes in one ear and out the other. He is incredibly naive and idealistic, especially when it comes to the Church. The only edict of the Church he feels the least bit uncomfortable about is the law requiring Dead children be put to death. Questioned about this practice, Saryon will become very grave and defensive and will repeat all Bishop Vanya's sermons on the subject verbatim.

Those meeting Saryon after his encounter with Joram will find that the Priest is evasive, secretive, and seems constantly preoccupied with some inner turmoil. Any direct question regarding Joram will draw an evasive, confused response, as will questions regarding faith in the Almin or the Church and its practices. The secrets he bears tear at Saryon's body as well as his spirit. He eats little, he cannot sleep, he is nervous and fearful. This eventually leads to the stroke that nearly claims his life.

Those who meet Saryon after Joram's return from Beyond will discover that the Priest, while having purged himself of his secrets, has changed little. The peace he found when he sacrificed himself for Joram is gone. His broken and scarred hands bear witness to man's inhumanity and lust for power. Saryon knows the Church is corrupt. He has no faith in a God that could let this happen. His primary concern now is for Joram and Gwendolyn. His first and only loyalty is to both of them. Never, under any circumstances, will he leave or betray either of them. When his faith is restored and he knows that Joram has found peace with himself, Saryon will be able to leave him to become Prince Garald's friend and mentor in the brave, new worlds Beyond.

SARYON (Catalyst)
PHANTASIA STATISTICS

ATTRIBUTES

Attack	44	Defense	54	Health	59
Strength	45	Dexterity	57	Movement	5
Intelligence	61	Intuition	61	Senses	52
Form	human	Size	58	Resistance	44
Renewal	100	Capacity	100	Lifewell	300

ABILITIES	TALENT	STATION	SCORE
Combat	—	—	—
Movement	—	—	—
Health and Healing	—	—	—
Form and Size Altering	—	—	—
Information	11	15	26
Life Transfer	17	22	39
Tool Crafts and Skills	1	1	2
Telepathy and Empathy	9	19	28
Illusions	5	10	15

Gwendolyn (Player Character)

Gwendolyn in Merilon: Sixteen years old, Gwendolyn is a pampered, sheltered, young woman of the upper-middle class. She is pretty, though not beautiful, with golden hair and blue eyes and an attractive figure. People are instantly attracted to her smile. She is one of those humans who walks in sunshine and flowers. She loves everyone, she loves being herself, she loves life.

Gwen is charming and outgoing and flirtatious. She has just discovered the power women hold over men, and she is exploiting it to its fullest. There is a simplicity and modesty about her, however, that is very appealing. She is naive and knows nothing about the world outside Merilon.

Gwendolyn is initially attracted to Joram for his darkly handsome looks and the air of romance and mystery that attends him. As time passes, her infatuation for him deepens into an affection that is both physical and spiritual, for Gwen can see how desperately he seeks and longs for love. Gwen is the more mature of the two in the relationship. Her love is a giving love, while Joram's is a taking.

As Saryon foresees, this love is doomed unless Joram

changes. Should something happen and Joram not discover the truth about himself but gain his dream and become rich and powerful, his marriage to Gwen would turn out most unhappily. He has lied to the world and himself so long that he would be unable to tell the truth. The web of lies would slowly bind up and smother their love.

GWENDOLYN (BEFORE GOING BEYOND)
(Quin-alban)
PHANTASIA STATISTICS

ATTRIBUTES

Attack	45	Defense	49	Health	49
Strength	45	Dexterity	58	Movement	5
Intelligence	55	Intuition	50	Senses	54
Form	human	Size	57	Resistance	20
Renewal	240	Capacity	360	Lifewell	1,000

ABILITIES	TALENT	STATION	SCORE
Combat	5	1	6
Movement	9	8	17
Health and Healing	2	4	6
Form and Size Altering	26/10[1]	10	36/20
Information	—	—	—
Life Transfer	—	—	—
Tool Crafts and Skills	1	1	2
Telepathy and Empathy	—	—	—
Illusions	7	6	13

[1]The score before the slash indicates the character's score whenever casting a conjuration spell in this mystery. The score after the slash deals with all other types of the mystery.

Gwendolyn After the Return: As Joram relates, many of the magi crossing the Border go insane. It is as if a person who has been living for sixteen years in a small room filled continually with bright sunlight were suddenly thrust out into an open field during a dark, moonless night.

Gwendolyn is a Necromancer, born to the Mystery of Shadow. This would have been apparent from her birth had her parents not instantly (and probably unconsciously) squelched any obvious leanings in that direction. The shock of her passage through the Border threw her back into her true nature, doing so with such violence that she cannot escape.

True Necromancers were able to dwell in both worlds — the material and the spirit. Gwen cannot. She dwells only in the world of the Dead. She can communicate with them, but not with the Living. The Dead will attempt to use her to warn the Living about the doom of Thimhallan, but they will be forced to do so indirectly, using parables similar to Count Devon's tale about the mice in the attic.

PCs seeking to question the Dead through Gwen will not meet with any direct answers but must sift through irrelevancies, parables, stories, and legends. Joram is very protective of his wife. Either he, Father Saryon, or Gwen's parents will be with her at all times. Under no circumstances can Gwen come out of her madness until the magic is freed.

GWENDOLYN (AFTER THE RETURN) (Aluava)
PHANTASIA STATISTICS

ATTRIBUTES

Attack	45	Defense	49	Health	49
Strength	45	Dexterity	58	Movement	5
Intelligence	55	Intuition	50	Senses	54
Form	human	Size	57	Resistance	20
Renewal	240	Capacity	360	Lifewell	1,000

ABILITIES	TALENT	STATION	SCORE
Combat	5	1	6
Movement	5	1	6
Health and Healing	2	4	6
Form and Size Altering	26/10[1]	10	36/20
Information	15	1	6
Life Transfer	—	—	—
Tool Crafts and Skills	—	—	—
Telepathy and Empathy	35/10[2]	10	45/21
Illusions	7	6	13

[1] The score before the slash indicates the character's score whenever casting a conjuration spell in this mystery. The score after the slash deals with all other types of spells of the mystery.

[2] The number before the slash indicates the talent of the character when attempting telepathy or empathy with the dead. The number after the slash indicates the talent for all other types of Telepathy & Empathy.

Simkin (Nonplayer Character)

Joram makes two observations about Simkin: first, that Simkin plays the game for the game's sake, and second, that he is magic personified.

Simkin is completely and totally amoral. He cares for nothing and no one. He will act for or against someone as it takes his fancy. He will tell the truth, on occasion, but it is often so jumbled up with blatant lies that it is impossible to believe a word he says.

Because he is amusing and (apparently) harmless, Simkin is much like the classic court Fool in that he is able to exhibit the follies of people to themselves. He pounces instantly on the weakness of any person present and will exploit that to the fullest. Amid the fawning and pretensions of the royal courts, this barbed truthfulness is oddly refreshing.

The one startling fact about Simkin that no one knows (or will find out in these first Darksword books) is that he is immortal. Simkin hints at this when he tells Prince Garald that he was present when the Prophecy was given following the Iron Wars. Of course no one believes him, but in this instance Simkin is stating fact. He *was* present. He was present when Merlyn and the magi left the Ancient World. Just how long Simkin has been around is open to conjecture, but he may have been giving Adam and Eve tips on how to dress. Since Simkin *is* magic, his power has no limits except those that he puts upon himself. The remarkable things we see him do are only a very minute part of the miracles he could perform if he wanted. He takes nothing seriously, however, and Players who attempt to get Simkin to help them by performing some tremendous feat of magic will only find themselves in worse trouble.

Human life means nothing to Simkin. After all, he's met millions of people. He is, in fact, fascinated by death, and thus most of his lugubrious stories deal with death in grotesque forms. His stories are rarely pointless, often having some relevance to the discussion at hand, be it only a play on words.

Since life is a game and the game is everything to Simkin,

he enjoys placing humans in difficult and even dangerous situations to see how they react. He will do so in such a way that he always appears completely innocent.

Simkin is unpredictable, and thus can be a very dangerous companion. Yet, he can also be extremely valuable if he chooses. Simkin loves adventure and will gladly accompany any party of adventurers on any quest. He will tell them anything they want to hear in order to convince them to let him come with them. (He would, in fact, probably go with them whether invited or not! More than one adventurer has discovered a teapot in his knapsack!) There is a strong chance that Simkin has information or can help the party in attaining their goal. He will make things as lively and interesting for them as possible on the way, however. Woe betide the group if Simkin gets bored!

Simkin has been to all the royal courts and will be welcome in any of them. He is on familiar terms with all people of influence. He will be able to take Players any place they want to go—from the home of the Faerie Queen to the marvelous Zoo in Zith-el, to the palace of the King of Sharakan, to Bishop Vanya's private chambers, to the subterranean meeting place of the *Duuk-tsarith*. Getting out again may be an entirely different matter, however!

Simkin remembers the ancient world very well, and he has no desire to cross the Border until he discovers the wonders of Technology that have been developed in his absence. After Joram's return, it occurs to Simkin that Thimhallan is extremely boring and he could find all sorts of new adventures in the "brave, new world." To cross over into the other world disguised as Joram will be a wonderful joke on everyone concerned.

Simkin's death at the end is all too real—Technology destroying Magic. If Joram does not free the magic, both Simkin and the magic remain dead. By freeing the magic, however, Joram brings Simkin back to life, and there is undoubtedly the possibility that Joram's son, who goes out to seek his fortune in the worlds Beyond, will find himself accompanied by a companion in pink silk trousers carrying an orange silk scarf!

SIMKIN[1]
PHANTASIA STATISTICS

ATTRIBUTES

Attack	N/A	Defense	N/A	Health	N/A
Strength	N/A	Dexterity	N/A	Movement	5
Intelligence	N/A	Intuition	N/A	Senses	N/A
Form	human	Size	61	Resistance	N/A
Renewal	N/A	Capacity	N/A	Lifewell	N/A

ABILITIES	TALENT	STATION	SCORE
Combat	N/A	N/A	N/A
Movement	N/A	N/A	N/A
Health and Healing	N/A	N/A	N/A
Form and Size Altering	N/A	N/A	N/A
Information	N/A	N/A	N/A
Life Transfer	N/A	N/A	N/A
Tool Crafts and Skills	N/A	N/A	N/A
Telepathy and Empathy	N/A	N/A	N/A
Illusions	N/A	N/A	N/A

[1]Simkin is the personification of magic. As such, his magic has no limits. Many Attributes and Abilities for Simkin are listed with a "N/A" result for "Not Applicable." This means that the scores for these Attributes or Abilities may be any number limited only by the desires of Simkin himself.

Mosiah (Player Character)

A Field Magus, Mosiah is far stronger in magic than he realizes. Given sufficient Life, he could develop his skills and become a truly powerful magus. He is uneducated—at least as far as reading or writing. He knows a great deal about farming, however, and about the seasons, real weather (as opposed to magically controlled weather), plants, and animals. Having spent time in the Sorcerers' village, he can work with his hands as well as with his magic, although he will always feel uncomfortable around Technology.

Mosiah is an affectionate son with deep respect for his parents. He is a loyal friend to Joram, knowing that—deep inside—Joram truly cares for him.

Mosiah is not particularly ambitious, beyond learning to

read and write and utilizing his full potential to magic. Life in the big city fascinates him until he gets there. Because of his down-to-earth nature, Mosiah can see through the glittering facade of the people of Merilon and discovers that they are shallow and base beneath. Mosiah is far more comfortable facing dangers in the Outland than he is in pursuing the empty pleasures of the city.

Mosiah's major fault is his blind admiration for Joram. He will follow Joram anywhere, though common sense warns him against it. He even puts up with Simkin for Joram's sake. Although Mosiah dislikes Simkin, it is more because they are completely opposite personalities than that he actually knows the Fool's true nature.

In any social situation Mosiah is shy and awkward and will immediately give himself away as the simple peasant that he is. He is deeply religious, respectful to all in authority. He understands dangers present in the wilds of the Outland, but he only gradually comes to learn the more insidious dangers of court intrigue. Naturally trusting, he might open up and talk to anyone who professed a strong interest in his past life as a Field Magus, life in the Sorcerers' village, Joram, or the Darksword—freely imparting all information he knows about any of these subjects.

Mosiah is good-looking in a raw-boned, athletic fashion. His character can be seen in his face, which is open and honest. Mosiah is invariably truthful and can be trusted implicitly. When granted sufficient Life, he has the ability to change into any form of were-animal. This is his primary means of both attack and defense.

MOSIAH (Pron-Alban)
PHANTASIA STATISTICS

ATTRIBUTES

Attack	50	Defense	48	Health	53
Strength	51	Dexterity	53	Movement	5
Intelligence	47	Intuition	44	Senses	53
Form	human	Size	62	Resistance	20
Renewal	240	Capacity	360	Lifewell	1,000

ABILITIES	TALENT	STATION	SCORE
Combat	5	8	13
Movement	5	5	10
Health and Healing	2	1	3
Form and Size Altering	$32^1/10$	10	33/11
Information	–	–	–
Life Transfer	–	–	–
Tool Crafts and Skills	2	10	12
Telepathy and Empathy	–	–	–
Illusions	7	8	15

[1]The score before the slash indicates the character's talent whenever casting spells dealing with *permanent* conjuration in this mystery. The score after the slash indicates the character's talent whenever dealing with any other type of spell structure in this mystery.

Garald, Prince of Sharakan (Nonplayer Character)

In his late twenties, Garald is an extremely handsome man. Elegantly but tastefully dressed, he is all that is good and noble in the world of Thimhallan. He is a true gentleman in every sense of the word.

Garald is still unmarried, rather an unusual circumstance, especially for the only scion of a royal house who is expected to produce heirs to the throne. Court gossip hints at a tragic romance when the Prince had just turned twenty. He was away from home, visiting the royal family in Avidon at the time. The King of Avidon had a very beautiful daughter who died of a sudden illness that the *Theldara* could not cure. Was Garald in love with her and did he bury his heart in her grave? No one knows for certain for the Prince will never discuss what happened to him in Avidon. All anyone knows is that, upon his return, Garald was subdued and melancholy. He threw himself into his work and began holding lavish parties (where he met Simkin). Though he is gallant and charming to all women, he never shows romantic interest in any of them, much to his father's concern.

Prince Garald is *Albanara*, born to rule. He takes his duties very seriously and works day and night for the good of his people. He is a classic example of the benevolent ruler and will make an excellent king. Indeed, Garald is king in all but name, for his doting father has turned over most of the reins of government to his son. His people—from the lowest field worker to the highest noble—admire and respect him. Anyone meeting Garald realizes that his country comes first.

Garald enjoys people, however. He takes an interest in those he meets and is sympathetic to their problems. (One thing that endears him to his followers.) Thus he goes out of his way to help Joram. This sympathy is due, in part, to the influence of the wise Cardinal Radisovik, who was Garald's childhood tutor and is now his trusted friend and mentor.

A handsome, clever child whose mother died at his birth, Garald was in a fair way to be spoiled by his father. He might have grown up much like the Emperor of Merilon—shallow, insensitive, mired in court intrigue—had not the Cardinal taken the boy's education in hand. With love and discipline and the best tutors in Thimhallan, Radisovik taught Garald what it means to be a good man as well as a good king. Radisovik's teaching and the shadow of his own early sorrow have tempered Garald's character and forged a man of honor with a deep sense of commitment to his people and himself.

PCs meeting the Prince find him to be gracious and charming. He keeps himself properly aloof, however, and they are never allowed to forget that they are in a royal presence. Garald is a master of court intrigue. He will politely discuss all subjects, but those talking will often find that they are inadvertently being drawn into revealing more information to him than he will to them. The Prince is fascinated by all things military and his talk will become increasingly warm and animated on this subject.

Garald is guarded at all times, day and night, by two members of the *Duuk-tsarith*. These men and women are unfailingly loyal to the Prince and will instantly act to protect the Prince if he is threatened. Those in the presence of the Prince will have the uncomfortable feeling that they are constantly under surveillance, even if they cannot see the black-robed warlocks.

GARALD (Albanara)
PHANTASIA STATISTICS

ATTRIBUTES

Attack	47	Defense	49	Health	53
Strength	50	Dexterity	44	Movement	4
Intelligence	50	Intuition	53	Senses	58
Form	human	Size	61	Resistance	40
Renewal	640	Capacity	1,360	Lifewell	2,500

ABILITIES	TALENT	STATION	SCORE
Combat	12	20	32
Movement	9	16	25
Health and Healing	5	5	10
Form and Size Altering	5	10	15
Information	1	15	16
Life Transfer	—	—	—
Tool Crafts and Skills	1	5	6
Telepathy and Empathy	1	1	2
Illusions	5	15	20

Bishop Vanya (Nonplayer Character)

The rotund Bishop is a huge man, extremely fat and flabby. He is a gourmand, doting on food and fine wines. He hires the best chefs in Thimhallan, his dinner parties are the most lavish in the empire.

The ranking catalyst in the country of Thimhallan, Bishop Vanya is extremely intelligent and very powerful. He knew early on in his life exactly what he wanted to achieve, and every act from that point on went to furthering his ambition. He knows how to ingratiate himself to those above and below him. He knows who is useful and who is not. He knows a threat when he sees one and will not hesitate to remove it or nullify it.

Bishop Vanya is the true ruler of Thimhallan—the emperors and kings of the city-states being (for the most part) merely puppets under his control. This was true until the King of Sharakan decided to rebel—a situation that Vanya finds intolerable. The Bishop fears this, for if Sharakan succeeds in throwing off the yoke of the Church, then he knows that other city-states will not be far behind. This is why he is taking such an interest in Merilon.

Vanya also fears the Prophecy. The Bishop's relationship with the Almin is not that of servant and master, but more like two business partners working toward a common goal. Vanya believes he knows the Almin's will—it coincides with his own, of course. Vanya assumes that the Almin has chosen him to the deal with this Prophecy, and he attempts to do just that, even if it means sending innocent children to their deaths (or keeping Joram imprisoned for life).

No one sees the Bishop without a scheduled appointment, which is extremely difficult to obtain. Only high-ranking catalysts and nobility would ordinarily be granted an audience with His Holiness. Most catalysts who live and work in the Font rarely even see him. By some chance should the Players gain an audience with the Bishop, Vanya will be quite charming. The group will immediately sense, however, that they are in the presence of a powerful, dangerous man. If questioned about the Prophecy, Bishop Vanya will appear terribly astonished to hear such a thing, deny having any knowledge of it, and will laughingly regard the matter as some child's tale. He will then immediately detain the person or persons asking the questions on some charge or other, summoning the *Duuk-tsarith* to deal with the prisoner. It is more than likely that these people will unaccountably drop out of sight.

BISHOP VANYA (Catalyst)
PHANTASIA STATISTICS

ATTRIBUTES

Attack	42	Defense	58	Health	60
Strength	47	Dexterity	54	Movement	5
Intelligence	60	Intuition	68	Senses	52
Form	human	Size	58	Resistance	67
Renewal	100	Capacity	100	Lifewell	300

ABILITIES	TALENT	STATION	SCORE
Combat	—	—	—
Movement	—	—	—
Health and Healing	—	—	—

ABILITIES	TALENT	STATION	SCORE
Form and Size Altering	—	—	—
Information	13	33	46
Life Transfer	14	35	49
Tool Crafts and Skills	1	1	2
Telepathy and Empathy	11	37	48
Illusions	5	25	30

MINOR CHARACTERS, BOOK ONE

Elspeth, the Faerie Queen (Nonplayer Character)

Elspeth is by no means the only faerie queen in the world, but she is the eldest and rules over all the rest who are her offspring. Though to all appearances a young and beautiful woman, Elspeth is as old as Thimhallan. She is immortal. There is no power in the world that can harm her as long as the magic is in the world. What happens to the faeriefolk when the magic is freed is a mystery, though many believe that they were able to fly with the magic into the universe and are currently establishing their secret colonies on any number of other worlds.

Elspeth bears one child a year—always a daughter. The child must be fathered by a human male, obtained either by luring him into the enchanted ring of mushrooms or by other means that the faeries use to entrap humans. Elspeth never raises her children but sends them off as babies with a colony of faeries who take care of the girl until she is old enough to be their queen.

To any male adventurer Elspeth will appear to be the most beautiful, desirable woman he has ever seen in his life. It will take a great deal of discipline or willpower to resist her advances. (Not even the *Duuk-tsarith* are immune to her charms.) Those who succumb to her and spend one night with her will find themselves unable to leave her. Once Elspeth is pregnant, she will have nothing more to do with her lover and will cast him aside. The madness and chaos of the faerie kingdom will eventually drive the man insane. Human women entering the faerie kingdom will be selected by Elspeth as her companions and will be forced to entertain her with stories of humans (whom Elspeth finds fascinating) until they, too, fall insane or can manage to talk their way back to the world above. (See *Faeries* page 172.)

ELSPETH (FAERIE QUEEN) PHANTASIA STATISTICS

ATTRIBUTES

Attack	25	Defense	61	Health	83
Strength	47	Dexterity	73	Movement	5/6/35[1]
Intelligence	72	Intuition	53	Senses	73
Form	human	Size	60	Resistance	55
Renewal	1,190	Capacity	3,260	Lifewell	3,450

ABILITIES	TALENT	STATION	SCORE
Combat	30	20	50
Movement	35	15	45
Health and Healing	12	35	47
Form and Size Altering	17	35	52
Information	—	—	—
Life Transfer	—	—	—
Tool Crafts and Skills	—	—	—
Telepathy and Empathy	45	23	53
Illusions	56	22	78

[1]Ground/Water/Flying movement rates.

Anja (Nonplayer Character)

A woman of indeterminate age who might once have been pretty, Anja is now haggard and wild-looking. PCs will see no resemblance between her and the boy she claims is her son. Anja wears a faded, torn green dress that must once have been elegant. Clumsy attempts have been made to patch it. Her hair is filthy and matted, her face is dirty, her hands are grimy from her work in the fields. She will go out of her way, if possible, to avoid talking to Players, giving the pathetic impression that she is far superior to those around her. A mention of Merilon might rouse her interest. She will tell the Players that she plans to return there shortly so that her son can claim his birthright.

Anja is convinced that Joram is her natural-born son. No amount of argument or persuasion will shake her conviction. If anyone mentions the Stone Watchers, she will become hysterical and fly into an incoherent tirade against the catalysts. She will openly insult or spurn any catalyst in the party. The sight of a warlock will send her into a frenzy of terror. Her first thought will be to escape with her son.

ANJA (Albanara)
PHANTASIA STATISTICS

ATTRIBUTES

Attack	47	Defense	45	Health	64
Strength	48	Dexterity	52	Movement	4
Intelligence	54	Intuition	53	Senses	59
Form	human	Size	58	Resistance	40
Renewal	640	Capacity	1,360	Lifewell	2,500

ABILITIES	TALENT	STATION	SCORE
Combat	13	20	33
Movement	9	16	25
Health and Healing	5	3	8
Form and Size Altering	5	10	15
Information	1	15	16
Life Transfer	—	—	—
Tool Crafts and Skills	1	1	2
Telepathy and Empathy	1	1	2
Illusions	5	18	23

Blachloch (Nonplayer Character)

An undercover member of the *Duuk-tsarith*, Blachloch is an extremely powerful and dangerous warlock. He has been planted in the Sorcerers' midst so that he can lead them blindly into war and then betray them. He is highly disciplined, highly skilled at his work. He is capable of killing without mercy.

Although Blachloch knows about the Prophecy, as do all the *Duuk-tsarith*, he does not know about Joram's involvement. The only thing he knows is that he has been given orders by Bishop Vanya to watch Joram carefully.

The warlock covets the darkstone and will stop at nothing in his attempts to discover where Joram found it and what he knows about it.

Blachloch is playing a part, not only to the Sorcerers but to his henchmen, most of whom are common criminals the *Duuk-tsarith* allowed to "escape" and join up with him. He plays his role so well that even other members of the *Duuk-tsarith* (Prince Garald's bodyguards, for example) will not be able to easily discover that he is not what he claims—a renegade warlock.

BLACHLOCH (Duuk-Tsarith)
PHANTASIA STATISTICS

ATTRIBUTES

Attack	67	Defense	52	Health	52
Strength	60	Dexterity	57	Movement	5
Intelligence	62	Intuition	66	Senses	56
Form	human	Size	61	Resistance	40
Renewal	640	Capacity	1,360	Lifewell	2,500

ABILITIES	TALENT	STATION	SCORE
Combat	20	20	40
Movement	16	7	23
Health and Healing	—	—	—
Form and Size Altering	14	3	17
Information	—	—	—
Life Transfer	—	—	—
Tool Crafts and Skills	—	—	—
Telepathy and Empathy	30	8	38
Illusions	15	5	20

Andon, Leader of the Sorcerers (Player Character)

A man in his late sixties, Andon looks older, having lived a very hard life in the Outland. He regrets bitterly the Sorcerers' involvement with Sharakan, believing that a return to the world will only involve them in trouble again. Andon fears Blachloch, but if the old man is pushed to his limit, he will stand against the warlock. Andon advocates passive resistance, however, and is opposed to the blacksmith's militant plans for outright rebellion. Andon is uneducated and can neither read nor write. He knows something of the past glories of the Sorcerers, but only by legend. Under no circumstances will he reveal the location of the hidden books of the Dark Arts to anyone. (Joram discovers them through Simkin.)

ANDON (Sorcerer)
PHANTASIA STATISTICS

ATTRIBUTES

Attack	51	Defense	51	Health	62
Strength	63	Dexterity	57	Movement	5
Intelligence	60	Intuition	52	Senses	46
Form	human	Size	61	Resistance	20
Renewal	240	Capacity	360	Lifewell	1,000

ABILITIES	TALENT	STATION	SCORE
Combat	3	7	10
Movement	2	5	7
Health and Healing	1	1	2
Form and Size Altering	13	10	23
Information	—	—	—
Life Transfer	—	—	—
Tool Crafts and Skills	24	15	39
Telepathy and Empathy	—	—	—
Illusions	5	1	6

Deacon Dulchase (Player Character)

Saryon's only friend in the Font, the irreverent Deacon is quite a bit older than Saryon, which perhaps accounts for his liking of the young man, since most of Saryon's peers consider him a bookwormish bore. Like many catalysts, Dulchase had no choice but to join the Church when he was young. He discovered Church life was just what he thought it would be—dull and restricting. The carefree and easy life of a university student would have suited him far better. As it was, Dulchase was constantly getting into scrapes in his student days at the Font and came near expulsion several times. He was saved by his wealthy family and their equally wealthy and high-placed friends in Merilon.

Dulchase has not let himself become bitter over his fate but takes full advantage of his role as clergyman whenever possible—(invites himself to dinners, bestows "special" blessings on buxom widows, makes certain he has the best seat at all the Illusionists' shows.) Dulchase is currently under the protection of an extremely powerful nobleman, who enjoys the Deacon's sharp tongue and bold speech. Dulchase thrives on life at court. He is friends with everyone, hears and repeats all the gossip, knows who is in favor and who is out. He will not hesitate to impart any of this information to anyone who asks.

After Joram's "death" Dulchase travels to Zith-el, where he is a high-ranking catalyst in the court and takes an uncommon interest in the Zoo.

DEACON DULCHASE (Catalyst)
PHANTASIA STATISTICS

ATTRIBUTES

Attack	42	Defense	44	Health	56
Strength	47	Dexterity	61	Movement	5
Intelligence	54	Intuition	63	Senses	47
Form	human	Size	58	Resistance	20
Renewal	100	Capacity	100	Lifewell	300

ABILITIES	TALENT	STATION	SCORE
Combat	—	—	—
Movement	—	—	—
Health and Healing	—	—	—
Form and Size Altering	—	—	—
Information	10	5	15
Life Transfer	14	10	24
Tool Crafts and Skills	1	1	2
Telepathy and Empathy	12	3	15
Illusions	5	5	10

MINOR CHARACTERS, BOOK TWO

Lord Samuels (Player Character)

Gwendolyn's father is a stalwart member of the upper-middle class with a firm ambition to rise higher. A Guildmaster, he has worked hard all his life to obtain his position and has risen to the top by honest and fair means. Wise investments allowed him to increase his wealth, and now he wants only the title and the prestige to go with it. He looks on all young men of noble birth as eligible suitors for his daughter's hand.

Lord Samuels is also keenly interested in politics and, after Gwen's disappearance, seeks solace in involving himself in the political intrigues in court to help ease the bitter pain he feels at her loss. He is secretly part of an ever-growing number of noblemen in Merilon who are banding together in opposition to Xavier and Bishop Vanya.

Lord Samuels loves his daughter dearly. He will not force her into an unhappy alliance, but he sees no reason why she shouldn't fall in love with a rich man rather than a poor one. Lord Samuels, following the Turning, knows a considerable amount about the Prophecy and has discovered the truth about Joram. His fear of Emperor Xavier will make him extremely hesitant to share this information with anyone.

LORD SAMUELS (Pron-Alban)
PHANTASIA STATISTICS

ATTRIBUTES

Attack	50	Defense	50	Health	52
Strength	56	Dexterity	61	Movement	5
Intelligence	59	Intuition	52	Senses	59
Form	human	Size	62	Resistance	50
Renewal	890	Capacity	1,860	Lifewell	3,000

ABILITIES	TALENT	STATION	SCORE
Combat	5	7	12
Movement	5	10	15
Health and Healing	2	5	7
Form and Size Altering	35^1/10	25	60/35

ABILITIES	TALENT	STATION	SCORE
Information	—	—	—
Life Transfer	—	—	—
Tool Crafts and Skills	2	1	3
Telepathy and Empathy	—	—	—
Illusions	7	12	19

[1]The talent before the slash indicates the character's talent whenever casting spells dealing with *permanent* conjuration in this mystery. The score after the slash indicates the character's talent whenever dealing with any other type of spell structure in this mystery.

Lady Rosamund (Player Character)

A well-educated woman of her day, Lady Rosamund is the perfect match for her husband. She has done her part to elevate the family to the rank it now holds, and her ambition equals that of her husband. Her fondest dream is to be admitted into the ranks of the nobility. She has raised Gwendolyn from birth to believe that she is destined to be the wife of a wealthy nobleman whether she loves him or not. Lady Rosamund came to love her husband after they were married, and she sees no reason why Gwen can't do the same.

Lady Rosamund is elegant, handsome, and mistress of all situations, handling even the unexpected visit of the Emperor with aplomb. The loss of her lovely daughter is a terrible blow. She will be reluctant to discuss Gwen or Joram with any stranger and will look to her husband for guidance on what to say.

LADY ROSAMUND (Quin-Alban)
PHANTASIA STATISTICS

ATTRIBUTES

Attack	43	Defense	55	Health	56
Strength	50	Dexterity	57	Movement	5
Intelligence	59	Intuition	51	Senses	48
Form	human	Size	60	Resistance	40
Renewal	640	Capacity	1,360	Lifewell	2,500

ABILITIES	TALENT	STATION	SCORE
Combat	5	1	6
Movement	10	12	22
Health and Healing	2	5	7
Form and Size Altering	20/10[1]	20	49/30
Information	—	—	—
Life Transfer	—	—	—
Tool Crafts and Skills	1	1	1
Telepathy and Empathy	—	—	—
Illusions	7	15	22

[1]The score before the slash indicates the character's score whenever casting a conjuration spell in this mystery. The score after the slash deals with all other types of spells of the mystery.

Marie, House Catalyst (Player Character)

Upon his marriage Lord Samuels applied to the Church for a House Catalyst. He was given the resumés of several from which to choose, and he and his new wife selected Marie. Coming from a lower-class family in Merilon, Marie owes her education and position in life to the Church. (See *Catalysts*, page 264.) She was glad to acquire such a good establishment and soon became genuinely fond of her master and mistress. Marie has been forbidden marriage by the Church (no issue was foreseen), and she lavishes her love and affection on the children of the Samuels.

Marie is exceedingly fond of Gwen and sympathizes with Gwen's love for Joram. The catalyst was once in love herself but was forced to end the relationship when the Church forbade the union. She is a romantic at heart and will further Gwen's love affair with Joram all she can (without actually disobeying Lord Samuels.

Marie is in her forties, nearly the same age as Lady Rosamund. She is slender with a sweet face and disposition. She is a faithful daughter of the Church, but she is not in the habit of daily prayer or meditation beyond what a catalyst must normally perform to gain Life. Marie would rarely, if ever, be found in the family chapel.

MARIE (House Catalyst)
PHANTASIA STATISTICS

ATTRIBUTES

Attack	42	Defense	49	Health	54
Strength	45	Dexterity	55	Movement	5
Intelligence	57	Intuition	65	Senses	55
Form	human	Size	56	Resistance	10
Renewal	100	Capacity	100	Lifewell	300

ABILITIES	TALENT	STATION	SCORE
Combat	—	—	—
Movement	—	—	—
Health and Healing	—	—	—
Form and Size Altering	—	—	—
Information	11	3	14
Life Transfer	17	8	25
Tool Crafts and Skills	1	1	2
Telepathy and Empathy	15	3	18
Illusions	5	1	6

Cardinal Radisovik

Son of the Cardinal in Sharakan, Radisovik was raised in the royal palace side by side with the boy who would eventually become King (Garald's father) of that powerful city-state. The two were close friends. The only time they were separated was during the years Radisovik went to study in the Font. (The young Radisovik did manage to smuggle the young King into the Font via the Corridors. The two were purportedly going to explore the sealed-off Merlyn's Chambers. Caught by the *Duuk-tsarith*, the young men were sternly lectured and the King sent home.) The two young men did everything together, even falling in love with the same woman, a noble lady of Sharakan. Whom she preferred is open to question, but the Vision performed by the catalysts consigned her to the King. Radisovik accepted his loss with good grace. The three continued to be close friends, and on her deathbed the Queen gave her newborn son, Garald, into Radisovik's charge.

Radisovik took this charge seriously, becoming father, mentor, and friend to the young Prince.

Radisovik is in his fifties. He is handsome and refined looking, his black hair streaked with gray, not tonsured like the heads of most catalysts (the lack of tonsure is a sign of rebellion among the catalysts of Sharakan and is one way a PC can spot a rebellious or renegade catalyst). The Cardinal is responsible for formenting the rebellion of the catalysts in Sharakan. Their demands for change in the Church are many and include Free Life for everyone at any time and a removal of the Church from politics. It is interesting to note, however, that Radisovik is deeply involved in politics himself, and one wonders if he hasn't put forth these more radical views in order to gain moderate concessions.

Shortly after the magic was freed and the first terrible storm swept over the land, Radisovik was the only person able to determine calmly and logically what had occurred. Radisovik himself made contact with the "enemy," gaining the Marines' help in saving as many lives as possible. At the Cardinal's insistence, Major Boris led a rescue party to the Temple of the Necromancer, where they discovered Joram, Gwendolyn, and Saryon injured but alive.

Radisovik was mortally injured when a portion of a wall of the Cathedral of Life collapsed on top of him. He died in Saryon's arms, giving Garald into Saryon's charge, much as the woman Radisovik had loved had given her baby into his.

Radisovik is wise and intelligent and a very powerful catalyst. He respects his Prince but will not hesitate to tell Garald when he is wrong, although he will take care to do this out of the hearing of others. Radisovik will be charming to friendly PCs, including catalysts. He will discuss frankly his views on the Church, but will do this circumspectly, refusing to criticize it openly before strangers. He will not talk much at all about himself, always leading the conversation back to the PCs and their own adventures. Radisovik will always gain more information about someone else than he will reveal about himself.

The Witch, Head of the Order of *Duuk-tsarith* in Merilon (Player Character)

Members of the Order of *Duuk-tsarith* never use names and so hers is not known. The witch's background is similar to all other members of the warlocks' organization. When it was determined that she was born to the Mystery of Fire, she was taken from home as a baby to the warlocks' secret training place in The Mountain. She was immersed in the study of magic and the other rigorous disciplines of the warlocks. Intelligent, quick-thinking, she rose through the ranks to the top of her Order. Her one fault is her fiery temper, and she must exert considerable control over herself to contain it.

Like the others of her Order, the witch is strictly businesslike. She has no tender thoughts or feelings; she has no compassion. The word "mercy" is foreign to her. Those who by chance catch a glimpse of her face within the shadows of her black hood will note that she is very beautiful, but her beauty does not touch the heart. She is not cruel or sadistic and takes no pleasure in inflicting pain, yet she is not reluctant to torture a victim when necessary. It is all part of her job. The witch will do anything she must in order to locate Joram and the Darksword.

THE WITCH (DUUK-TSARITH) PHANTASIA STATISTICS

ATTRIBUTES

Attack	60	Defense	60	Health	67
Strength	61	Dexterity	63	Movement	5
Intelligence	66	Intuition	65	Senses	54
Form	human	Size	58	Resistance	60
Renewal	1,140	Capacity	2,360	Lifewell	3,500

ABILITIES	TALENT	STATION	SCORE
Combat	24	30	54
Movement	13	25	38
Health and Healing	—	—	—
Form and Size Altering	18	28	46
Information	—	—	—
Life Transfer	—	—	—
Tool Crafts and Skills	—	—	—
Telepathy and Empathy	27	25	52
Illusions	19	28	47

Xavier, *DKarn-ðuuk*, Prince of Merilon (Nonplayer Character)

The royal lineage of Merilon runs through the Empress's side of the family. At her death, therefore, her younger brother, Xavier, comes into power. Born to the Mystery of Fire, Xavier left his home as a child to undergo the secret, exhaustive training of the warlocks. However, because he was of royal birth and an heir to the throne of Merilon, Xavier was not forced to lose his identity as are other, lesser-born students of the warlocks.

Intelligent, ruthless, Xavier soon rose high in the ranks of the warlocks and qualified to become one of the elite *DKarn-ðuuk*—a War Master. He was content with this until whisperings among the *Duuk-tsarith* about what was transpiring in the Court of Merilon reached his ears. Xavier returned to Court immediately to find that the rumors were true—the Empress was dead, her corpse being given the semblance of life by magical means. By the law of succession Xavier could claim the throne.

Unfortunately the Prince is blocked by the Emperor. Supported by the might of the *Duuk-tsarith* and the power of the Church, the Emperor has made it an act of high treason for anyone to even hint that his wife is not in perfect health. Ostensibly the Emperor continues to rule Merilon in his wife's name. The true ruler is actually Bishop Vanya.

Joram's "death" and the discovery by the populace of the Empress's true condition allows Xavier to take control of Merilon. But The DKarn-Duuk, as he is known, becomes obsessed with obtaining the Darksword. He would give anything to acquire it. It is maddening to him to know that it is being held in the arms of a stone statue, right there for anyone to take, yet Xavier cannot take it.

Xavier's true age is not known, but he is probably in his mid-thirties. He is Joram's uncle and resembles his nephew—his hair is black and luxuriant; his eyebrows thick and black. He has the same intense stare, although the eyes are cold, not fiery like Joram's. The resemblance is such that anyone who knows Joram would find it startling. Even if they do not make the connection, they might wonder if they

had met this man before. Xavier's body is slender, not
muscular, for he has spent his life in the study of warfare
and magic. His face is pale, his lips are thin and bloodless.
Like all the warlocks, he rarely shows emotion. He dresses
in the crimson robes of the warlocks.

XAVIER (DKARN-DUUK)
PHANTASIA STATISTICS

ATTRIBUTES

Attack	68	Defense	65	Health	70
Strength	61	Dexterity	63	Movement	5
Intelligence	63	Intuition	61	Senses	48
Form	human	Size	60	Resistance	65
Renewal	1,290	Capacity	3,360	Lifewell	3,750

ABILITIES	TALENT	STATION	SCORE
Combat	17	35	52
Movement	6	20	26
Health and Healing	2	1	3
Form and Size Altering	2	15	17
Information	—	—	—
Life Transfer	—	—	—
Tool Crafts and Skills	—	—	—
Telepathy and Empathy	—	—	—
Illusions	5	25	30

Emperor and Empress of Merilon, Joram's Father and Mother (Nonplayer Characters)

An intelligent man, Joram's father is cursed with a weak
and indolent nature. Born to a well-to-do family of minor
nobility in Merilon, the young man was selected by Bishop
Vanya to marry the Empress after the Vision undertaken
by the catalysts showed that the nobleman could provide
the city-state with an heir.

Unfortunately the Vision did not show that this child
would be born Dead.

The Emperor has a pale complexion with red cheeks
from an overindulgence in wine. His face was once handsome but now tends to be jowly. He has black hair that he

wears short and uses magical means to keep it from turning gray. He has become extremely fond of fine living, wears the very latest fashion, the most elegant clothes.

The only person in the world the Emperor truly cares about is his wife. One of the most beautiful women in Thimhallan, the Empress has a vivacious personality that makes her the exact opposite of her husband. She is fond of him, though she does not love him, and even this affection for him dies with her baby. She never forgives her husband for turning his back upon their child.

The Empress's health has always been fragile. Following the death of her child, she becomes depressed and despondent and her health suffers still further. She has no care for anything except the gay court functions that take her mind temporarily off its sorrow.

The Emperor never ceases to love his wife and will do anything in his power to make her happy. When she dies, he is truly devastated. In the madness of his grief he refuses to believe she is dead and forbids the Druids from taking the body to be buried. Undoubtedly this is what gives Bishop Vanya—worried over what his role will be in a government run by the strong-willed Xavier—the idea of keeping the Empress "alive."

It is easy to convince the Emperor to go along with the scheme. The magically animated corpse seems so lifelike that he half convinces himself she isn't really dead at all. But gradually, as the corpse begins to decay and not even the most powerful Druids and catalysts can maintain the illusion of life, the horror of the situation sinks into the Emperor's soul. But he is trapped in the charade; the Bishop will not permit him to stop the grisly play-acting. Accustomed to a life of ease and unending wealth, the Emperor is too weak to give it up.

Under no circumstances will the Emperor claim Joram as his son, even though, when he meets him in Merilon, he is certain of the boy's true identity. The Emperor knows that to acknowledge Joram would bring about his immediate downfall, for Xavier and Vanya would lose no time in publishing the fact that Joram is Dead. But the Emperor is not completely devoid of dignity. His appearance at the Turning shows Xavier and Vanya that he is aware of what is taking place and gives both of them several uncomfortable moments.

The Emperor is vastly relieved when the Darksword breaks the spell surrounding the corpse of his wife. The horrible charade is ended. But now his life is in ruins. He has lost his beloved wife and his son—twice. Burdened with guilt and despair, the Emperor takes advantage of the confusion at the Border following Joram's escape to slip away from his bodyguards and disappear. The *Duuk-tsarith* start off in pursuit, but Xavier orders them to desist. He lets it be known publicly that the Emperor is insane. The Emperor never returns to the Palace but wanders the land, a stooped and broken beggar. His last act, before he dies, is to urge Joram to become the rightful ruler of Merilon.

EMPEROR OF MERILON (Albanara)
PHANTASIA STATISTICS

ATTRIBUTES

Attack	55	Defense	55	Health	60
Strength	56	Dexterity	54	Movement	4
Intelligence	54	Intuition	55	Senses	62
Form	human	Size	63	Resistance	72
Renewal	1,500	Capacity	4,760	Lifewell	4,100

ABILITIES	TALENT	STATION	SCORE
Combat	6	1	7
Movement	9	1	10
Health and Healing	5	1	6
Form and Size Altering	5	10	15
Information	1	42	43
Life Transfer	—	—	—
Tool Crafts and Skills	1	1	2
Telepathy and Empathy	1	38	39
Illusions	5	30	35

MINOR CHARACTERS, BOOK THREE

Major James Boris, Marine Commander and Leader of Expeditionary Force to Thimhallan (Nonplayer Character)

A military "brat," coming from a long line of soldiers, the Major's entire life is the Marine Corps. Born on Earth, the son of a colonel, the Major joined the Marines at the age of eighteen and has had a distinguished career. His colonel father refused to play favorites with his son, and Boris peeled his share of potatoes (a beloved tradition held over from ancient days) aboard many an intergalactic ship before his own skills and unfaltering courage led to advancement.

The Major studied the language and what else was known about Thimhallan before traveling to that planet, but his logical mind refused to believe most of it, and he truly thought the civilians who wrote the reports were exaggerating (or had indulged in mind-altering drugs). Boris is convinced that landing his troops on Thimhallan will be somewhat like invading the Intergalactic Science Fiction and Fantasy Convention—rounding up a bunch of weirdos in funny costumes. He is completely unprepared for the reality of the situation, and this leads to tragic results.

Boris is an honorable soldier. The thought of committing genocide horrifies him, but he has a responsibility to his men and to the high command who sent him here. He is fearful of Joram's proposed raid on his troops and attacks Merilon on the principle that the best defense is a good offense.

When the magic was freed and the terrible storm swept over Thimhallan, Boris immediately broke off the attack and put his soldiers and equipment to work helping the people of Merilon survive the chaos. As a result of the Marines' untiring efforts, thousands of people were saved who might otherwise have perished.

Major Boris is short and stockily built, with a bulldog chin, thick neck, and strong, muscular shoulders. He is blond and good-looking, brash and confident, and takes a common-sense, rules-and-regulations view of life. He is highly skilled in martial arts and an expert marksman with the old-fashioned projectile weapons that have become a hobby with many of the Marines.

Boris has never married, believing that the life of a Marine is no life for a wife and children. This may have something to do with the fact that, as a child, he traveled from one off-world military base to another and never made any lasting friendships. The Major has no close friends until he meets Prince Garald.

MAJOR JAMES BORIS (SORCERER/ TECHNOLOGIST) PHANTASIA STATISTICS

ATTRIBUTES

Attack	63	Defense	62	Health	54
Strength	61	Dexterity	59	Movement	5
Intelligence	47	Intuition	55	Senses	49
Form	human	Size	52	Resistance	27
Renewal	0	Capacity	0	Lifewell	0

ABILITIES	TALENT	STATION	SCORE
Combat	—	—	—
Movement	—	—	—
Health and Healing	—	—	—
Form and Size Altering	—	—	—
Information	—	—	—
Life Transfer	—	—	—
Tool Crafts and Skills	22	25	47
Telepathy and Empathy	—	—	—
Illusions	—	—	—

Menju the Sorcerer (Nonplayer Character)

Exiled from Thimhallan in his youth for crimes committed when he attempted to take over a dukedom near Zith-el, Menju was cast into Beyond. He was found, lost and wandering, by the Border patrols. Menju was one of the few magi who managed to maintain his sanity after the traumatic crossing from a world of Life into a world of Death. He saw quickly that what small amount of Life remained to him could be used to his advantage in his Dead world. Going into show business would not only allow him to use his talents in magic to make money, but it also gave him the perfect cover for his proposed criminal operations, allowing him travel freely.

Needing qualified middle managers for his criminal empire, Menju looked for others from his native land. He found most locked up in mental wards. But there were a few who were sane and who were eager to join up with Menju when he proposed that they turn their magical talents to crime.

Menju was quick to take notice of anyone the patrols found, and so he was among the first to visit Joram upon his arrival on Earth. Sympathetic, understanding, able to speak Joram's language, Menju befriended the confused, homesick, and grief-stricken youth. It was comforting to Joram to be able to talk about Thimhallan and purge his soul of his vast guilt, and thus Joram opened up to Menju more than he would have under normal circumstances. It was only when Menju—in the mistaken belief that he had Joram completely under his control—attempted to abduct Gwendolyn that Joram finally understood the man's true nature.

Joram spent the years in Beyond helping a secret government agency in its battle against Menju and his powerful organization that includes assassins, drug runners, smugglers, space pirates, and thieves.

Menju's death will temporarily disrupt the organization, whose top members will be forced into hiding when the government raids Menju's palatial home and discovers the names of his allies. But the return of magic into the universe will enable these men and women to change their appearance, move to other worlds, and it is expected that the organization will soon surface—stronger and more powerful than ever.

Menju the Sorcerer is in his sixties, although he appears younger through cosmetic surgery. He has thick, gray hair that is meticulously combed and deeply tanned skin. He is always dressed impeccably in the most expensive and well-tailored suits. Menju has a radiant smile; a deep, cultivated voice; and hands that are noticeable for their dexterity, grace, and long, supple fingers. He is adored by audiences throughout the galaxy, donates millions to charities, runs a school for aspiring magicians, and is a stalwart member of

the Stage Actors' Union. There has never been a breath of
scandal attached to his name. He has been married several
times (he likes young, beautiful women) but is currently
single. His former wives have lots of money and no complaints.

Menju's plan is to capture Thimhallan and use it as his
base of operations for his crime syndicate. The Sorcerer
will kill any male magi he captures without hesitation. He
will take young and lovely female magi prisoner, planning
to use them later to start his own dynasty of magicians. All
catalysts are immediately taken prisoner, and Menju will
attempt to force them to give him Life. Since there is a
surplus of catalysts, any who refuse will meet a quick end.
Although Menju is enamored of his ability to use his magic
once more, he is a novice magus—unskilled and uncertain.
He feels far more comfortable relying on Technology and
will use the magic mainly to intimidate men like Major
Boris. Menju knows of the Darksword and its power and
wants it for his own.

MENJU THE SORCERER)
PHANTASIA STATISTICS

ATTRIBUTES

Attack	55	Defense	58	Health	53
Strength	55	Dexterity	56	Movement	5
Intelligence	58	Intuition	54	Senses	54
Form	human	Size	62	Resistance	10
Renewal	100	Capacity	100	Lifewell	300

ABILITIES	TALENT	STATION	SCORE
Combat	3	8	11
Movement	2	7	9
Health and Healing	1	15	16
Form and Size Altering	7	9	16
Information	—	—	—
Life Transfer	—	—	—
Tool Crafts and Skills	20	20	40
Telepathy and Empathy	—	—	—
Illusions	5	10	15

Appendix II

Adapting to Other Game Systems

There are undoubtedly those veteran gamers who—like a small friend of ours with a most unfortunate habit for "acquiring" things—would like to visit Merilon but are currently adventuring in other worlds. For those of you coming from other game systems to Thimhallan, we offer suggestions on how to make the transition and a few hints on what your PCs might find on their arrival.

Those of you interested in adapting our system to your own should study it and then feel free to do with it as you want within the context of your own game.

Beginning the Adventure

The PCs in their old world are lost and wandering in whatever dreadful place the Gamejudge decides to dump them. This may be a bog, a wood, a desert, a mountain. They have no idea where they are. They come upon a very faint path. Study reveals (1) it is very old, (2) it was apparently used by a great number of people, (3) no one has used it since. Any magic-user of any alignment will feel a tingling of excitement when he or she sets foot upon the path and the irresistible urge to follow it. So overpowering is this urge that he or she will do so even without the rest of the company.

The path leads to two glowing pillars (see description of the Portals of Passage in the History part of this volume, page 196). Beyond the pillars is a void. It is as if the PCs have come to the edge of the world. Nothing can be seen on the other side. Any PCs who are not magic-users and attempt to go through the pillars will find themselves unable to enter by any means. An invisible force field bars their way. (Stubborn fighters who insist on hurling themselves at the field will eventually take damage!)

A magic-user approaching the pillars will cause them to glow even more brilliantly until the light is blinding to the eye. Magic-users of good and neutral alignment will instantly have the feeling that they are being called home after wandering for years in a cold and uncaring world. They may experience visions of great magi of the past standing in the pillars, beckoning to them. Magic-users of evil alignment will sense that power beyond their wildest dreams lies through those pillars. It is as if the source of magic itself is shining upon them like the sun. So strong will these impressions be that the magic-user will do his best to persuade or otherwise induce the members of his party to enter with him. If this fails, the magic-user will abandon the party and rush through the pillars to vanish in the void beyond.

If the party chooses to go with the magic-user, the magic-user will enter between the pillars first and all may follow safely. If the magic-user leaves the group and enters on his own, the group standing behind will notice the glow of the pillars beginning to fade. They have only moments to decide if they want to follow their magus. If the glow disappears completely, they will have lost the opportunity (unless they can find another magic-user). If they choose to follow, they may do so if they keep the image of the magic-user in their minds.

The journey is extremely difficult. Reduce PCs at least one level because of the rigors of the trip through space and time. (First-level players will remain at that level.) Magic-users may be penalized even further, with additional reduction of physical strength based upon their level and the number of people traveling with them.

Depending on where the PCs arrive in Thimhallan, the Gamejudge should immediately begin a secret encounter check once every few rounds to determine if they have been discovered by the *Duuk-tsarith*. For PCs arriving in the Outland, below the sea, or in the Wild, the odds against the *Duuk-tsarith's* finding them are small but will increase the longer they stay in Thimhallan. Any use of a magical object will increase these odds tremendously, however. PCs materializing in a city can expect to encounter the *Duuk-tsarith* within ten to fifteen minutes following their arrival.

PCs will find other changes in Thimhallan as follows:

1. Clerics will lose all powers, including those of healing. The only god in Thimhallan is the Almin. Clerics will begin to feel a most remarkable sensation, however. On first arriving, the cleric will notice that he feels empty, as though he is a vessel without anything inside. Whenever he touches anything in the new world, however, he will experience a most pleasurable sensation of Life flowing into his body. This will begin as soon as his feet touch the ground and grow stronger the more he comes into contact with objects around him. Assume for game purposes that the cleric is turning catalyst and is slowly absorbing the magic of the world. He must, however, figure out what to do with it. How long this absorption takes before he can give Life to another is up to the Gamejudge. Such a thing would probably happen accidentally, in the excitement of battle: the cleric touching the magic-user and the magic-user suddenly feeling a surge of additional strength. After this, however, clerics will need to follow the rules laid down for Transference of Life found in this book. Any catalyst they met could easily tell them how this works. Clerics of good alignment will absorb magic at a higher rate than those of evil alignment, since the Almin is a compassionate god.

2. Druids will suddenly discover that they have healing powers, all based upon their level when they entered the world. (It may take them a while to find this out!) Druids will also note many unusual things beginning to happen to

them—trees bowing in respect as they pass, or walking over to offer them shade or dropping fruit into their hands, plants twining themselves into comfortable cushions. Druids, depending on their level, will be able to call upon the forces of plant life to work for them (defend them or the group) almost immediately upon entering Thimhallan.

3. Magic-users will find that all magical objects they had in their possession have survived the journey and seem to be in good working order. Unfortunately all objects that are imbued with Life are considered to be Sorcerous in nature. The use of any Dead object that has had Life granted to it will immediately send a signal to the *Duuk-tsarith*, who will instantly begin searching for the object and its user.

A Nullmagic spell cast by the *Duuk-tsarith* (as they generally do upon first encountering a potential enemy) will instantly absorb all magic from any object, no matter how powerful, and render it useless until the spell is lifted by the warlock. The *Duuk-tsarith* will confiscate all such items, along with any other "Sorcerous" objects the group is carrying (swords, armor, daggers, tinderboxes, flints, torches, waterskins, quills, icons of other gods, pouches, anything with metal that has obviously been forged and shaped). The *Duuk-tsarith* will almost certainly assume the PCs to be Sorcerers. They will take them to their dungeons (with the exception of clerics, who will likely be turned over to the nearest Church official and undoubtedly sent from there to the Font). The PCs better be prepared to do some fast talking!

The only major city where the PCs might not instantly be taken into custody by the *Duuk-tsarith* is Sharakan, and this would only be in the years just prior to the coming of Joram. Sorcery is accepted in this city at this time, and while the high quality and unusual nature of the objects the PCs possess might lead them to be taken to the King for a meeting, the PCs will not be considered criminals unless their actions warrant such a charge.

PCs fortunate enough to stumble across a Sorcerers' village will find themselves treated almost as gods, though they may quickly lose every object they possess to the eager Sorcerers, who will carry them off for study.

Depending on their level, magic-users will slowly begin to absorb Life from the world around them. This absorption will be accelerated the longer they depend upon that Life alone. Magic-users bereft of all wands, rings, scrolls, will absorb magic at a higher rate than those who still cling to objects of their old world. A native of Thimhallan will be able to explain to the magic-user all about using Life in this world. At this point the Gamejudge should have the magic-user choose a Mystery under which he or she would like to develop further. (PCs wanting to become *Duuk-tsarith* or *DKarn-duuk* will be sent to The Mountain for rigorous and demanding training.)

4. PCs of classes that have no skills in magic (fighters, thieves) will be Dead to magic in Thimhallan and will not be able to attain it. Any fighter or thief with some degree of skill in sleight of hand will be able to pass himself off as being Alive (treat as Illusion for an observer). Those who don't have this skill better work at acquiring it quickly! The *Duuk-tsarith*, upon investigation of a Dead PC found *alone and by himself*, will be able to tell that he is Dead almost immediately. A group of magi can protect a Dead PC by keeping him always near them, thus using their own Life as a "screen" for his Deadness. Gamejudges should check periodically to see that this continues to work.

Those PCs with a small amount of magic (fighter/magi) will be able to acquire Life at a level proportionate with the magic they were able to cast in their old world.

Once the PCs manage to extricate themselves from the trouble they will undoubtedly experience on arrival, they will have a wonderful time exploring Thimhallan.

Good luck adventuring!

Life Attribute Aid Table

With each new station reached by a character, their Life Resistance, Renewal, Capacity and Lifewell Attributes increase automatically. This table will help you in determining the scores for these Attributes when only the station of the character is known.

Stat	Res	Ren	Cap	Life
1	1	10	10	50
2	2	20	20	100
3	3	30	30	150
4	4	40	40	200
5	5	50	50	250
6	6	60	60	300
7	7	80	110	400
8	8	100	160	500
9	9	120	210	600
10	10	140	260	700

Stat	Res	Ren	Cap	Life
11	12	170	360	900
12	14	200	460	1,100
13	16	230	560	1,300
14	18	260	660	1,500
15	20	290	760	1,700
16	22	340	860	1,800
17	24	390	960	1,900
18	26	440	1060	2,000
19	28	490	1160	2,100
20	30	540	1260	2,200
21	32	590	1360	2,300
22	34	640	1460	2,400
23	36	690	1560	2,500
24	38	740	1660	2,600
25	38	790	1760	2,700
26	42	840	1860	2,800
27	44	890	1960	2,900
28	46	940	2060	3,000
29	48	990	2160	3,100
30	50	1040	2260	3,200
31	51	1070	2460	3,250
32	52	1110	2660	3,300
33	53	1130	2860	3,350
34	54	1160	3060	3,400
35	55	1190	3260	3,450
36	56	1220	3460	3,500
37	57	1250	3660	3,550
38	58	1280	3860	3,600
39	59	1310	4060	3,650
40	60	1340	4260	3,700
41	61	1370	4460	3,750
42	62	1400	4660	3,800
43	63	1430	4860	3,850
44	64	1460	5060	3,900
45	65	1490	5260	3,950
46	66	1520	5460	4,000
47	67	1550	5660	4,050
48	68	1580	5860	4,100

Stat	Res	Ren	Cap	Life
49	69	1610	6060	4,150
50	70	1640	6260	4,200
51	70	1660	6360	4,220
52	70	1680	6460	4,240
53	70	1700	6560	4,260
54	71	1720	6660	4,280
55	71	1740	6760	4,300
56	71	1760	6860	4,320
57	71	1780	6960	4,340
58	72	1800	7060	4,360
59	72	1820	7160	4,380
60	72	1840	7260	4,400
61	72	1860	7360	4,420
62	73	1880	7460	4,440
63	73	1900	7560	4,460
64	73	1920	7660	4,480
65	73	1940	7760	4,500
66	74	1960	7860	4,520
67	74	1980	7960	4,540
68	74	2000	8060	4,560
69	74	2020	8160	4,580
70	75	2040	8260	4,600
71	75	2060	8360	4,620
72	75	2080	8460	4,640
73	75	2100	8560	4,660
74	76	2120	8660	4,680
75	76	2140	8760	4,700
76	76	2160	8860	4,720
77	76	2180	8960	4,740
78	77	2200	9060	4,760
79	77	2200	1,060	4,780
80	77	2240	1,160	4,800
81	77	2260	1,260	4,820
82	78	2280	1,360	4,840
83	78	2300	1,460	4,860
84	78	2320	1,560	4,880
85	78	2340	1,660	4,900
86	79	2360	1,760	4,920

Stat	Res	Ren	Cap	Life
87	79	2380	1,860	4,940
88	79	2400	1,960	4,960
89	79	2420	2,060	4,980
90	80	2440	2,160	5,000
91	80	2460	2,260	5,020
92	80	2480	2,360	5,040
93	80	2500	2,460	5,060
94	81	2520	2,560	5,080
95	81	2540	2,660	5,100
96	81	2560	2,760	5,120
97	81	2580	2,860	5,140
98	82	2600	2,960	5,160
99	82	2620	3,060	5,180
100	82	2640	3,160	5,200

PHANTASIA CHARACTER SHEET

CHARACTER NAME
CHARACTER CLASS (MYSTERY)

Attack	Defense	Health
Strength	Dexterity	Movement
Intelligence	Intuition	Senses
Form	Size	Resistance
Renewal	Capacity	Lifewell

Abilities	Talent	Station	Score
Fire: Combat			
Air: Movement			
Water: Health and Healing			
Earth: Form and Size Altering			
Time: Information			
Life: Life Transfer			
Death: Tool Crafts and Skills			
Spirit: Telepathy and Empathy			
Shadow: Illusions			

Notes

Index

Page numbers in boldface indicate where you can find statistics

About the Authors

Born in Independence, Missouri, Margaret Weis graduated from the University of Missouri and worked as a book editor before teaming up with Tracy Hickman to develop the *Dragonlance* novels. Margaret lives in a renovated barn in Wisconsin with her teen-aged daughter, Elizabeth Baldwin, and several pets. She enjoys reading (especially Charles Dickens), opera, and rollerskating.

Born in Salt Lake City, Tracy Hickman resides in Wisconsin in a 100-year-old Victorian home with his wife and four children. When he isn't reading or writing, he is eating or sleeping. On Sundays, he conducts the hymns at the local Mormon church.

The Darksword Trilogy marked Margaret and Tracy's first appearance as Bantam Spectra authors. They followed up with *Darksword Adventures*, a companion volume and game book set in the same world, then, the **Rose of the Prophet** trilogy. **The Death Gate Cycle**, a seven book series being published in hardcover and paperback, is their most inventive fantasy fiction yet. In addition to their collaborations, each is working on solo series. The first of these is *Star of the Guardians* by Margaret Weis.